CORRUPT VOW

FILTHY WICKED PSYCHOS #3

EVA ASHWOOD

Copyright © 2022 by Eva Ashwood

All rights reserved.

No part of this book may be reproduced in any form or by any electronic or mechanical means, including information storage and retrieval systems, without written permission from the author.

This is a work of fiction. Names, characters, organizations, places, events, and incidents are either products of the author's imagination or used fictitiously. Any resemblance to actual persons, living or dead, or actual events is purely coincidental.

Author's Note: This is a dark romance and includes themes that may be triggering for some. Please read at your own discretion.

*For the villains who aren't redeemed
by the woman they love...
but who would gladly
burn down the world for her.*

1

WILLOW

"I'll do it," I tell my grandmother, my voice shaking. "I'll marry whoever you want."

The words seem to hang in the air for a long moment, filling the space between us. Between *all* of us. I can feel the Voronin brothers react behind me as if their emotions are a physical force, anger and disbelief practically radiating from them. I know they still want to get between Olivia and me, to stop her from forcing me to do this, but I won't let them.

Because whatever they might try, it won't work.

My grandmother is holding all the cards right now.

As I stare into her eyes, bile crawls up my throat. In the weeks since we met, I've been getting to know her, coming to understand her. Or so I thought. Her eyes are hazel, not brown like mine, but I could see something in the shape of them that always reminded me of my own. They're the eyes of the one living relative I have left... but they might as well belong to someone I've never met.

Despite her outward appearance, Olivia Stanton is a cruel and calculating woman who's willing to blackmail me into marrying someone just to rebuild her empire. She's using me like a pawn in a game she intends to win. Before today, I would never have thought my grandmother was capable of something like this, but I guess that just goes to show how thoroughly she had me fooled.

The petite older woman smiles, seeming pleased, as if she's read my thoughts and knows I understand the threat she's holding over my head.

"Very good," she says. "That's the correct answer, Willow. You're making the right choice here. It wouldn't have gone well for you or your men if you'd tried to deny me."

"You—"

Malice bites off what probably would've been a string of curses, and he and his brothers step forward again. Their anger is even more apparent now, and I know they must hate this just as much as I do—being so out of control in this situation, having their fates decided by someone else.

A raised hand is the only reaction from Olivia at first. She stops them in their tracks, her eyes cool and her posture straight.

"Do I need to remind you of your position in all of this, Malice?" she asks. Her tone is pleasant, but edged with steel. "My husband got you out of prison, playing the part of 'X.' You would have been in there for many more years if he hadn't stepped in. And I could send you back with a snap of my fingers. I wonder if you would survive this time? Or if your brothers would." She looks to Ransom and Victor. "They've done criminal things for my husband and myself, and evidence of those things would probably be enough to put them away for a good long while too."

My heart clenches in my chest just hearing her make that kind of threat. I don't even want to imagine it.

I went from being afraid of these three brothers, to being angry at them for the way they pushed me around and seemed to want to control my life. But despite the rockiness of our beginnings, I've come to care for them, so much and so deeply that it's overwhelming.

So much that I know I can't let anything happen to them. Especially not going back to prison. Not when I know how hard it was for Malice the first time around, and how hard it would be for Ransom and Victor if they ended up there.

They've saved my life more than once.

They've come to my rescue when no one else would.

Now this is something I can do for them, and I'm determined to see it through.

I extend my arms out, holding them off. "Don't," I say, turning to look at each of them in turn. "Please. Don't risk this."

They're all bristling, anger tightening their expressions. Malice is almost shaking with it, as if the pressure inside him might explode outward at any moment. But they stay where they are, and when I'm somewhat confident that they won't move, I transfer my focus back to Olivia, glaring her down.

"I already agreed to do what you want," I snap. "I understand what's at stake. Leave them alone."

Olivia narrows her eyes, glancing between me and the brothers. There's a calculating look on her face, as if she's trying to evaluate how intense the emotions between us are. Maybe she's trying to see how far she can push this, or just trying to make sure that we all really do understand the threat she's making.

"Yes," she finally says, smiling again. Fine lines appear at the corners of her mouth, her eyes wrinkling slightly at the corners. I used to think that smile made her look kind, but now it just makes her look like a devil in a designer dress. "I do believe that you understand what's at stake here. That's good."

My grandmother's eyes move down to the grave we're still standing near, and I blink, caught off guard when I follow her gaze.

Misty's grave. The reason we're all here.

Less than half an hour ago, I was focused on burying my adoptive mother. It's hard to believe that things have gone so far off the rails since then. Everything has changed, my entire world shifted on its axis. Everything I thought I knew, thought I could rely on, has been yanked out from under me, and I still feel like I'm struggling to regain my balance in all of this.

As I stare down at the deep hole that contains Misty's casket, my throat gets tight. My adoptive mother was unreliable at best and a manipulative user at worst, but in comparison to my grandmother, she was a much better option. And now she's gone.

My stomach twists when it hits me that I'm honestly thinking of Misty as someone who treated me better, when Misty was never a good mother to begin with. She did the bare minimum, and even that was a stretch sometimes. In the end, there are only three people in the world who have ever truly stood up for me and protected me.

Malice, Ransom, and Victor.

They've saved me time and time again, put themselves between me and the people who wanted to hurt me, and promised that they'd keep me safe.

And that's why I have to do this. Why I have to protect them now.

I square my shoulders, clenching my jaw as I tear my eyes away from Misty's grave and look back to my grandmother. "What happens now?"

The smug, satisfied curl to Olivia's perfectly colored lips makes my blood boil, but there's nothing I can do about it. I can't attack her any more than the men can, even though for the first time in my life, I think I might be capable of the same sort of violence they are.

"You'll have to come with me," she says.

The guys tense all over again at that, a sound almost like a growl rumbling in Malice's throat, and my stomach drops. At the beginning of this funeral, all I wanted was to go back home with them and let them help me forget my grief. But that won't be happening now.

I turn to face them, my mind and my heart buzzing with so many things I wish I could say. I wish I could tell them everything that's building in my chest, but there's no time. And I couldn't say it anyway, not with Olivia listening.

Instead, I look at all three of them, my gaze lingering on their faces as if I'm trying to memorize them. The set of Malice's jaw, the brightness of Ransom's eyes, the intensity that sits just below the surface of Victor's expression. They stare back at me, and for the first time since I met them, they all look as lost as I feel.

"I'll be okay," I say, my voice low. "So please, don't... don't try anything. She's not going to hurt me if I do what she wants. She needs me, so as long as I do this, it'll be alright."

Malice grinds his teeth, glancing from my face to Olivia and then back again. "You don't have to—"

"I do, though," I tell him. "You know I do."

"Fuck," Ransom bites out. "Goddammit, I fucking hate this."

"Me too," Vic says quietly. "Willow..."

He doesn't finish the thought, shaking his head instead. His hand taps out a rhythm on his thigh, agitation written in every line of his body. They're all tense and furious, and it feels like they're half a second away from snatching me up and trying to make a run for it.

I take a step away from them, just to make extra sure that doesn't happen.

"I don't want you to go with her," Malice says, his voice so strained that it sounds like gravel.

"I know," I whisper, tears burning the backs of my eyes. "But I have to. It's going to be okay."

Okay. No matter how many times I say that word, it doesn't feel more true. Nothing about this situation is even remotely close to okay, and we all know it.

But I have to get them to let me go. None of it will matter if they try to get involved and end up getting thrown in jail or worse. Olivia has already shown that she doesn't give a shit about them as more than a means to an end or as leverage against me. They're pawns to her, just like I am. But unlike me, they're completely disposable in her eyes.

My chest feels like it's full of lead, but I try to keep my face from showing the despair I feel. There's no hope or optimism in my heart, but I don't want to make this worse.

Suddenly, as if something has snapped inside him, Malice strides forward. For a terrifying second, I'm afraid he's going to shove me aside and try to kill Olivia with his bare hands. But instead, he closes the distance between us, palming the back of my head and pulling me toward him as he leans down. At first I think he's going to kiss me, and my heart leaps, both with want and with fear. I don't know what Olivia will do if he kisses me right here.

But he just presses his forehead to mine, closing his eyes for a moment as his strong fingers thread through my hair. I cling to the front of his shirt, wishing desperately that I could bury my face there and let him make this all go away.

But in the end, I let go.

Ransom takes Malice's place as his brother steps back, and he looks heartbroken on top of being angry. He doesn't smile, just reaches up and tucks a bit of my blonde hair behind my ear, following the motion down so his fingers graze across my neck. I shiver at the touch, and he sighs softly, pain burning in his blue-green eyes.

For a moment, it looks like he wants to say something, but then he thinks better of it and steps back.

As Malice and Ransom stand side by side, I shift my gaze to Victor. He doesn't move at all for a long moment, just stares at me hard from where he seems rooted to the spot. My heart thuds in my chest, and as our gazes lock, a memory of our kiss in the kitchen flashes through my mind. It seems very far away right now, even though it wasn't long ago at all. Vic drums his fingers against his thigh, counting out a pattern only he knows, and then shakes his head as if snapping himself out of his stasis.

He moves in closer, stopping with several inches still between us. He swallows hard as his hand stretches out, and he grazes his fingers over my cheek, feather-light and soft. He barely lingers, and my breath catches as he pulls away.

I can still count on one hand the number of times he's touched me, but this one... this one means a lot.

I blink away the tears blurring my vision and cement the image of them standing there in my mind, then turn back to Olivia. Lifting my chin, I take a deep breath and will my voice not to shake as I say, "Let's go."

She nods, then jerks her head imperiously. I follow her as she leads the way out of the cemetery, toward her car.

With every step I take, I can feel the distance between me and my men growing. I can tell that they haven't moved, still standing in the exact spots I left them in, watching me get farther and farther away.

And as the distance between us grows, my gut twists, dread at what's to come rising in me.

2

WILLOW

When we reach Olivia's sleek, expensive car, we both climb into the back.

I slide across the seat, almost pressing myself up against the door on the opposite side of the car just to get away from her. I've never felt so stiff and uncomfortable around Olivia before. Just sharing air in this confined space with her makes my skin crawl.

In contrast, my grandmother seems relaxed and confident, radiating the kind of satisfaction that comes from getting your way so completely.

I hate that. I wish I could do something to shake her up, to make her realize she hasn't won the way she thinks she has, but there's nothing. Because she's in control right now.

Once we're settled in the back, Olivia says something to her driver, and he starts the car, taking us away from the cemetery.

As we roll down the street, I can't stop myself from glancing over at my grandmother, wondering how in the hell I never saw beneath her facade. She played the role of being a kind old woman who wanted to help me so well, and I fell for it time and time again.

It's a good lie, I guess. But still a lie, like so much of the world of the ultra-wealthy. Everything in her world is all about appearance, people lying about who they are on the inside and selling you on the glittering masks they're always wearing.

My mind goes back to the three Voronin brothers as my fingers twist together tightly on my lap.

Not one of them has ever made any effort to hide who they are. That's what scared me about them at first. Malice looked me in the face and told me that he and his brothers weren't heroes from the get-go, and none of them ever tried to convince me otherwise.

But unlike Olivia, at least I can take them at face value. I knew exactly who they were when I started to care about them, which makes me feel like I can trust my feelings for them.

It makes those feelings seem more real, because they're grounded in something I know is true.

Hell, that may be the *only* thing I know to be true right now.

The driver doesn't say a word as he navigates us through the streets of Detroit, and I'm grateful for the silence in the car. I can't imagine trying to make small talk with my emotions in turmoil like this.

I slump in my seat, looking out the window, watching the trees pass and wondering how this is going to go. I can feel Olivia's eyes on me at one point, critical and assessing, but I ignore her, not glancing over.

"Sit up straight," she says eventually. "Slouching isn't becoming of someone of your status."

I want to say I can't believe she'd be concerned with appearances at a time like this, but I guess that's the whole point. She's blackmailing me into being her puppet, and now she's pulling on my strings, making me conform to what she needs me to be. That thought makes fury and disgust rise inside me, but I don't want to find out what will happen if I disobey her.

So I sit up straight, gritting my teeth and seething with hatred for my grandmother.

Luckily, or maybe not, we arrive at Olivia's house just a few minutes later.

The large estate is familiar since I've been here many times, but everything about it feels wrong now. I shudder as we walk into the entryway, remembering how grand and impressive it all seemed the first time I saw it.

Now everything feels oppressive, all the chandeliers and pieces of art on the walls and vases full of flowers coming together to form some sort of a gilded prison.

"Come along, Willow," Olivia says crisply. She snaps her fingers, her low heels clicking on the marble floor as she leads the way deeper into the house.

We end up in one of the sitting rooms, and my heart starts to pound in my chest. I don't know what she's going to do with me. There are a lot of rooms in this house, and she could easily pick one and make that an *actual* prison for me, locking me up until Troy Copeland shows up to claim his prize and drags me away to a church to marry me.

As I wrap my arms around myself, glancing around warily, a man I've never seen before strides into the room through another doorway. He's tall and broad shouldered, with a bearing that makes me think maybe he's ex-military or something, and his bushy eyebrows rise slightly as he looks toward Olivia.

She nods, inclining her head slightly in my direction.

He walks right up to me, and I flinch away from him immediately.

Olivia tuts under her breath, giving me a sharp look. "What did I say about your posture?" she asks.

I have to bite my tongue to keep from snapping back at her, but I don't want to piss her off right now. Not when I don't know what's about to happen.

The man circles me slowly, and everything in me wants to bolt away from him. He reaches out and grabs my wrist, turning it over so that the smooth underside of it is facing upward.

He pulls out something that looks like a big syringe from his pocket, and my heart lurches, adrenaline spiking through my veins.

Instinctively, I try to jerk away from him. I don't know what that is, but it can't be anything good. I can hear my pulse thudding in my ears, and fear washes over me, cold and intense.

Behind me, surprisingly strong hands grab on to my shoulders, and as I suck in a breath, my nostrils fill with the scent of Olivia's perfume. She's holding me still, making sure I can't run away.

"Behave," she snaps. "This doesn't have to be painful, but it can become quite unpleasant if you give me any trouble."

The man doesn't even react to her words. He takes the syringe and places it against my wrist, pressing down on the plunger until something sharp stabs into the sensitive skin.

I flinch at the burst of pain, my mind reeling and my skin turning clammy as I try to figure out what the fuck he's doing to me.

"I want it deep enough that it won't be easy to dislodge," Olivia says. "She can be surprisingly clever when she has the proper incentive, and I need to keep an eye on her."

"Yes, ma'am," the man says, his deep voice curt and professional. "Unless she wants to dig around in her own arm with a knife, it's not coming out."

They talk about me like I'm not even present in the room, and my head spins for a moment before latching on to the words.

When the man pulls the syringe back, there's a small cut seeping droplets of blood where the tip of the syringe was placed, and when I flex my wrist, I can feel a deep ache in the muscle. I blink down at it, my breath hitching as I realize what's just happened.

Olivia had him put a tracker in me. Under my skin.

I shudder hard, unable to hold back the revulsion that fills me. I hate the thought of being marked like this. Tagged like livestock or property, so I can't get away. It makes me feel like Olivia doesn't even see me as a person, and I have to wonder if she ever did. When she came to see me in the hospital after I escaped from Ilya, she looked so relieved to have found me, so concerned for my well-being. But even back then, even from our very first meeting, she knew exactly what she wanted to use me for.

And like she told me back at the cemetery, when I didn't let her manipulate me into doing it the "easy way," she decided to force my hand and blackmail me into doing what she wanted instead.

This is the "hard way," and I have a feeling I'm only getting a small glimpse of how awful the hard way will be.

My wrist throbs dully, blood welling to the surface from the puncture. I fight to keep my emotions off my face, not wanting to give away how much agony I'm in physically and emotionally right now.

I don't want to give her the satisfaction.

The burly man steps away, and Olivia lets go of my shoulders, passing me a handkerchief to stem the bleeding. I take it, but don't press it to my arm, indulging in this little act of defiance. I hope I get blood all over her fancy furniture.

But Olivia doesn't even seem to notice.

"The range is as we discussed?" she asks the man.

He nods. "Yes. Nowhere to hide with one of those in her skin. You'll get a ping for significant events, and you'll be able to pinpoint the location within half a mile or so."

Olivia nods. "Very good. That's exactly what I need."

She says it casually, as if she hires men to put trackers in people all the time. And maybe she does. Maybe she and her husband —*my grandfather*, I remember with a sickening little lurch—did stuff like this often, blackmail and extortion, throwing their money around until they got what they wanted.

I rub my arm, finally dabbing at the blood with the silken material in my hand just because I can't stand to look at it any longer. I feel sick, my stomach roiling as the man packs up his things and takes his leave with another nod to Olivia.

"It's just a bit of extra insurance," my grandmother tells me once it's just the two of us. "I know you won't run or try to get away. Because I know you understand that I have enough resources to hunt you and your men down if you try to leave Detroit." She gives a sharp smile that makes her look like a viper decked in pearls. "That won't be very pleasant for anyone involved. I know you understand how serious I am. So you'll be smarter than to try to get away from me. Won't you?"

There's a clear warning in her voice, and I swallow hard, nodding jerkily.

"Good." She clasps her hands together, her smile widening. "Now, I will inform Troy that your engagement is confirmed, and then there will be a brief period so that we can all get ready for the wedding the two of you deserve. It will be a big, lavish affair, befitting the union of two such prominent families."

I know she means that honestly, but it sounds like a joke to me. Troy is a disgusting lech, and since Olivia has shown her true colors, I can't help but think that the Stanton family isn't much better. But maybe she's right. Something elaborate and fancy on the outside, but shallow and forced underneath is exactly what this wedding is going to be like. It's exactly what it deserves.

"Then you'll be married," she continues, nodding as if I've said something in response. "And I can finally get to work rebuilding the Stanton legacy as I always intended to."

It's so clear that this is nothing but a business arrangement for Olivia. She doesn't care about me or my feelings. She'll be tying her empire to Troy's, gaining more money and power through the union—helping to improve her standing and her wealth after her husband was betrayed by his business partners and apparently lost a good bit of their money.

The truly disgusting thing is that from what I've seen, Olivia is still very wealthy. She doesn't even need to do this. But she wants to be as obscenely wealthy as she was before, wants to claw her way back to the top of Detroit's upper-class echelon, and she's willing to do whatever it takes to get there.

Even if it means she has to essentially pimp out her granddaughter to the highest bidder for a marriage I don't want.

I swallow past the lump in my throat, my stomach in knots and bitterness on my tongue.

"What does Troy get out of this?" I ask her, wadding up the bloody handkerchief in my hand. "I know he's not doing it out of the goodness of his heart."

"Our family name still carries a lot of weight in Detroit. And I have business connections that can help him and his family. It's a smart match." She looks at me, her lips twisting downward a little as if she's tasted something sour. "On top of that, Troy has always been... intrigued by you. I had hoped to have a virgin granddaughter to auction off, and I was highly disappointed that the Voronin brothers ruined that plan. But it turns out that Troy is somewhat more forgiving of that failing than other men might be. He's more fascinated by the fact that your adoptive mother was a prostitute, and that you were raised by trash."

Her tone of voice makes it sound like she's disgusted by that, but the little smile on her face says that she's pleased with it. Whatever makes him open to this arrangement is apparently a good thing in her book, but the way she talks about his *fascination* with me makes me want to throw up.

I knew Troy was a lecherous creep from the moment I met him, and this just confirms that. I remember how he looked at me when I was at the country club trying to learn how to golf, how he ran into me and Joshua and made those insinuations about what kind of person I must be after being raised by Misty.

I thought he was just a rich boy who thought he could get away with saying shitty things, but it turns out it was even worse than I could have imagined.

Olivia doesn't even seem to register the effect her words have had on me. She keeps talking, returning to the subject she cares most about as she adds, "I'm very hopeful that this marriage will help return my estate to its former glory."

"I'm so happy for you," I can't resist grinding out, irritated at the tone of her voice.

Her eyes snap to mine, narrowing for a moment before she shakes her head. Her gray hair is pulled back from her face in a classic style, and she runs a hand over it even though there isn't a single strand out of place.

"This didn't have to be this way," she reminds me, her tone cool. "And I honestly don't understand why you're so resistant to all of this. This is your *family*, Willow. This estate is your birthright. It's in your blood, and you didn't make the right choice for it. I thought I was teaching you to see the bigger picture and to understand the importance of our legacy and making the necessary sacrifices for it. You are the one who forced my hand here."

Anger rises up in me in a hot rush, and I glare at her, not flinching away from her stare.

"I don't give a shit about that," I snap. "I don't care about the money, or the Stanton legacy, or your standing among the other wealthy families of Detroit. It doesn't mean anything to me."

And why should it? For most of my life, I've been considered trash. Raised by a hooker, working overtime and then some just to be able to get by, missing so much school that I didn't even get my GED until several years after I should've graduated. People like my grandmother have been handed everything on a silver platter, and it's still not enough for them.

Olivia's face hardens, any hint of softness vanishing from her features.

"You're too much like your father," she says. "Too willing to follow your feelings, only thinking of yourself. He was never interested in what it took to maintain our family's legacy either."

I blink, caught off guard. "What do you mean?"

"I had a perfectly acceptable woman lined up for him to marry. Someone who would have lifted our family to a higher station and benefitted both families in the process. But that wasn't good enough for him." She sneers. "No, he fell in love with a woman far beneath him. Someone he had no business being with in the first place, who would have been very bad for our reputation. So when I found out about her and the fact that they'd had a baby together, I took care of it."

"You... took care of it," I echo on a whisper, not even sure what to make of that.

Before today, I would have thought she meant that she helped them, gave them money to take care of the baby, and made sure they didn't have to struggle to get by. But after what I've seen? I know that's not what happened.

"What do you mean?" I press, and my lips feel numb as I force the words past them. I'm not even sure I want to know the answer, but I can't stop myself from asking.

Olivia lifts her chin, holding my gaze, her face impassive.

"I killed her in a fire," she tells me. "The woman he was so in love with. And I had hoped it would take care of the problem of the baby as well. A clean slate, if you will."

Her words hit me like a slap in the face. *The problem of the baby*, she said.

Me.

I was the baby.

When I first met Olivia, she told me that my mother died in a fire that my mother herself had set. She had mental and emotional issues, supposedly, and it was her fault I was burned so badly.

But that was a lie.

Olivia has clearly stopped trying to pretend that she's a good person, or that she's ever cared for me at all, because she just flat-out admitted that she killed my mother. That she tried to kill *me*.

I stand frozen in place as I stare at her, stunned. There are too many emotions clogging up my chest for me to process them all. Hurt and anger are at the forefront, but everything else is just a confusing jumble.

Before I can think of anything to say, another man comes walking into the room. I jump, startled by his sudden appearance. I don't recognize him either, but he's also tall and muscled, dressed in a black suit and wearing dark gloves.

Olivia waves a hand at me, looking annoyed by my skittishness.

"Jerome will take you home," she says. "And make sure you don't do anything foolish." She smiles, but it's that cold, sharp-edged one. Her true smile, I'm coming to realize. "I'll be in touch soon. There will be a lot to do to get ready for the wedding, and there's no time to waste."

I'm escorted out of the sitting room, and then out of the house altogether. Jerome opens the door to a nondescript black car, and I get in without argument, my head in a daze. Part of my mind rebels at the idea of letting a stranger take me anywhere, but the truth is, my situation can barely get worse than it already is. And no matter where he ends up taking me, at least I won't be stuck in Olivia's house any longer.

Just like Olivia's other driver, the man she called Jerome doesn't speak at all. I sit in the back of the car, the fingers of one hand wrapped around my still aching wrist, as I gaze blindly out the window, barely aware of the scenery passing by.

After what feels like an eternity, we pull up outside the luxury complex where Olivia helped me rent an apartment.

"Get out," Jerome tells me, jerking me out of my thoughts.

I scramble to comply, but when I slip out of the car and head toward the front door of my building, the vehicle doesn't pull away. Instead, Jerome just sits there, and it occurs to me that he's probably been given orders to watch the place, making sure that I'm under guard. Between that and the tracker she had put in me, Olivia has made it impossible for me to slip away easily.

My feet carry me up to my apartment unit, and once I get inside with the door closed behind me, the heaviness of everything that's happened hits me in a vicious rush.

I drag in a sharp breath and then another, but it feels like glass in my lungs, stabbing me over and over again. I keep seeing Olivia's cruel smile, hearing the way she spoke to me, the threats she made.

I keep thinking of my birth mother, killed in a fire for the sin of loving a man with an evil harpy for a mother.

Olivia wanted me dead. She called me a problem that she needed to correct. But now that I'm grown up and have reappeared alive and well, she wants to use me. She never cared about me or my happiness. She never wanted to be my family. Not in the proper sense. She just wanted another pawn. Someone else to use on her path to more money and power.

She never loved me.

The first sob hits me hard, and I put my hands over my face, tears spilling down my cheeks as my shoulders shake.

Several more wracking sobs tear through my body, and as I drag in a ragged breath, a soft sound to my right catches my attention. My head snaps up, panic already bursting through me. I'm half expecting it to be Jerome or some other employee of my grandmother's, sent here to drag me back to her house.

But instead, I look over to see Malice climbing through my window, followed by Ransom and Victor.

3

WILLOW

I stare at the three brothers in shock, tears still in my eyes.

"What are you doing here?" I ask, and my voice comes out raspy and pained.

The three of them are a flurry of movement. Vic shuts the window as Malice nods to Ransom, who nods back, heading into my room.

"We're getting you out of here," Malice says grimly. "We won't let you do this. We can get you away, help you escape this."

"I—"

Before I can get the words out, Ransom is calling from the bedroom, "I'm leaving the fancy clothes here. I know they're nice, but I don't think you want anything that bitch bought, right?"

"Traveling lighter is a good idea," Victor chimes in, heading for the bathroom. "Only grab the essentials."

"Wait," I stammer. "You can't do this."

"Solnyshka, I know you think you need to protect us, but—"

"*Stop!*" I practically shout. My voice echoes around us, and Malice and Victor both blink at me in surprise. "I can't go anywhere. I can't leave."

Malice's face hardens, anger shining in his dark gray eyes. Vic looks pissed too, and Ransom comes out of the bedroom, running a hand through his messy brown hair.

"We don't really have time to argue about this right now," he says, his eyebrow ring catching the light as he shakes his head. "We can do it once we get you out of here, okay?"

"You don't understand," I tell him, stepping away from the door. "You have to go. Now."

That seems to set Malice off even more. He gets right up in my face, the way he used to when he was pissed off at the way our lives had collided and had no idea how to handle it.

"No, *you* don't understand," he snaps. "You need to come with us. I know you're trying to be noble or whatever the fuck, but we're not letting you marry this asshole just to keep us safe. We're not letting you sacrifice yourself for us!"

"Listen to him, butterfly," Vic murmurs quietly. "Please. None of us want to see this happen to you."

"I don't want it either," I say desperately. "But I don't have a choice."

"Yes, you fucking do!" Malice explodes. He backs me up, pressing me into a corner of the room until my back hits the wall. "You don't get to make this call, Solnyshka." His voice is a low growl, anger and frustration taking over. "There's no goddamn way we're letting you do this. I'll kill any other man who tries to fucking touch you."

I shake my head, trying to get my thoughts together. Everything is a confusing scramble in my head, all the emotions about what I learned from Olivia warring against the fact that I really do wish I could just run away with the brothers.

Malice takes advantage of my daze, reaching out to grab my arm and hauling me away from the corner.

"Get the bag," he snaps to Ransom, and then he starts towing me toward the door.

That jerks me back to my senses, and I struggle against him, trying to yank my arm away. He's stronger than I am, but I dig my heels into the plush carpet on the floor, hitting his hand where it holds me.

I claw at his arm, doing everything I can to stop him from taking me from the apartment, my breathing coming in harsh, short pants.

"No," I rasp. "No. *No!*"

Malice finally stops, turning to stare at me.

I must look wild and terrified, but that's how I feel. Hysteria is bubbling up in me, making the room spin a little as I fight to get air in my lungs. Each breath feels like it's too shallow, not giving me enough oxygen to keep going, and the stress of the day is slamming into me like a ton of bricks.

Concern flickers across Malice's face, a small line appearing between his dark brows as he drops his head to meet my gaze.

"Solnyshka, what—"

His grip on me loosened a little when he stopped, and I take advantage of that fact to rip my arm free, stumbling backward and away from him.

"Stop! *Please* just stop. I can't go with you. I *can't*... You don't understand, I—"

It comes out sounding like broken gibberish, and I realize there are tears streaking down my face. My chest hurts from breathing so hard, and I'm shaking from head to toe as if I'm freezing.

I wrap my arms around myself, trying to hold myself together even though I feel like I'm splintering apart.

The brothers exchange glances, something unspoken passing between them, and Malice doesn't make a move to grab me again.

"Willow," Ransom says gently, taking a few cautious steps toward me. "What happened? What did she do to you?"

I shake my head, and it takes me a few tries to get any sound to come out of my mouth. It's hard to speak, the words sticking in my throat like shards of glass, but I have to tell them so they don't make this worse than it already is.

"There's a guard outside," I manage first. "He... he dropped me off here and he's still out there in his car."

Malice whirls to face the closest window, glaring down at the street below.

"Fuck. So she's watching you," he growls, hands curling into fists at his side.

"And that's not all." I hold up my wrist, the one that Olivia had her man put a tracker in. "She's tracking me too. If I leave a certain area, she'll know immediately, and she'll know how to find me."

Just saying it out loud makes it hurt even more. My wrist throbs where the skin was broken to put the tracker in, and the tears fall faster down my face. I can't even be bothered to wipe them away, just sniffling, trying to keep it together.

"She has a whole plan," I explain. "For how the engagement to that... that asshole is going to go. How we're going to get married." I swallow again.

"That fucking *bitch*," Malice explodes. He pivots away from the window, his fist lashing out to punch the wall with a heavy thud. "She can't do this."

"She can," I whisper. "She's already doing it. She said if we try to escape, she'd come after us. And she could do it. Her estate may not be what it once was, but I know she has the resources, and she'd be so angry that..."

I shake my head, a sob bubbling out of my throat before I can finish that sentence.

But I don't need to.

Everyone in this room knows what Olivia Stanton is capable of now, and she's made her threats well.

"That doesn't change anything," Malice says, turning back to face me. "We still have to get you out of here. If she thinks she can make you marry someone just to save her fucking empire, she's in for a rude awakening."

"He's right." Vic nods, his face serious. "We can outrun her."

The tears fall harder and faster. I stare at the three of them as they look back at me—still so determined to get me out of here, and still so wrong about everything.

"No, we can't," I whisper. "You don't understand. She already tried to kill you once. She'd kill me if she decided I wasn't useful."

"No way. She needs you too much," Ransom objects. "You're her family."

"She doesn't give a shit about family." It comes out harsh, edged with anger and hurt and the rasp of my tears. "She told me so herself. She told me that she killed my mom."

"What?" Vic asks, his eyes narrowing sharply.

"My real mom," I tell him. "Olivia told me… when we first met, she told me that my birth mom was unstable and had mental problems. She said that my mom was the one who set the fire in our house, the one that left me with these scars. But it was Olivia. My mom wasn't 'good enough' for my dad—Olivia's son—so Olivia got rid of her."

I glance down at myself as I finish speaking. Just looking at my body now makes me shudder with revulsion. Olivia killed my mother. She tried to kill me. And I wear the scars of that every day.

"She thought she killed me too, when she set the fire," I murmur. "I have no idea why I didn't die. Maybe my mom was able to get me out somehow, or maybe someone found me in the wreckage afterward and kept it secret. And then I ended up in the system, where I was adopted by Misty."

My heart feels like it's breaking as I say it out loud, the weight of all of it bearing down on me. I shake my head, clenching my jaw and tightening my arms around myself, steeling myself against every argument I know these men will try to make.

"I can't let that happen to you," I say. "I can't let her get her hands on you. I can't lose you too. She's already taken away my family, and I can't… Please. Please don't do this."

My pulse beats a frantic rhythm in my chest, and I stare at the three of them, trying to get them to understand just how important this is. I know they can be impulsive and reckless, I know they're used to danger, but this is too important. If they get hurt, if Olivia kills them or sends them to prison, I don't know how I'll survive.

The Voronin brothers all stare at me, their expressions so similar despite the differences in their features. Their eyes are intense, but at least I can tell they're listening to me. They can hear how serious I am about this.

The silence stretches on for a heavy beat, and then Malice strides forward.

He reaches for me, and I half expect him to start trying to get me to leave again. But instead, he pulls me into a hug, his strong arms going around me, holding me tight.

He enfolds me in a crushing embrace, and that's so much better than me holding myself together that I immediately melt into it, clinging to him for dear life.

He's strong and sure, and he smells comfortingly of leather and spice and something smoky, the way he always does.

"It's okay," he murmurs gruffly. He smooths a hand down my back and drops a kiss to my head. "It's okay."

He only speaks those two little words, but that's all it takes. I break down, sobbing into his chest, the stress and anger and horror of the day getting the best of me as I cry until my throat is raw.

Ransom and Victor move in to stand close, and Malice just keeps holding me, strong and silent and solid.

4

MALICE

In the time since I first met Willow, I've rewritten my thoughts on her a few times.

At first, I thought she was some frail little thing, in the wrong place at the wrong time and doomed to pay the price for that. It wasn't my problem, and I was willing to do what I had to in order to protect my brothers.

Then I realized she was stronger than I gave her credit for, and that strength became fucking intoxicating, drawing me to her like a moth to a flame, undeniable.

Holding her now, it's almost like she's a mix of those two things. Fragile enough to be sobbing herself apart in my arms, but strong enough to stand up to me, to stand up to all three of us, to keep us safe.

Her fucking grandma, that bitch, wants to use her as a pawn, but she doesn't realize that Willow could never be a pawn. She was always meant to be a queen.

I hold my Solnyshka a bit closer, almost crushing her in my grip, but I can't help it. Willow doesn't seem to mind. The tighter I hold on to her, the more she responds in kind, her fingers bunched into the fabric of my shirt, clinging to me like I'm a lifeline.

My head is spinning, and my emotions are a fucking mess right now. The need to protect her and get her away from here is at war with the need to make that pained, desperate, hysterical look on her face disappear.

Every time her body shakes with a sob, I run my hand up and down her back, trying to comfort her. I whisper soothing nonsense, promising it's going to be okay, that we're all here for her, but at the same time, my head is full of one question.

How?

How the fuck are we supposed to keep her safe when she's trying to do the same for us, and there's a crazy, megalomaniac bitch pulling the strings?

One fucking step at a time, I guess. Or die trying.

For the moment, I just focus on the here and now, holding Willow and letting her cry herself out.

Ransom is on her left side, stroking her arm, running his fingers through her hair. He's quiet, which isn't like him, but there's a storm of conflicted feelings on his face, so I get it.

Vic's on the other side, and he has one hand stretched out, like he wants to touch her but can't quite get there. He steps in as close as he dares to and finally lets the fingers of that hand tangle in the fabric of Willow's dress. Close enough, I guess.

"We'll figure it out," he promises her, and the heaviness of those words isn't lost on me. It's what Vic always promises when he plans to throw his whole self into something, and he doesn't do it for just anyone.

Eventually, the shaking and sobbing eases up, and Willow lifts her face from my shirt. Her cheeks are red and her eyes are puffy from crying, but she seems calmer than she did before.

I pull back reluctantly, not wanting to let her go.

She still has tear streaks down her cheeks, the wetness clumping her pale lashes together, and I reach up, using one thumb to wipe them away.

Even in this state, she's still so fucking beautiful to me. She's the most beautiful woman I've ever known, and she always will be.

"Listen to me, Solnyshka," I tell her, keeping my voice low. "We don't have any plans to let your fucking grandma kill us or send us to jail. But there's also no way we can let you be forced to marry someone else. Especially someone that bitch picked out for you, knowing full well that he's a piece of shit. So we'll have to come up with a third option."

"What's the third option?" she murmurs, her voice rough from crying.

"Plan C," I say. "We'll just have to come up with it."

Hope blooms in her eyes, and although it's just a tiny spark, nearly drowned out by the pain and fear, it's still there. And it's really fucking good to see.

"You know, this is something we've gotten good at," Ransom puts in, grinning. "We're always coming up with a new plan on the fly, changing things up, figuring out a way around obstacles. If we weren't good at that shit, we'd be dead by now. We can do it this time too."

Something flickers through Vic's eyes, and he peels away from our little group, moving through the living room, checking things carefully. Once he's satisfied in here, he moves into each of the other rooms, being thorough in a way that only he can be, and probably subconsciously cleaning as he goes.

"Okay," he announces when he comes back. "The place is clean."

Willow gives him a confused look, and he clarifies. "I was checking to make sure she didn't have any bugs planted in here. To listen in on you."

"Only you would think to do that," Willow murmurs. "I guess it's kind of your area of expertise, huh?"

Her lips turn up in a halfhearted smile, but it's nice to hear her joking again.

Vic smiles back, inclining his head as his blue eyes meet hers. "Exactly."

Ransom goes to the window and peeks out, keeping his head low. "Black car?" he asks. "Some kind of SUV?"

"That's the guy who drove me home," Willow confirms.

"Ransom?" I cock a brow at him, and he hears my unspoken question, giving me a rundown of what he sees outside.

"One guy in the car, behind the wheel. Probably armed, but hard to tell. We didn't see anyone else on our way in, but that doesn't mean she doesn't have other guards stationed somewhere in or around the building."

Willow rubs at the spot on her wrist where she said some guy put a tracker under her skin. "She doesn't need other guards," she murmurs. "She's holding all the cards."

"For now, maybe," I tell her. "But we can come up with a way to fuck that up for her."

I guide Willow to the couch, sitting her down. Ransom and I sit on either side of her, and Vic takes his usual chair, although he scoots it closer to the couch. This is the way my brothers and I usually come up with plans, the three of us sitting in our living room, ready to bicker and pitch ideas until we have something we're happy with.

Before we even start talking, Ransom pulls Willow into his lap, and she goes easily. She melts into his touch, and my younger brother lets out a quiet sigh, as if being close to her is helping him stay calm as well.

My own palms tingle, itching to have my hands on her, to have her in my own arms again. But I know she needs this. She needs to feel grounded by all three of us in whatever ways we can make that happen.

Ransom's always been good with her, a hell of a lot better than I am most of the time. He's good at getting her to open up and feel comfortable with him, and right now, she needs that comfort.

I want that for her, after the fucking mess of a day she's had.

"Let's go over the facts first," Vic says, taking point. "Today was... a lot. A lot of new information came to light, and we haven't really had a chance to sort through all of it."

"Well, we know Olivia fucking Stanton is X." Ransom snorts. "Biggest surprise of the day, I'd say."

He's right about that. This whole time, we'd been picturing some well-connected man, sitting in the shadows, pulling the strings. We'd considered the idea that it was someone we knew personally before, someone who had a personal stake in our lives and knew how to push our buttons.

But we never could have expected it to be Willow's grandmother.

"Is there any chance she was bluffing?" Vic asks. "Any chance she lied about that?"

I glance at him, aware that he's just asking the question to be thorough and cover all our bases. But we all know the answer.

"No," I say. "She's definitely X. She knew too much, and unless she's somehow someone even bigger than X, someone X might've been answering to, she had to have been telling the truth."

Vic nods, his dark hair glinting under the overhead lights. "Then we know she's not bluffing. She has the ability to send Malice back to jail—and to possibly put us all away if she wanted to. We have no idea how extensive her network might be, both in the criminal world and the legit side of things, but we know she plans to keep close tabs on Willow. Did she say anything about making you move in with her?"

He addresses that last question to Willow, who shakes her head, straightening a little from where she's leaning against Ransom's chest.

"No," Willow murmurs. "But I assume she'll want me to live with Troy after we get married."

That last word sounds bitter as it comes out of her mouth, and it makes my jaw go tight, my hands unconsciously clenching into fists.

Vic hesitates, and I can tell he's grappling with what she just said too. Then he clears his throat and responds. "Well, she's clearly taking steps to make sure you can't run away, even if she's letting you stay on your own for now. Either way, escaping would be dangerous, and as you said, Olivia has the resources to hunt us down."

"You sound like a real ray of sunshine right now, Vic," Ransom mumbles, pulling Willow closer in his lap. He nuzzles against her, and she rests her head against his, both of them looking at Vic to see where he's going with this.

My twin rolls his eyes, although the rest of his expression barely changes.

"I'm laying out the facts," he says. "We have to know what we're working against if we're going to figure out a plan."

"It makes sense," Willow murmurs. "I don't want to miss something because we... weren't looking at all the facts."

Vic shoots Ransom a look, and our younger brother grimaces but nods. The fact of the matter is, there's not a lot of wiggle room here. Olivia Stanton is an evil bitch, but she's an evil bitch with connections and resources that we could only dream about.

"We could just kill her," I mutter under my breath.

"No," Willow says immediately. "She's not like Carl or any of the other people you've gone after. Her death can't be covered up that easily. She's a prominent member of society, and even if the people in her circle are as two-faced as she is, they'll ask questions. You can't do that."

I shrug one shoulder, slumping down on the couch even more. "I was kidding. Mostly."

Because fuck, it would feel good to take her out after all the pain she's put Willow through.

"No murders," Vic agrees. "But there might be something in the fact that she's X that we can use to our advantage."

"What do you mean?" Ransom asks.

"She threatened to use the jobs we've done for X against us, but maybe we can do the same to her. We could try to get evidence that links Olivia to all the crimes she had us commit."

"And then turn her in?" Willow wants to know. "Wouldn't that just link you to the crimes as well?"

Vic shakes his head. "No. We don't turn her in. We blackmail her. People like Olivia value their reputations more than anything, so if we threaten to expose her if she doesn't let you go…"

"Then she might be willing to do it without trying to fuck us in the process," I finish. "It's an idea."

"How do we get the evidence we need?" Ransom asks.

Vic's eyes flick to Willow. "You're the only one who has access to her house. To her, really. You'll have to find a way to snoop around her mansion and see what you can find."

Determination fills Willow's eyes, and it settles something inside my chest. That hopeless, panicked look is finally starting to be chased away, and I'm glad to see it gone. She should never have to feel like that.

"I can do that," she agrees with a nod, resolve clear in her tone.

Pride fills me at the sound of it. She's steel all the way through, our girl, and she's going to find a way out of this.

My fingers itch to touch her, and just like that, I decide Ransom has had enough time cuddling her or whatever. I pull her into my own lap, and she comes willingly, settling in and melting against me just like she did with him.

Fuck. I like that a lot.

She's a warm, comforting weight, and I wrap my arms around her, nuzzling into her hair, breathing in the scent of her shampoo and her skin.

"It's the best idea we've got," I murmur after a moment, agreeing with Vic's plan. "But we need a backup. If this plan doesn't work, we're still not letting Willow marry Tony."

"Troy," Willow corrects, her lip curling.

"I don't give a fuck," I shoot back. "You're not marrying him.

We'll run for it and deal with the consequences of that, whatever they may be."

"Malice," Willow starts, drawing back a little to look at me. "We can't—"

"No, Solnyshka. That's non-negotiable," I say, cutting her off. "It's not fucking happening."

She stares at me for a second, her eyes bouncing between mine. I let her look for as long as she wants, my expression making it clear how goddamn serious I am about this.

After a moment, she sighs, nodding her agreement.

"Good girl," I growl. Palming the back of her head, I pull her into a kiss.

I can never seem to hold myself back when it comes to her, but I'm starting to learn that Willow doesn't need or want me to. She meets my kiss, not flinching at the rough, possessive way I hold on to her and how I slide my tongue into her mouth, sweeping through it like I'm laying a claim.

She trembles slightly against me, but this time it feels more like it's from pleasure than the panic of earlier. She makes a soft noise against my mouth, and I nip at her bottom lip before pulling back.

"Ty vyydesh' za drugogo tol'ko cherez moy trup," I growl. *"Ja ub'ju ego, esli on dazhe popytaetsja."*

I wind one hand up and into her soft blonde hair, fisting it near the roots and making her look at me. Her pupils are blown wide, darkening her gold-flecked brown irises, her lips pink and wet, and she looks fucking perfect.

"You're ours," I remind her, my voice firm and intense. "No matter what happens, that's never gonna change. We'll never let you belong to anyone else."

5

WILLOW

Malice's words hit me hard, both in the heart and in places a bit lower.

I stare into his stormy eyes as he finishes speaking, believing with all my heart that he means it. Even though I'm still terrified and freaked out about everything, the conviction in his tone helps soothe me.

He means what he says, and he's willing to face the consequences. All of them are.

I nod, acknowledging his words.

Malice holds my gaze for another long second, then slowly unwinds his fingers from my hair, letting me feel the power and control in his grip.

"Good. Then that's settled," Ransom says as the moment slowly breaks, leaning back on the couch. "It's not the best as far as plans go, but..."

He shrugs, grimacing slightly.

"But we don't have very many options," Vic agrees with a sigh. "This was hard enough when we were just trying to figure out who X was. Now that we know, the stakes are much higher."

"I'm sorry," I murmur, feeling like this is somehow my fault. I'm the one who brought Olivia into our lives, after all. Maybe if I'd turned down meeting my biological grandmother all those weeks ago at the hospital, we wouldn't be in this mess—although judging by how well Olivia takes hearing no for an answer, I'm sure that's not likely. The second she realized I was still alive, the first domino fell, and there was no way to stop what came next.

Vic flicks his eyes up to me, a frown passing over his face.

"It's not your fault," he tells me, his tone serious. His way of speaking isn't as intense as Malice's, but I can tell he means what he says just as much. "Your grandmother took advantage of you, butterfly. And we'll do whatever it takes to make sure it doesn't get worse."

I swallow hard, nodding at him. "Okay."

He nods back, those clear blue eyes of his seeming to see right through me.

"We should probably go," Ransom says after a quiet moment. "Just in case the guard does a sweep or something. It's probably not a good idea for us to be found here."

Malice's face darkens, but Vic nods again, already getting up from his chair.

Ransom and Malice each kiss me one more time, and although Vic doesn't, he gives me a look full of meaning as they head for the door.

"Let us know if you need any help getting dirt on your grandmother," he says. "We'll do what we can."

"Thank you," I tell him. All of them.

Watching them go makes me feel like I'm being torn in two, as if my heart is going with them. In a practical sense, it's a good thing that they're leaving, because I was worried about the guy watching my place finding them here, but I miss them as soon as they're gone.

That feeling I had when I first moved in, of this apartment being too big and too empty, is multiplied now. Especially now that I know it wasn't so much a gift as it is a fancy prison for Olivia to keep me in until she makes me marry Troy. She might not have decided to make me live under her roof until the wedding, but this isn't much better. It's just an extension of her power, another piece of proof that she never cared about me in the first place.

I stand in the middle of the living room for a minute, gathering myself together, and then start trying to do normal things—anything to take my mind off the panic that still lurks at the edges of my consciousness. My stomach growls loudly, and as it does, I realize I haven't eaten anything since before the funeral.

It's crazy to think that this is the same day, when it feels like the girl who was most concerned about laying her adopted mother to rest this morning was a completely different person than I am now.

I go into the kitchen and heat up some canned soup, watching the liquid bubble in the pot. I make toast to go with it, the way I used to when I was a kid, but by the time I settle at the kitchen table with the steaming bowl, I don't even want to eat it.

I feel hungry, but my stomach twists in knots, my appetite low.

But I force myself to take small bites, dipping the bread into the broth and eating half of it before I give up and dump the whole thing into the sink. I run the garbage disposal, the harsh grinding sound grating against my ears before I flick it off.

As I move back through the living room toward my room, I turn off the lights. It's evening by now and has gotten dark outside, and I hope that keeping it dark inside as well will keep the guard on the street from watching me too much. Just thinking about him out there, maybe reporting my movements to Olivia, makes me shudder and feel sick.

I also feel dirty, grimy from the long day and everything that's happened, so I run the shower as hot as I can stand it and step under the spray, scrubbing myself clean.

It doesn't really help. All I can think about is how if I have to marry Troy, I'm never really going to feel clean again.

Back in my old place, when I was feeling like shit, I'd stand under the hot water until it started to run cold, letting that be the signal for when I'd been in for too long. Now I don't have that signal, since the hot water heater in this apartment is much better, so I have to force myself to get out, shivering as I dry off and walk back into my room to put on pajamas.

As I get dressed, I glance at the places where I put the cameras back up. I know they're still on, and I hope Vic is watching me. It makes me feel less alone to think of him in his room, sitting at his desk, keeping an eye on me.

I get into bed and grab my phone, opening my text chain with Vic. But instead of sending him a message, I decide to call him instead. I just want to hear his voice right now.

"Willow," he murmurs, picking up after the first ring. "Is something wrong?"

"Hi," I whisper. "No, nothing's wrong, I just.... well, a lot is wrong, but nothing new is wrong."

"That's good. I think you're full up on things being wrong for the time being."

I let out a messy sigh. "You can say that again." I glance at the cameras once more. "Have you been watching?"

"Yes," he says. "I always want to watch you, but now I want to make sure you're okay."

Hearing him admit that warms my heart. It's kind of hard to believe that I once thought Vic was cold and robotic. He feels things just as deeply as his brothers do—he just has less of an idea what to do with those feelings.

Closing my eyes, I take a deep breath and then let it out, still holding the phone to my ear.

"Will you stay on the line as I fall asleep?" I ask quietly, my cheeks flushing a little. "We don't have to talk. It would help just to hear you on the other end of the line. I don't want to be alone right now."

"Of course. You should get some rest if you can."

"I know. I'll try. Goodnight, Vic."

"Goodnight, butterfly."

I shift around, making myself more comfortable in bed, holding on to the phone like it's my most precious possession. The sound of his steady breathing is as soothing as I hoped it would be, but I'm still too wound up and tense to fall asleep.

After a moment or two of silence, I speak up again. "Hey, Vic?"

"Hm?" he asks.

I open my mouth, but nothing comes out. There are so many things I could say. I could tell him how much I appreciate him, or how glad I am that I've gotten to know him better. I could say I still think about the time he kissed me, and how I wish he'd do it again. Or I could tell him that I think I'm falling for him. It's right there on the tip of my tongue, but I chicken out before I can say anything like that.

Instead, I just swallow hard and whisper, "Thank you. For everything."

"Of course," he repeats, as if everything he and his brothers have done for me is the simplest, most natural thing in the world.

I can hear him typing on his keyboard through the phone, and I imagine that he's doing what he always seems to do best—working away at his computer, using the skills he taught himself to try to help his brothers and me. The steady clicking noises join the soft pattern of his inhales and exhales, and after a while, my eyes drift shut as I listen.

But even when exhaustion finally pulls me under, I don't sleep easy.

6

WILLOW

My dreams are *weird and disjointed, jumping from one thing to the next.*

My grandmother stars in all of them, standing like a statue with her ramrod straight posture and that cold look in her eyes. When she smiles, it's chilling, and no matter where I try to run to, she's there.

I dream of being back in the hospital, but there are bars on the windows and the door is locked from the outside. It's in the aftermath of when Ilya kidnapped me, and the police lead Olivia through the door and into my room.

My heart pounds in my chest, panic sweeping through me. Unlike when I met her in real life, this time I know just from looking at her that she's not a good person.

"Wait!" I call as the police officer starts to leave us alone together. "Don't leave me with her. She's a murderer. She's evil."

The cop frowns, giving me a look filled with pity, as if he thinks I've lost touch with reality.

"She's your grandmother," he says, his tone placating and patronizing. "And she wants what's best for you. She's never done anything wrong."

"That's a lie!" I scream, trying to kick off the sheets. "She killed

my mother. She tried to kill me. You have to get her away from me! Please!"

I try to throw myself out of the hospital bed, desperate to get away, only to find that I'm chained to it. Thick steel cuffs are wrapped around my wrists and ankles, and when I try to move, they rattle against the thick bars at the sides of the bed.

"She's hysterical," Olivia says to the cop. Her voice isn't the cold, brusque tone she used when she told me I'd have to marry Troy, but the kindly one she used in the beginning to lure me in and make me trust her. "She's had a terrible ordeal, but what she needs most right now is her family. I'll take care of her from here. Don't worry."

The cop nods, and I shake my head, my entire body jerking as I fight to wrench my wrists free of the cuffs. "No, please! Don't believe her! Help me!"

Olivia comes closer to the bed, and I struggle harder, the clanging of metal on metal filling my ears as the chains rattle and shake.

But there's nowhere to go.

She's closing in on me.

Leaning down and—

My eyes snap open, and I drag in a ragged breath. I'm thrashing in my bed, and cold relief fills me when I realize I'm not chained down to it. Instead of scratchy hospital sheets, I'm lying on the soft, Egyptian cotton sheets Olivia picked out for me, which honestly doesn't feel much better.

My heart is racing, and I feel off balance and jittery from the nightmare.

"Willow?"

I jump at the distant voice in my ear at first, but then realize it's Victor. The phone is still there, on my pillow, and although morning sunlight is streaming through the window, he stayed on the line all night with me. Just like he said he would.

"Are you alright?" he asks as I press the phone more fully to my ear, and even though his voice sounds mostly neutral, the way it usually does, I can imagine the way he'd be looking at me if he was here.

"I... had a nightmare," I tell him, dragging my free hand down my face. Having him with me makes me feel better. Even if we're not in the same room, I know he can hear me and see me, and he's watching out for me.

"Do you want to talk about it?" he asks.

I shake my head and swallow hard. "No. Did you sleep at all? Or were you hunched over your computer all night?"

He huffs a little laugh, and it makes me smile to imagine the way his own smile would be pulling at his lips.

"A little," he says. "Not long after you fell asleep."

That makes me feel even better, thinking that we were connected somehow all night. It might be the closest I'll ever get to cuddling with Victor.

"How are Malice and Ransom? Malice seemed... really pissed off yesterday."

"He was really pissed off," Vic replies. The *we all were* is unspoken, but I hear it all the same. "And he still is today. He's slammed every cabinet in the kitchen, it sounds like. Ransom is... out of sorts. He's in the garage, but I don't hear him working on anything."

I can definitely picture that. Malice stomping around like he has a storm cloud of rage over his head. His own localized hurricane, whipping around him and making it dangerous for anyone other than a chosen few to get close to him.

It's a bit harder to picture Ransom out of sorts, just because he's usually so cheerful, at least compared to his two brothers, but this is a big, weird situation, so it makes sense that he would feel some kind of way about it.

"They'll be okay," Victor is saying, shaking me from my thoughts. "We're more worried about you, anyway."

"I'll be okay too." I try to make my voice sound convincing. "I'm going to do what I can, and—"

I'm cut off by the sound of the line beeping, a signal that I have another call coming through. When I pull the phone away from my ear to look at the screen, I shudder to see that it's Olivia.

"I have to go," I tell Vic hurriedly. "She's calling me."

"Okay," he says, but I can hear the strain in his voice. "Take care, butterfly. Be careful."

"You too."

He ends the call on his side, and I answer my grandmother's, all the comfortable, warm energy I was feeling from speaking with Vic disappearing in less than a second.

"What?" I say, not even bothering to pretend to be polite.

"You will not be answering the phone like that for much longer," Olivia replies, her voice crisp and businesslike. "You're lucky I don't have the time to deal with your disrespect right now, but you *will* learn to behave like a lady of society. I won't have you embarrassing me."

I clench my jaw and breathe in through my nose, trying to settle the angry feeling in my chest. Olivia needs me for this deal, but I can't say what she'd do to me if I pissed her off too much. Or to the guys, who don't have the benefit of being needed for her empire to flourish.

"Sorry," I mutter. "What is it?"

"That's better, if only just. You need to come to the house today," she says. "Get dressed, in something appropriate, and come downstairs. Jerome will drive you."

I want so badly to tell her to go fuck herself. To tell her that she has no power over me and I don't have to do what she says. But none of that is true. She has all the power, and if I don't do it, people I care about will suffer.

"Fine, okay," I mumble.

I don't really want to gamble with keeping her waiting, and I definitely don't want Jerome to come up here and have to handle things himself, so I make it quick, pulling on one of the outfits Olivia bought for me a while ago and brushing my hair.

When I get downstairs, Jerome is there at the door waiting. He doesn't say anything, just leads the way to his car, opening the back door for me. I slide in, and it's a silent ride to Olivia's mansion.

My stomach is in knots the whole way, wondering what hell my grandmother plans to drop in my lap today. I can't imagine this whole awful scenario is ever going to take a turn for the better. Not where she's concerned, at least.

Of course, when I get to the house and follow one of the staff to the sitting room, Troy is there. My heart lurches, my footsteps stuttering as soon as I catch sight of him.

I knew this was coming, but seeing him in person makes it so much more real than it was before.

He's sitting on the couch, a drink in his hand, looking like he thinks he's some kind of king on his throne. But as soon as our gazes meet, his expression changes. It goes from neutral, even bored as he listened to whatever Olivia was talking about before I entered, to that lecherous grin that I hate so fucking much.

My fingers curl themselves into fists, and I tuck my hands behind my back, trying to breathe through my disgust and revulsion for this man.

"Ah. My darling fiancée," he says, drawing the last word out. "There you are."

I swallow back bile, glaring at him, and don't respond.

His grin only grows at my obvious reticence.

"Oh, don't be that way," he chides. "Your grandmother told me the good news. My bid to marry you has been accepted. We should be celebrating."

I bite down on my tongue hard, trying to keep the flood of things I want to say from spilling out of my mouth.

But he doesn't seem to need any verbal response from me one

way or another. He rises from his chair and strides over to me. When he reaches me, he makes a slow circle around me, taking me in and inspecting me like I'm a new car he wants to buy or something.

"She knows how to dress herself, at least," he comments, talking to Olivia like I'm not even present. "Hair color is good, but it needs to be styled by someone who knows what to do with it." He fluffs one of my blonde locks with his fingers, and I fight the urge to flinch away, not wanting to give him the satisfaction. "Soft. Nice. Hygiene is good too. You can never tell with people raised on that side of the city, you know? Some of them crawl out of their gutters and think they can just mingle with regular people, no questions asked."

Rage rises in me, but I still don't reply. I stare straight ahead, keeping my gaze focused on a flower arrangement in the corner and wishing I could set it on fire with my eyes.

"Of course, her background knocks a couple points off her value," Troy continues.

"But her pedigree adds much more," Olivia counters.

Troy nods, his classically handsome features morphing into an easy grin as he flicks a glance toward my grandmother. "Granted."

He completes his circle and comes to stand in front of me again, reaching out to grip my chin. I jerk away, and he smirks.

"Fiery. I like that. So, I know you're not a virgin. That ship has sailed and is probably sunk to the bottom of the sea by now, right? But I want to know when it started."

"What?" I ask, glaring at him. "What is that supposed to mean?"

"When did you first start sleeping around? When did you become the little slut standing in front of me?" he asks, amusement glinting in his brown eyes as he cocks his head. "Did your mom pimp you out as soon as you got old enough? Did she offer two for one deals to help make rent?"

It hits me like a slap in the face, and I can hear my heartbeat rushing in my ears. It's not true, of course, but I can think back to some of my mom's clients touching me once they were done with her, or while they were waiting for her to be done with another client. She never explicitly gave them permission to do any of that, but she never did enough to protect me from them either.

"No," I say, biting the word out. "She didn't offer *two for one deals.*"

"Pity," Troy replies, grinning. "I bet you wanted her to. I bet you listened to her getting railed and wished it was you. Is that what happened the first time? How you popped your little cherry? You heard your mom getting fucked, and you wanted to know what it felt like, so you grabbed something and imitated it?"

His eyes are shining with some combination of fucked up entertainment and what I recognize as lust. He's getting off on degrading me and trying to get me to say demeaning shit about myself. It's just a game to him. A sick and twisted joke.

When I don't respond to his question, Troy doesn't seem bothered. He picks his inspection up again, grabbing my chin once more and pulling me in closer. He turns my face this way and that, then uses his fingers to pry my mouth open so he can look inside.

I'm so startled that I don't even react, my heart lurching in my chest as I try to swallow.

"Not bad," he murmurs. "Could be worse, considering where you're from."

My cheeks flood with heat from the humiliation of it all. He's treating me like I'm some kind of horse, some piece of livestock he's about to bring home.

He lifts one arm and then the other, running his fingers along them. "No track marks. Good. Unless you're hiding them somewhere else?"

"I don't do drugs," I snap.

"I don't doubt her about that," Olivia says. "Whatever habits her mother engaged in, Willow seems to have been too bright to get involved with them."

Before, I might've considered her words a compliment, but now all I hear in it is condescension.

Troy runs his fingers up my arm slowly, holding my gaze. "Good." Then his gaze drops to my chest, and I have to fight the urge to cover it. "Nice tits. Could do with being a bit bigger, but they have surgeries to correct that. I like a girl I can hold on to."

He winks and steps in even closer to me.

"So there's one last thing to check," he says, his voice dropping low. "Before I fully agree to this marriage."

Before I can say anything, he's shoving his hand down the front of my pants.

I gasp, caught off guard, and I can't even move as he works his fingers past the lips of my pussy so he can thrust one deep into me.

It hurts, and I shudder in utter revulsion as he feels around, like he's checking to make sure I really don't have a hymen or wants to see how tight I am or... fuck, I don't even know what.

My stomach rolls with nausea. It would serve him right if I threw up all over him, but I don't want to deal with the fallout from that, so I swallow back the bile that tries to rise up. My cheeks burn, anger and humiliation battling for dominance in my gut.

Olivia just sits where she was when I walked in, calmly sipping her tea like this isn't happening in front of her, or like she doesn't care one way or another that it is.

After another long moment of prodding, Troy pulls his fingers out of me and then out of my pants and finally steps back, putting some much needed distance between us. He smirks at me, running his tongue over his lip, and then looks to Olivia.

"She doesn't seem that damaged," he says. "I'm surprised, honestly. I'll take her."

My grandmother smiles, setting aside her tea on a small tray. "Excellent. Then the deal is done."

Those words are one push too far for me, and my stomach

finally revolts, ignoring all my attempts to keep it down. I spin on my heel and dash out of the room, gagging as I run down the hall toward the bathroom. I make it just in time to fall to my knees in front of the toilet, throwing up in a rush.

Every part of me feels disgusting. It's like I can feel the phantom traces of Troy's touch on my skin and between my legs. I wish I could shower. I wish I could go back in time and make sure none of this could happen.

Tears well in my eyes, but I blink them back, shaking my head with a low groan. I don't have time to fall apart here. If I take too long in the bathroom, then Olivia will likely send someone after me. Maybe even Troy, and he's the last fucking person I want to see right now.

I also don't want him to see me like this. Letting him see any weakness in me would probably be a bad idea.

So I drag in a deep breath and drag myself up, flushing away the evidence of how badly this has rattled me. I wash my hands and then rinse my mouth out in the sink, trying to pull myself together.

Reluctantly, I leave the bathroom, heading back down the hall toward the sitting room. On the way, an open door on one side of the hallway catches my attention. It's cracked a few inches wide, and I push it a little wider and peer in. The room is a bit more practical looking than the rest of the house, although it's still decorated elaborately, with large paintings on the wall. There's an expensive looking wooden desk and a couple of chairs in one corner, several file cabinets, and bookshelves lining the walls.

This must be Olivia's office. The door has always been closed when I've come to her house, so I've never seen the inside of it before.

A spark of hope lights in my chest, burning away some of the dread. There must be dozens of papers and documents in that room. Maybe there's something in there that we can use. Something that will link her to all the terrible shit she's done, and the things she's made the Voronin brothers do for her.

At the very least, it's a good place to start my search, and that's more than I was expecting to get out of this visit.

I close the door a little and head back to the sitting room where I left Troy and Olivia, but as I step inside, I realize that Olivia is gone now. It's just Troy, leaning back in his chair as he finishes his drink.

He smirks when I enter, and I have the sudden urge to flee the room.

"You know, you should be grateful," he drawls smugly. "I'm doing you a huge favor here."

"I promise you, you're not," I bite out between clenched teeth, debating if I can leave now that he's had his little moment, without being dismissed by Olivia first.

"Not many people would want to take on someone like you." He gets up and comes closer to me, circling me again. "But I like a challenge. I know what they say about you, all the whispers among the society women, but there's something fun about the idea of turning a whore into a housewife. Plus..." He reaches out, grabbing my ass and pulling me in tight against his body. "I have some particular... appetites, let's say. And I think the daughter of a hooker might just be able to keep up. Better than any of the frigid bitches in the country club set, at least."

"Get off me," I snarl, trying to push away from him. He's surprisingly strong, and he doesn't let up for a second.

"Maybe I'll try you out right now," he whispers, leaning in and dragging his tongue up the side of my neck. His breath smells like whiskey and something stale, and it makes my stomach heave all over again. "Give you a little spin, huh? Make sure I'm getting the best deal here."

He shoves me backward, and when I stumble, he takes advantage of that, pushing me onto the couch. I don't have time to scramble away before he's on top of me. His weight is unpleasant and stifling, and when he grinds his crotch down against mine, adrenaline shoots through my veins like a flood of ice water.

"What the hell are you doing?" I shout, writhing beneath him. "I said get the fuck off me!"

I struggle hard, trying to find a way to get him off or to get out from under him. My heart races, and I reach up, about to slap him—but he's quicker than me. In a flash, he grabs my wrist and pins it over my head.

His creepy grin never falters, and he stares down at me like it's turning him on even more to see me fighting and struggling against him.

"Fuck, yes," he mutters under his breath. "This is gonna be fun."

Footsteps enter the room, and my heart skips a beat. I turn my head to see Olivia coming back in, her heels tapping lightly on the floor. I'm almost happy to see her, thinking that she'll tell Troy off or something, but she doesn't say anything. She just lifts one eyebrow and stands there, making no move to stop him.

Hatred for both of them boils in my blood, tinged with a sick sort of despair.

Is she going to watch him assault me? How far will she let him go?

But luckily, Troy takes her appearance as his cue to get off me. He gives my wrist one more painful squeeze, then releases it, getting back to his feet and readjusting his well-tailored clothes. There's a slight flush on his cheeks, his usually perfectly styled hair a little mussed.

"Well," he says, turning back to Olivia as he smooths his hair. His tone is perfectly casual, as if he wasn't just trying to force himself on her granddaughter in the sitting room. "Now that the deal is set, we'll need to have an engagement party."

Olivia nods. "Of course. It deserves to be celebrated. And I'll be in touch to settle the guest list with you. It's important that we invite all of the top families in Detroit. I want them to know about this deal."

"Alright. We can hammer out the details soon," Troy agrees.

He smirks at me one last time and then takes his leave. Once he's gone, Olivia looks at me. I haven't moved, and I can only imagine that I look like a mess, still half sprawled across the couch.

"You did well," she says. "Or as well as can be expected."

I don't even know what to say to that, so I just pull myself up and try to breathe. "Can I go now?" I ask.

"You can go when you're dismissed," she replies curtly.

I grit my teeth. "I would have thought you had other things to do today, that's all."

"Oh, I do. I have big plans. For you and for those men of yours."

"What?" My blood runs cold. "I thought you were done with them. I thought that was the point of this."

Olivia smiles, cold and cruel. "No, the point of this is for you to finally do something to benefit your family. And to keep me from sending them to prison, I imagine. But that doesn't mean I'm going to let them off the hook that easily. They're quite useful, and I have many more things they can do for me. They're attached to you, which makes them very malleable. So why wouldn't I use them?"

My stomach drops, my limbs feeling heavy and numb. I stare at her, once again left breathless by how evil she is. How was I so blind before? How did I not see how manipulative she is? Was I really so blinded by my need for family, by the hope that I had finally found the connection I had craved for so long?

"Good help is so hard to find these days," Olivia continues. "So I plan to get every last drop out of those brothers. And when they're dead, I'll find someone new to move on to."

"You can't do that," I say thickly, shaking my head. "That wasn't part of our agreement. It's not—"

Olivia holds her hand up, cutting me off smoothly. "Our agreement was about you getting married and keeping your men out of jail. There was no agreement that X would stop using their services." She picks up her teacup again, raising to her lips as she tips her chin toward the door. "*Now* you are dismissed."

My jaw snaps shut. My legs shake as I get to my feet and slip out of the room, my head spinning and my heart clenched with worry.

I agreed to marry a monster to protect the Voronin brothers.
But have I truly managed to protect them at all?

7

VICTOR

The tension in the warehouse we live in has never been higher, which says a lot.

Even before a high stakes mission or when we were planning out the death of Nikolai Petrov, things weren't this tense.

Malice and Ransom have almost gotten into arguments enough times that I sent them to opposite ends of the place to cool off a couple of hours ago. Neither of them are angry with each other, just the situation, and since there's nothing to take it out on right now, they're lashing out at each other.

I can't blame them, really.

I feel antsy in a way that I hate. It's as if there are bugs under my skin, skittering across my nerves and making it impossible to relax as I sit at my desk, watching the feed from Willow's apartment. She's not there, having gone off to do whatever it was her grandmother wanted from her, but it eats at me that I have no idea what's going on. That I can't see her when she's away.

I want to see her all the time. I always want eyes on her, to make sure she's safe.

The front door slams, and I know that must be Malice coming home. Annoyed with being put in time out, he went out on his own for a bit. I hear him stop to say something to Ransom, but at least this time it doesn't sound like they're bickering.

Their voices come closer as Malice stomps up the stairs, and I don't even bother to get up since I know they're coming to me anyway.

The two of them have been in my room a lot more often than usual, wanting to see Willow on my screen just as much I as do.

Honestly, I don't love it.

I work hard to keep my space just so, organized and tidy, everything in its place. Malice and Ransom don't mean to, but they usually mess that up, even just in small ways. One of them will sit on the bed and rumple it. Pillows will be jostled out of place. Ransom always leaves behind some odd or end that he's picked up to fiddle with, and Malice just looms in the space, filling it up in a way that's hard to balance.

But I know they want to keep eyes on Willow, so I don't tell them to stop.

"Fucking asshole," Malice snarls as the two of them walk in.

"Who this time?" I ask, turning in my chair.

"Ethan fucking Donovan. I ran into him this morning, and he was all in my face about the fact that he and his shitty little gang managed to cut into our business."

With everything going on, our ongoing issues with the Donovan gang seemed pretty small in comparison, but clearly since our meeting with them went sour all those weeks ago, they've been busy.

"Bold of him to rub it in your face," I say.

"Right? I could have fucking killed him right then and there."

"No you couldn't," Ransom says. "I mean, you *could* have, but that would fuck everything up, so you wouldn't. Plus, it's not that big a deal. Even though business is down with the chop shop right now, if the plan we made with Willow works out, we'll be fine. Better than fine."

He's right. Blackmailing X is our ticket to getting Willow free of her grandmother and getting Olivia off our backs in general. Without having to run around doing shit for X, we can focus all our energy on growing our business.

Malice seems to know Ransom is right, because he sighs, raking a hand through his hair. It's almost exactly the same color as mine, but where I keep mine shorter and more neat, his is longer and wilder.

"Yeah, yeah," he grunts. "I fucking know. I just hate how smug he was."

"He is a piece of shit," Ransom agrees, crossing his arms over his chest. "But we have bigger fish to fry."

Some of the tension eases out of the room, which is a relief. It makes the air a little easier to breathe. I turn back to my computer just in time to hear the ping of an incoming message.

Almost as if the universe is laughing at us, the message is from X.

"Motherfucker," I hiss under my breath. I start running decryption program that will allow us to read the message, and Malice frowns.

"What is it?"

"Speak of the devil..."

My words trail off, but that's all it takes for him to catch on.

"Mother*fucker*," my twin curses, even louder than I did. "This is fucking bullshit. She can't do this."

"Apparently, she can," I point out. "Because she is. And she knows we won't tell her no."

Malice's tattooed arms flex, and he looks like he's about to punch something, which makes me wince just thinking about it. I don't need a hole in my bedroom wall, and even a dent would irritate me to no end.

The decryption takes a while, and although Malice doesn't put his fist through the wall as we wait, he does start pacing the room like an angry predator in a cage.

"Here we go," I say once the message has loaded, and the two of them gather around to read it with me.

It's another job, standard sabotage. Find some info, destroy the evidence. Probably someone who had the misfortune to cross Olivia or her husband when he was alive.

Malice goes back to pacing once we've read it all, dragging a hand through his hair.

"This is such garbage," he spits. "We're just handing her more stuff to hold over us. More shit she could use to turn us in if we don't do what she wants. But it's not like we have a fucking choice, because if we don't do it, then she'll turn us in for everything fucking else!"

Ransom sighs. "Yeah. It blows."

"Agreed," I say. "But Malice is right. It's not like we have any wiggle room here. Not with Willow in the mix."

I scan the email again, and the smug tone of it makes my hackles rise. Olivia knows how boxed in we are, knows that she's the one with all the power, and that all we can really do is fall in line—and it's clear that she's enjoying it.

I'm with Malice. This really does fucking suck.

"I need a goddamn drink," my twin grumbles.

"Same here," Ransom agrees. The two of them head back downstairs, but I stay put, not wanting to leave the comforting bank of my computers. Still, I have too much nervous energy to just sit still, so I pull out my weights and do a few reps, trying to burn off some steam.

I count each movement, making sure that both sides are balanced and even as I lift the weights. My form is perfect, and I put all my energy into focusing on that and not the chaotic spiral things have become in our lives.

Once I feel more centered, I go back to my desk and start researching the job we have to do for X. If we have to do this shit for her, then I want to make sure we have all the information we need, so we're not just walking in blindly. She's set us up on jobs designed to fail before, and although I don't think she wants to kill us anymore now that she's using us as leverage against Willow, I don't trust her enough to count on that.

Out of the corner of my eye, I notice movement on the feed from Willow's apartment a few minutes later, and my heart unclenches as I see her walking into her place.

At least she's back home where I can keep an eye on her. Safe, if not sound. I glance over periodically while I work, and it's comforting, in a way. If it wasn't for everything hanging over our heads, it would be almost... nice.

But it's easy to pass the day like that, watching Willow putter around her apartment as I work at my keyboard.

I go downstairs for a quick bite around seven, and then head right back upstairs. A few hours later, I watch her crawl into bed, and I glance at my phone on the desk, waiting for her to call. Hoping for it, even. But then I see her put her hands over her face, her shoulders shaking.

She's crying.

I grab the phone and pull up her number, pressing the button to call her.

There's a slight sniffle when she answers the phone. "Hi."

She's trying to keep the tears out of her voice, but I know they're there. "What's wrong?" I ask. "What happened? What did your grandmother want with you?"

"It's just..." Willow trails off and takes a shaky breath. "It was so fucking terrible."

"What was?" My stomach tightens into a knot. "What did she make you do?"

"Just the whole thing. I went over there, and Troy was there. They talked about me like I was a car or a cow or something. Talking about how it was a deal between the two of them, like I wasn't even a person. It just sucked, and he sucks, and now I have to marry him."

I narrow my eyes, and even though she doesn't say as much, I can tell she's not telling me the full story. Something else happened, but she doesn't want me to know.

Which... makes sense, in a way. Nothing good could have happened over there, and it's not like we can go kick down Olivia Stanton's door to make her pay for it. We can't even go after this Troy fucker without stepping out of line and making things worse.

"Willow..." I don't even know what to say to comfort her.

"Can we just... talk about something else?" she asks. "I'm just too freaked out and sad about all of this to keep harping on it right now."

"Of course," I say, agreeing instantly. I can't do much to help her, but I can at least do that.

"Thanks. What did you do today?"

Even that's a tricky subject, considering that her grandmother just gave us another job, but I leave that part out.

"I played babysitter for Malice and Ransom a bit. They spent most of the morning snipping at each other like children, so I had to put them in time out."

Willow giggles softly, which makes me smile a little. "I can't imagine Malice in time out."

"It didn't last long. He stomped out of the house about five minutes later."

"*That* I can picture. What else?"

"I rearranged my room a bit. Well, put it back in order, I guess. Ransom is always leaving little bits and pieces behind, and I chucked them all back in his room."

"Did you organize them first?"

From anyone else, that comment might seem like a taunt, but when Willow says it, I only hear warm familiarity in her tone.

"No," I tell her. "I closed the door, and he can deal with it. Did you eat something today?"

"Yeah. I didn't have much of an appetite, but I made a peanut butter sandwich when I got back. It made me think of you."

I sit back in my chair, thinking about the first time I made her a sandwich. "Was it good?"

"Mm-hm. How's your stash holding up? Or did Malice and Ransom raid it again because they were out of their devil peanut butter?"

I chuckle. "I made them buy the big family sized jar, so it hasn't happened again. I saw Ransom double dip his knife between the peanut butter and the Nutella the other day, and I almost banned him from the kitchen entirely."

"Eww," Willow says, and I glance at the screen to see her smiling softly.

There's a pause, comfortable silence falling between us, then Willow takes a deep breath.

"Can I ask you something?" she murmurs.

"Of course."

"Well, I was thinking about the times you've fed me, you know, and how... how that one time you kissed me. And then you left. I was just wondering why."

My shoulders tighten, the feeling of ease vanishing as her words spill into my ear. I drag in a deep breath and grit my teeth. "Why I kissed you or why I left?" I ask.

"Both, I guess."

I don't want to talk about this at all... but even though I feel awkward and uncomfortable, I want to keep distracting Willow from her fear. And I don't want to lie to her. So I tell her the truth.

"I kissed you because I wanted to. Because I couldn't help myself. You were sitting right there, and I just—I needed it. And it was too much for me, apparently."

"What do you mean, too much?" she asks softly.

"I... came just from kissing you, butterfly." I draw in another breath, trying to keep my voice measured, controlled. "I've seen you with my twin and Ransom. I've seen them fuck you until your eyes rolled back in your head and you fell apart completely for them. And I know I could never do that."

"Victor..."

"My control snaps entirely whenever I so much as touch you," I tell her. "And I need that control. I can't... I can't touch you without losing it, and I can't deal with that feeling. It's too much. I'm not like them, and that's so..."

I trail off, not even sure how to finish that sentence. I can hear the frustration and shame in my voice, and I close my eyes, gripping the phone tight.

Fucked up. I'm so fucked up.

8

WILLOW

My heart thuds hard in my chest as I listen to Vic breathe through the phone's small speaker. His words are still hovering in my ear, and I bite my lip as I process them. He sounds so frustrated, so fed up with himself, and probably a little embarrassed too. Vic prides himself on his control and being able to keep his cool and do what needs to be done, and then I came along and shook all that up.

It's clear he wishes he were better at this, more like his brothers, and that it's a new feeling for him. He sounds like he wants to give up, like he's expecting *me* to give up on him.

But I won't.

And even though he might be embarrassed by what happened between us in the kitchen, he has no reason to be. I would never hold that against him.

And in truth, part of me likes knowing that he needs me so much that he could come just from kissing me.

"I'm sorry," he says after a long beat, picking the thread of the conversation back up. "I shouldn't be putting all of this on you. I'll—"

"No," I interrupt. "It's okay. I asked, and I'm glad you told me.

I'm glad I know. And Vic, there are lots of things we can do without touching. You remember, right?"

I glance to the cameras as I say that last part, recalling the time when I touched myself the way he wanted while he watched me and listened to me fall apart. He told me what to do, and just hearing his voice giving me directions was one of the hottest things I've ever experienced.

It sends a shiver down my spine just thinking about it, and I can tell from Vic's sharp inhale that he's thinking about it too.

"Is... is today a day when you usually jerk off?" I ask him, my heart speeding up its cadence in my chest.

"Yes," he replies, his voice thick. "This is one of the days."

My tongue darts out, licking my lips quickly. This is a progression of what we did before, when he watched me, and I don't know if it's a good idea to ask for more, but I want it. And now that I know he left the kitchen because he felt overwhelmed and embarrassed, not because of something I did wrong, I feel less unsure.

"Can I... watch?" I whisper. "I'd really like that right now."

Vic is quiet on the other end of the line for a moment, and I keep going.

"You've watched me lots of times," I say. "Alone, with your brothers, putting on a show just for you." I smile a little, dragging my bottom lip between my teeth. "You can watch me too. But I want to see you come, Vic, just for me. Just the two of us. I want to experience it with you, like this."

Vic takes a breath, and I can hear it shuddering in and out of him. He's out of control again, probably. I've thrown a wrench into his carefully cultivated planning and schedule. But maybe that's for the best. If we both want this, then maybe it has to be a little awkward first.

"Willow..." he breathes.

"Please?" I say. "I want to see it. Watching you jerk off in the bathroom that night was one of the hottest things I've ever seen. I felt your cum soak my pussy, and it felt so fucking good. I've... god,

I've thought about that so many times. I want to see you come again."

I'm surprised how easily the words roll off my tongue. I feel a bit awkward about it, dirty talk not coming naturally to me or anything. But my time spent with the brothers, listening to Malice and Ransom say filthy things to me in the heat of the moment, has helped it feel more natural than I ever thought was possible.

They're still better at it than I am, but I know I have to take the lead more with Victor than the other two. I have a feeling that if he did ever let himself go, he wouldn't be restrained at all, but he always holds himself in check so much. He needs someone to help him come out of that shell and get what he wants.

I wait to see what his answer will be, and I'm surprised when the screen of my phone lights up, the call switching to a video call. Vic's face fills the screen, and I smile, taking in how handsome he is. He's got similar facial features to Malice, but somehow, it looks different on each of them—especially now that I've come to know them so well. His jaw is strong and angular, and he has strong cheekbones that somehow draw attention to his blue eyes, making them stand out even more.

Seeing him on my phone's little screen makes me miss the days when I lived with them and I got to see him all the time. When we had these little conversations in their kitchen, over peanut butter sandwiches or coffee, talking about our families or the nature of Vic's work. Even though things were still a bit stilted and awkward back then, it was a closeness that I needed. That I still need.

Even more so now, honestly.

"Hi," I whisper, giving him a little wave through the phone.

A smile tugs at his lips, and even though he looks unsure and even a little bit afraid, he seems happy, at least.

"Hello," he says back. Then he grimaces slightly. "I don't... I'm not sure..."

"It's okay if you don't want to, but... will you try?" I ask quietly. "Don't think about it too much."

He snorts. "Have you met me, butterfly? Thinking about things so much is my job. Someone in this family has to do it."

I chuckle. "Okay, fair. But not right now. There's no crisis right now. Not one we can do anything about, anyway. It's just you and me."

"Right," he repeats, his voice dropping a little. "Just you and me."

We stare at each other for a while, and it's interesting how different this feels from anything we've done before. Usually, Malice and Ransom are there, leading the way, touching me, kissing me, fucking me. Giving Victor something to watch and me something to focus on.

Even when I put that show on for Victor before, it was different. More one-sided. I touched myself and got myself off to the sound of his voice, but I couldn't see him.

Now that we're staring into each other's eyes, even over the phone, it's different.

"I want to see you too," Vic says, and his eyes are intent as he watches.

"Okay," I breathe back.

I lick my lips and get situated, piling the pillows against the headboard and making myself comfortable. I hold the phone so that Vic can see the line of my body, barely covered by the tiny shorts and oversized shirt I threw on for bed.

"Beautiful," he murmurs, sounding entranced. "I wish..."

He shakes his head, not finishing that thought, but I can guess where it was going.

"Me too," I murmur back.

I slip my hand under my shirt, skating my fingers along the soft skin of my stomach. There's a patch of scar tissue on the right side, and before, I used to avoid touching it whenever possible, embarrassed and ashamed of how rough and ugly the scars were, even when it was just me alone.

But after that time with Vic, I've started to get more comfortable with it. Touching them doesn't make me shudder anymore, and instead, I explore the way the scars feel in contrast to my other skin. Going from soft and smooth to more textured and rough.

"Let me see," Vic says, leaning in closer. He's probably watching both through his phone and via the cameras, getting the best angles and close-up views of what I'm doing.

I nod, hiking up my shirt to show off where I'm touching. I dip one finger into my belly button and then drag it over to that patch of scars, stroking the edges of it lightly.

A moan spills from my lips, and Vic's eyes follow my finger so closely that it's almost a physical sensation, like there's a phantom touch right after my own. It makes me shiver as I keep going.

"Perfect," he says. "You're so good like this, butterfly. Beautiful. Chaotic."

"I know you like it," I say back, and my voice is already getting breathy from how worked up I'm starting to get.

Some of the nerves are falling away, leaving only need in their wake.

But it's still one-sided.

I drag my hand and the fabric of my shirt up even more, pulling it up over my breasts so he can see them. I grip one tightly, rubbing my thumb over the nipple and feeling the jolt of pleasure that it sends through me.

"You too," I tell him. "I want to see you too."

"Okay," he says.

There's a moment where he sits there, staring at me, and I can see his lips moving the slightest bit. I realize he's probably counting to himself, trying to recenter, to get some control over what's going on.

I wait, watching, and eventually I'm rewarded by Vic slumping down a bit in his chair. The camera follows down his body, and he lets me see him starting to undo his pants.

I swallow hard, taking in the sight as he pulls his cock out. It's already half hard, just from watching me, and I feel a flutter of aroused pride at that realization.

"Keep going," he urges me as he wraps his hand around himself.

I nod, getting back to it.

Somehow, it's even easier when I have the sight of his cock right there in front of me. Even through the phone, it's the closest I've ever been to it when I wasn't already blissed out of my mind from pleasure, and my body craves more.

My mouth waters, and I think about what it would be like to take him between my lips. To suck him off, taking as much as I can, taking him all the way down to the root maybe, while he fills my throat.

I moan just from that thought, tweaking my nipples, rolling one between my fingers and pressing down hard for that zing of pain.

"You like that," Vic says breathlessly. "When it hurts a little."

It's not a question, but I nod all the same. "Y-yeah. It always feels good. I love it when... mmm... when I can really feel it."

"Tell me what you're thinking about," he urges, and I swallow hard again.

"You," I admit. "Your cock. Taking it in my mouth and... and letting you fill me up."

"Fuck. Fuck, butterfly."

"Yeah. I want... I want you to put your hand in my hair and make me take it at your pace. Whatever you want."

"You'd look so good like that," he rasps. "Your perfect mouth around me. I've thought about it... fuck, I've *dreamed* about it."

My eyelids flutter, almost falling closed as I pinch and pull at my nipples, but I force them to stay open. I don't want to miss anything. I watch as Vic fists his cock slowly, almost methodically, keeping a measured, even rhythm.

Every once in a while, he'll squeeze the base, holding there for a second like he needs to catch his breath before he explodes.

"Your cock is so fucking big," I whisper, pulling the phone

closer so I have a better view of it. "Fuck, Vic. You're maybe even bigger than Malice."

He chuckles roughly, something flashing through his eyes. "Don't let him hear you say that. He'll be dead set on fucking you until you can't walk to prove it doesn't matter."

I moan because he's right, and I can picture exactly the scenario he's describing.

"Would you watch?" I ask, my hands roaming my body restlessly. "Would you watch your brother fuck me into the mattress and then maybe come over and fuck me too, once I'm all loosened up and sloppy?"

My cheeks burn, and I can't quite believe the words that are coming out of my mouth right now. It barely sounds like me, but it's hard to hold back when I want that so bad.

It's so easy to imagine, Malice holding me down, forcing me to take it as he fucks me to within an inch of my life, his cock pounding in and out of my willing core. Then leaving me a mess, dripping and exhausted, but not done yet.

And Vic, who would have been watching the whole time, coming over, flipping me over maybe, so he can see my face, sliding in where his brother just vacated. Malice's cum would be like lube, making it even easier for Vic to push his way inside me.

My pussy throbs with need, and touching my breasts and nipples isn't even close to enough anymore.

"Fuck, butterfly, the way you talk..." Vic trails off, breathing hard. Precum has already started welling at the head of his cock, and he strokes his palm over the tip of it, dragging that wetness back down as he strokes slowly. "I remember when you couldn't even say the word cock. When you would turn into a little mouse at the idea of being fucked by my brothers. Now look at you."

My cheeks are still on fire, but his words only make me that much more turned on. My hips buck up, like they're searching for something to grind against, and I moan low in my throat.

"I can't help it," I whimper. "You guys just... just bring it out in me."

"Good," he says, and his voice is different than I've ever heard it. Strained and rough and possessive. "I like that we're the ones who get to see this side of you. That you do this for us and no one else."

I nod eagerly, dragging my hand down my stomach, taking the phone along as well so Vic can see that I'm about to start touching myself in earnest.

"Yes," he groans. "Let me see. Show me how wet you are for me. Please. I need to see it."

The desperation in his voice is such a fucking turn on, and I practically rip my shorts off, showing him both that I'm not wearing any underwear under them and that my pussy is already soaking wet from this.

"Fuck," he breathes, and inhales raggedly. "Fuck."

"I wish you were here," I tell him. "Even if you didn't touch me, even if I had to get myself off, I want you to watch. I want you to see me fall apart."

"Show me. Show me how it would be."

I don't hesitate to follow his command, stuffing two fingers into myself, the slickness of my arousal easing their way in. Months ago, that might have been enough to satisfy me, but now, it's barely even close. I've learned so much more about what I like, how rough I can take it, and what truly turns me on.

My body throbs with need, and I work my fingers deeper into myself, moaning and arching on the bed.

Vic's breathing is harsh as he watches, and I glance at the screen to see his hand moving faster on his cock, like he's getting close to losing control.

I move my fingers in time with his hand, pretending it's him thrusting into me. The fantasy of that makes my heart race, but it's still not enough, and I make a frustrated sound.

Vic's fist stops moving, tightening around the thick base of his shaft again. "What's wrong?"

"Nothing," I reassure him. "This is so good. It's just..."

"You're used to more than your own hand now, aren't you?" His fingers flex and then loosen, a vein on his cock pulsing.

"Yes," I whisper, my cheeks burning.

"That would have been enough for you before, wouldn't it?" he continues. "Just your fingers in your pussy, working yourself up. You could come from just that, but now you need more. Your body is used to being filled up completely."

"God, Vic," I moan. "Fuck..."

It's kind of incredible the way he does this. His voice is shaky from his own desire, but he manages to make his dirty talk sound so precise, like he's listing off the sexiest scientific facts known to man.

And of course he's right.

Of course my body craves more. Wants it deeper, harder, thicker.

Even though it's not quite enough, I'm still so worked up, still so close to the edge already, and I can tell Vic isn't that far off either. He squeezes the base of his cock again, letting me see how beautiful and flushed it is, and I watch as a thick drop of precum runs down the head, sliding over the curve of it in a way that makes me wish I was there to lick it up, to taste the salty sweet tang of it.

He takes a shuddering breath and then another, and I see him counting again, tapping the fingers of his other hand against his knee, getting himself back under control.

"I want to make it last," he explains, even though I didn't need him to. "I don't want to come before you do."

Just him talking about me coming has my pussy spasming with need again, and I suddenly have an idea.

I pull my fingers free of my soaked entrance and then roll over so I can get to the nightstand drawer. Inside are a couple of things that still make me blush to think about. I was embarrassed to buy the toys, but based on what I did with the guys, and how much I craved sex when we were apart, I figured they would be good investments.

So I get them out and put them on the bed, letting Vic see.

He chokes out a quiet noise, thumbing the head of his cock as he watches me.

"Holy shit, butterfly," he whispers. "When did you get those?"

"I bought them before I put the cameras back up," I tell him. "I just... I needed something then. I missed you all, even if I wouldn't let myself admit it."

"Fuck," he groans, sounding almost wrecked. "Have you used them both already?"

"No," I admit. "Just one."

"Which one haven't you used?"

Practically holding my breath, I lift up the first toy, a smooth, black plug with a yellow gem on the end of it. It's small enough to fit easily in the palm of my hand—I was too intimidated to go for anything bigger.

"You've never had that inside you before?" Vic asks.

"No."

"Do you know what to do with it?"

My heart flutters. "Yes."

I watched a few videos, so I'm familiar with the basic idea. I don't admit aloud the reasons why I bought it, or how turned on I got thinking about the idea of my ass and pussy being filled at the same time, but maybe Victor can read my mind, because he lets out a low, hungry sound that goes straight to my clit.

"Will you show me?" he murmurs. "Will you let me see?"

I swallow hard and then bring the plug up to my lips, licking and sucking at it slowly, answering silently by letting him watch as I drag my tongue around the smooth, flavorless silicone.

I prop the phone up against the blankets so that Vic has a clear view of my pussy and ass, then I grab the bottle of lube I bought and drizzle some over the plug and over my fingers. Breathing hard, I start working myself open, using my slick fingers to ease my ass open a little before I attempt to press the plug in.

Even though it's small, it feels much bigger once it starts working its way inside me, and I suck in a sharp breath as the widest part stretches me, pulling my rim wider until it's seated all the way in.

"Fuck," I pant, squirming in place as my clit throbs.

"Beautiful," Vic groans. "How does it feel, butterfly? Tell me."

"Mmm, it feels… different, but good," I whisper, clenching around the plug a little. "I feel full, but it's still not enough."

"What else do you have?"

I hold up the other thing I bought, swallowing hard. It's a thick vibrator, shaped like a dick, smooth and shiny. It's not quite as big as any of the Voronin brothers, but it's close.

"What are you going to do with that?" he asks, his voice husky.

"I'm going to fuck myself with it," I tell him, boldness rising in me as my breath comes faster. "I'm gonna fill my pussy and my ass, and I'm gonna think about you the entire time."

There's a choked sound on the other end of the phone. Vic goes quiet for a long moment, and I blink, lifting my head to look at the camera on my screen. His hand is still wrapped around his cock, and I can see how heavily his shaft is pulsing, little dribbles of precum sliding down the side. Another sound reaches my ears, and I realize he's counting aloud this time—still under his breath, but loud enough that I can hear him.

"Are you okay?" I murmur. "Is this too much? I can stop if you—"

"*No.*" The counting breaks off as he answers immediately. "Don't. Stop."

The ragged desperation in his voice is enough to send my pulse into overdrive. This might be a lot for him, but I can tell he wants it, and suddenly, it feels like the most important thing in the world to get this toy inside me. To fill myself up so Vic can watch, to fuck myself on it until I fall apart.

I don't even need the lube for this one. All I have to do is rub it against my pussy, and the slickness of my arousal coats it easily.

As I drag the silicone toy through my folds, the head of it slides against my clit, and I gasp as a jolt of sensation shoots through me, lighting up my entire body.

"Ahh!" I hiss out.

The pleasure spreads like a wildfire, fierce and sudden. I try to hold it off, but I'm so turned on from everything we've been doing that an orgasm rises up and tears through me before I can stop it. My back arches, a cry spilling from my lips as I grind against the solid weight of the silicone, pressing it hard against my clit.

"Fuck." Vic's voice is harsh, as if he's got his jaw clenched so tightly he can barely get the word out.

"Oh... god," I breathe, pulling the toy away from my clit as the orgasm finally starts to fade. "That was... an accident."

"I'm not mad about it."

He laughs softly, and despite how lost in pleasure I am, I file the sound away in my memory bank. It's one of the best things I've ever heard, and I want to be able to replay it over and over.

My heart is beating heavily in my chest in the aftermath of my climax, but just like Vic said earlier, I want this to last. I haven't seen him come yet, and even with one orgasm down, I'm still craving more. My pussy clenches, and I give in, ignoring how sensitive I am as I press the head of the toy to my entrance.

I hold the phone with my other hand, letting Vic get a close-up as I push the thick length in slowly, my body swallowing it up inch by inch.

He curses under his breath, and when I glance down at the screen, he's working his cock again. Slowly and carefully this time, like he's trying to measure out the sensations so he doesn't explode.

"Victor." I moan his name, arching my hips as I shove the last few inches of the dildo into myself hard. I'm even more aware of the plug inside my ass now, the feeling of fullness unlike anything I've ever experienced. "Fuck, it feels so good."

"You look..." He trails off, and I can hear the quiet, wet sounds of him working his cock. "Keep going. Show me what you like."

I nod breathlessly, then start working the toy in and out of my pussy. Each drag of the silicone against my walls makes me shudder, and when I let it bottom out again, it hits a spot inside me that has me seeing stars.

"Never seen anything so fucking perfect," Vic mutters, and I don't even know if he's aware that he's talking anymore. "So perfect. Pretty and pink and tight. I can see every time you clench, butterfly, the way your body wants more. Move the phone down a little... right there. *Fuck.*"

"Please," I sob, desperate to keep hearing his voice. "Keep talking, Vic. Oh god, please."

"Willow," he breathes, and my name sounds so good on his lips. "I can't stop it. I'm gonna—"

"I'm so close too. Come with me. Right now. *Please.*"

Vic's hand is moving faster now, and I watch, transfixed, as he chases his own pleasure. My own hand shakes as I hold the phone and use the other hand to fuck myself with the slick toy, and just as my toes curl into the blankets, Vic sucks in a sharp breath.

He crashes over the edge a second before I do, both of us groaning and shaking, and I watch as he spills over his fingers, bending a bit at the waist as if the force of it is taking something out of him.

It's beautiful, the way he strokes himself through it, the way his cum splatters over his hand and down his shaft. I feel more connected to him than ever, caught up in the throes of my own orgasm, and I whimper his name over and over.

When my muscles finally unclench, I drag the dildo out and set it on the bed, then work the plug out of my ass too. We're both still breathing hard as we try to come down, and I roll over onto my side, holding the phone in both hands to keep it steady.

"Oh my god," I whisper, and then laugh softly. "You know, that last time, I came mostly from watching you finish on your own hand. So, it's not that different than you coming from a kiss."

He snorts, raising the phone back up so I can see his face. He looks good. More rumpled and mussed than I've ever seen him before. There's a warm, satisfied look in his eyes, and he seems less tightly wound than usual.

"I'm not sure I believe that," he says. "But... thank you."

I nod, smiling back. Affection and such strong attraction to this man wells up in my chest, along with a soul-deep wish that he was here with me. Or that I could be there. As long as we were together, I wouldn't really care where we were.

The phone sex helped push the realities of what's going on away for a while, but not long enough. It's all still right there, weighing on me.

"Are you alright?" Vic asks after a moment of comfortable silence.

"With what we just did?" I grin, although I can tell it's a little wobbly. "More than alright. With everything else? Not really. I'm... scared," I admit.

"I know. But what Malice said is true. You're ours. And we're going to keep you. No one else gets to have you."

"You'd better mean that," I tell him. "Because I want to keep you too."

Vic smiles on my screen, and it's so different than his usual smile. It's beautiful and bright, like nothing I've ever seen before.

It's perfect.

9

WILLOW

After getting cleaned up a bit, Vic and I talk for a while, murmuring over the phone in low voices. We talk about stupid things, anything and everything, and it's nice just to hear his voice.

I don't know how long I make it before my eyelids start to droop, but after a while, I fall into an exhausted sleep. The stress of the day, combined with the relaxing after-effects of a couple of good orgasms, knocks me out hard, which means that I thankfully don't have any dreams—or at least, none that I remember.

When I wake up in the morning, I feel more determined than ever. Feeling so connected to Vic last night, hearing him say that he and his brothers are going to keep me... it makes it even more clear what I have to do. Even if I don't want to.

My fingers shake as I grab my phone and scroll through my contacts to call Olivia.

It rings for a few seconds, and then she answers.

"Willow. What can I do for you?" She sounds surprised to hear from me, and my stomach twists, thinking about how her saying those words used to make me feel safe and cared for. Like someone was looking out for me.

Now it just makes me feel sick.

"I want to make the most of what I can't avoid," I tell her. "If

I'm going to be getting married to Troy soon, I need to know how to survive and thrive in this world—your world."

"I see," my grandmother says. "I was under the impression that you didn't care much for 'my world,' as you put it."

"I don't," I admit. "I hate it, honestly. But you've made it pretty clear that I have no choice in the matter, so I'd at least like to not fall on my face when it comes to navigating this life. I want to know how to hold my own. To... to fit in."

I don't even have to pretend to sound resigned to it. It's how I felt even before all of this happened, like I was a fish out of water, not sure how to act when she invited me to things. It's easy enough to tap into those feelings, along with not hiding the fact that I don't want any of this.

If I tried to act otherwise, she'd be too suspicious to believe it. But she knows that she has a lot of leverage over me, and that I'm willing to do what I have to as long as it keeps the guys safe.

And as far as she knows, there's no way out for me now.

God, I hope she's wrong about that.

Olivia is quiet for a moment, and my stomach twists as I wonder if she's seen through me or guessed that I have an ulterior motive. But when she speaks, she sounds pleased.

"Good. Very good. You may not want this, but at least you realize your role in all of it. It would be a shame to have you embarrassing the family name, so yes, I will help you."

I don't even really know what to say to that. *Thank you* would be a step too far, so I settle on, "Okay. Should I come over?"

"Yes," Olivia agrees. "We'll get started right away. Adam will drive you."

After ending the call, I get dressed in another Olivia approved outfit and head downstairs. A guard is still stationed outside my place—someone other than Jerome today, presumably Adam—and he watches me as I head toward his car and get in.

When we arrive at Olivia's mansion, I'm ushered inside by one of the house staff. My grandmother is waiting for me in the sitting room, but at least Troy isn't there with her today.

She has tea laid out, and she sits primly in her chair, watching as I step awkwardly into the room and settle on a couch across from her. The maid who led me in offers me some tea too, and I take it, even though the paranoid part of me can't help but worry that my grandmother drugged it or something. But I don't see how that would serve her right now, and she's nothing if not cold-heartedly pragmatic, so I lift the cup to my lips and take a small sip.

Once the maid steps out of the room, Olivia clears her throat, fixing me with an assessing look.

"Now, I know you haven't had a very good example of what it means to be a wife at all, let alone a wife in this world," she says. "Your mother died, of course, but I highly doubt she would have been a good role model to begin with."

It takes me a second to realize she means my birth mother, not Misty, and I clench my fingers around my tea cup, dragging in a deep breath.

Olivia doesn't even seem to notice, caught up in her little lecture.

"Men with money like to believe they are untouchable. That is what you must first understand. They buy into the idea that they're the man of the house, that their word is law, that they have all the power. And we let them think that, because it's easier when they're happy."

"Was my grandfather like that?" I ask before I can stop myself. Learning anything else about my toxic family seems useless at this point, but still, I want to know.

She smiles, and it seems truly fond, which only makes me hate her more.

"He could be, at times. He liked things a certain way, and he could be very demanding. But that doesn't mean I let him do whatever he wanted. In this world, behind every powerful, rich man, should be an equally powerful and savvy woman. My husband was the face of the Stanton family, and everyone believed that he was in charge, but I had my ways of guiding him to do what I wanted."

"How?"

"It comes from knowing the man. Knowing what he likes, knowing what makes him listen. I would make suggestions, while making sure his glass was full. I would speak with him over his favorite meals and use his good mood to make him think that my ideas and plans were his ideas and plans."

I frown, staring down into the murky depths of my tea. "So... you manipulated him."

She waves a delicate hand carelessly. "Call it what you want, but it worked out well for both of us. You just have to know how to handle your man."

"Well, I don't think that's going to work for me," I mutter, bitterness rising up in my throat. "Troy doesn't even like me, much less respect me."

Olivia waves her hand again, giving me a patronizing look. She sets her teacup down and leans a little closer, as if we're sharing a secret. "You're just not looking at it the right way. You have something Troy wants, and you can use that to your advantage if you're smart."

It takes me a few beats to catch on to what she means, and when I do, I stare at her, disgusted.

She saw Troy on top of me when she came back into the room yesterday. She's heard him talk about me, and she clearly knows that he's only interested in me because he thinks it's somehow hot that I'm the daughter of a prostitute. He thinks that's going to make the sex better or some fucked up thing, and judging from the look on Olivia's face, she wants me to go along with that.

"Oh, don't give me that look," she says crisply as she notices the horrified expression on my face. "A woman in this society has to use every tool in her arsenal, even if that means you have to give in to what he wants. *Whatever* he wants you to do, you will do it. You will give him anything he demands, because that will benefit you. And in turn, it will benefit me."

My stomach roils, and I feel like I'm going to be sick.

I want to tell her off, to tell her I'm never going to do that and she and Troy can both go fuck themselves, but I bite my tongue.

I asked for this, in a way. I asked for her 'grandmotherly advice,' and this is it. But as disgusting as her ideas of how to get by in this world of hers are, it got me into her house, so that's the win I needed.

"I need to use the restroom," I tell her, getting up and setting my cup down, not bothering to hide the quaver in my voice. "I don't... feel well."

I can feel her eyes on me as I make my way out of the sitting room and down the hall, and I put my hand on my stomach to sell the idea that I'm about to go vomit again.

Once I'm out of Olivia's eyeline, I straighten up a little, my steps quickening. It's easy to find my way back to the room I passed by yesterday. The door is shut this time, and I take a second to make sure that none of the house staff are nearby before I try the handle.

The door isn't locked, thank fuck, so I slip quietly into the room.

My pulse is racing, the need to rush making my hands shake. I probably only have five minutes or so if I'm trying to match the time an actual trip to the bathroom would take. Any longer than that, and Olivia might get impatient and send someone to fetch me... or even worse, come after me herself.

Dragging my phone from my pocket, I walk quickly over to the file cabinets and slide the top drawer of one open. I don't have time to take pictures of all the documents inside, so I snap a photo that shows all the little tabs at the top of the hanging file dividers. I'll have to show it to the guys and see if they recognize anything as relating to a job they've done for Olivia.

I repeat the process with the other file drawers, opening and closing them as smoothly and silently as possible as I count down the seconds in my head.

By the time I get to what I think has been four minutes, my heart is in my throat. I snap a few more quick pictures and then shove my phone back into my pocket. Taking a second to run my sweat dampened palms over my clothes to dry them a little, I force myself to drag in a few slow breaths to calm my racing heart. Then I make my way back to the sitting room.

My skin prickles with awareness, but Olivia doesn't seem to have noticed anything amiss, and as I take my seat on the couch again, she resumes the lesson in her coolly brusque tone.

I settle in, listening carefully and nodding whenever it seems appropriate.

She goes over everything from how I should be dressing to the kinds of conversations I should be having with people at social gatherings. There are apparently unspoken rules for everything, and my head is spinning with information by the time she finally comes to a stop.

She flicks her gaze over me and sniffs, lacing her fingers together on her lap.

"I don't expect that you'll pick it all up from one or two lessons," she says. "And the best teacher is experience, of course."

"Of course," I mutter.

"You will have ample opportunities to learn, but learn fast."

"I'll do my best."

She gives me a look that clearly says she doesn't think very much of my best, and I sigh, already anxious to be done with this.

"That will do for today," she says. "I have other things to do. Organizing a wedding on such a short schedule is no easy task." She gives me a look as if that's my fault, then adds, "We'll meet again tomorrow. We have a dress fitting scheduled. You need something for your engagement party, and I know you don't own anything that would be suitable."

"Okay."

I nod curtly, hating that by calling her this morning, I basically deprived myself of the one day I might've gotten to spend without seeing my awful grandmother. But at least I got something useful out of it.

She tells me where we'll be meeting, but I barely bother listening, because she also makes it clear that she'll have one of her men drive me there.

Once she's finished giving me instructions for the morning, I stand up and glance toward the sitting room door. Since no maid has come to fetch me, I'm about to see myself out, but before I can, Olivia stops me by speaking again.

"You know, your little trio of men will be doing a job for me this evening," she says, examining her perfectly manicured nails. She glances up at me through her eyelashes, not even bothering to lift her head. "But you don't need to worry. If they do it right, it's unlikely they'll come to any harm."

Hatred fills me, and I entertain a little fantasy of punching her right in her smug face, but I try not to let any of that show in my expression as I give her a tight smile and then stride from the room.

We have a plan.

If the plan works, then all of us will be free of her and her bullshit forever. I just have to focus on that.

10

RANSOM

"Last one!" I call out, throwing a rock through the window of the storage unit and reaching through to open the door from the other side.

"You don't need to yell, Ransom," Vic says, moving past me into the unit.

It's neat and organized, but that's not going to last long.

This latest job for X is pretty simple, at least compared to some of the other ones we've had to do. There's no tailing anyone, and probably not much room for anyone else to get hurt, which is a fucking relief.

The bitch wants something from a storage unit in this block, so we're dividing and conquering. Vic and I trash other units, to make it look like a random break-in rather than a targeted thing, and Malice goes to get whatever the fuck it is X wants. I don't know, and I didn't ask.

I just want to be done with this so we can get the fuck out of here.

Vic and I move through the small unit, smashing things, denting boxes, rummaging around to make it look like someone broke in to do a smash and grab.

It's the same thing we did in a few other units nearby, picking them at random, though I could tell it bothered Vic to not have some kind of order to it.

Usually, I would tease him about that, but I'm not in the mood.

"Think that's good enough?" I ask him, glancing around at the mess we've made.

"I think so," he replies. He kicks another box for good measure. "Let's meet Malice."

We've all got ski masks on, even though Vic disabled the surveillance before we got here. But if someone shows up to investigate, they won't be able to tell who we are. The last thing we need is to be recognized by some bystander who happens to be passing by and get busted for what should be an easy job.

"We're done!" Vic calls.

"Hold your fucking horses!" Malice shouts back.

Vic rolls his eyes, which is a funny expression in the ski mask, and we start to head out, smashing another couple of windows as we go.

We make it back out to the street, and we can hear the sound of sirens in the distance as we leave.

"Not close yet," Vic murmurs. "We have time."

Malice's shoulders relax. "Someone must have heard all the smashing and called the cops."

"Nothing for them to find, at least."

We covered our tracks well. The cops will get there, and it'll be deemed a random act of vandalism. If they have insurance on their shit, then it'll be fine.

We jog down the street to our car and get in, peeling out.

Vic is in the driver's seat, the way he prefers to be, driving careful and precise, even at breakneck speeds. Malice has shotgun, and I'm in the back, as usual. Little brother seat.

"That went smoothly," Vic says, signaling before merging into a new lane.

"Yeah," Malice agrees. "Almost too smoothly, but it was a

fucking smash and grab. Either the bitch is insulting us or she just wants to keep us busy."

"I'd bank on the latter. It doesn't really matter what she throws at us anymore."

Malice grunts, and I fold my arms, ticked off. Once upon a time, these jobs for X were just an inconvenience, but it was a price worth paying to keep Malice out of jail. X popped up every month or couple of months, made us do something annoying, and we got her off our backs until the next time.

But now we're helping the woman who's essentially holding Willow captive, forcing her to do whatever she wants.

It makes each job that much harder.

"It fucking sucks," Malice grumbles. "I don't know who that bitch thinks she is. She's just going to keep using us for her own fucking kicks. Just because she can. Just because she's the goddamned worst."

He slams his hand down on the center console, and Vic shoots him a sharp look.

"Stop it," he says.

"Fuck off, Vic. Don't tell me you're not pissed about this shit too."

"I am, of course I am. But don't take it out on my fucking car."

It's not new for Malice to be pissed off, but it kind of surprises me how angry I am about it all. Usually I'm able to let this kind of shit go, letting it roll off my back because we didn't have a choice. We still don't, but it's so much worse now.

I curl my hands into fists, and I want to hit something. Someone. I don't know. There's all this energy under my skin, violent and turbulent, and it needs to go somewhere. My leg bounces up and down, and I glare out the window as the streetlights and trees whip by.

I fucking hate this, and I hate how Willow is caught up in the middle of it all. Trapped in this fucking shit show because she's trying to protect us.

It's not right, and she doesn't deserve it. Not for a fucking second. The worst part is there's no clear way out right now. We have a plan, but who knows how long that's going to take to work? We have to just deal with this shit for now, and keep doing X—Olivia's bidding—like good little boys until Willow gets the information she needs.

And we don't have that much time anyway.

We get back to our place, piling out of the car.

"I'll go do the drop," Malice says. "Get this shit over with."

Vic nods. "Check in when you get back. I'll be upstairs."

They split off, Malice going to his car and Vic heading to his room, and I stand there for a second, not sure what to do. I've got all this anger in me, and it feels like there are wasps under my skin, buzzing around, demanding attention.

I need to do something to distract me from how fucking agitated I feel, so I stalk into the garage, grabbing tools and starting to work on my bike.

Usually that centers me, or at least distracts me from feeling bad, but this time it's not enough. I tighten a bolt here, adjust something there, but all I can focus on is the angry pulse of my heart, the sound filling my head.

I keep thinking about Willow and how scared and lost she looked when Olivia was detailing everything to her at the funeral. How she shook and cried in Malice's arms when she got back to her place later.

She's trying to be strong about this, but I know she's still scared. I know she feels trapped.

I can't get my mind off it, and the deep breathing exercises that Vic showed me once don't seem to be doing anything at all to help.

"Fuck this. Fuck it!" The words explode out of me as the irritation boils over, and I throw my wrench across the room, where it lands with a sharp clang on the concrete.

This is a waste of time. There's only one thing that will soothe me, I know that, and there's no use pretending otherwise.

I get on the bike and rev it up, peeling out of the garage and heading toward Willow's place without even really thinking about it too much.

When I get to her building, I park at a distance.

I'm sure her guard is still hanging around, and I don't want him to see me, so I walk around to the back side of the building. Some guy has the door propped open while he takes a smoke break, and I nod to him and then slip inside like I'm supposed to be there, taking the stairs up to Willow's floor.

Something rises in me as I make my way down the corridor toward her unit. Something protective, possessive, and almost beast-like. Primal. It sits solidly in my chest, urging me to claim Willow. To take her and mark her, leaving something on her to make sure she knows beyond a shadow of a doubt that she's mine.

Ours.

We may share with each other, but no one else. And definitely not some skeezy rich boy with her shitty grandma's approval.

That feeling pulses through me with every second, and I stride up to Willow's door, knocking heavily when I reach it. If she doesn't answer, I'm already planning on breaking in through the window like we did last time, but Willow comes to the door a second later, looking exhausted and wary.

Her eyes widen when she catches sight of me, and she opens her mouth.

"Ran—"

That's all she gets out before I haul her into my arms, kissing her hard and fast.

11

WILLOW

I GASP SOFTLY as Ransom's lips crash into mine.

It's not the first time we've kissed by a long shot, but I'm caught off guard by how intense it is. It's almost more like kissing Malice than Ransom, but I'm immediately swept up in it.

Despite the shock of his sudden appearance, my body has no problem keeping up, so even as my mind reels, my arms wrap around his shoulders and I kiss him back, responding in kind.

It's so much easier to focus on this, rather than how awful I feel and how worried I am about the future, so I throw myself into it. I kiss him wildly, biting down on his lower lip, grasping at his clothes, wanting to touch him everywhere.

"Fuck," Ransom groans against my mouth. He takes another step inside and kicks the door closed behind him. "Come here."

"I'm here," I gasp back. "I'm right here."

He works one thigh between my legs, and I moan his name, grinding against him.

"Just like that, angel," he mutters. "Right there."

He kisses me again, his lips trailing down my neck to where I'm sure he can feel my pulse hammering against my skin. With his arms wrapped tightly around me, he keeps walking me backward. I stumble a little, but he steadies me, pulling me close and letting me find my balance.

My head spins as we keep kissing, lips and hands and teeth and tongues colliding, our bodies melding together. Someone watching would think we haven't had our hands on each other for months, and even though I know that isn't true, it feels like it may as well be.

It almost feels like back when I first started living with them, back when every time I let myself indulge in these men, it felt like something I wasn't supposed to be doing.

It was fast and hard and illicit.

Terrifying and electrifying all at once.

The backs of my knees hit the edge of the couch, and we go down together, him on top of me. He braces his arms on the cushions, keeping his weight from crushing me and cushioning me from the fall.

Our lips finally separate, and for a long second, we gaze at each other, breathing hard. Ransom reaches up to brush my hair back from my face, smoothing his fingers over my cheek and down to my neck.

It sends a pleasant shiver down my spine, and I lick my lips, feeling the lingering tingle from where he bit and sucked at the bottom one.

"What are you doing here?" I ask. It feels a bit late for that, now that he's already been kissing and groping at me, but I want to know.

He sighs, and there's no trace of his usual smile on his handsome face.

"I just... had to see you," he says.

The words drag up a memory, an echo of a time when he said something so similar. He and his brothers weren't fully in my life yet, just hovering at the edges of it, and he came to my school one day on his motorcycle. When I asked him what he was doing there, he said he just wanted to see me... or that maybe he just wanted *me* to see *him*.

That sentiment hits so much deeper now. It's like he needed a reminder that he's always in my thoughts, just like I seem to be in his.

I reach up and cup his face, stroking my thumbs along his cheekbones.

"I missed you," I admit, and it comes out sounding raw and breathless. "And... I want you."

His face lights up, something that was hard and intense in his eyes turning warm and bright. He rolls onto his back so that he's beneath me, then pulls me down and kisses me all over again, peppering my face, my cheeks, my forehead, and my nose.

He runs his hands up and down my back and then grips my ass, dragging me flush against him.

My mouth falls open, and I gasp softly at the sensation, feeling that he's starting to get hard under me. I can't help but roll my hips, seeking out more of that pressure and friction, giving in to the urge to take more.

"You have no idea how much I want you, angel," he murmurs, his voice rough. "How much I've been thinking about you."

"Probably as much as I've been thinking about you," I tell him softly, nuzzling against his neck.

He chuckles, and I can feel the vibration of it all the way through my body.

When his hands start to move over me again, they have more purpose this time. He pushes down my stretchy lounge pants, sliding them over my hips and thighs, dragging them off along with my underwear.

"Have you been thinking about me naked?" he teases. "Have you been thinking about my cock?"

I can feel the flush rise up my chest, but I don't even try to deny the truth. "Yes."

"What else have you been thinking about?"

As he speaks, he helps me sit up enough that he can pull my shirt over my head, leaving me completely bare. His hands skate over my curves, and when he grabs a handful of my breast and pinches my nipple, I gasp softly, arching against him.

"This," I whisper. "You touching me. The way you always seem to know just what I need."

"You've been thinking about my hands? The way they feel on your tits? What else?"

He tugs my nipples away from my body, making it hard for me to focus enough to answer his question, but I manage to gasp out, "Your mouth. Your tongue. All the dirty things you say and do with it. The way the piercing feels when you lick me."

"Fucking hell, angel."

He groans, sitting up suddenly and replacing his fingers with his tongue as he drags it over my nipple. I hiss, clutching at his hair, but then he pulls back, letting cool air rush over my damp breast. A hungry smile curves his lips, and when he lies back down, I expect him to pull me with him so that my upper body will drape over his.

But instead, he grips my hips and tugs me upward, shifting me higher and higher until I'm straddling his face.

I tense up, because I've never done this before. I've been eaten out by the guys plenty of times, but I've never been on top, sitting on someone's face like it's a throne and I'm their queen. It makes me shy just to think about it. I have no idea what I'm doing, and I don't want to hurt him if I do it wrong.

I try to get up, to move off him, but Ransom's hands have a firm hold on my hips, and he pulls me right back down.

"You don't have to—" I squirm a little, shaking my head. "What if I smother you? What if—"

He cuts me off, gripping my hips tighter.

"I want to drown in you, pretty girl," he murmurs thickly. "I want you to soak my face with everything you've got. I want to suffocate in your pussy."

God, that mouth of his.

His words are like an immediate aphrodisiac, and I can't help the little moan that spills from my lips. I'm breathing hard now, looking down at him. He stares right back up at me, a smirk on his face.

He can clearly see how turned on I am despite my apprehension, and his tongue darts out to lick my thigh before his teeth graze the delicate skin, making me shiver.

"Be a bad girl," he urges me. "Ride my face, angel. Take everything you want."

I lick my lips, warring with myself for a second. But more than anything else, I trust Ransom. If he says he wants this, I believe him. And judging from the desperate, possessive way he kissed me when he first walked in, maybe right now he *needs* it too.

So I settle back down, still trying not to hurt him or cut off his breathing. But I let him have access to my core, allowing him to spread me open even wider as he tugs me into position right where he wants me.

When the first touch of his tongue on my pussy comes, I moan, low and deep. It feels so good, and Ransom has learned exactly what I like by now. He licks and laps along my wet folds, teasing me a little by dipping his tongue in and out of my entrance, but never pushing all the way in.

"Oh, god," I gasp out when he drags the tip of his tongue along my clit, making me shudder hard. "Ransom, that feels—"

He chuckles, the sound muffled in my wetness. "I haven't even gotten started yet, pretty girl. I'm gonna make you scream."

"Fuck," I groan, my lower belly going tight.

Ransom doesn't stop. He doesn't even slow down. It's like he wants to feast on me until he's devoured me whole, and from the way my body is shaking and trembling for him, it's clearly on board with that.

When he finally pulls back a tiny bit to get a breath, his lips and chin are shiny with my arousal. He makes a show of dragging his tongue along his lips in a slow line, holding my gaze the entire time.

"Fuck, you're so goddamn delicious," he says, his blue-green eyes hazy with desire. "The more turned on you get, the better you taste, did you know that? The sweetest fucking thing I've ever eaten. I can't get enough of you, pretty girl."

He dives right back in, and this time, he does thrust his tongue all the way into me. It's not quite like a dick being in there, or even a few fingers, but it feels good in a different way. I can feel the top and bottom balls of his piercing now too, adding a fresh sensation to the mix.

Ransom spears his tongue in and out several times, working me up until I'm soaking wet before lapping at me like he wants to taste the arousal that belongs to him.

"There you go," he murmurs encouragingly. "Don't think about anything else, just let yourself take this. Let me feel what a dirty girl you are."

My body starts trembling even more, and I brace my hands on the armrest of the couch, holding on for dear life. The part of my brain that was unsure about this has definitely switched off, leaving only the part that wants it so badly.

"Fuck, fuck, fuck, fuck..."

It comes out almost like a chant, each word accompanied by a roll of my hips. I can't help the way my pelvis grinds against his tongue, and the warm, wet pressure against my clit sends an endless wash of pleasure through me.

Ransom keeps going, his fingers tight enough to leave bruises on my hips and thighs, his tongue going into overdrive as he pulls me down so hard that I truly am sitting on his face.

"You're so good at that," I whimper, my eyelids falling shut. "Oh my god, you're so fucking good..."

The words keep coming, an endless babble, and I know I couldn't hold them back if I tried. I don't even register wanting to say them or trying to say them. It's just a reaction to the intense sensations shooting up my spine and pooling in my belly.

"Your mouth, Ransom. Your fucking mouth. I just—it's so—"

I choke off the words with a moan, tipping my head back as ecstasy threatens to pull me under. Everywhere Ransom's tongue touches, everywhere he licks, feels electrified. My body hums with it, buzzing like a hive of bees, and I feel filthy and powerful in the best way. Like his face really is my throne, and this is how he wants to pay tribute to me.

Instead of holding on to the armrest, I thread my fingers through his hair, fisting the soft brown strands as I grind against him, doing exactly what he wanted me to. I can't help it, urged on by need and the frantic beat of my pulse.

And Ransom lets me. He moans into my soaked flesh, and I know if I had it in me to look back over my shoulder, I'd be able to see how hard he is in his pants already. How badly he wants this.

The way I'm pulling at his hair seems to unleash something in him, and he attacks my pussy even harder, sucking on my clit and leaving no inch of me untasted.

I work my hips, humping his face, gasping for air, giving in to the desperate feeling that courses through me.

"Oh fuck," I moan. "I'm so—I'm gonna—"

Ransom reaches up blindly and palms my breasts, then applies himself to playing with my nipples. He pinches and rolls them between his fingers, tugging them away from my body in a way that makes more heat shoot straight through me.

I tip my head back, a wordless moan of pleasure spilling out of my mouth. I'm so close. Right there on the edge, trembling on the precipice of something huge and intense.

With one hand still on my breast, Ransom lets his other hand slide downward, skating it down my back and over the swell of my ass. He slips one finger between my cheeks, and as it presses into my back hole, I let out a choked sound of shock and pleasure.

The sudden burst of sensation is enough to snap the tension

that's been building inside me, sending me flying headfirst into an orgasm more intense than anything I've ever felt before.

I'm coming, coming undone and coming apart, and I bear down into it, but it feels different. For the first time ever, my orgasm leaves me gushing, and I can feel a hot rush of liquid spilling from me as I shake through the pleasure of it all.

I pull my hands away from Ransom's hair and rise up a little, embarrassed and horrified.

"Oh my god, I'm sorry!" I manage to squeak out, breathless. "Th-that's never happened before."

Ransom's lower face is soaked, but when he looks up at me, there's no disgust in his expression. Only scorching heat.

"Sorry?" His voice is raspy. "For what? That was the hottest fucking thing I've ever felt. You letting go for me like that, soaking my face? Fuck, angel. I'll remember that forever."

A blush rises in my cheeks, but before I can respond, he lifts me up like I weigh nothing, sliding out from under me. He sets me down with my knees on the floor and my upper body draped over the couch, then stands up behind me. When I look over my shoulder, he drags a hand over his chin and licks his fingers and his lips, like he doesn't want to miss a drop.

My heart flutters, another trickle of wetness seeping from me as my swollen pussy clenches at the sight.

Ransom's gaze skims over me, and he tugs his shirt over his head before shoving down his pants and kicking off his shoes.

"I want you to soak my cock now," he tells me. "Just like you did my face."

He kneels down behind me as he finishes undressing, and I shiver as he skates his hands down my back. He grabs two handfuls of my ass, pulling my cheeks apart wide enough to bare both of my holes to his gaze.

"Look at that gorgeous pussy, so wet and ready for me," he rasps. "Jesus, I could come just from looking at you."

He grabs one of my wrists and then the other and pins them at the small of my back. I squirm a little, testing his grip, and he tightens his hold, giving me nowhere to go. I love that feeling, the sensation of being held down, knowing he's about to fuck me hard, and my body shakes with the anticipation of it.

With his free hand, he guides his pierced cock into me, sliding it right into my core and ramming it home. The shock of being filled so quickly punches a gasp out of my body, and I turn my head so my cheek is resting against the soft fabric of the couch.

His thick shaft is so much, so good. I can feel every single inch of it as he thrusts in deeper, every ridge of his length and every bump of the piercings along the underside.

They feel different from this angle, and the way they rub against my inner walls is driving me crazy. I can barely take the barrage of sensations, my nerve endings firing over and over again, leaving me gasping and shaking where I kneel on the floor.

All I can focus on is the hard, punishing thrust of his cock again and again and the way it makes me feel. I arch and writhe beneath him, and Ransom holds on to me tight, keeping my arms pinned, holding me in place with his muscled body.

I gasp for breath as his hand moves across my ass, groping and squeezing at the flesh there.

"Everything about you is perfect," he groans. He digs his fingers in, spreading my ass cheeks again with one hand. "Everything."

"Ransom," I choke out, his name sounding desperate and needy. "Please. Fuck."

"I've got you," he murmurs, and I can hear the promise in his tone.

He rubs that hand over my ass, and when I feel his fingers creeping toward the place I want them most, I nearly choke on the moan that spills out of me.

His fingers drag over the sensitive skin between my cheeks, and my eyes fly open wide when I feel him probing at my puckered hole. Just like before, it should feel weird, but it doesn't. It feels electric and exciting, and every time the pad of his finger brushes over my rim, I get that much closer to the edge.

Ransom laughs, the sound breathless and deep, and I can't help but push back against him, craving more of his touch. More of everything.

"You like this, don't you?" he teases me. He works the tip of one finger in, moving it shallowly in my tight hole. It's just one finger, and just the tip at that, but it feels so much bigger, so much more.

"F-fuck," I choke out, squirming in his hold.

"You do," he murmurs, and I can hear the grin in his voice. "Dirty girl. You want all your pretty little holes filled, don't you? You want me and my brothers to make sure you get fucked the way you deserve."

"Ransom, I—"

I can't make the rest of the words come out, and I don't even know what I was going to say, honestly. Everything is a jumble in my head, mixed up with the lust and desire and pure need I'm feeling.

"I know, angel," he says soothingly. "I know how bad you want it." He punctuates each word with a deep thrust, and I moan with pleasure as it shoots through me. "I know you want a nice hard dick in your pretty, tight ass. Maybe one day I'll fuck you there. Would you like that? Me fucking your ass while Malice fills your perfect pussy?"

I nod, breathless and more turned on than I think I've ever been. "Please, please, please."

It spills out like a chant, like something I can't hold back. Just picturing what Ransom is saying is enough to have me right there, trembling on the edge of my orgasm.

And he doesn't let up. He fucks into me hard and fast, making sure I feel every inch of him. The piercings rub against my inner walls, and before I'm ready for it, that hot fire is spreading, burning through me with an intensity that takes my breath away.

I scream as I come, face down on the couch, struggling to breathe while I work my hips back, desperate for every drop of pleasure that Ransom can give me.

He keeps fucking me through it, not slowing or hesitating for even a second. His hand is tight around my wrists, and he keeps that one finger working into my ass, making it impossible for me to come down. Each aftershock builds and builds until it's like a continuous wave of pleasure that I couldn't stop or deny if I wanted to.

It feels like it'll never stop. Like each wave is going to drown me, holding me under until the next one comes along. Ransom's thrusts get wilder, deeper, and I know he's close too.

I want him to come. I want to feel it when he loses it the way I am.

Instead of finishing inside me though, he pulls out at the last second. I can hear him stroking himself, the sound of skin on skin, the way his breath shakes and stops for a second when he hits his own orgasm.

And then there's the wet splash of his cum spattering over my back, painting me as if he's marking his territory.

I like that. Fuck, I like it more than I ever knew I would.

I slump over the couch, breathing hard, my heart going a mile a minute. Ransom slips his finger out of my ass and drags it through the mess on my back. Then he returns to my back hole, using his own cum as lube as he presses that thick finger deeper inside, fucking me with it.

The aftershocks keep coming, and I whimper, just on this side of too sensitive as he keeps going.

My body is quaking with full body shudders every few seconds, my pussy clenching around nothing, sore but needy.

Finally, Ransom takes mercy on me and pulls out entirely, then leans down to kiss me. He strokes the limp, sweaty strands of hair back from my face and smiles at me before he stands up.

My body feels like overcooked spaghetti, but in the best way, and he has to gather me up and into his arms to move me.

"You... wore me out," I whisper, my head lolling on his shoulder.

"Good," he says warmly, pressing a kiss to my hair. "That was the idea. And now, pretty girl, it's time for a bath."

12

WILLOW

I curl up against Ransom's chest as he carries me through the living room and down the hall to the bathroom, letting him take charge completely. I'm too worn out to move yet, and the man holding me is warm and steady.

That was pretty close to the most intense thing I've ever experienced, a few times with Malice notwithstanding. Being with these men is like a crash course in sex, in all the things I never knew I would want—or tried to deny I could ever want. I had no idea how badly I needed that release, but after the last couple of days, it's clear that I really did.

Now I feel boneless and fully relaxed for the first time all day.

Ransom draws the bath, grabbing some of the bottles I keep lined up along the back ledge of the tub and sniffing at them. He tips in a little of the peony and rose scented bath oil, and the soothing scent curls through the bathroom along with the steam from the tub.

Once it's full, he helps settle me in and then climbs in behind me.

This apartment has started to feel a little like a prison sometimes, but the tub is nice and big, with plenty of room for both of us to stretch out comfortably.

For a while, we just soak in silence, and I close my eyes, inhaling the floral scent and letting the hot water soothe my sore body. Ransom drags his hands over my skin, his fingers wet and leaving trails down my arms and over my shoulders.

It's relaxing and comfortable, and I nestle against him, drifting pleasantly.

"You know, I almost don't want to wash this cum off you," he says thoughtfully.

"Perv," I tease without opening my eyes.

He snorts. "I just wish I could leave it there, as a reminder of who you belong to."

I smile at the thought of that. "Possessive perv," I amend, but it's pretty clear from my tone that I'm not upset about it at all.

"You love it."

"Yeah... I do. I like the idea of belonging to you and your brothers," I admit. "I've never really belonged anywhere before. Or to anyone. But I feel like I do now."

He strokes his hands up and down my skin, and the rhythm is so comforting, soothing me even more as I speak.

"I think... well, I think that's what hurt so bad when I thought you guys had betrayed me with that video. Because it felt like I had finally found a place to belong and then lost it. It felt like it had all been a lie, and that really sucked."

"I know. I'm so sorry it felt like that," he says gently. "You always have a place with us. Always. No matter what happens. And from here on out, there will be no more secrets or surprises like that. We won't keep anything from you, not even to protect you. The four of us are a team."

I smile at that, nestling deeper into his arms. "I've never had that. A team. A family. I like the way it sounds."

He holds me closer, as if he can keep the loneliness away with just the power of his arms around me. And maybe he can.

"What was it like when you were younger? Having two brothers you were so close with?" I ask, curious.

Ransom hums under his breath a little. "Sometimes it was pretty great. Sometimes it was a huge pain in the ass. You know how Vic and Malice can be."

I laugh at that. "Stubborn. Angry. Impulsive. Well, not so much Vic for the last one, I guess."

"True. But yeah, for the most part, it was great. Even though I'm the baby of the family, they never really treated me like I was a burden or anything. They let me tag along with them for the most part, and when they didn't, I could tell they were trying to protect me. Mom was really big on family."

I listen closely as he talks about it, wondering what it would have been like to grow up in a house like that. With siblings, with a mother who actually cared and wasn't always drunk or high or trying to take advantage of me.

"Malice would tease me sometimes, you know? Like big brothers do. He'd take my toys or Mom would tell him to share half of his cake with me and he'd take the bigger 'half.'" He makes air quotes with his fingers. "But that was all superficial shit, really. If I got into it with some asshole at school, Malice was the first person to show up and make it clear what happened when you fucked with his family. He taught me how to throw a punch and defend myself, and Vic showed me how to care less about what idiots thought."

"That sounds really nice," I say, and I can hear the wistful tone in my voice.

"It was. Mom made sure we all had each other's backs. I remember one time when Malice and Vic were having a fight about something. I don't even remember what, so it was probably something stupid. But Malice ended up not waiting to walk home with Vic after school, and Vic got into it with some bullies from the next town over. He held his own, but it definitely would have been easier with Malice, you know? Mom was pretty pissed when he came home all bruised up and asked where Malice had been. Vic didn't rat him out, just said he'd walked home alone that day, but

Mom knew. She always knew. She sat us all down and told us that we always had to be there for each other. That brothers were supposed to make sure everyone was taken care of. We took that to heart."

It's kind of amazing, hearing these stories and seeing how much they really did take that to heart. All three of them have each other's backs, always, and even though they bicker and disagree, I've never seen one of them leave another behind.

"I can tell," I murmur. "I remember thinking that when I first met you guys. That you seemed like such a strong team, even though you all have such different personalities."

Ransom nods. "Sometimes I joke that if we weren't brothers, we wouldn't be able to work together at all, but it works out somehow."

"Because you love each other."

"Sure," he says, smiling. "It's funny that our mom taught us what family is, because our dad taught us what family isn't. Just because we're all related to him by blood, it didn't mean shit. So we also learned that family is what you choose to make it."

Family is what you choose to make it.

It's a good point. Olivia is related to me by blood, but look how that turned out. Misty adopted me, and she was far from being a good parent, but at least she never tried to do anything like what Olivia's doing.

"I'll remember that," I tell him. "It's a good way of looking at things."

"I tell myself that whenever I feel shitty about being just a half-brother, you know?" His voice goes soft as he speaks. "Even if we're not fully blood related, we're family because we choose to be."

Something about the tone of his voice makes me turn in his arms, pressing my breasts against his chest. I look up into his face, taking in how open and relaxed he looks now. It's a big difference from the stormy way he pushed himself into my apartment hours ago, and I'm glad to see he seems to feel better now.

I wrap my arms around his neck and nuzzle against him, breathing in the scent of his skin.

"I think you should tell them," I whisper against his neck. "Malice and Victor. It won't weigh on you anymore if you just tell them, and I know it won't change the way they see you."

"How can you be sure about that?" he asks, an uncharacteristic note of uncertainty in his voice.

"Because of everything you just told me. You're family. You're a team. I know they'll still believe that even after it comes out. They've loved you and looked out for you for years. Why would they love you any less just because your DNA is a little different than theirs?"

He sighs. "I'll think about it."

Before I can say anything else, he tips my face up and then leans down to kiss me. It's hard to keep the thread of what I was thinking about when his mouth is on mine, so I let it go, falling into the connection between us all over again.

THE NEXT MORNING, I wake up in Ransom's arms, warm and content. The floral scent from the bath we took last night still lingers on our skin and on the sheets, and I wish I could float in this haze of contentment forever.

I curl up against him, feeling comforted by his presence—especially considering what today is going to bring.

Olivia is expecting me, and we have to go dress shopping for the engagement party. I don't want to. Not even a tiny little bit.

"What's on your mind, angel?" Ransom asks, his voice raspy from sleep.

It sends a shiver up my spine, and I look up into his eyes and sigh. "I have to go shopping with Olivia today. I need a dress for the engagement party she's throwing."

Immediately, his expression hardens. He looks so much like

Malice in this moment that it almost startles a laugh out of me, but I hold it back.

He doesn't say anything, just glares for a moment, darkly furious. Then he pulls me in closer and kisses me hard.

The intensity of it takes my breath away, and I clutch at his shoulders to anchor myself as I kiss him back. There's so much purpose here, so much intent, and I can feel it coursing through me as the kiss heats up.

Ransom's hands are everywhere, skating down my back and over my ass, and then back up, coming over my shoulders and then down to my breasts. He squeezes them hard, and I gasp, breaking away from his mouth for a second to suck down air.

When I look at him, his eyes are still intense. There's a storm swirling in those blue-green depths, and a spark of determination there that makes my heart skip a beat.

"What—" I start to ask, but I'm cut off by him rolling me onto my back and then climbing over me, looming with his hands on either side of my head.

He dips down and kisses me again, his mouth rough against mine. His tongue presses between my lips, and he kisses me hard and fast, swiping his tongue through my mouth like he wants to devour me—or make it so no one else can.

When he pulls back, his teeth graze my lower lip, and I arch against him, my naked body rubbing against his.

"Fuck," he grunts. "Fuck, I want…"

Whatever he was going to say is eaten up by a low groan as he moves his mouth to my neck. He drags his tongue over the sensitive skin, making goosebumps pop out, and I can feel my heart racing in my chest.

My pussy is getting wet, and I spread my legs automatically, wanting more. Needing this.

If I could start every morning before I had to see Olivia like this, then maybe it would be less terrible. Just a little.

Ransom seems determined to make sure I can't think about

Troy or Olivia or the engagement at all. He grabs a handful of my breast again, squeezing hard before giving me a sly smirk.

His mouth moves down further, kissing a trail along my neck and collarbones until he gets right to the valley between my breasts.

It feels like a jolt of electricity when he licks his way down that stretch of skin and then moves to take one of my nipples into his mouth.

The heat is incredible, and I hear myself whimper as I writhe on the bed, clutching at him with desperate fingers.

Ransom licks and sucks at that sensitive little bud until I'm practically dripping between my legs, arching and squirming under him, needy and on fire with it.

Then he switches to the other side, giving the other nipple the same treatment. He worries at it with his teeth a bit, and the pricks of pain mingle with the pleasure in the way I like, and I can feel myself getting closer and closer to falling apart. Just from this.

"Ransom," I moan. "Fuck, Ransom. I'm—"

"Not yet," he rasps, glancing up at me. "Hold on for a bit, angel. I want you to come, but I want it to be with my cock buried so deep in you that you can't feel anything else."

"Fuck," I whimper, bucking my hips up. "Yes. God, yes."

He grabs the base of his cock, flushed and jutting out from his body, and then lines it up with my pussy. As soon as the head touches my sensitive flesh, I gasp, arching up, urging him closer. When he drives himself into me hard and fast, I rake my nails against his back and wrap my legs around his waist like I'm trying to bind us together.

"Perfect," Ransom pants. "You're so fucking perfect."

I don't have the breath to respond, so I just hold on for dear life as he sets a hard, punishing pace. I know I won't last long, and from the way he's fucking me like it's his entire purpose in life, I doubt he will either.

He fucks into me with wild abandon, the sound of skin on skin echoing in my room. The bed creaks, shuddering under the force of our movements and providing a counterpoint to our breathless groans.

"Keep going," I choke out as tingling warmth starts to spread through me. "I'm gonna come. Oh god, Ransom, I'm so close."

"That's it," he groans. "That's it, pretty girl. Come on my cock. I wanna feel it."

I nod frantically, and when he thrusts again, he hits something inside me that sends my climax bursting through me like a firework. I bury my face against his neck, muffling my cry of pleasure against his warm skin.

Ransom keeps thrusting, chasing his own pleasure, and when his orgasm hits, he slams inside to the hilt, pouring his cum deep into my pussy.

I pant for breath, my heart racing and my head spinning, arms and legs still locked around him. When Ransom kisses me again, it's softer this time, and I melt into it as our bodies soften together.

"Now you have something to remember our night together by," he murmurs against my lips. "I want you to go to this stupid dress fitting with my cum inside you, so you can remember that your grandma can never truly keep you from us. From the men you belong to."

I shiver at the words and the sentiment, and it does make me feel better. I grin and lean up to kiss him, feeling filthy and cherished and happier than I have in a while.

We both get out of bed not long after, and I don't shower, just putting on clothes and some makeup and brushing my hair. Ransom kisses me one more time and then slips out of my apartment—and hopefully out of the building without being seen.

I give it a few minutes and then meet Jerome downstairs so that he can take me to meet Olivia.

Of course, the place we pull up to is lavish and fancy. The name of it is in French, and I don't even try to parse out the elegant script of the sign above the door. Jerome drops me off at the front and then goes to park, and I push my way inside, immediately intercepted by a blonde sales woman with a blinding smile.

"Hello," she greets me. "Can I help you?"

"This is my granddaughter," Olivia says, coming around a corner.

"Oh!" the woman replies. She turns her smile up another few watts. "It's fantastic to meet you. Your grandmother says you're shopping for a dress for your engagement party. Congratulations."

For a second, I don't even know what to say to that, but Olivia gives me a sharp look, and I blink and try to contort my features into something that looks like excitement. "Oh, um, thank you."

"Please, let me know if you need anything, Mrs. Stanton," the sales woman says and rushes away.

Olivia gives me an analytical once-over and then leads the way to the sales floor proper. There are racks and racks of dresses, in every shade imaginable. Different cuts, different necklines, different sleeves.

Once upon a time, shopping in a place like this would have been exciting, a new thrill for someone like me, but now it means nothing.

I know all this lavish fanciness just hides ugliness underneath.

The sales woman, whose name is Juliette according to her name tag, comes back with glasses of champagne and delicate little cookies on a tray. She rambles a bit about the new fall line that's just arrived, and Olivia listens for a while before sending her away with a little wave of her hand.

I just stand there, letting my grandmother direct everything. It's easier that way, and I wouldn't even know where to start in a place like this.

Olivia walks along the racks with a critical eye, picking out dresses and putting most of them back. She has Juliette gather a few after a while, all in neutral, elegant colors, and then comes back to me.

"Try these on," she says. "Come out between each one so I can see."

I take the dresses and step into the fitting room. There are mirrors on every wall, which is a little disorienting, but I quickly strip out of the clothes I came in and start putting on dresses.

I come out in the first one, a dusty rose number with a scooped neckline and long sleeves.

Olivia makes me turn for her and then shakes her head. "No, too frumpy. Next."

"Why are we buying a dress off the rack anyway?" I ask her as I step back into the large fitting room to put on the next dress. "I thought you would have had something custom made." The disdain for her general snobbery is barely held back in my tone.

"This is faster, since we need it on short notice," she says. "And it will still be custom. These dresses are just the base. Once we've picked one, it will be tailored to fit perfectly. One of a kind."

I roll my eyes and slip into the next dress before coming out again.

Talking to my grandmother makes me cringe, and I'm tempted to try to get through the entire fitting in silence, but I still need to know more—about her, and about her world. I have to understand Olivia Stanton if I'm going to beat her.

"The color on this one is good," Olivia says, walking around me after I emerge wearing the third dress. It's a dark green gown that does seem to make my pale skin almost glow. "And it covers your unsightly scars. With a shorter hemline, and perhaps shortening the sleeves, it could work. You'll need new shoes, obviously. And accessories."

"I've never really accessorized before," I tell her.

Olivia pins me with a stare, seeming annoyed by my lack of interest in fashion. "You do now. Your outfit will be impeccable, and it will be the same way whenever you go to a function where you are representing our family. Do you understand how important this engagement party is?"

"I guess," I mutter quietly.

"Do not mumble at me," she replies sharply. "This marriage is joining two very important, very influential families in Detroit. *Everyone* who matters in this city will want to come out to see the happy couple. So you will look as good as possible to make the right impression."

"So we're just showing off for your peers?"

"Exactly," she says.

I shake my head, huffing out a breath. "All you people care about is appearances."

My grandmother just gives me a hard look. "Yes," she agrees. "We do. And you had better play your part well."

She holds my gaze for a moment, as if she wants to make sure her threat is sinking in well. Then she waves me back into the dressing room to try on another dress.

"At least it won't be as bad as the last time I took you out into society," she says, speaking quietly almost like she's talking to herself. "Misty can't show up and cause another disturbance."

I narrow my eyes, pausing in hanging up the green dress. Something about Olivia's tone makes my stomach twist, a strange sort of tension spreading through my limbs. She sounds self-satisfied. Almost... smug. Like the reason Misty isn't around anymore to embarrass her is because...

My hand flies to my mouth, stifling a choked gasp.

Nausea rises up immediately after, and I clamp my palm tight over my lips, bending over a little as I close my eyes.

Olivia killed my birth mother. She openly admitted it to me and talks about it like it's something she's proud of. She saw my birth mother as an impediment to the success of the Stanton family legacy, so she took care of it in the way only a sociopath would think to do.

And she saw Misty the same way.

Misty embarrassed her by causing a scene at the art museum gala. And my adoptive mother also had the audacity to show up and demand money from Olivia.

So Olivia... took care of the problem.

"The overdose," I whisper, my words slightly muffled by my hand. "That was... that was you. It wasn't an accident."

There's a moment of silence, and I'm not sure if Olivia heard my words with the dressing room door between us. Then she sniffs, and I can almost picture her lifting her chin. "She was an addict who'd ruined her life. She was beyond saving, and it was only a matter of time before she overdosed on her own."

"But she didn't." I shake my head, horror ricocheting through me. "She didn't do it on her own. *You* were the one who—"

"I did what I had to." Olivia's voice is closer now, as if she's stepped nearer to the dressing room door. "Which is what I always do. Misty couldn't be allowed to disgrace you anymore. She was trash, and she was disposed of accordingly. It's not as if the world will miss her." She exhales sharply, a breath that sounds almost like a little laugh. "Even you won't miss her."

My throat goes tight, my heart hammering in my chest. Her words cut through me like poisoned knives, sending pain lancing through me.

This hurts even worse than learning about the murder of my birth mother. Because Olivia took both of them from me. And because... Olivia is partly right. Misty and I had a complicated relationship, to say the least, and there were times when I wanted her out of my life. I was ready to cut ties with her entirely by the end, but that doesn't mean I wanted her dead.

I step out of the dressing room, tears stinging my eyes as my hands shake.

"You're *vile*," I snap. I know I shouldn't give in to the anger coursing through me, and that poking at Olivia could be dangerous, but I can't help it. The words just keep coming. "You play with people's lives like you think you're some kind of god. Just because you don't like someone or you think they're an embarrassment, you think you can just... just get rid of them. Who the fuck do you think you are? How could you just—"

Before I can finish the sentence, Olivia's arm snaps out. Moving so fast that I barely see it coming, she backhands me across the face. The blow is hard enough to cut me off, the sudden burst of pain making stars dance before my eyes as I rock back on my heels in shock.

Her cold hazel eyes narrow, her delicate features pulled tight as she stares at me. For a moment, a look of venomous hatred passes through her expression. Then she squares her shoulders, her face smoothing out as she steps back.

"The green dress will do for the engagement party," she says. "For the wedding, we will be having a dress custom made. It will have to be completely one of a kind if we want to make the right impression."

I blink, my cheek throbbing dully as I stare at her. The way she just shifted so quickly between psycho bitch and elegant society woman leaves me reeling. It's like there are two completely different versions of her, the mask she wears so perfectly refined that I'm finally starting to understand how she fooled me for all those weeks after we first met.

She really is a fucking sociopath.

That thought sends a wash of fear through me, chilling my skin. I already know that she's killed at least two people who stood in the way of what she wanted, and that makes the threat she's holding over the Voronin brothers feel all the more real.

"Troy and I have gotten hung up on a few points in the negotiations for the terms of this arrangement," my grandmother continues, still talking in that calm, neutral tone, as if she didn't just admit to murder and then slap me. "But it will all be worked out soon."

I nod, still massaging my aching cheek as fear curls in my belly. I have no idea what she means about them getting 'hung up on a few points of the negotiations.'

But judging from what I know of my grandmother, it can't be anything good.

13

RANSOM

THE NOISE of the grinder squeals through the garage as I hold it steady, cutting through the metal of the frame on the car. Sparks fly, and I'm grateful for my goggles, keeping the worst of it back from my face.

When I cut through the connection, Malice yanks on one end, pulling it away and separating out the parts.

The whole time, I can feel eyes on us, and it makes my shoulders climb up toward my ears.

I force myself to take a breath and relax my posture, but this shit is so irritating. I can tell from the look on Malice's face that he's not thrilled about it either, but there's not much we can do.

Work is work these days, and we need the money.

The guy who brought us this car to chop is some kind of low-level criminal. Scum, basically, and not the kind of person we'd normally do business with. Most likely, he was sloppier with the theft of this car than someone more professional, and that means there are more chances he could lead the cops right to us if they decide to investigate.

But work has been so lean lately that we've been strapped, and we need cash on hand more than ever these days. If we're gonna be able to protect Willow from her grandmother, then we need some resources.

We can't even dream of the kind of resources Olivia has, so we need all we can get.

It doesn't help that the ratty little fucker who brought the car in insisted on hanging around to watch the work. "I wanna make sure I'm getting my money's worth," he'd said, and Malice had almost decked him right then and there.

I was able to calm him down with a look, but the longer this dude has been standing there, watching us work, the more I wish I'd just let Malice go off.

"There might be a lot more where this came from," the guy is saying. His eyes dart around, but it doesn't even seem like he's looking at anything in particular. "Buddy of mine has a buddy who's a valet." He waggles his eyebrows significantly. "Lots of fancy cars left overnight in weird places, you know? You know?"

Malice ignores him, focusing on the job, and I nod, just to acknowledge him before I fire the tools back up again, thanking fuck for the sound drowning out this dude's voice.

Finally, over an hour later, we finish with the car. The guy hands over a stack of bills, and then he and his buddy load the parts up into another car.

I flip through the money as they head out, counting the stack. It was a lower rate than what a job like that probably deserved, but we got paid, so that's all that matters.

"Fuck," Malice groans, mashing the button to close the garage door. "I thought that fucker was never gonna leave."

"We need a new policy," I mutter. "Drop it off and we'll call you when it's done."

"We need better fucking clients. Not greasy little rat fucks, who are likely to get us arrested one of these days," Malice fires back.

I shrug and give him a look. "Right now, we have to work with what we've got."

Malice rolls his eyes and pushes open the door between the garage and our living space. I follow him, moving into the kitchen and washing my hands in the sink.

Vic comes down a second later with his laptop, settling at the kitchen table. "Ransom," he says, and I roll my eyes.

"I know, I know. I'm cleaning it up."

I grab a towel and wipe up all the grimy water that splashed on the counter, giving Vic a look as I hang the towel back in place.

He just arches an eyebrow and looks back to his computer.

"We got another message from X," he says.

As if this fucking day couldn't get more annoying.

"Are you fucking kidding me?" Malice demands. "We just finished doing shit for this bitch."

"I know," Vic says. "It's bullshit, but it's clear she's trying to prove a point. And it's not like we can argue with her about it. Not yet anyway."

Malice grumbles and then so does my stomach.

I open up the snack cabinet, the one that Malice and I share because Vic thinks we're slobs. I rummage through it, looking for the crackers that I like, but the box is gone.

"Did you eat all my fucking crackers?" I ask, turning to glare at Malice.

"I bought the damned things," Malice says, shrugging. "So yeah, I had a few."

"You bought them because I asked for them. And you had more than a few. The box was half full last week."

Malice just shrugs again, and I glance at Vic.

"Don't look at me," he says, not even glancing away from his laptop.

"Vic. My favorite brother. The best of us." I lay it on thick, batting my lashes even though he's not looking at me. "Do you have any crackers?"

"I might," he says. "Because unlike the two of you, I keep track of what I have and don't eat like I'm afraid the food is going to disappear if I don't get it in my stomach fast enough."

"Hey, that's mostly just Malice," I shoot back. "Can I please have some of your crackers? I'll replace them. I promise."

Vic rolls his eyes. "I've heard that before."

"I really will this time! I've had a hard day, Vic. And all I really want is some of those garlic crackers with some cheese spread. Please?"

"Just eat something else," Malice suggests. He grabs an apple from the bowl on the counter and doesn't even bother to wash it before dropping into one of the kitchen chairs and biting into it with a decisive crunch. "We've got plenty of snack shit."

"If you spray apple juice on my laptop, I'm going to kick your ass," Vic says calmly to Malice. "You can have some crackers, Ransom. Just take a whole sleeve."

"See?" I say, pointing at Malice. "This is why Vic is my favorite brother."

Malice just rolls his eyes and takes another big bite. "I don't give a fuck."

Under Vic's watchful eye, I take a sleeve of the crackers and then make sure to fold the box lid down the way he likes it before putting the box back where it was. Vic nods, and I grin before grabbing the cheese spread and sitting down at the table with them.

"What made today so hard?" Vic asks. "Was there a problem with the job?"

"Not with the job—"

"With the fucking idiot who brought the car in," Malice chimes in. We fill Vic in on what happened and how much we got paid, and he sighs.

"We used to charge more for shit like that."

"Yeah," I agree. "I thought about that too. But with how things are right now…"

He nods. "Any money is better than nothing."

"It fucking sucks," Malice grumbles. We all kind of nod at that because he's right. This isn't where any of us wanted to be, and having to take shit jobs just to try to stay on top of things is dangerous as well as annoying.

I shrug a shoulder though, leaning back in my chair. "We've been through worse, and we've always figured it out. We can do that again."

Malice nods, his face set into determined lines. "Yeah, we can. And even with all this shit we're up against, it's worth it."

I know without him having to say it that he's talking about Willow. He only gets that look in his eye when he's talking about her.

The same spark I see in his face lights in my chest. "You're right. It's definitely worth it."

I smile a little, memories of this morning playing in my head for a second. And last night too.

I can see Willow, bent over the couch, taking my cock and begging for more, taking everything I could give her. She's so fucking responsive, arching into every touch, coming undone so easily under my hands and my cock. Somehow, she's still so sweet, after everything that's happened to her... and that's *still* happening to her.

And her sweetness is edged with something wicked, something delicious that gives her a good girl/bad girl dynamic, and it's intoxicating. Both of those sides of her are real and truly her, and she's the brightest light in any room she's in.

At this point, I'm beyond addicted to her. That was a good word for it at first, for the way I craved being around her, but now it's so much more than that.

More than addiction. Something deeper.

I'm falling for her, and I know it. All the way down to my soul.

Malice catches my eye and we share a look. It feels like he can guess the direction of my thoughts the same way I figured out his a second ago, but that's not weird. Willow is on all of our minds a lot these days.

Vic nods his agreement too. "It's worth it. No matter what, it will be worth it."

There's a soft ping from his laptop, and it draws his attention back to the screen. The new message we got from X earlier today must be finished decrypting.

"What's the damage?" I ask, already feeling unease settling in the pit of my stomach. X's jobs have always had a level of risk to them, but knowing what we know now, there's no way Olivia's going to be content with sending us on fetch quests and sabotage missions for too much longer. It just doesn't seem to be her style.

Vic's eyes move rapidly as he scans the message, and when worry flashes across his face, the feeling of dread in my gut kicks up a notch.

"It's another job," he says, stating the obvious. "But this one's just for Malice."

14

WILLOW

A COUPLE of nights after the dress fitting disaster, I'm in the car with Olivia, being driven somewhere. She didn't see fit to answer me when I asked where we were going, so I just sit on my side of the large back seat, waiting for us to get there.

Honestly, I was almost glad when I got the call from her earlier today. She had Jerome bring me over to her house first, which gave me another chance to poke around a little.

Not that I found much at all. But I'm still trying.

I managed to peek around a few other parts of the house while Olivia was getting ready for whatever this is, and it made me more convinced than ever that the stuff I need is in her office somewhere.

The rest of the house is largely decorative, ostentatious and meant to intimidate outsiders and show off Olivia's wealth. She's not leaving anything incriminating lying around in the areas she wants people to see.

The office is the one room that seems private and utilitarian. It's where she manages her estate, so if I'm going to find anything, it has to be in there.

"Troy and I are nearing the end of our negotiations," Olivia says suddenly, startling me out of my thoughts. I blink over at her, disgust rolling in my gut.

"I guess you're happy about that," I mutter, not even bothering to pretend it brings me anything other than irritation to hear it.

"He's been very... difficult." Her lip curls a bit as she speaks, her pleasant facade cracking a little. "He believes that since you are 'damaged goods,' he should get better terms in all of this."

I narrow my eyes, glaring out the window. "I thought he was into that."

Just saying it makes me feel sick.

She clicks her tongue softly against her teeth. "Personally, perhaps. But socially, being married to someone everyone knows was raised by trash will affect his standing." She grimaces. "And then there's the fact that my own estate is currently not as strong as it could be. He's trying to push any advantage he can."

"Isn't that what you people do?" I ask. "You try to fuck over other people to make yourselves look better or have more money or whatever."

"Do not 'or whatever' me," Olivia says, her voice cold. "I'm willing to concede a little where these negotiations are concerned, because they'll get me what I want in the long run, but I won't let our family get the short end of the metaphorical stick."

It's on the tip of my tongue to tell her that she's not any family of mine and I wish I'd never met her. Knowing what I know now, I would've preferred to spend my entire life having no idea where I came from.

Luckily, Olivia is still rattling on about Troy, so she doesn't notice the mutinous look on my face as I bite back the comment.

"Tonight will settle things between us once and for all, and it will be the last part of the negotiations," she tells me.

It all sounds very final, and I frown, not really understanding what she means. I don't know what this will entail, and when the car finally pulls to a stop at our destination, I'm even more confused.

From the outside, it looks like nothing. Like some kind of warehouse or factory that's been abandoned from its original purpose and turned into something else.

Olivia puts on sunglasses and adjusts the head wrap she has on, and I narrow my eyes. It's almost like... she wants to hide herself as much as possible. To keep her identity hidden.

Where the hell are we?

"Come along," she says sharply to me, getting out of the car and waiting impatiently for me to follow.

I do so, and she leads me around the building to a back entrance.

I blink as we step inside, caught off guard by the florescent lighting and the loud noise. It's unmistakably the sound of a crowd, laughing and jeering, and the scent of sweat and blood hangs in the air.

Before I can ask anything, Olivia is striding away, her shoes tapping on the pitted concrete floor as she walks, and I have to hurry to follow after her.

We go up some stairs and then step through a doorway into a small room, and I realize it's like a private box at an arena or something. We have a view of the space below, and I can see loads of people packed around what looks like a fighting ring.

I blink as it all starts to make sense.

Well, at least some of it. I understand what this place is now, but I still have no idea what we're doing here.

Olivia relaxes once she takes a seat, removing her sunglasses and taking off her headscarf. The glass that separates us from the rest of the onlookers must be one way, so she's clearly not worried about being spotted anymore.

"There you are."

The deep voice behind me makes me jump, and I turn around to see Troy walking in with all his usual lecherous swagger.

He nods respectfully to Olivia and then smirks at me, looking me up and down.

"Ah, my future bride," he drawls. "You couldn't have put on something a little sexy for me?"

I glare at him, my cheeks heating with fury. Before I can snap at him that I'd rather die than cater to any of his gross little kinks, Olivia speaks up, addressing me.

"Troy loves these fights," she says. "He comes here and bets on them the way others might do with horses."

"What does that have to do with your negotiations?" I ask, the word tasting bad in my mouth.

"This is the last of them, as I said. A wager on the fight. Although I'd hoped for something a bit more..." She glances around the sparse space with distaste. "Suitable."

Troy shrugs. "The nice one that Julian Maduro owned burned down. So this is the best we've got right now. It's a shame, but it's been busier than ever, which is good." He shifts his attention to me, his grin a little unhinged. "Have you ever seen something like this before?"

I shake my head warily, not answering with words.

"Ah. Guess you still have some cherries to pop after all." He winks and licks his lips. "But you've probably seen stuff like this in whatever slum you grew up in. Bare knuckle fights, no weapons, no backup. Just two people beating the shit out of each other to see who can last the longest. It's intense and raw, and if we're lucky, someone might have to be wheeled out of here before the end of the night. If they don't die, they might end up eating through a tube for the rest of their life."

The way he talks about it is the same way other people talk about football or basketball, but he's clearly into watching these fights for the blood and violence and the possibility of seeing someone die. It's not surprising.

But it still doesn't make sense for me to be here. If Olivia and Troy want to bet on a stupid fight, then they don't need me around to do it. I haven't been present for any of the other negotiations surrounding our marriage, so I don't know why I'm suddenly being included now.

I'm about to give in and ask when a voice crackles over the shoddy PA system to announce the next fight.

I barely register most of it as the announcer gets the crowd hyped up for more bloodshed, but over the cheers of the audience, a name stands out, and it makes my blood run cold.

One of the fighters is Malice Voronin.

I'm going to have to watch Malice fight, and if it's anything like what Troy's been talking about, it's not going to be pretty.

My stomach drops, and I whip my head around to stare at Olivia, horrified.

There's a smirk on her face, and I grit my teeth, filled with more hatred than ever for this horrible old bitch. She doesn't care about these fights, and she probably could've found another way to negotiate with Troy if she really wanted to.

This is just a power trip for her. Her way of showing me that she can make Malice do whatever she wants. And a way for her to hurt me on purpose, just because she can.

I turn away from her, not wanting to see that smug look on her face for another second. I look out into the crowd, knowing that I can see them but they can't see me. At first, it's just a teeming mass of people, barely distinguishable from each other, but I finally find the two faces I've been searching for.

Ransom and Victor are down there.

Both of them are staring at the ring, tense expressions on their faces. Ransom leans in and says something to Vic, and Vic just nods, looking grim.

This must be another job that X gave them. Olivia either signed Malice up to fight, or she just told them that one of the three of them had to volunteer, and Malice stepped up. Neither of those scenarios would surprise me, knowing how protective Malice is of the people he cares about. And I'm glad his brothers are here, at least.

Even though I really, really hate all of this.

A few seconds later, the fighters walk into the center of the ring. Malice looks stoic and determined, cracking his knuckles as he sizes up the other guy. His opponent is smaller than him, but he looks wiry and fast, and there's a sharp grin on the guy's face as he stares right back at Malice, unafraid.

The announcer calls the beginning of the fight, and the guy lunges across the ring quick as a flash, trying to land a hit on Malice. The crowd screams as Malice twists out of the way, grabbing the guy's arm and yanking it back hard.

Behind me, Olivia and Troy discuss terms.

"So if your man wins," Troy is saying, "Then you get the stake you want in my family's company. But if my pick wins, then I get more of your estate's holdings."

"I'm aware of the deal," Olivia replies, her tone cool. "But I have picked my fighter carefully."

My eyes are glued to the fight, even though I don't want to see it. But it feels like if I look away, something terrible might happen.

It's a brutal brawl. Malice's opponent is quick on his feet, and he lands a few good hits on Malice just by out-speeding him. I wince at the sound of his fist connecting with Malice's jaw, which is audible even from our box behind the glass, and Malice spits blood out onto the floor.

But it doesn't stop him, and he attacks right back, using his size and strength to his advantage. He punches the guy right in the face, and there's a sickening crunch as his nose sprays blood. He seems dazed, and Malice uses that to his advantage. He keeps hitting him, landing blow after blow until the man's face is a bloody, bruised mess.

Even with the hits he took, Malice seems to be in good form, and while I hate seeing this, I have to admit that he's a good fighter. I wonder if it's something he picked up as a kid, defending his brothers the way their mom taught him to, or if prison brought it out in him, since he had to fight to defend himself so often.

The rule is that the bout doesn't end until one of the men is incapacitated enough to stop fighting, and my nails dig little crescent shapes into my palms as it drags on. But finally, Malice catches his opponent with a vicious right hook that sends his head snapping sideways. The man crumples to a bloody heap on the ground, and although I can see him moving a little, he doesn't get up again.

Olivia smiles, turning to Troy with that look of smug superiority on her face. "I believe that's my win," she says. "I'll have the contracts drawn up—"

"Wait. Let's do double or nothing," Troy cuts in, scowling. "If you win this time, you can have an even bigger stake in the Copeland Corporation. I'll give you a seat on our board of directors."

Olivia's cold eyes glitter as she considers it. She's already won, so she doesn't have to accept his new offer, but I know before she even says anything that she will.

She's too greedy to do anything else.

Still, when she inclines her head in agreement, my heart sinks.

15

WILLOW

Worry turns my stomach inside out.

Fuck.

Fuck.

I don't want to see Malice fight again. He came out of the first bout okay, but he did take a couple of really hard hits. There's already a nasty bruise darkening on his face, a cut above his eye, and a trickle of blood sliding from one of his nostrils.

The other guy looks much, much worse, but the moment of relief I had at this all being over is well and truly shattered as fear and adrenaline start pumping through my veins all over again.

Two guys come out and help Malice's first opponent to his feet, basically dragging him out of the ring as he shuffles along.

The announcer says something that I don't hear over the roaring in my ears, and I watch Malice's jaw tighten. My gaze flicks to Ransom and Vic in time to see them exchange a glance, and then the next fighter enters the ring.

He's close to Malice's size, with hard eyes, and Malice looks him over as if he's trying to gauge his weak points. This man is bigger than Malice's first opponent, but I hope that means he'll be slower too. Then it will just be brute force against brute force, and

I have to believe that Malice can come out on top again in that situation.

I'm just starting to talk myself down from my initial panic, taking a few deep breaths to steady myself... when another man walks out into the ring.

I blink, my brows drawing together. *What the fuck? What is he doing?*

The second man comes to a stop beside the first one, the two of them standing side by side as they face Malice, and the implications slam into me.

It's not going to be a two-way fight, or even a three-way fight.

It's going to be two against one.

"What the hell? He has to fight them both?" I leap up from my seat and round on Troy, furious and terrified. My heart slams in my chest, and I want nothing more than to smack the self-satisfied look off his face.

"What is the meaning of this?" Olivia demands, also sounding upset. "This isn't what we agreed on."

Troy just shrugs, still smirking. "Don't look at me. It's the rules of this place. The undefeated fighter has to take on two new fighters if he wants to continue in the ring. If you didn't know that, that's on you." Olivia bristles, but Troy doesn't back down. "But if you want, we can call the deal off entirely...?"

She presses her lips together into a thin line, clearly considering her options here.

"No," she finally says.

Troy nods and settles in, looking like he couldn't be more pleased.

I ball my hands into fists at my side, trying to make myself breathe evenly so I don't fall into a full-blown panic attack. My stomach churns with worry, and anger burns through me like fire. Anger at Troy for being such a slimy, manipulative piece of shit, and at Olivia for putting us in this situation in the first place.

Troy's a fucking cheater, but Olivia is the one who signed

Malice up for this, and now he has to fight two men—who, unlike him, didn't just finish another bout and are fresh and uninjured.

The announcer calls the start, and the crowd goes wild, everyone in the stands screaming and hollering as if they're losing their minds. I step closer to the glass, holding my breath as the new bout begins.

Malice stands loosely, dressed in athletic pants and a tank top. His scars and tattoos are on full display, his muscled arms gleaming with a sheen of sweat. For a moment, he and his two opponents continue to size each other up—and then all three of them move.

The men both lunge in at once, and Malice ducks and twists out of the way of their fists, managing to clip one of them with a punch as he slips away. But it's a glancing blow, not hard enough to do the kind of damage he'll need to.

It's not like the first fight, where it felt even until Malice got the upper hand. This is a bit more of a free-for-all, the two opponents trying to take opportunities to get at Malice where they think they can.

The two men might both be trying to take him out, but it's clear they've never fought as a team before. Their attacks are uncoordinated, and Malice uses that to his advantage. They both lunge at the same time again, and Malice elbows the bigger one in the throat, making him stumble back and get in the way of the other man.

He uses that as a distraction to sweep the first guy's legs out from under him and gets in a few good hits before he has to dart back, out of the reach of number two.

His skill is clear to see, and even though he's breathing hard, his eyes look clear from here, as if he's channeling his anger and strength into every hit he can land.

Just watching the way he moves is breathtaking, and I wonder what it says about me that I find him mesmerizing and oddly beautiful like this. I can't look away.

The fight continues, Malice holding his own while his opponents seem to almost work against each other, giving him the upper hand. But it doesn't take long for that to shift, and they seem to realize that working together is the best way to come out on top.

There's no moment of agreement that I can see, but they stop getting in each other's way so much and start focusing on teamwork.

One of them darts in, ready to crack Malice across the jaw, and when Malice blocks that hit and dodges back, the other one is ready with a hit of his own, knocking Malice back.

Malice wipes a smear of blood from his face and launches himself back in, but he can't seem to make much headway. No matter what he does, there's always one of them waiting in the wings to knock him back.

He takes heavy punches to the face, to the stomach, to the chest. He manages to block some of them, but most of them connect with horrible cracking sounds as he starts to get overpowered.

When he stumbles, they press their advantage, lighting into him and making him drop down to one knee on the ground.

His chest heaves, and his shirt is stained with blood and sweat. The crowd is screaming, stomping on the floor, demanding to see more.

It's clear that they don't care who wins, they're just here for the spectacle.

"Get up," I whisper, my hands curling into fists as I stare down at Malice. "Come on. You can do it."

"Not a fucking chance," Troy says gleefully, stepping up beside me. "He's done for now."

Olivia makes a noncommittal noise, but she leans forward in her seat on my other side, watching intently. Distantly, I wonder if she's going to work out some punishment for the brothers if Malice loses this match.

But thinking about that makes me feel sick, so I push the thought to the side, focusing again on the fight.

The two opponents clearly smell victory, and they step toward Malice, ready to finish the job. Malice's head is hanging down, and he looks defeated, which makes my heart stop for a second.

But as they close in on him, he moves, almost too fast to track. He grabs the leg of the guy nearest to him, yanking hard and bringing him down in a heap. There's a loud crack as his head hits the ground, and the crowd *oooooooh*'s in sympathy.

The man is dazed, and that's enough for Malice to lunge in and drive his knee down into the guy's windpipe, leaving him wheezing and passed out on the ground.

"Fucker," I hear the other one grunt, and Malice's head snaps to him. He looks so tired, but he's not done. He surges up, fury snapping in those stormy eyes.

The last opponent tries to block him, but he's not ready for the force Malice hits him with. Malice punches him so hard in the jaw that I'm almost positive the crunching sound is bone breaking, and then he grabs the man's wrist, wrenching his arm back and probably dislocating it from the socket.

The man howls in pain and crumples to the ground, leaving Malice the only one standing, breathing hard and dripping blood onto the floor. The referee calls out a five-count, giving both of Malice's opponents a chance to get back up... but neither of them do.

As the count ends, the crowd explodes, screaming and cheering. I can just make out the announcer declaring Malice the winner over the noise.

In the chaos, Malice turns and limps his way out of the ring, and Olivia stands up primly and faces Troy, looking pleased and sure of herself.

"Well, I believe that settles things fully?" she says, arching one finely plucked brow. "The terms are set. The engagement party will be soon, and then the wedding will follow a week after."

Troy makes a sour expression, glaring at Olivia as much as he dares. Then he shrugs and steps closer to me. Transferring his focus from my grandmother's face to mine, he leers down at me, using one arm to pull me tight against his body as his other hand trails down my side.

"Oh, well," he says, vindictive heat flashing in his eyes. "I guess I'll just have to make sure to get my money's worth out of you when you're my wife."

He says it loud enough that Olivia can hear, but the words are meant for me.

I shudder in disgust, ripping myself away from him as his hand slides over my ass. He snorts a laugh and then stalks out of the room, leaving me alone with Olivia.

Instead of commenting on what just happened, she pulls the scarf over her hair again and then gestures sharply with one hand.

"Follow me," she says, and I obey.

We head back downstairs, but instead of retracing our steps to the entrance we came in through, we walk down a dingy hall. When we reach the end of it, she pushes a door open, leading us into a small locker room.

It's empty, except for where Malice sits on one of the benches, sweaty, bruised, and bloody. The bruise on the side of his face looks much worse up close, and I know he's likely going to have more littering his body.

He looks up when we step into the room, and when he sees me standing behind Olivia, his eyes flash with something I can't identify. I have no idea what he's thinking right now, but it's pretty clear he didn't know I would be watching his fights.

After a second, he jerks his gaze away from me to glare at Olivia. "What the fuck was that?" he snarls. "When we got the job, X failed to mention there would be more than one fight tonight."

Olivia shrugs one shoulder, seeming unbothered. "Well, that's because there wasn't supposed to be. It was an... unexpected development. But I knew you could do it."

Malice snorts, rolling his eyes. "Not my first rodeo," he mutters.

She smiles. "Yes, I'm aware. Your time in prison prepared you well for this kind of thing, didn't it? You aren't unused to being outnumbered or thinking on your feet."

There's something in her tone that makes me glance over at her, and Malice must hear it too, because his head snaps up.

"What the fuck is that supposed to mean?" he demands.

"It means that I know you've been ganged up on before. Quite literally, in fact. How many men forced themselves on you when you were in prison? I know you were raped by at least one, but was it more than that? And you survived and then came back to kill their leader, making his gang back off. I knew you were the type to fight against the odds, which is why I chose you for this assignment instead of one of your brothers."

Malice stiffens, his jaw going tight and his shoulders bunching. He doesn't meet my eyes, staring at Olivia like he wishes he could pick her up and break her in half. My grandmother doesn't even flinch, though. She just smirks, as if she's proud of herself for having learned enough of Malice's traumatic past to use it to her advantage now.

Meanwhile, my heart is breaking for Malice and what he's been through. He's told me some of what happened to him in prison, but not everything. I knew he had been jumped by a gang, and I knew that he killed one of them and got sent to solitary for it, which is why the number twenty-four is significant to him.

But I had no idea he'd been assaulted like that.

Malice hasn't looked away from Olivia, and I brace myself for what she might say next, and what he might do when she says it, but then her phone starts ringing in her bag.

My grandmother sighs and pulls it out, and her face twists into a look of annoyance when she sees who it is.

"Troy," she mutters. "He'll be trying to renegotiate something even now." She cuts her gaze to me. "Honestly, I didn't expect *him* to be the difficult one in all of this."

Maybe you should be blackmailing him instead then, I think, but I keep those words locked behind my lips as she walks toward the door, looking annoyed.

"I'm going to go find Troy to put an end to this nonsense, and then we will be leaving, Willow," she calls over her shoulder.

I don't even respond, waiting until the clacking of her heels fades away and the door closes.

Then it's just me and Malice left in the locker room.

Somehow, I don't know what to say to him. After hearing what happened to him in prison, I feel like I should comfort him or do something to make sure he knows that it's okay and I don't think less of him or anything like that, but the words get stuck in my throat.

It must show on my face though, because when Malice finally looks at me, his face goes hard.

"Whatever the fuck you're thinking right now, you can stop," he snaps. "I don't want your goddamned pity."

16

MALICE

My jaw clenches as my words hang in the air between us.

My body fucking aches.

I'm not a stranger to fights, not even to fights where I'm outnumbered, as that bitch Olivia so helpfully pointed out. But it's been a while since I had to go all-out, and my muscles are screaming from exhaustion and overuse.

My chest aches even more, though.

I hate the way Willow is looking at me right now. Like she doesn't know what to say and wants to be careful of my *delicate* feelings, when I sure as fuck don't have any.

I hate the memories of that time. I hate thinking of the helplessness that I felt when I was jumped and then held down and raped. I never wanted to feel that way again, and I made sure I never did. I became stronger and tougher, and built myself a reputation that makes people think twice before fucking with me. But no matter how much distance I put between myself and that moment in time, the memories are still there, haunting me.

Willow swallows hard, and her gold-flecked brown eyes go soft. She closes the distance between us and then climbs onto my lap. Even though my entire body is tense and on edge, her weight is a soft, welcome addition.

Not seeming to care that I'm sweaty and bloody, she reaches up and cups my face with both hands, and it's a struggle not to lean right into the comforting feeling of her hands on me.

"I *don't* pity you," she says softly, responding to my earlier words. "I don't. But I hate that that happened to you. You didn't deserve it, and I wish I could kill the men who did that to you."

A surprised breath huffs out of me. It almost makes me smile, hearing her say something that sounds so... well, so like me, I guess. It unwinds some of the tension in my chest, making it easier to breathe. Easier to look at her. My fierce Solnyshka, with the spirit of a fighter inside that delicate, fuckable body of hers.

I pull her closer against me, needing to feel her. Needing to be close.

"I already killed one of them," I remind her. Not smug, just a statement of fact.

"Good," she whispers. "The rest of them deserve it too. I just... you didn't deserve that."

"They sure fucking seemed to think I did," I mutter. And I never talk about this when I can help it, but it's easier to say the words with her soft body pressed against mine, her gentle fingers tracing paths along my jaw. "Those fuckers had it out for me in a big way. They almost killed me."

She blinks, looking appalled. "That's the gang you told me about before?"

I nod. "Yeah. Same assholes. It happened not long after our mom... after Nikolai killed our mom. It was a shitty time, you know? I almost gave up when I found out. I was in there because we'd killed our shitbag father to protect her, and finding out our mom had died anyway almost broke me. I didn't think I was going to make it out, and I didn't have the energy to fight off every fucker that wanted a piece of me. My heart was just... shattered."

Willow wraps her arms around my shoulders, holding on tight. From anyone else, it would feel claustrophobic and demeaning, but from her, somehow, it doesn't. I know she just wants to be there for me, so I let her.

"But you didn't give up," she murmurs, and it's not a question.

"No, I didn't. I decided I couldn't go out like that. I couldn't let them kill me. So I kept fighting, and that's when I came back and took out the leader of that gang as a warning to the rest of them."

"And then they put you in solitary, right?"

I nod. "Yeah. The warden thought that was going to be some big punishment, but for me, it wasn't like that. For one, it gave me space away from everyone who had it out for me, and I spent most of the time just thinking about shit."

"Like what?"

"Like… I dunno. All the stuff that was keeping me going. All the reasons I was fighting in the first place. For the longest time, it was my family. Even while I was in there, I knew I had to make it back to them. I wanted to see my mom smile again, see her reading her favorite books, see her build a better life without our dad. I wanted to see Vic and Ransom and do all the things we'd talked about before I went to prison. But even after Mom died, her memory kept me going. Once I really thought about it, I knew she wouldn't want me to fall apart just because she was gone. It was the only thing I cared about, and focusing on what was left of my family kept me from losing it in solitary. Even when I got out of that cell and then out of prison altogether, they were all I cared about. The rest of the world could burn as far as I cared, but as long as my family was safe, I wouldn't give a shit."

"They're lucky to have you," Willow murmurs. "Your brothers. And your mom was too. You love harder than just about anyone I've ever known. You care so much."

I shrug a shoulder, the intensity and sincerity of her words hitting me right in the chest.

"I've added a couple other things to the list of stuff to care about now," I murmur. "And I'd do anything to keep them all safe."

I meet her eyes as I speak, watching to make sure she understands what I'm saying.

Her breath catches, her full lips parting a little. Then a smile spreads across her face, lighting it up and making her look even more fucking gorgeous than she already did.

She leans in and kisses me, her mouth soft and warm on mine. It's such a fucking contrast to the beating I was taking a little while ago or the smug, cold way Olivia taunted me before she walked out. This is just affection and care, pure and sweet in the way that only Willow can be, and it feeds something inside me even as it makes me ravenous for more.

I kiss her back, gripping her hips harder. She sets the pace for it at first, and I fall into her rhythm, letting it be deep and slow. Our mouths only separate when we need to snatch breaths of air, and then we're right back together, tongues tangled, bodies close.

There's so much goddamned meaning in it, but I'm starting to realize that every kiss with Willow is like that. Not just a kiss, but so much more on top of it.

It's only a matter of time before the heat starts to build though, and that's how it always is with her too. It starts to get deeper, hotter, us chasing the need to be as close to each other as we can.

She's like a fucking drug. Just having a taste of her always makes me crave more. Kissing isn't enough, and I need as much of her as I can get.

"I need you, Solnyshka," I mutter against her mouth. "I need to be inside you. I fucking need it."

She moans softly and then nods, her eyes bright when I pull back to look at her.

"Yes," she pants. "Please."

That's all I need to hear. I growl under my breath and move quickly, lifting her up and spinning her around so she's facing away from me.

I work her pants down just a little as she reaches back to drape an arm around my neck. It's a little awkward in this position, but I know we don't have time for more than this. I leave her pants and panties bunched up around her thighs, the fabric pinning them together, and just thinking about how tight she'll feel as I fill her up has my cock pulsing.

I fumble with the elastic waistband of my own pants quickly, shoving them down too, and my shaft springs free, rock hard and ready. Willow moans when the tip of it presses against her, and she trembles against me as I lift her up and start to work my way inside her.

"Fuck," I hiss, curling my fingers against her skin. "Goddamn, you're so fucking tight like this."

This position and the way she's pinned mean I can't go as deep as I want, but it's good enough. I pull her down onto my cock, and her head falls back onto my shoulder as her chest rises and falls fast.

"*Yes,*" she pants. "Fuck me, Malice. Make it hurt a little. I want to feel some of your pain."

"Shit," I groan, shoving up into her hard and fast. We don't have time to do anything else, and I don't know any other way to be. Willow makes me want her completely. Makes me want to consume her. It's hard, brutal, and messy, no finesse to it, just the need to be inside her, to claim her, to seal this connection between us.

Especially now, when she has to be at her grandmother's beck and call.

When we both do.

"You feel so fucking good," I grunt, shoving my hips up harder and relishing the sound of our skin slapping together. It echoes in the locker room along with her moans, primal and filthy. "You like this? Is this what you need?"

"Please—I can't—" she chokes out. Her thighs strain at the fabric that pins them, and she writhes in my lap.

"Touch yourself," I rasp. "Rub that pretty pink pussy of yours until you fall apart for me."

She whimpers, but she does what I say, managing to work her hand between her legs so she can find her clit. Willow moans at her own touch, her hips bucking as she grinds down on my cock at the same time.

"That's it," I murmur, urging her on. "Let me see you. I wanna see you come, Solnyshka."

"Malice," she moans. "Fuck. *More.* I need—"

"I know what you need. You need it to hurt a little. I've got you."

I slam my cock into her harder, and she bites back a scream as her fingers fly over that sensitive little nub.

We're playing with fire, and I know it. Her grandma could come back at any time. Anyone could find us like this, Willow writhing against me as I fill her up.

"You like that?" I pant to her, my fingers digging harder into the softness of her hips. "You like knowing anyone could walk in here and see this? See you getting fucked like your life depends on it and begging for more?"

"Malice." My name sounds so fucking good on her lips like this, and I keep going, wanting to drive her insane.

"They'd know right away. As soon as they laid eyes on you. They'd see what a little slut you are for my cock and how you can't get enough. How you'd let me fuck you all night if we could."

"Yes," she moans. "Yes, please, fuck. I don't care if they see. I want them to see."

Fuck, that's hot. I can hear the truth in her words, and it makes my balls tighten.

"Good girl," I growl in her ear. My cock pulses inside her, and even though I don't want this to end, I'm too fucking close. I know she is too, from the way the walls of her pussy are clenching around my shaft. "You're such a perfect slut, aren't you? Say it. Tell me you're a dirty little slut for my cock."

She whines softly, her face flaring with heat, but her lips part.

"I—I'm a dirty slut for your cock," she manages to get out in a rush. "For you and for your brothers."

"Fuck," I groan. "Fuck."

Willow comes fast and hard, her sharp cry of pleasure cut off as she slaps a hand over her mouth. That's enough to push me over the edge too. I thrust up into her a few more times, pulling her down to meet my strokes so I can get as deep as possible, filling her up and biting down on her neck as I ride out my orgasm.

We're both panting and breathless as my cock pulses inside her one last time.

I rest my head on her shoulder, right in the crook of her neck, breathing in the smell of sweat and sex and blood. And beneath it all, there's the scent that I'd recognize anywhere in the world. The scent that's started to feel like home to me.

The scent that's indescribable except by one single word.

It's just her.

Just... *Willow*.

17

WILLOW

As Malice's broad chest rises and falls against my back, I can't move for a moment. My legs are like jelly from straining against the tight constraints of my pants, and my heart is still racing.

I know I should move, and quickly too, because there will be hell to pay if we get caught like this. But I just can't.

It feels too good to be here like this with Malice, connected to him, as if the rest of the world doesn't even exist. His cock is still inside me, slowly going soft, but hard enough that I feel impaled and filled, and I never want to move.

I wish we had time for him to fuck me again. For him to pin me against one of these lockers and take me from behind, fucking me until my legs really do give out.

Even though I just came, the thought of that is enough to make me bite my lip, and my clit pulses with renewed arousal.

I give in to the urge and reach down and start stroking it slowly, teasing my fingers around that sensitive area, whining softly as the pleasure spikes. It doesn't take long, since I'm already so sensitive from the orgasm before, and soon enough I'm moaning, squeezing around Malice's cock as I come again.

He groans, the sound vibrating against my back as he nuzzles my neck.

"You greedy, filthy little thing," he murmurs, his voice warm and low in my ear. "You just can't get enough, can you?"

I shake my head, breathing hard. "I always want more of you," I admit.

"I know," he breathes. "And I love that. I love how much you want it. How well you take me. No one has ever ridden my cock as well as you."

He presses a kiss to my neck, and we stay like that for another second before he sighs. Slowly, he lifts me up and draws out of me. I make a plaintive little noise, and I can feel my pussy tightening around him as if it's trying to pull him back inside. But we both know that we can't stay like this, as much as we might want to.

Malice helps me get dressed properly once more, pulling up my pants and tugging my shirt back into place. Then he stands up himself, wincing as he moves. He tucks his cock away and drags the waistband of his athletic pants back into place.

The bruises and gashes from the fight stand out on his tattooed skin even more now, and he grimaces a little, limping as he moves.

"Are you okay?" I can't help but ask.

"Yeah. I've had worse," he reassures me.

Or at least, I know that's what he's trying to do, but his words don't really make me feel better. Worry curls in my gut, making me frown.

"I know, but…" I bite my lip. "We probably shouldn't have just done that. You just fought three guys, back to back. You're hurt."

Malice reaches for me, grabbing my shoulders and pulling me into a hard kiss. It takes my breath away for a moment, leaving me blinking in a daze.

"It doesn't matter," he says as our lips part. "It doesn't matter how many guys I fought. Doesn't matter if I'm cut up or bruised, or how bad it hurts. I'll *always* want to be inside you, Solnyshka. Nothing short of death itself could stop me from wanting to fuck you."

I swallow hard and rest my forehead against his chest, listening to the beat of his heart. I breathe him in, the scent of sweat and blood tickling my nose, and his rich scent buried underneath it.

"I'm sorry she made you do this," I murmur after a while.

Malice snorts. "Like I said, I've been through worse."

I sigh, wrapping my arms around him, my fingers trailing over the broad muscles of his back through his tank top. "You know, I have a dream that maybe someday you won't have to say stuff like that. That you'll get an easy life, where you and your brothers can work on cars and not constantly be in danger of being hurt or killed. And it won't be a matter of having been through worse, because things will be so good."

He runs a hand over my hair, smoothing it down.

"I want that too," he murmurs, his voice uncharacteristically soft. "I've lived my whole damned life surrounded by violence. Outside and inside my own mind, it's always violence. I never really let myself consider what it would be like to have peace. But now that I've had a taste of it, I want more."

My brows furrow, and I pull back to look at him. "What do you mean? What taste?"

As far as I can tell, it's just been him and his brothers fighting and scrapping against the world for so long.

"You." His tone is quiet and simple, his stormy gray gaze holding mine. "Having you is the closest thing to peace I've ever felt."

Sudden tears blur my vision, but before they can fall, Malice grips my chin between his thumb and forefinger and drops his head to kiss me deeply. I go up onto my tiptoes to meet him, sliding my fingers through the sweat-slicked dark hair at the back of his head.

When we finally break apart, my heart aches. I don't want to walk away from him after all of that, don't want to let this moment end, but I know we only have a little time.

"I need to go find Vic and Ransom," Malice tells me. "Before they start thinking I fucking died back here or something."

I laugh, but there's no real humor in it. He could easily have been killed tonight if things had gone differently in the ring.

"I'll come with you," I murmur, and I fall into step with him as we leave the locker room.

Another fight is going on, but I consciously avoid looking toward the ring. I've seen enough violence tonight to last me for a long while.

Vic and Ransom have moved away from where they were sitting to watch Malice's fights. They're standing at the edge of the crowd, talking with their heads together, both of them looking a bit anxious. Vic spots us first, scanning the space as we head toward them. Something flares in his blue eyes when he sees me, and he nudges Ransom, who looks up as well.

"There you are," Ransom says as we near them. "We were about to head down there and make sure you hadn't collapsed in a heap somewhere."

Malice rolls his eyes. "I'm insulted you think a fight like that would've been enough to take me out."

"You fought well," Vic says. "They didn't think you would."

"That's why they got laid out, and I didn't," Malice retorts.

Even with all the joking, I can tell they're all pissed that Malice had to fight at all. And they have every right to be.

My phone buzzes in my pocket, and I know before I pull it out that it's going to be Olivia. And I'm right. It's a text from her, telling me to meet her at the car.

Of course she decided not to go back to the locker room to fetch me. She probably can't take the chance that someone from the crowd will see her and spread the rumor that Olivia Stanton of all people watches low-brow fights like this.

"I have to go," I tell the brothers, already sad to be leaving them behind. "Malice, you did a great job. I'm glad you're okay."

He smirks and gives my hand a squeeze.

Ransom pulls me into a hug, holding on tight. "You're taking care of yourself, right?" he asks. "Staying out of trouble?"

I laugh and nod. "Yeah. As much as I can. You do the same, okay?"

"Oh, only the best trouble for us," he replies, giving me a crooked grin.

When he steps back, Vic steps in. He hesitates and then reaches out, placing a hand on my shoulder. I can feel the way his fingers tremble a bit, but I'm just pleased he's touching me at all.

"We're here if you need us," he murmurs. "Always."

"I know," I tell him. "You're always there for me."

I swallow hard, and it's a struggle to make myself step away from them and head back outside to the car.

Olivia meets me there, sliding into the back seat all brisk and businesslike, and without comment, the driver begins to navigate us away from the fighting ring.

There's an attitude of smug satisfaction that seems to surround my grandmother like an aura, and I clench my jaw, anger rising in me.

"Did you get everything you wanted out of tonight?" I ask her, bitterness coating the back of my throat.

"Yes," she says, folding her hands in her lap. "Troy had to cave on some of his terms, and his overconfidence was his undoing. It took him down a peg, and that's good. It went well." She leans back in the seat with a little sigh. "I knew it was the right call not to kill the Voronin brothers after they defied 'X' by refusing to deliver you as a virgin. I considered it, but in the end, I decided not to. And it was a good thing, because they've proven themselves to be very useful."

I don't have anything to say to that. I just clench my jaw, staring straight ahead as I grapple with my emotions. Even though I was angry with them for that video they made of me, I know now exactly what they were trying to save me from, and I can't help but feel grateful for it. Even if in the end, Olivia twisted things around to get what she wanted anyway.

Despite my silence, my grandmother isn't content to let the

subject drop, though. She looks over at me as we turn a corner, her head tilted to one side.

"You love them, don't you?" she asks, staring at me like she's trying to read my mind. "Because it's clear they love you."

My heart lurches in my chest, slamming hard against my ribs.

Do I love them? Do they really love me?

I know whatever exists between us is big, but I haven't given a name to it yet. It's scary to do, and scary to think about.

My mind races, my fingernails dragging over the fabric of my pants as I look down, trying to hide my face from her a little. I can't help but wonder if Olivia is bringing this up now because she wants more leverage against us.

Because the truth is, even if the brothers and I do love each other, it's dangerous to admit that right now, when we have someone who's trying to use our feelings against us.

Silence fills the car for several blocks, but rather than forcing an answer from me, Olivia changes the subject, breaking into my thoughts as she speaks again.

"Now that things are settled with Troy, the engagement party will be announced tomorrow," she says. "You'll need to be ready."

A new wave of fear washes over me, and I close my eyes to steady myself.

I'm running out of time.

18

WILLOW

The day of the engagement party comes so much faster than I'm ready for it to—especially since it means the wedding isn't far off either. I have a pit in my stomach the whole morning, making it hard for me to eat or focus on anything else.

In the late afternoon, I get ready to head over to Olivia's house. She wants me to prep for the party there so that she can oversee all of it and make sure I look perfect, everything done according to her standards.

As much as I'm dreading it, that's a good thing, really. It's been a couple days since I last went over to her house, and hopefully I'll have another chance to snoop around today.

I've managed to snap pictures of several more files and documents in her office and send them to the guys, but after poring over them to see if they relate to previous jobs they've done for X, they couldn't find anything that looked promising.

And with the countdown seeming to tick by faster every day, I have to keep digging.

My phone buzzes as I'm about to walk out the door, and I frown as I pick it up, my brow furrowing as I read the text message that just came through.

APRIL: Hey Willow. I heard about your engagement, congrats! We miss you at school.

I blink, making a face. Back when I was still going to school at Wayne State, April and her followers dedicated a lot of time to making my life miserable, so this message from her makes absolutely no sense. She's acting like we're old friends, as if she didn't spend an entire semester bullying me and mocking me for being poor.

But I guess that explains it, right there.

I'm not poor anymore. And even though she was still willing to mock me behind my back after she found out I was Olivia's granddaughter, now that my engagement to Troy has been announced publicly, I'll be tied to yet another wealthy family in Detroit.

The only way April measures a person's worth is by their money and status, so she's probably hoping that if she kisses my ass now, I'll help her advance her social standing after Troy and I are married.

I wonder if she knows that my supposed fiancé is a sick fucking creep. Would it change her opinion if she knew? Somehow, I doubt it.

Well, fuck April. And fuck Troy too.
Fuck all of this.

Instead of bothering to text her back, I gather my things and let Jerome drive me to my grandmother's house.

As soon as I walk in the large front door of her mansion, Olivia descends on me. I'm not late, but she's in control freak mode, prodding me up the stairs and to a bedroom where a professional stylist is waiting.

"I'm so pleased to have this opportunity, Mrs. Stanton," the woman says, practically gushing.

"Yes, well, I just want my granddaughter to look perfect for her big night." Olivia's smile is as fake as she is, but the stylist doesn't seem to notice.

The woman ushers me into a seat and starts fussing over me, talking about colors and curlers and whatever else. I'm barely listening as she and Olivia confer, sitting there like a doll while my hair is brushed out and different colors of foundation are tried against my skin.

"Not that one," Olivia says at one point, shaking her head. "It needs to look more natural."

"Oh, of course," the stylist agrees. "I was just thinking that with her... features..."

She trails off when Olivia gives her an arch look and then replaces the makeup she had been about to use. I can imagine what she meant by 'features.' It's her impulse to want to hide my scars. And I doubt that Olivia vetoing the stylist's choice isn't because my grandmother thinks I look fine just as I am. She just doesn't want me to be caked in makeup for this party.

Either way, no one cares what I want, so I keep my mouth shut, letting them get on with it. I tilt and turn my face where the woman's soft fingers guide me, closing my eyes and pursing my lips and doing whatever she says, just to get this over with.

After a while, Olivia makes an impatient noise, and I open my eyes to see her frowning at her phone.

"The caterer, again," she mutters. "I don't understand how hard it is to get this right."

She answers the call, sounding brusque and annoyed, and I don't envy the poor person on the other end of the line. Olivia walks out to deal with whatever the issue is, and my pulse jumps as I realize this might be my best chance.

It has to be now, while she's distracted.

"Um," I say, straightening up a little. "I'm sorry, but I really need to use the bathroom. I'll be back in a minute, okay?"

The stylist blinks, surprised, and I give her an apologetic smile as I slip out of my chair and quickly leave the bedroom.

It's blessedly quiet in the massive house, and I move quickly, darting downstairs and into the office. As usual, I start a countdown in my head, scared to give myself more than five minutes or so to look. I haven't gotten caught rifling through my grandmother's office yet, and I can't afford to get sloppy now.

As I ease the heavy wooden door closed behind me, my gaze darts around the room, scanning the walls, shelves, and file cabinets. I've looked in every one of the file drawers by now, and I've even managed to open every drawer in the big desk. Where else would she keep valuable documents and stuff? I know she has stake in a few different companies, but I don't think she has an office outside her house. And even if she did, I would've expected her to keep anything potentially incriminating close to home, where it's easier to keep hidden.

So where the fuck is it?

My eyes scan the bookshelves again, my fingers tapping my thigh in a more agitated and less rhythmic version of what Vic does. Would she keep things hidden behind the books? *Inside* the books?

Maybe the most important documents are upstairs in her bedroom. Maybe they're—

I freeze, my gaze snagging on one of the paintings on the wall. It's a portrait of Olivia and the man I'm guessing must've been my grandfather, along with a boy who looks to be about ten. Olivia is obviously younger in the painting, and I try to ignore the way that this more youthful version of her bears an even stronger resemblance to me. Instead, I focus on what caught my eye in the first place.

The painting is slightly crooked.

In any other house, that wouldn't mean anything, but for Olivia? For the most exacting, viciously controlling person I know? It's weird.

It's already been at least thirty seconds since I entered the room, and I have to give myself extra time to get back upstairs, so I step forward quickly, making a beeline toward the large painting. I don't know what I'm looking for, exactly, but I feel around the edges of it, putting my face up against the wall and trying to see behind it.

When I give a soft tug on the frame, it pops away from the wall, and I have to stifle my yelp of shock. For a second, I'm terrified that I've accidentally knocked the painting off the wall and it's about to come crashing down, drawing Olivia and every member of her house staff.

But instead of falling, the portrait swings outward, revealing a large safe set into the wall.

My heart lurches again, excitement filling me as I stare at it. Then I shake myself and snatch my phone from my pocket, holding it up and taking several pictures of the safe. I make sure to snap a photo of the keypad on the front as well as the embossed text identifying the brand name, and once I think I have enough, I swing the painting back into place.

There's no way I'm going to be able to get inside the safe right now. I have no idea how to crack one, and I only have a minute or two left before I have to get back upstairs. So I pull up Vic's contact on my phone and text all the pictures to him, sending along a message right after.

ME: Just found this. Do you know how to open it?

My hand shakes a little as I shove my phone back into my pocket, and I crack the office door to make sure no one's coming before darting back into the hallway. I take the stairs two at a time, giving myself half a second to calm my breathing before I re-enter the bedroom where the stylist is waiting for me.

"I'm sorry," I tell her, offering an apologetic smile as I settle back into the chair. "Too much coffee this morning."

She nods politely and gets back to work.

By the time Olivia walks back into the room, the stylist is setting curlers into my hair, and my grandmother examines my face with a critical eye.

"Lovely," she says, nodding. "With the curls and the dress, she'll be passable."

Passable. Fantastic.

After over two hours of primping and prodding, Olivia finally declares me ready to go. I don't even feel like myself, and every time I glance in the mirror, I have to stare.

If circumstances were different, it might be nice to be so dressed up, with my hair falling around my shoulders in soft, voluminous curls. I might even enjoy the chance to go out in a beautiful dress and have a good night.

But instead, it feels like being led to an execution. All I can think of is how Troy will leer at me, and the engagement ring that Olivia unceremoniously shoved onto my finger after the stylist finished up feels like a heavy weight dragging me down.

Olivia got herself dressed and made up while the stylist was busy with me, and the two of us slide into an expensive looking town car to head to the event.

I haven't been involved in the planning at all, so I have no idea what to expect when we pull up outside a large building and walk up a wide set of stairs—but of course, the place is opulent as fuck. Olivia and Troy's family have clearly spared no expense for the occasion.

There are chandeliers dripping with crystal, and honest to god ice sculptures on a couple of the refreshment tables. Waiters in tailored black uniforms circle the room, holding out fancy little hors d'oeuvres on trays, and an orchestra in one corner plays music over the whole affair.

I can't even imagine how much money was spent on this. Probably more than I've made in my entire life.

There are already tons of guests, a huge crowd of people milling around, eating the food and sipping champagne and expensive wine while they schmooze with each other.

A few faces stand out, people I recognize from school whose families were influential enough to snag invites to this party.

I scan the room, and my gaze lands on Colin DeVry, standing with people who look like his parents.

My heart lurches in my chest, a sudden rush of memories washing over me. He was so nice to me once, going out of his way to invite me to a party, to make me feel like I was welcome at a school where so many people treated me like an outsider and a pariah. But then it turned out that he only wanted to fuck me because I was a virgin and he thought I would be easy.

I watch as he struggles to hold his champagne glass, his hand shaking slightly. None of the easy confidence I remember him having is present as he tries to avoid spilling it all over his mother, and she shoots him an irritated glance.

Something savage and fierce rises up inside me, a dark sort of satisfaction that floods my chest before I can try to convince myself that it's wrong. Maybe it *is* wrong, but I can't help being glad to see that his hands haven't completely healed, or that they haven't healed well.

Malice broke every single one of Colin's fingers because of what he did to me, and it's clear that he's still dealing with the fallout from that.

Part of me wants to keep looking at Colin until he glances my way, but I decide he's not worth the time. So I make my way slowly through the crowd in a different direction as Olivia greets several of the guests, the mask she wears in public firmly in place.

Ignoring the waiters and their trays of food, I swivel my head, scanning the crowd to see if I recognize anyone else that my grandmother invited to this sham of a party.

When my gaze lands on three familiar figures, I have to do a double-take, shocked and unsure if I'm actually seeing Malice, Ransom, and Victor standing among the guests or if it's just some kind of illusion brought on by wishful thinking.

But even after I blink twice, they're still there, standing together, dressed in the same suits they wore to the museum gala.

Malice's face still bears marks from the fight last week, although the bruises and cuts on his face are healing.

They're here.

Malice is glaring in Colin's direction, but I couldn't care less about that right now. My feet are already moving, carrying me toward them as if I'm being pulled by some invisible tether to their side, my eyes wide.

"What are you doing here?" I hiss, my heart pounding in agitation as I reach them. "Did you crash my engagement party?"

The consequences of that would be... bad. Really bad. Olivia wants this to be perfect, and as much as I know the Voronin brothers don't want me to marry someone else or have to go through with this, I didn't think they'd do something as risky as showing up to my engagement party.

Before any of them can answer me, someone clears their throat sharply behind me, and I turn to see Olivia coming up to stand with us.

All three of the brothers immediately level glares at her, but my grandmother doesn't even seem to notice, let alone care. She gives me a tight smile and nods to them.

"I invited them," she says. "They were a last minute addition to the guest list."

It takes a good few seconds for that information to be processed in my head, and even when it penetrates, I can't quite believe it.

"Why would you do that?" I ask her, stunned.

Her eyes narrow a little, her expression serious. "Much like your father, you have a tendency to be... unruly. Given our conversation in my car the other night, I thought you could use a little reminder of why you're doing this."

Do you love them? Because it's clear they love you.

Her words echo through my mind, and I can feel myself going pale, the blood draining out of my face. She invited the three brothers to give me a visceral, immediate reminder of the threat she holds over them. If I don't do this, if I step out of line or say the wrong thing in front of her guests, she'll have them sent to prison, and I'll probably never see them again.

"You understand, then," Olivia says, smiling as she takes in my expression. "Good. Now come along. There are *actual* guests you need to meet."

With that, she takes my arm, sweeping me away before I can say another word.

19

VICTOR

Olivia practically drags Willow away, and I watch her go, my gaze glued to her.

Malice and Ransom are beside me, and I can feel the tension and irritation rolling off them strongly enough to taint the air. I can't judge them for that. I'm just as irritated, being here, seeing the way Willow's grandmother treats her like a pawn. It's sickening.

I take a few deep breaths, trying to calm myself down. I count out the taps of my fingers against my crossed arms, and when that doesn't work, I start mentally rearranging the decor in the room, sorting it into something more pleasing to my brain.

But that's not really doing the trick either.

It's not a surprise. For the past several weeks, my usual ways of keeping my emotions under control haven't been working as well. I keep feeling things more than I'm used to, getting slapped across the face with some emotion out of nowhere, with nothing to do but try to ride out the wave of it.

It's as if Willow ripped my skin off, and now everything is touching the raw heart of me. Sometimes it feels good, like when I'm with her. I don't want a layer of separation there, I just want to feel her and be with her.

But sometimes it feels fucking awful. It makes me feel like there's an electric current inside me, or a hot poker being pressed right up against my nerves, making it impossible to calm down or find my usual focus.

"Fuck this shit," Malice mutters under his breath beside me. "Look at these assholes."

Ransom and I take in the guests with him, gazing around the room at the who's who in Detroit's upper echelon. Unsurprisingly, they're almost all scum.

Colin DeVry is there, the piece of shit who thought he could get away with assaulting Willow, and I know Malice hates him in particular.

"Breaking his fingers wasn't enough," my twin growls. "Should've broken his face in while I was at it."

"Well, don't do that here," Ransom cautions, shooting him a look. "I know you hate this, we all do, but we need to keep our shit together. We're here as insurance, but we've got our own agenda, remember?"

Malice drags in a deep breath and then nods. "Yeah. Yeah, I know."

Ransom is right. If we get kicked out of here, then we won't be able to do what we came here to do.

There's some commotion near the front of the room, and when I look over, I see that the 'man of the hour' has arrived.

Troy Copeland comes striding in, and some people go so far as to applaud his appearance. My lips press together as I watch people move forward to greet him, shaking his hand and clapping him on the back.

He soaks up the attention with a sly, pompous expression on his face, and then Willow is ushered over to him by her grandmother, looking like she'd rather be anywhere else.

Olivia says something to Willow that I can't hear before giving her a little push forward.

Willow moves in, smiling thinly at Troy, and then leans in and kisses him right on the lips in greeting.

I don't have to look at Malice to feel the rage coming off him. It's practically searing into my skin with its intensity.

Ransom clutches his glass so hard it's probably about to shatter in his hand, and I take a deep breath, trying again to keep my own feelings in line.

"It's fake," I remind them in a low voice. "She doesn't want to be doing this anymore than we want her to. It's all a lie."

In the back of my mind, I know I'm convincing myself as well as them. My own jealous possessiveness is there, roaring up, making me want to march over there and yank Willow away from that piece of shit.

Or fuck her in front of all these people so they'll know who she belongs to.

That thought surprises me, and I shake myself a little, not giving in or going down that path. Not right now.

I keep my eyes on Willow instead, watching as she greets people at Troy's side. Her smiles are tight and forced, and I wonder if any of them can tell. Or if they even care.

Finally, after almost half an hour of schmoozing, Willow slips away from Troy's side.

"I see my opportunity," I murmur to my brothers and then melt into the crowd, following Willow at a distance.

She walks into the ladies' room, a single occupancy bathroom, and I pick up speed to follow, shoving the door open wider to slip inside after her.

Willow startles, whipping around, but when she sees that it's just me, her face relaxes a little.

"What are you doing?" she whispers. "We can't—"

"I got your text about the safe," I tell her, speaking low and fast. "And I did some research based on the info and the picture you sent. It's a top of the line brand, no surprise there, but it's not uncrackable."

"Really?"

"Really." I pull a small device out of my pocket and show it to her. "This will help you crack it. She has an electronic keypad, and this will run every possible combination. It'll take a few minutes, but it should get you in."

Willow sucks in a breath, staring at me for a second, her brown eyes wide. Then she makes a quiet noise and throws her arms around me.

My body reacts instantly. My cock stiffens in my pants, every inch of me on fire from her touch. I hesitate, not really sure what to do as tension crawls through me, my pulse picking up. My fingers flex and extend, and instead of burying them in her hair like I want to do, I end up giving her a loose pat on the back.

Maybe she can tell that this is awkward for me, because she pulls back, smiling a little sheepishly.

"Sorry," she murmurs.

"No, it's... it's fine. I was just surprised."

"Thank you for doing this. I didn't know how I was going to get into that safe otherwise."

I nod, smiling at her. "Of course. It's what I do. Thank you for sending me that last piece of information. I wouldn't have been able to work it out without that."

I give her a quick rundown on how to use the device, and she repeats the instructions back to me, letting me know that she understands. The look on her face is serious and intent.

When I pass the device to her, our fingers brush as she takes it. Just that little touch has sensation shooting up my arm, and I suck in a breath as I watch her tuck the small object into her cleavage.

Judging from the light flush on her cheeks, she noticed that as well.

She looks back up at me once the device is stashed away in her dress, and suddenly, that possessiveness I felt outside in the main room comes rushing back. Unsure what I'm doing, but unable to stop myself, I lean in and press my lips lightly to hers.

It's just a small kiss, barely more contact than the brush of our hands a moment ago, but it's as if someone has poured pure fire into my veins. There's an immediate explosion of sensation, a jumble of feelings I don't even know how to identify or control. My heart races, my already hard cock throbbing in my pants, every part of my body demanding more.

It's too much, and I'm already too close to the edge.

I'm losing control, staring over the edge of the abyss and wondering how bad the fall will be.

I have to pull away, and we both stumble back a little as if it took physical strength to separate ourselves. I'm breathing hard, my nostrils flared as I suck in air through my nose.

Willow seems breathless too, and I want to say something to her—whether to apologize for kissing her like this, or to apologize for stopping, I'm not sure.

But I can't find the words, so I just take another step back, clearing my throat as I try to quell the torrent of feelings rushing through me.

"I'll... leave first," I tell her, my voice so strained that I barely recognize it.

Willow nods, the specks of gold in her brown eyes seeming to glint as she stares at me. Before I can get lost in their depths, I turn and slip out, leaving her alone in the bathroom.

20

WILLOW

I STARE after Victor as the door shuts behind him, my lips still tingling from the feeling of his mouth on mine. It was soft and far too brief, but somehow just what I needed.

My body hums with desire, and I have to swallow hard, fighting against the urge to go after him and beg for more.

Fuck, I crave him so much. So badly.

And with every hint I get that he craves me just as much, I become more and more desperate for him to let go and take what he wants.

But I know it's a process. I know it's not easy for him, and I won't rush him.

Dragging in a deep breath, I shake my head to clear it, refocusing my mind a little. Since I'm already in the bathroom, I pee and wash my hands, checking my makeup to make sure that Vic's light kiss didn't smudge anything.

Once I'm sure there's no way Olivia can tell what happened, I leave the peaceful stillness of the bathroom, stepping back out into the party.

It's loud and grating, with people coming up to congratulate me every few minutes. The food is probably good, since Olivia spared no expense, but it seems tasteless and dry in my mouth. I force myself to swallow the salmon puffs and little canapés and whatever else, smiling perfunctorily and playing my role.

A large redheaded woman positively dripping with shiny jewelry comes up to me several minutes later, grinning.

"Congratulations," she says, reaching out to take my hand. She covers it with hers, patting it hard enough that I can feel her rings knocking against my skin.

"Thank you," I manage, trying to smile and look happy about any of this.

The woman winks. "Troy Copeland is quite the catch, wouldn't you say?"

"He has a great reputation," I answer, feeling my stomach go sour. I can't say that Troy Copeland is a piece of shit who deserves to have his face beaten in, but I can't quite bring myself to call him a catch, either—not even to keep up appearances.

The red-haired woman talks my ear off for a few minutes, then wanders away, only to be replaced by someone else. Most of the women who greet me seem to want to talk about how handsome Troy is, but honestly, I don't even see it anymore. He's got a classically attractive face, and if I didn't know him at all, I might think he was good looking, but when I look at him now, all I see is a lecherous asshole.

But I play my role just the way my grandmother told me to, determined not to give Olivia any reason to lash out at the brothers. I let myself be paraded around with Troy, like some kind of prized horse or new car, and I pretend to be happy.

Every time he touches me, my skin crawls, and I have to fight the urge to jerk away and put as much distance as possible between us. I hate being near him, but I know I can't show that, since we're trying to sell this thing.

Eventually, I manage to get some space. Some of Troy's golf buddies call him over, and he laughs.

"Time for some man talk," he says, winking at me and then walking over to them with all of his usual swagger.

I take advantage of his absence to get some air, slipping up the stairs and down a short hallway to an outdoor terrace. I just need a break from the noise and the people, and my cheeks hurt from fake smiling so much.

It's so much quieter outside, and the night air is cool against my skin. I breathe it in, trying to shake off some of the agitation from this evening.

After a few minutes, a quiet sound alerts me to someone else coming out onto the terrace, and I glance over in time to see Ransom step up next to me. He keeps his distance, leaning on the railing a few feet away from me. If anyone looked out and saw us, it would seem like we don't know each other. Like we're just two people who needed to get some air away from the party.

That's a good thing for appearances, but my heart aches, wanting to be close to him.

I stare out at the view over the city, the twinkling lights of buildings and the blur of headlights on the highway off in the distance. I swallow hard, wishing for so many things I can't have.

"How are you holding up?"

Ransom's voice startles me out of my thoughts, and I turn to glance at him.

"I—" My voice cracks, and I can feel the tears prickling behind my eyes, wanting to fall. I have to swallow again, not wanting to break down here. Not when I don't have time to put myself back together before I have to go back into the party and pretend to be happy. Not when I can't just lose myself in Ransom's arms.

So I drag in a deep breath and try again. "I'm okay. I just... hate this."

He glances over at me, and I can see the pain and longing in his eyes. It mirrors the feelings in my heart, and I want to reach for him so badly.

I curl my fingers around the cold metal of the wrought iron rail instead.

"Hey. Look behind you," Ransom murmurs.

I frown, but do as he says, glancing behind me. There's a small door a couple yards to the side of the arched doorway that leads back inside. It looks utilitarian rather than fancy like so many other parts of this building, so I'm guessing it leads to some sort of equipment room. Judging from the soft hum I can hear coming from behind the door, it might be where an AC unit and fan are kept.

"What about it?" I ask.

"Go inside," he tells me. "It's unlocked. I already checked."

I furrow my brow, confused, but I trust Ransom completely, so I do it. The door opens at my touch, and I slip inside, blinking in the darkness.

It's loud in here, the sound of the fan's constant churning drowning out the pounding of my heart. A moment later, Ransom follows me in, and he closes the door behind him.

He wraps his arms around me from behind, pulling me against his body. His hands roam, up and down my front and then over the curves of my hips, smoothing over the fabric of my dress. I can feel the firm warmth of his body pressed against me, and I relax into it, closing my eyes and inhaling deeply.

The smell of machine oil and grease fills my nose, but Ransom's scent is there too, soothing and familiar.

He leans in, and I can feel his mouth at my ear. When he speaks, his breath tickles against my skin, making goosebumps spread.

"Remember how I sent you to your dress fitting with my cum inside you?" he asks.

"Yes."

"Well, I want to send you back to that asshole fiancé of yours with my cum dripping from your pussy. Malice, Vic, and I have watched you with him every second of tonight, and even though you're doing an amazing job of pretending, I can see the sadness in your eyes. And I hate it, pretty girl. I hate it so fucking much. I want to wipe it away, just for a minute. Will you let me?"

My blood heats, and I moan softly, grinding my ass against his growing hard-on. I know it's probably a bad idea, but tears sting my eyes as the weight of this evening bears down on me, and all I want right now is what Ransom is offering.

A reminder of who I truly belong to.

A reminder that there are good things in the world, not just lies and manipulation and cruelty.

"Yes," I whisper. "Fuck, I wish we didn't have to hide. I wish I could just be yours. All of yours."

"You *are* ours." He presses a kiss to my temple, his large hands gathering the skirt of my dress as he pulls it up to my waist. "You always will be, even if this is all we can have right now, these little stolen moments. You're written in our bones, on our souls, and nothing can change that."

The tears that I've been holding back slip down my cheeks, two small droplets trailing down toward my chin, and I lean back against him, feeling his warmth and solidness as I close my eyes.

"Fuck me," I beg softly. "Troy's ring might be on my finger, but I want your cock inside me."

He shudders, his arms tightening around me as he hitches me close against his body. His lips find the side of my neck, pressing warm kisses there, and then he slowly loosens his hold on me.

"Bend over," Ransom rasps. "Keep your skirt hiked up."

I swallow hard and do what he says, bending at the waist as I hold the fabric of my dress up and out of the way. His fingertips skate lightly over my skin, then hook the waistband of my panties, dragging them down to my ankles.

I moan softly. Even in this dimly lit little room, I feel like Ransom can see everything, and my cheeks flush, but I don't want to hide. Not from him.

"There you are, angel," he murmurs, his tone almost reverent as he slides a finger along my slit. "Fucking beautiful."

"Ransom," I whisper, blinking back another tear before it can fall. Even now, I'm aware of the fact that I can't afford to mess up my makeup, and I hate that I have to worry about it. That I have to think about anything except how much I need what's about to happen. "I can't wait. Please. I—"

"You don't need to beg, pretty girl. Not this time. I couldn't deny you even if I wanted to. Instead, I'm gonna fuck you like you deserve to be fucked, okay?"

There's so much promise in his tone that it makes my heart stutter in my chest. I nod, my body tightening in anticipation, and over the sound of the fan running, I can hear Ransom's belt jingle as he undoes his pants and draws his cock out.

Just like he promised, Ransom doesn't make me beg or wait. He rubs the head of his cock against my slick entrance for a second, gathering my arousal, and then he's pushing his way in. I whimper softly as my body stretches to take him. I can feel every ridge in his cock, every single bump of his piercings, as he fills me up like he's coming home.

My mouth falls open on a quiet noise, my legs shaking a little as his hips press flush against my ass, his shaft buried to the hilt inside me.

"You good?" he asks, adjusting his grip on my hips.

"Yeah," I answer, even though *good* isn't the right word. I still haven't found the right word for how perfect it feels to be fucked by this man, but that one doesn't even come close.

"That's my girl," he murmurs. "Now hold on."

The first press inside was slow, but when he draws out and slams back in again, I realize exactly what he meant when he told me I was about to get fucked like I deserved.

This is what he was talking about.

The pace he sets is hard and fast, and all I have to hold on to is the fabric of my dress, so I grip it hard, fighting to keep my head up as my eyes roll back. He digs his fingers into the soft flesh of my hips, holding me up and keeping me steady. Each time he bottoms out in me, it's with an almost punishing snap of his hips, and it sends sparks cascading down my spine.

When Malice made me come in front of a crowd of people at

that museum opening, it felt filthy and wrong and somehow arousing to know that anyone could look up and see us. This isn't like that. We're more hidden away up here, no chance of prying eyes catching sight of us. But it still feels illicit in the best way, a stolen moment just for the two of us, so removed from the elegant facade downstairs.

"Touch yourself," Ransom pants. "Touch that pretty little clit."

I obey him, holding my dress with one hand and sliding the other between my legs and circling my clit. It draws a little whimper of pleasure out of me, and I bite my lip hard to hold back my noises. I know the fan is louder than we are, but I still don't want to risk getting caught.

"Slide your hand lower," he groans, pulling me into another hard thrust. "Can you feel the way your body takes me in? Feel how fucking perfect that is, and then tell me you weren't made for me."

My legs feel like jelly, my head spinning from the rush of blood in this position, and when I move my fingers downward, spreading them around the place where my pussy swallows up Ransom's cock with each drive of his hips, a shuddering breath escapes me. I've never done this before, never felt the connection between us so viscerally, and it makes something tighten in my chest even as it turns me on.

"I *was* made for you," I whisper. "For you and Malice and Vic. No one else."

"We were made for you too, angel," Ransom groans. "We're yours. You fucking *own* me, you understand? I've never felt this way about anyone."

Wrapping one arm around my waist to steady me, he shoves my hand away with the other, taking over, pressing down on my clit and rubbing it in hard circles. I buck against him, not sure if I should be grinding back against his cock or grinding into his hand. He slaps my clit lightly, and I whimper for him, my toes curling inside my fancy heels.

He stops thrusting suddenly, and my eyes widen when I feel him working a finger into my pussy along with his cock. It hurts, the additional stretch pushing my body to its limits, and my moan is half pain, half pleasure.

"Oh my god," I gasp. "Ransom—"

"You can take it," he whispers, his upper body leaning over mine. "You want me to stop?"

"No!" I choke out, clutching at the arm that's holding me up. "Don't stop. Don't ever stop."

My core throbs, caught on the edge of pleasure and pain, and it's almost too much. My head is spinning, and even though he's barely thrusting inside me, every small movement of his cock and that thick finger adds to the sensations spiraling through me.

"Put your fist in your mouth, pretty girl," he murmurs, his teeth grazing my ear as he rolls his hips again. "Because when you come, I want you to scream my name, even if I'm the only one who gets to hear it."

His palm grinds against my clit as he presses his finger deeper, and I barely have time to press my fist to my mouth, biting down on my knuckle as a garbled, muffled scream gets trapped behind my lips. It feels like the orgasm is ripped out of me, my knees wobbling so hard that I'm almost afraid Ransom won't be able to hold me up.

He does though, and as pleasure ricochets through my body, he drags his finger out of me and settles his hands on my hips again, pounding into me with choppy strokes. His thrusts lose all measuredness, and he groans low in his throat as his cock pulses inside me.

He drags out and then presses back in one more time, sending a trickle of cum spilling down my leg.

"Fuck," he mutters under his breath. "Fucking hell."

There's a moment of silence between us, broken only by the sound of the fan and our harsh breathing, and then he pulls me upright, withdrawing his cock as I keep my dress hiked up around my waist.

"Let's get you all cleaned up," he murmurs softly, dropping to his knees behind me.

He uses two fingers to gather up his cum and stuff it back inside me, and I suck in a breath as my still sensitive clit throbs. Carefully and tenderly, Ransom pulls my panties back up my legs, dragging them over my hips. He runs a hand between my legs again, pressing the fabric of the crotch against my opening and letting it soak up the extra cum. He makes a noise in his throat, then drops a kiss to the back of my upper thigh just below my ass before standing up.

He takes the skirt of my dress back from me and smooths it down, fluffing it out and making sure it hangs okay. Then he turns me around to face him, dropping his head a little and running his thumbs beneath my eyes to wipe away the tear tracks.

The soft care he takes with me makes me want to cry, but I hold it back. I can't afford to streak my makeup any more.

"Are you gonna be okay?" he asks, searching my face in the dim light of the equipment room.

"Yeah," I whisper back, forcing myself to nod. "Yeah, I'll be okay. The party can't go on for that much longer, right?"

"Right," he agrees, although we both know that the awfulness of this situation won't end just because the party does.

Unable to help myself, I lean into him and hold on for a moment, not wanting to let go. I breathe him in, closing my eyes, trying to pretend that we're back in the garage at their place, or on his bike going somewhere—anywhere—else.

We separate after a moment, and he tells me that he'll hang back for a few minutes so that we won't be seen going back downstairs together. I slip out of the equipment room, letting the night air cool my heated cheeks a little before I go back inside.

When I get back down to the party, it only takes a few minutes for me to find Troy again. He has a glass of champagne in his hand and is holding court with a group of people who seem to be hanging on his every word.

"Ah. There she is. My lovely wife-to-be," he says, greeting me with a cool smile. "Willow, let me introduce you to some of the board members of the Copeland Corporation."

I put on my fake smile and barely pay attention as he introduces me to the people he's talking to. I won't remember any of their names, so I don't bother trying to retain them now. I let the conversation wash over me as they shift from talking about the upcoming wedding to discussing some new development in the business world.

As they speak, Troy drapes an arm around my shoulders, pulling me closer against his side. His head drops as if he's about to press a kiss to my hair, a performative gesture of possessiveness—but then he suddenly freezes. His body goes stiff next to mine, and he shifts his attention back to the group in front of us.

"I'm sorry, will you excuse us for a moment?" he asks.

They all nod, and Troy's arm stays around me like a vise as he pulls me away from them, steering me across the room. He drops his champagne glass on a tray as a server passes by, then releases his hold on my waist and grabs my wrist instead, tugging me after him with a grip tight enough to bruise.

"What are you doing? We need to get back to the par—"

My breathless words break off as he yanks sharply on my wrist, dragging me into a little side room where the extra crates of wine and champagne are stored. The second we're inside it, he shoves me against a wall and looms over me, his hand shooting out and gripping my chin tightly.

"Get off me," I hiss, not wanting to draw attention but desperate to get him away from me. "What the hell do you think you're doing?"

"I could ask you the same question," he fires back. "Where were you just now? I lost track of you in the crowd for a while, and then you suddenly reappeared."

"I went to get some air," I snap. "I was on the terrace upstairs, okay? Let me go."

Troy snorts, and there's a harsh light in his eyes. "Right. Sure. Then would you care to explain why you came back from the terrace smelling like sex?"

My stomach drops all the way down to my shoes, fear skittering through my veins and making me feel sick.

Fuck. Oh no. Dammit, we were too reckless.

"I... I don't know what you're talking about," I say thickly, pressing against his chest and trying to turn my face away as he lowers his head and inhales deeply.

A harsh, knowing smile spreads over his features as he draws back. "Oh really? Tell me, was it just one of them who fucked you, or all three?"

His free hand roams over my body as he speaks, skating up my side and then down to my ass where he gropes me. He uses that hold to haul me closer to his body, and he grinds against me, pinning me tighter against the wall.

"I know what you've been up to, you little bitch," he murmurs in my ear. "Running around with those three criminals. I thought the big tattooed one looked familiar when he fought in the ring, and now I know why. He and his buddies were at that museum gala. I couldn't figure out why the fuck they showed up here tonight too, when they clearly don't belong in either place, but I finally put it together. They were on *your* side of the guest list, weren't they? Do they work for your family or something? You doing a little slumming with the help? Huh?"

I blink, my mind racing as I try to figure out what to say.

I'm shocked that he's guessed so much, but he's clearly more observant—and more jealous—than I gave him credit for. There's no way Olivia would have straight-out told him about the brothers working for her, and I doubt anyone else here thinks much of Malice, Ransom and Vic's presence. To most people, the three of them probably just look like random guests, but Troy saw through that.

"It's none of your business," I finally say, shaking my head as he drops his grip on my chin.

"Oh, it's every bit my fucking business," he bites out. "You're mine now, and if you've got a thing for those lowlifes, then I should know about it, shouldn't I? Should've figured that's what does it for you. Getting railed by three fucking criminals—at the same time, probably. Is that what you like? You like it rough? You like it filthy? Well, I'm not scum like them, but I can make it rough for you."

He grabs my shoulder and spins me around, forcing me against the wall. My breath catches, and I struggle against him, but he crowds me in, pinning me there with the weight of his body.

"Fuck you," I hiss, jabbing my elbow back and managing to catch him in the side. It's enough to make him grunt and pull away, and I slip away from the wall, breathing hard as I put distance between us.

His eyes narrow, and he starts to lunge for me again—but before he can reach me, the door opens.

All three of the Voronin brothers step inside, fury flashing in their eyes.

"Lay a fucking hand on her, and you'll pay for it," Malice snarls, his hands curling into fists.

Troy scoffs, his lip curling. "You can't touch me. I know you're under Olivia's thumb. I don't know who the fuck you think you are, but you don't get to tell me what to do with my fiancée. She belongs to me now."

He moves toward me again, but Malice is faster, putting himself between me and Troy. Vic and Ransom follow, forming a wall with their bodies that keeps him away from me. The tension cranks up another notch, and if I felt sick before, it's nothing compared to the pure terror that shoots through me now.

Oh god. We're so fucked.

21

WILLOW

Fear lances through me as I shift my gaze between Troy and the three muscled men facing off with him. Malice seems barely restrained, and the other two aren't much better.

If Troy takes one more step toward me, I know they'll attack him.

They're protective and angry, gunning for a fight, and Troy doesn't have the good sense to see that all the money in the world won't keep them from ripping him apart right here and now, so he's likely to do something stupid and push them past their breaking point.

Olivia's words of warning are still echoing in the back of my mind, and I know that the lives of the three men I care about hang in the balance here. If they attack Troy, Olivia will retaliate, and the fallout will be awful.

"Stop!" I blurt, the word almost ripped out of me in my desperation to keep them safe. "Please, don't do this. Not here." I slide around the Voronin brothers so that I can look each of them in the eye, holding my hands out. "It's not worth it, okay? It's not. Just let it go."

Malice drags in a deep breath, and the wildness in his eyes flares for a second before dulling into something a bit less intense.

"Please," I whisper, willing him to listen. "For me. Don't do this."

It feels like trying to talk down a group of feral animals, and my pulse is hammering in my chest, dread building in my gut. But as I murmur quiet words, the three of them finally drop their aggressive stances, although they don't take their eyes off Troy for a second.

Just as the horrible tension in my shoulders finally starts to drain away, the door opens again.

All five of us glance sharply toward it, and my heart crawls up into my throat as Olivia steps into the room.

My grandmother glances around, taking in Troy's angry posture and me standing between him and the guys. She's clearly trying to get a read on the situation, and I want to tell her to just please fuck off and not make this worse.

But I hold my tongue, biting down on my lip so hard I'm surprised I don't draw blood.

This is all so dangerous. Shit could go bad at any moment, and if it does, there will be no taking it back.

"Troy," Olivia finally says, addressing him in a cool voice. "You're ignoring your guests. As this party is partly for you, it would be rude to neglect the people who came out to celebrate with you. We have appearances to keep up."

Her words are polite on the surface, but I can hear the steel of the command underneath them. She's used to being obeyed.

"You shouldn't have invited trash to the party if you're so worried about appearances," he snaps back, tugging at the lapels of his jacket to straighten them.

Olivia narrows her eyes, her lips pressed into a thin line. I'm not sure if she's guessed how much Troy knows about her arrangement with the men, but she doesn't look happy about it.

She jerks her head toward the main room, and after a second, Troy relents. He steps around the three brothers, but before he leaves, he stops and looks at me over his shoulder.

"I'm keeping track of all the things you'll have to pay for once you're my wife," he hisses. "I'm looking forward to giving you every single one of your punishments."

I shudder at the vicious promise in his words. He doesn't have to be more explicit than that for me to guess what he means, and the guys can clearly read between the lines as well, because they tense as Troy stalks out of the room.

Olivia ignores the brothers, instead grabbing my arm and pulling me out of the room as well.

It aches like a physical pain to keep being dragged away from the three of them, but I don't protest. Not when things are already so tense and on edge.

I want to protect them, and this is the best way right now.

On the way out, I catch Ransom's gaze, and I can see pain and guilt in his eyes. He's probably blaming himself for this, and I hate that. It's as much my fault as it is his.

We got reckless and stupid, carried away by our need for each other.

And now we're all going to pay the price for it.

Olivia is clearly angry about the near fight between the guys and Troy, and her manicured nails dig into my arm as she leads me around the edge of the crowd.

"I'm going to have to do something about them," she mutters, her tone sharp. "I thought having them here would keep you *all* in line, but clearly I was wrong. They're forgetting their place and getting too unruly."

Worry fills me, but I do my best to keep my expression neutral, not wanting to stir up my grandmother's ire any further by showing my true feelings in front of her guests.

Thankfully, the rest of the party goes by in a blur. I let Olivia steer me around, and I smile and nod and do what I'm supposed to do until it's all over.

Troy gives me a big kiss at the end, pulling me close as people clink their silverware against their champagne flutes. As he bends me backward a little, hiding my face from the crowd, he bites my bottom lip, muffling my yelp of pain with his mouth.

His lips find my ear as he murmurs, "Every. Single. One."

I don't dare look in the direction of the three brothers, and I'm not even sure if they're still present when I'm finally ushered out by Olivia. Her car pulls up out front, and as we slip inside, she tells the driver to bring us back to her house.

The ride is tense, and I can't even enjoy the relief that the party is over. Olivia doesn't say anything, so neither do I, the two of us sitting in loaded silence until we get back to the house.

She leads me up to the bedroom where I got ready, then sweeps her gaze over me.

"Take all of that off," she says curtly. "And put it away neatly. It has to go back."

I blink, about to ask where it has to go back to, but then I realize that it all must be borrowed. She wanted to put on a show of wealth that she doesn't actually have. Of course, she still has more money than most people could ever dream of, but she wants to seem like she's better off than she is, and this was a part of it.

It must be why she's so obsessed with rebuilding her estate.

Rather than leaving, Olivia just stands there, watching impatiently, so I start undressing, removing the sparkling earrings and placing them back in the box they came from and then going for the fancy shoes to put them away as well.

Something digs against my skin, and I realize in a flash that if my grandmother keeps watching, she's going to see the device that Victor gave me. My heart slams against my ribs as my brain scrambles to think of what to do.

I stall, taking off the necklace and bracelet I'm wearing with exaggerated care, making sure to line each piece up in their velvet lined boxes.

Olivia lets out an annoyed breath, but luckily, rather than marching into the room and forcing me to strip faster, she turns and leaves without a word.

My legs wobble with relief, and after pausing for a few heartbeats to make sure she's really gone, I finish undressing quickly. I hang the dress up and put my street clothes back on, shoving the little device in my pocket.

Olivia still hasn't come back by the time I'm done, and I chew on my lip for a second, debating with myself. It's dangerous, but I don't know when I'll have another chance. And after the shit that happened tonight, we need leverage over Olivia more than ever.

It has to be now.

I dash down the stairs and head straight to the office, pushing the door open silently.

The portrait of my grandparents and my father rests on the wall where it's always been, and I make a beeline toward it, replaying the instructions Vic gave me about how to use the device to crack it.

I pull back the painting and follow his directions step by step, my hand shaking as I attach the device to the keypad the way he told me to. At first, I don't think it's working, but then I hear a soft whirring sound. He told me it wouldn't take more than a few minutes, but my foot still taps on the floor urgently as I wait, glancing over my shoulder once or twice.

When the door finally clicks open, I have to stifle a tiny sound of triumph.

I yank the door open, prepared to grab whatever documents look most promising and stuff them under my clothes, but as I reach inside, all my hand touches is cool metal.

I blink, peering into the safe.

It's completely empty.

No. That doesn't make any sense. I was so sure.

"Well, you must be devastated."

Olivia's voice comes from the office doorway, cool and slightly amused. I whirl around to find her standing behind me, still dressed in the outfit she wore to the party.

"Carrie told me you snuck off during your styling this afternoon," she says. "I checked my security tapes and realized you were poking around in my office. I know what you're trying to do, Willow, and it won't work. It's impressive that you managed to get the safe open, but you have to understand, I'm not going to let you win this game."

I swallow hard, still not speaking. I'm not sure what she'll do now. I'm more worried about the brothers than myself, since she needs me if she wants to get her estate back to its former glory, but considering how tonight went at the party, she might choose to lash out at them harder than before.

"Sit down," Olivia says suddenly, gesturing to a chair in front of the desk.

Her command surprises me, but I do it, settling onto the seat as she moves around the desk and sits on the large, plush office chair.

Lacing her fingers together, she rests her hands on the desk, studying me in silence as a clock on the wall ticks away the seconds. Then she sighs softly.

"I am tired of making threats, Willow," she tells me. "But perhaps there's another way to keep you pliant and in line."

"What do you mean?" I ask, my heart skipping a beat.

"Instead of threatening you, I am going to sweeten the deal. If you go through with this wedding, with no more trouble or incidents, I'll release the Voronin brothers from our deal. They will be free from X. No more jobs, no more blackmail. It will be over."

I stare at her, stunned, and she keeps talking.

"I underestimated how much you care for each other. And how headstrong and unruly you can be." She gives me an arch look. "But this is an arrangement where we can both win. I get your *true* compliance, and they get their true freedom."

Her words die out, but even though the office falls silent, I swear I can still hear them echoing around us.

She's basically just offered the guys a ticket out of this mess, the freedom to live their lives without having to worry about doing jobs for X that will inevitably get them killed one day. Without having to ever think or speak of Olivia again. Without her threats and manipulations constantly hanging over them.

True freedom.

As long as I actually go through with the wedding.

"I'll give you a bit of time to consider it," Olivia tells me, her cool voice breaking into my thoughts. "But don't forget what's at stake if you refuse my offer, Willow. There are many more jobs that X could send them on, and some of them are quite dangerous. You can stop all of that, if you choose. It's up to you."

She leans back in her chair, her hands still folded on the desk. Her hazel eyes scan my face, and then she gives a small nod, as if satisfied by what she sees there. As if she already knows what my choice is going to be.

And maybe she does.

22

MALICE

It's been a few days since the engagement party, and we haven't heard much at all from Willow.

It's got all of us on edge, wanting to know she's safe and find out if her grandma came down on her for what happened at the party, but it's not like we can just march in there and find out.

We have to be cautious so we don't get her in trouble, but waiting around has never been something I'm good at. It makes me feel like I've got ants under my skin, and it's fucking impossible to relax.

I hate this. This distance from her. This feeling of not having her close.

The wedding is in less than a week, which means a big red countdown clock is ticking over our heads. And in the meantime, we still have X breathing down our damn necks, giving us job after motherfucking job. We can't say no or tell her to go fuck herself, because she could easily send me back to prison or take out her anger on Willow, and neither of those are an acceptable possibility. So we have to keep playing her damn errand boys while we search for some kind of leverage to get her off all of our backs.

Today's little 'errand' was a mostly routine job, but Vic got hurt in the escape. It's not too bad, but he definitely needs to be patched up.

Ransom is in a pissy mood too, stomping into the warehouse and slamming the door as soon as we get home.

"This fucking sucks," he snaps. "We're going to be Olivia's bitches forever. Until we slip up and one of her stupid fucking jobs kills us."

He's been more on edge than usual lately, and I know it's because he blames himself for the shit that went down with Troy at the party.

"She's not gonna kill us," I grunt back, steering Vic to the couch and sitting him down.

"It's fine, Malice," my twin says, sounding worn thin.

"Shut the fuck up," I tell him, but there's not much heat in it. "You need to get stitched up."

I push his sleeve up so I can see the gash on his arm, then make quick work of threading a needle so I can do the few stitches he needs.

Vic grits his teeth. There's barely any expression on his face as I work, although he looks a bit annoyed that my stitches aren't as precise as his would've been.

"Did you hear anything else from Willow?" I ask him. The last update we got was that she'd gotten into the safe, but that there was nothing useful there. So now she has to keep searching the house, trying to find some other place where Olivia would keep her incriminating shit.

"No," Vic murmurs. "Nothing so far."

Ransom paces the living room, then stops and kicks at the coffee table, nudging it out of place by a few inches. Vic gives him a look, but Ransom doesn't seem like he gives a shit.

"So that's it then," he says. "Time's up. We need to start prepping for plan C."

Plan C is the last resort. The one where we all just get the fuck out of here with Willow, even if it means Olivia hunts us forever.

I clench my jaw and glance up at Vic, sharing a look with him. Neither of us really wanted it to come to this, but when he nods, I know Ransom is right.

We're basically out of time.

"Fuck." I let out a sharp breath, sitting back on my heels. "Guess we don't have another choice."

"We knew it could come to this," Vic agrees. "We'll have to put a few things in motion before we can go. And we'll need to find a way to talk to Willow without alerting her grandmother or Troy. We need as much of a head start as we can get."

Ransom opens his mouth to say something, but he's cut off by a knock at the warehouse door.

We all exchange glances, instantly on alert. None of us would put it past Olivia to send someone out here to 'deal' with us, so we move as a unit for the door, ready for a fight if it comes to that.

But when Ransom swings the door open, it's not a threat standing outside.

It's Willow.

"What are you doing here?" Ransom asks. "Are you supposed to be here?"

"What's wrong?" I demand. "What happened?"

"Let her come inside," Vic interjects.

We all move back so Willow can come in, and as she steps inside, worry turns my stomach into a rock. I should be glad to see her in our space again, back at the warehouse where she belongs, but given the shit that's gone down recently, it's not as simple as that.

"Nothing is wrong," Willow assures us, offering up a little smile, but it doesn't look right. "I'm okay. It's okay."

"Then what are you doing here?" Vic questions, and I can practically see him trying to work out the puzzle in his mind.

"Olivia said I could have one night to myself, away from her place or my apartment," Willow explains. "I think it was supposed to be a nice gesture, since the wedding is coming up so soon and she still thinks I'm going to go along with it."

Ransom frowns. "I don't think she expected you to come here though, right? And she'll know. The tracker will show her right where you went."

Willow nods. "I know. But she already knows where you live, so it's not like I'm giving her any information she doesn't already have. And... this is the only place I wanted to go."

Fucking hell. This woman.

Reaching out, I pull her into my arms, needing to have her close after all those days apart. Her scent tickles my nose, and I breathe her in, closing my eyes and letting it settle the irritation that's been right there on the surface since the party.

Then Willow gasps, and I pull back, looking down at her. "What?"

"You're bleeding," she says softly, running her fingers over my arms like she's checking for where I'm hurt.

Shit. I forgot I was covered in some of Vic's blood.

"It's not mine," I tell her, jerking my chin at him. "It's his."

Not seeming at all soothed by that, she glances at Vic, seeing the stitched up wound that he's got covered in gauze now. It's nothing big, but her eyes still go wide. Ransom got dinged a little too, although his wasn't enough to need stitches, and as she sees the blood seeping from the cut on his arm, she presses a hand to her mouth.

"Oh my god. What happened to you all?"

The three of us exchange glances, silent communication passing between us. We promised her we wouldn't hide things from her anymore, but this feels different. She has enough on her fucking plate already, without this adding to it.

But she must be getting better at reading us, because she looks at each of us in turn and then frowns.

"Stop it," she says. "Don't try to figure out how much you can hide from me. Just tell me what happened."

Ransom sighs, dragging a hand over his face. "It's not as bad as it looks. We just got a couple scratches from a job."

"A job from Olivia," Vic adds, as if that's not pretty clear by now.

Willow's eyes widen, and she gasps softly, looking horrified. "What happened?" she demands. "What did she have you do?"

"Just some stupid shit," I tell her. "Breaking and entering. It should have been easy, but there were some... complications."

"What kind of complications?"

I glance at Vic, and he nods before taking over. "The security system wasn't as easy to disable as it should have been," he explains. "Namely because the facility had dogs. She neglected to mention that."

Grief and anger war in Willow's eyes for a second, and she swallows hard. "I can't believe she's doing this to you. I mean, I *can*, but... is it always like this? Are all the jobs this dangerous?"

Ransom shrugs a shoulder. "Not always. Sometimes it's routine shit. Busywork. The problem is she's running us into the fucking ground. We barely get a day or two to breathe between these jobs."

"She's running you ragged," Willow murmurs, almost to herself.

"Yeah," I agree. "She's fucking with us because she knows she can, but it's not a big deal."

"How is it not a big deal?" Her head whips up, her voice rising. "She's putting you in life-threatening situations over and over again, and there's nothing we can do to stop her!"

"It's not a big deal," I say again, keeping my voice even.

"It really isn't," Vic agrees. "We hate working for her, but it's to keep you safe. And anything is worth that."

"Yeah. We'd do a hell of a lot worse to make sure you were alright," Ransom chimes in.

Worry is still churning in Willow's soft brown eyes, and I hate Olivia fucking Stanton just a little more for putting us all in this position.

Willow glances around at the three of us, drawing her bottom lip between her teeth. Tears well up in her eyes for a moment, a look of intense pain flashing across her face. Then it seems like something settles inside her, and some of the tension drains from her shoulders. She draws in a deep breath and nods.

"I know you would," she whispers.

"Anyway, it doesn't really matter now." I pin her with a look, returning to the subject my brothers and I were discussing before she arrived. "We're out of time. So we've gotta run."

Her mouth falls open. "What?"

"The wedding is supposed to be happening in just a few days. We need to get out of here. We should run now. Head out of the city. Maybe we'll be able to get enough of a head start to evade whoever Olivia sends after us."

"No!" Willow says sharply. She shakes her head. "No. It's too soon to give up. I can still get the evidence we need to blackmail her, and that'll be better than her hunting us. You know I'm right. I just need a little more time."

I frown at her, narrowing my eyes. "How much more time do you want?"

"Until the wedding." She sees me open my mouth to object and puts her hand on my chest, continuing quickly. "I'll be over at Olivia's house a lot in the days leading up to the ceremony. That will give me more chances to search the rooms I haven't gotten to yet. And I heard her snapping at a maid about how her bedroom is only supposed to be cleaned by certain staff members, so I think she might keep something important up there. Please, Malice. Let me try."

"And if you can't find it?" I grit out, wrapping an arm around her and pulling her tight against my body.

"Then we'll go." Her hand is still pressed to my chest, trapped between our bodies. "We'll set up a meeting point, and I'll find you there. It will be easier for me to slip away that day anyway, in the chaos of everything, with caterers and florists and last minute fires for my grandma to deal with."

"That does make some sense," Ransom murmurs grudgingly. "The more distracted Olivia is when we run, the better."

Willow nods. "Exactly."

I still don't fucking like it. All I want is to throw her over my shoulder like a fucking caveman, toss her in the back seat of the car, and get the hell out of here right now. But I know her argument has some logic to it, and I hate that even more.

"Solnyshka…"

I shake my head, but Willow fists her hand in my shirt, tilting her head up to meet my gaze. Her small body is molded to mine, and I can feel the thrum of her heartbeat in her chest.

"We can figure out the details later," she says. "I only have this one night away from my place, and that's not what I came here for."

Her tongue darts out to wet her full, pink lips, and before I can ask her what she did come here for, she shows me, rising up onto her tiptoes and crushing her mouth to mine.

23

WILLOW

Malice reacts immediately, releasing his hold on my waist so that he can cup my face in both hands. He angles my face to meet his, his fingers delving into my hair as he nearly bends me backward, his lips ravenous on mine.

This kiss was only meant to be a distraction.

I just wanted him to stop talking about leaving right now, for all of them to stop thinking about running away. In their minds, it's the last ditch option for us, but I know it won't work. We'd never truly be safe. Olivia would hunt us to the ends of the earth, just like she threatened to, and we'd never have a moment of peace.

Victor's blood smears over my fingertips as I grab on to Malice's arm, anchoring myself against the onslaught of his desire. I don't want to see any of these men bleed again. I can't stand the idea of them hurting or dying.

I won't let that happen.

"Fuck, Solnyshka," Malice mutters, barely stopping long enough to speak. "Is this what you wanted? Is this what you need?"

"Yes," I whisper, and it's not a lie.

He shoves his tongue between my lips, and I open for him, letting him lay his claim. He kisses me like he wants to erase every time someone he doesn't approve of has touched me, and I melt against him, clinging to his arms as I gasp into his mouth.

When he finally pulls back, his eyes are dark and stormy, and I can feel my heart racing.

"Is that all you came for?" he asks, his voice rumbling in his chest.

"No."

"What else do you want, then?"

Not answering with words this time, I shift my gaze to Ransom and Vic. I can feel the split second of hesitation in Malice, an instinctive unwillingness to let go of me. I'm sure if it were for anyone else besides his two brothers, he never would, but it's a testament to the bond between them that he releases his possessive grip on me, sharing this moment with them.

I turn to Ransom first, and he opens his arms, welcoming me in. When we kiss, it reminds me of how it felt when we snuck into that equipment room during the engagement party. The pressure of his lips is hot and hungry like always, but there's an edge of desperation to it.

We all feel it, I know we do: the knife's blade hanging over us. The threat that all of this might end horribly.

He clings to me, and I let him, kissing him deeper. Behind me, Malice steps in closer, pressing himself along my back. His hands run up and down my sides, and his mouth finds my neck, leaving kisses there that rock me to my core.

Every touch of their mouths or hands or bodies against mine works me up higher, making me go soft and pliant between them. The entire room seems to heat up, the air thickening as I turn to look at Vic.

He doesn't move to kiss me, and I don't take that step either, not right now. But there's something there, a spark that passes between us when our eyes meet. His go gratifyingly dark, and he moves in closer to us, not looking away for a second.

He's near enough now that I feel surrounded by all three of

them—Ransom at my front, Malice pressed in behind, and Vic just off to the side. I can feel Malice and Ransom getting hard, their cocks filling as they press against me.

I can't help but grind against them both, pushing back against Malice and then forward to rub against Ransom. I lean up and catch Ransom's mouth in another kiss, and when he drags his teeth over my lower lip, I groan into the little spark of pain and pleasure.

"I... I missed you," I breathe.

"We missed you too, Solnyshka," Malice says roughly. "Can you feel how much?"

His hands are on my hips, and they slip under my shirt, moving over my scars and caressing my skin. I can feel the roughness of his calluses, and it makes my breath hitch.

"Yes," I whisper. Then I grin against Ransom's lips. "But you should probably keep showing me anyway."

Ransom chuckles, and when he pulls away to let me breathe, Malice drags a moan out of me with his mouth on my neck. His hands skate up to my chest, and he shoves my bra up and over my breasts so he can cup them in his hands.

I gasp softly when he starts rolling and pinching my nipples, and Ransom's eyes gleam.

"Is that turning you on?" he murmurs. "You like when Malice does that? Is he gonna get you nice and wet for us? All slick and swollen and needy?"

Before I can even get an answer out, Ransom is reaching down between my legs. He cups my pussy through my jeans, but I know that not even the layer of clothing will hide how hot and wet I am from this.

Ransom grinds his hand against me, finding my clit with ease, and I let out a shuddering breath. I feel caught between the two of them, with Ransom's hand working me up and Malice pulling and pinching at my nipples.

Neither of them are gentle, but they never really are, and my body has learned to crave this kind of intensity from them. My arousal is already soaking into my panties, and I'm wearing far too many clothes. So are they, for that matter.

As if he can read my mind, Malice yanks my shirt up and over my head and then makes quick work of my bra, tossing it aside. I shiver a little from the sudden rush of cooler air, and my nipples go impossibly harder.

"Fuck," Ransom groans. He steps back enough to let his eyes roam over my bared upper body, and the heat in his blue-green eyes flares bright. "Now that's a sight for sore eyes. Jesus, pretty girl. Your tits are gorgeous."

"Such a sweet talker." I start to roll my eyes, but then he dips his head and takes one of my nipples between his teeth, teasing at it with sharp little bites. My eyes roll back for real, my head lolling against Malice's shoulder as his muscled, tattooed arms hold me steady.

"He's not wrong, though," Malice murmurs, and I can feel his voice vibrating through me. He flicks my other nipple with his thumb, making me hiss out a breath. "They look even better with our mark tattooed on them. Right over your heart. Right where it fucking belongs."

"Yes," I moan, my eyelids drooping.

He pinches my nipple again, kneading my breast. "I bet we could make you come just like this, couldn't we? You wouldn't even need Ransom's hand back between your legs. His mouth and my fingers right here would be all it takes to have you falling apart for us."

He's right, I think. It's a different kind of pleasure, feeling them play with my nipples, but it sends little bolts of sensation zapping through me, and every time they pinch or tug at the little nubs, my clit throbs.

I arch my back, leaning more of my weight on Malice as I silently offer myself up to their ministrations, and Ransom makes a noise in his throat. Instead of biting my nipple again, he sucks hard on my breast, drawing it into his mouth with a hungry pull.

"Oh fuck," I blurt, my hand latching on to the back of his head.

Warmth drips down to my clit as if there's a direct line from my breast to my pussy, and as Ransom sucks harder, Malice gives a sharp tug on my nipple, making me writhe between them.

"You don't even know what you look like right now, do you?" Vic asks.

His sudden words catch my attention, and I shift my gaze to him, taking in the flush on his face and the way he's palming his cock through his pants.

"Tell me," I ask, practically begging. "What do I look like?"

"Like ours," Malice answers for him. "Like our perfect, needy little slut."

"You look beautiful, butterfly," Vic says, his words following after Malice's as if they're a continuation of the same thought. "So fucking stunning."

Ransom releases my breast from his mouth with a wet pop, laving my nipple with his tongue and making me shiver. He looks up at me through his lashes as he keeps teasing my nipple, blowing a breath on it before murmuring, "You'll look even better when you come for us. The way your mouth drops open and your cheeks get all flushed, the noises you make as you try to ride out your pleasure? That's the stuff of wet dreams right there."

As if talking about it has made him even more determined to see it, he nudges Malice's hand away and starts teasing my other nipple with his mouth. Seamlessly, Malice moves his hand over, picking up where Ransom left off. They switch back and forth, working me up until I'm gasping and squirming. The lack of friction against my clit is driving me mad, but with every swipe of Ransom's tongue or tug from Malice's callused fingers, I spiral higher and higher.

Finally, Malice's deep voice vibrates against my back as he murmurs, "She's had enough. Make our girl come."

I didn't realize that the two of them were holding back up to this point, but they clearly were. In unison, Malice gives a sharp twist to one nipple at the same time Ransom bites down on the other, flicking his tongue over the sensitive tip.

In a rush, all the pleasure that's been slowly and incrementally building up inside me tips over, and I grab on to both of them as I come hard, a full-body, rolling climax that leaves me panting for breath.

Somewhere in the middle of it, my eyes must've fallen shut, and by the time I open them again, Ransom has straightened up in front of me, a sexy half-grin on his face.

"Told you," he says, satisfaction in his voice. "The stuff of wet dreams."

Grinning back, I reach down and palm Ransom's cock through his pants. He lets out a hissed breath, stepping forward to close the distance between us and give me better access. Shifting my position, I turn a little between the two of them so that I can do the same thing to Malice, rubbing both of them through their clothes at the same time.

"Shit," Malice groans as he grinds himself against my palm, grabbing my hand to press against it even harder. "You got me so fucking hard for you. It's been too goddamn long."

Ransom makes a wordless sound of agreement, and my heart swells. It makes me feel filthy and powerful to be sandwiched between them like this, to have them both so close, so turned on.

They bring something out in me that no one else does.

That no one else ever could.

They make me feel beautiful and sexy for all the things I crave, not sick and disgusting.

"It has," I murmur. "I want..."

My words trail off as my mind races a little, overwhelmed by all the things I could say. I want so much from these three men, honestly, but right now, there's one thing I crave most. One thing I need from them to heal the hole I can already feel growing inside my heart.

"I want you to fuck me. I want your cocks inside me. I want—I *need* you to fill me up."

It's addressed to all of them, even Vic, even though I know he's not ready for that yet. But I need all of them in any way I can have them right now.

Malice pulls back a little, looking at me with heat in his dark eyes.

"You've come a long way, Solnyshka," he says approvingly. "From that little lost girl who stumbled over her words the first time, who could barely say pussy as she described her dream to us. And now look at you, taking what you want, begging for cock like a fucking pro. It's hot as hell."

He leans down, his lips hovering just over my mouth.

"Maybe this time there won't be a warmup," he murmurs. "Maybe this time I'll fuck you first."

"No." The word slips out of me before I can really consider it, and Malice's dark brows shoot up in surprise. I clear my throat as I add, "Not first or second. I want you to fuck me at the same time."

Understanding flashes through his gray eyes, and a new kind of heat blooms on his face.

"Fuck," he groans. "Jesus fucking Christ."

He presses in closer, and I find myself crushed between the two of them again. It's as if my saying those words flipped a switch in them, dialing everything up to eleven.

They grope and kiss me, practically devouring me as if they can't get enough. I lose track of whose hands are where as they touch me, and don't even try. It doesn't matter, because I belong to each of them equally.

"Are you sure?" Malice mutters, his mouth moving against the skin of my neck. "You know I don't fuck gentle. It'll be a lot. You think your tight little body can take us both?"

I nod eagerly, my stomach fluttering with nerves. "I want it," I tell him. "I can take it."

He growls approvingly, and the sound goes straight to my core.

24

WILLOW

Between the three of them, they get me to the living room. Malice and Ransom don't stop touching me, and Vic is only a few feet away, even though his hands aren't on me.

We stop in front of the couch, but before they can lay me down on it, Ransom stops suddenly. He frowns, turning to look at all of us.

"You know what? No. Enough of this couch shit. If we're gonna do this, we need a bed."

Malice arches an eyebrow at him. "What do you suggest then? It's not like we have a bed that's big enough for all of us."

"And it's not like we're not gonna be all on top of each other," Ransom fires back.

"Not mine," Vic says, and I can't help but smile at him. He's into this, I can tell from his dark gaze and the tent in his pants, but he probably still doesn't want to deal with cleaning his brothers' fluids from his sheets. "And Malice's room is a fucking mess," he adds.

"Hey," Malice snaps back. "It's not that bad."

"It is that bad," Ransom tells me in a low voice. "We'll use mine."

"Fine, whatever," Malice relents.

The four of us make it upstairs in a rush, and as soon as we get into Ransom's room, he and Malice are on me.

I'm already shirtless and braless, and Malice hauls my pants down while Ransom gets down on his knees to help me step out of them. They work together until I'm naked for them, and I can feel Vic's ever present gaze on me, taking it all in, not giving me anywhere to hide.

Ransom pulls me over to the bed, and I go down easily, Malice following and looming behind me.

My heart races with the knowledge of what we're about to do. I've fucked them in so many different ways by now, but this is new and different, and I know it's going to be intense—right at the edge of what I can take.

That's why I need it so badly.

If this really is our last time together, I want it to be something that will stay seared in my memory forever. Something I can carry with me for years.

My eyes go to Victor, standing at the foot of the bed. His hand rests on his crotch as he palms himself, alternating between rubbing his dick and squeezing it through his pants.

"Will you stay?" I ask, even though he doesn't look like he has any intention of moving. "Will you watch?"

He nods, his gaze never leaving mine, and Ransom grins, tilting my face toward him for a kiss.

"Don't worry," he murmurs. "We'll put on a good show for him. But we've gotta get you all needy and worked up first."

"I'm already worked up," I tell him, panting against his mouth.

He just smirks, and it's clear he doesn't think that's good enough. He and Malice share a look, and the two of them push and pull my body until I'm sprawled out on the bed for them just the way they want.

Ransom kisses my mouth and then down to my throat, his lips warm and intent.

Malice starts lower, and there's the edge of teeth in his kisses as he nips along between my breasts and then down lower to my stomach.

I squirm under them, my eyes glazing over as they work me up and take me apart between the two of them. Ransom's mouth finds my nipples again, and he goes from one to the other, tongue circling the peaked buds, sending jolts of pleasure down to my core.

Malice trails his tongue down from my belly button to land between my legs, and when his large hands spread my legs wider, I try to relax my muscles, letting him push them open.

His mouth finds my pussy, and I whimper, my back arching.

"Fuck! Malice!"

His tongue doesn't let up, and Ransom trades off between his mouth and his fingers on my nipples as the two of them work in tandem until I'm practically babbling with the need to come again.

But they don't let me. Instead, they draw back at the same time, and I blink as I gaze up at them.

"We'll take your ass first," Ransom murmurs, his voice raspy with arousal. "Then fill your pussy. Since you're new to getting fucked in the ass, it'll give you a chance to bail if it's too much to take us both."

I nod, my heart swelling in my chest at his care. If it turns out to be too much, I'm sure none of them would hold it against me. But I know it's going to be fine.

I can take it.

I want so badly to take it.

"Up on your hands and knees," Malice says, and his hands urge me into the position he wants, surprisingly gentle.

He drags one hand down my spine as I get settled, and I moan softly, enjoying the sensation. Ransom tosses him some lube, and my heart thunders in my chest.

I hear Malice uncap the lube and drizzle some over his fingers, and then a second later, there's a probing sensation at my ass. It's nothing that I haven't felt before, and I force myself to let out a ragged breath and then drag in another one.

"Good girl," he growls. "There you go."

He slips in another finger, and I drop my head, my breath going shaky.

"You're doing so well." Ransom smooths his hands over my hair and tips my face up so he can kiss me. "Isn't she, Vic?"

"She's perfect," Vic agrees. I can hear the strain in his voice, deepening it a little. "So fucking good."

Malice spends several more minutes stretching me out, and just as I'm starting to get used to the feeling, his fingers slip out of me. I hear the wet sound of more lube being poured. When he comes closer again, something much, much thicker than his fingers presses against my ass.

I inhale sharply, my toes curling against the blankets. His tattooed cock is so massive that it's always been a stretch to fit it inside my pussy, and it feels even bigger now as he starts to work it into a tighter hole.

It hurts a bit, even as it feels good, and I whimper, biting down on my lip while my arms tremble, trying to hold me up.

"That's it," Ransom soothes me. "You're doing so fucking well, angel. You're amazing. Look at you."

"You can do this," Victor murmurs, and even though I know he's still standing at the foot of the bed, it's almost like he's whispering the words directly into my ear. "I saw what you did with that plug. How much you wanted it. How much it turned you on. You were getting ready for this, weren't you? Even if you didn't know it yet."

A guttural moan builds in my chest, heat crashing through my veins as I realize he's right. I *was* preparing for this, and the thought of Vic watching me then and watching me now fills me with the same hungry determination I felt that night.

Ransom keeps touching me, grazing his hands over my breasts and my stomach and my shoulders, giving me something else to focus on while Malice keeps working his way in. But it's impossible to keep my attention away from the intrusion in my ass. It's so much, so overwhelming, and it feels a bit like I'm being ripped apart.

Malice curses roughly behind me, and the sound of his raw pleasure is enough to make my clit throb. The orgasm that was so close earlier is hovering right at the edge of my awareness, ready to come rushing back at any moment.

It takes a while for him to get fully seated, and when he's finally balls deep in my ass, I'm nearly crying from the sensations.

"You're so fucking tight," he hisses. "Jesus fuck."

"Willow?" Ransom asks, calling my name to get my attention.

I lift my head to look at him, and there's a question in his eyes.

"Y-yeah. I want it. Please."

"Okay." He kisses my forehead and then moves, sliding in under me as Malice helps keep me steady. With his cock in one hand, he guides himself to my pussy and starts easing into me.

As soon as the head breaches my entrance, my whole body feels like it's on fire.

It's so much. It's so fucking much.

The bumps of his piercings make it even more intense, and I hear myself sobbing as he presses into me, filling me up. I'm overwhelmed, gasping for breath, trying to find some equilibrium to hold on to.

Malice's hand grips my jaw from behind, his lips brushing the shell of my ear.

"Remember what you told me that day in the shower, Solnyshka?" he murmurs as Ransom shifts his hips upward, sliding inside another inch. "You told me I didn't need to worry about breaking you, because you were already broken. Well, I don't think you're broken. I think you're so fucking strong. Look at the way you're taking my brother. I should've known it would end up like this the first time I watched him fuck you. You were so greedy for it then, and you're still greedy for it, aren't you?"

I'm nodding without even realizing it, agreeing wordlessly with everything he says, and when Ransom makes a choked noise beneath me, I look down and realize that he's fully seated himself inside me.

His blue-green eyes flash up to meet mine. "Ready?"

I nod again, my pulse racing.

"We'll try to go easy on you, Solnyshka," Malice grits out. "But I don't know if I can. Fuck, you feel too good. Your ass is like a goddamn vise."

As the two of them start to move, finding a rhythm inside me, my head spins. I glance up and see Vic standing by the head of the bed, watching us intently. His eyes track his brothers' movements, and every shiver and shudder that my body gives in response.

"Vic," I gasp, and I already sound so wrecked. "Please?"

"What do you need?" he asks. His voice is even more strained than before, either because he's holding himself back or because he wishes he wasn't.

"You. Just... I need you closer. I need you here too."

He hesitates, looking unsure for a second, but then something slides into place behind his eyes and he nods, crawling up to join us on the bed. I expect him to stop a couple feet away, but instead, he keeps going until he's kneeling beside the three of us.

When he takes my face in his hands, I gasp in shock from his touch. His palms are warm and firm, and when he pulls me into a kiss, I go eagerly.

It's a brand new experience, kissing Vic this way. The closest thing to compare it to would be our kiss in the kitchen, but this is like that one on steroids. His mouth is hot and intense, and he kisses me with a deep, all-consuming hunger, like he wants to match everything his brothers are doing with just his lips and tongue.

It makes me dizzy and hot, and as my body adjusts to the push and pull of Malice and Ransom fucking me in different holes, pleasure edges out pain until it's all I feel.

"Fucking goddamn," Malice grunts. "You're taking us so well. I knew you could do it, Solnyshka. Knew you'd be perfect like this."

I moan against Vic's mouth at the dirty praise, my ass tightening around Malice as my pussy clenches around Ransom's cock.

There was never a question of me lasting very long like this. With Ransom and Malice both driving into me and Vic's lips on mine, everything is so intense and overwhelming that it only takes a few minutes for me to hurtle over the edge.

I whimper, tilting my head up to kiss Vic harder as I fall headfirst into the breath-stealing pleasure of an orgasm. My body writhes between them, my fingernails digging into Ransom's chest. I feel so connected to all three of them in this moment, caught up between cocks and mouths and hands and hearts.

Vic makes a noise in his throat, his hand palming the back of my head. His lips become more desperate on mine, and I can tell from the way his breath hitches and his body jerks that he's coming.

A sudden rush of fondness and gratitude fills my chest at the knowledge that he did this for me. That he kissed me and then came for me, just because I was falling apart too.

"Shit," Ransom curses. "Fuck. I'm—"

"Yeah," Malice grunts, right on his heels.

Their thrusts get harder and deeper, and Malice slams himself hard into me, coming in harsh spurts. Ransom is right behind him, filling me up with a low groan as Vic presses his forehead against mine, grounding me through it all.

In the aftermath, it takes a second for us to sort out how to separate. We're all breathing heavily, and I'm sticky and sweaty. Our limbs seem tangled together, our bodies so deeply connected that it almost feels wrong to break that connection. I can barely move, and as Malice and Ransom carefully pull out of me, I wince at the sudden feeling of emptiness.

Once no one is holding me up, I collapse onto the bed, too tired to do anything else. Three of them follow suit, making the mattress shift beneath me.

Even Vic sprawls out on the too-small bed, and I glance over at him, catching sight of his flushed cheeks and mussed hair. He's still dressed, his softening cock tenting his pants a little and his cum staining the fabric. I bite my lip to hide my smile, not calling attention to the fact that he hasn't pulled away from us yet, just letting it be.

"Holy fucking shit." Malice runs a hand through his dark hair. "If I'd known it was gonna feel like this, I would've suggested we do that a long time ago."

Ransom snorts. "Now you're gonna want to fuck her in the ass all the time, huh?"

"Maybe. I don't think she'd complain."

"We're going to need more space," Vic murmurs. "Because I don't really enjoy having Ransom's foot in my back."

"Aww, you love me," Ransom counters. "You know it's worth it."

"That's debatable."

"Rude."

"The truth can never be rude. It's just the truth."

The sound of their good-natured bickering fills my ears, and I let my eyes drift shut as I listen to them, basking in their closeness and trying desperately to hold on to this feeling of perfect bliss while I can.

They're talking about the future and doing this again, and I wish so badly that I could have that future with them all.

But I can't.

The warmth in my chest fades a bit as cold reality washes over me.

When Malice asked me why I came here tonight, I didn't answer, because I was certain they'd try to stop me if they knew.

The truth is, I came to say goodbye.

25

WILLOW

A FEW DAYS LATER, I stand in the bedroom of my apartment, staring at myself in the mirror.

This is the last time I'll be here. The last time I'll wake up in a bed that's only my own.

Today is my wedding day.

I try to keep the fear and sadness off my face, but it churns in my chest, making my heart beat hard and fast.

As far as the Voronin brothers know, I'm going to meet them at the designated rendezvous point today, so that we can all try to skip town before Olivia catches us. I don't want to give any hint that that's not what's gonna happen, just in case Vic is watching through the cameras. I need them to think the plan is going ahead as scheduled, so that they won't try to stop me.

It's the only way.

I drag in a deep breath and square my shoulders, trying to find some courage. What I'm heading toward is terrible, but I don't have any other choice.

There's a car stashed behind my apartment building so that I can drive myself to the rendezvous point without being spotted by Olivia's guard, but instead of heading toward it, I leave the building and march right toward Jerome's ominous looking SUV.

"Are you ready?" he asks, glancing at his watch.

"Yes." I nod sharply, then climb into the back.

With every block we drive, my stomach knots itself tighter and tighter. My fingers are tangled together so tightly that my knuckles turn white, and I have to keep telling myself that I'm doing the right thing. This is the only way to keep the brothers safe and get them out of Olivia's clutches. That's all that matters.

When Jerome drops me off at the church, Olivia is right there waiting for me as I walk up the stairs to the grand entrance. She looks smug and almost proud, giving me a smile that looks slightly genuine for once.

"You're a smart girl, Willow," she says, nodding. "I'm glad you accepted my offer. You know how to play the game, and that will serve you well. And in the end, this marriage will be the best thing for you. You're going to have a life that's better than anything those men could have given you."

I bite my tongue so that I won't blurt out what I'm actually thinking, but it's so ridiculous that she still thinks, even now, that I should be grateful for this. That the chance to marry into the wealth and power of the Copeland family is more important than anything else.

My fingers twitch, wanting to curl into fists, but I force them to stay loose at my sides. I hate this woman so much. Now more than ever.

She's taken so much from me, and she still has the nerve to pretend like she's giving me something. That this is for my own good and I'll realize that one day.

"I just want to get this over with," I tell her, my tone cool. It's the best I can do to hold my temper and not lash out at her.

Everything has to go smoothly today, or it won't matter what I'm giving up.

Olivia's eyes skate over my face, as if looking for a sign that I'm lying or ready to run. Whatever she sees must be good enough, because she nods and then leads me to the back where I can get ready, leaving me in a little room by myself.

My wedding dress is hanging from a hook on the wall, an elegant and expensive testament to the life I'm condemning myself to now. It's perfectly tailored to me, and I hate the sight of it.

The woman my grandmother hired to help get me ready arrives a few minutes later.

"Are you ready?" she asks, knocking on the door as she opens it.

"Yes," I say dully.

She holds out the dress so I can step into it, lacing up the bodice and arranging the fabric before beaming at me.

"Oh my goodness, you look absolutely beautiful," she coos.

I nod, but I don't even glance at my reflection.

She sits me down in her chair and starts in on my hair and makeup, and we don't talk. Her sunny demeanor fades a little, and it's all silent and businesslike, with none of the excitement and happiness that should go along with a wedding.

All I feel is dread, and either the stylist can pick up on that or Olivia has trained her not to ask questions, because she works quickly and efficiently and then steps back, declaring me ready.

I finally look in the mirror, and I barely even recognize myself. My hair is overdone, and the makeup is understated, but I don't look like myself. My eyes are flat and dull, and there's no smile on my painted lips.

I can't even enjoy the fact that the dress hugs my curves perfectly, showing off a tasteful amount of cleavage before trailing down to the floor in a short train. Faceted beads catch the light around the bodice, just enough to draw the eye, but not so much as to be gaudy.

On any other occasion, this dress would make me feel like a princess.

Now I just feel like a prisoner.

The engagement ring I've been wearing has been removed and is sitting in a little dish on the vanity, but my hand doesn't feel any lighter without it—because I know it will be replaced by something much worse soon.

A wedding ring.

My mind wanders to the guys, and my heart and stomach clench at the same time. Surely they've realized by now that I'm not coming. It's past the time we were supposed to meet. Have they texted or called?

I don't move to check my phone. I don't want to know.

Well, I do. But I'm afraid that if I check, my resolve will crumble.

Once the stylist slips away, I pace the room alone, curling my fingers into fists and releasing them, trying to focus on breathing and not freaking out. A glance at the clock tells me it's almost time for the wedding to start, and I wait for Olivia to come get me and drag me into my new life.

The door opens, and I draw in a breath—then let it out in a rush when I see that it's not Olivia, but Troy.

He shoots me a lascivious grin, and as he moves closer, I can smell booze on his breath.

"It's the big day, wifey," he drawls, leering at me. "I just came to see if you're up to snuff."

"I'm sure I am," I mutter. "Everything I'm wearing is Olivia approved."

"Yeah, but she's not the one you need to impress anymore, is she?" He arches an eyebrow, pressing his tongue against the inside of his cheek. "I'm the one you'll need to please, starting today. And I should warn you, I can be a little... exacting."

He walks around in a circle as he speaks, taking me in the way he did when he 'evaluated' me back at Olivia's house. His eyes are everywhere, examining my hair and makeup and the way the dress shows off my body. He leans in and trails a hand over my hip, then up to my chest, where he squeezes my breast hard.

Pain shoots through me, and I clench my jaw, my stomach churning with anger and disgust.

"Yeah, I guess you'll do." He shrugs idly, squeezing harder. "You know, some of my friends think I'm a fool for agreeing to this. Your grandma is a bit of a has-been, but her husband was once a major figure in our world. You, though? We all know you're nothing. You're just a piece of trash she plucked out of a dumpster and shined up a little."

I swallow hard, biting back the urge to spit in his face or slap him. I never wanted to be forced into any marriage, but why the hell did it have to be this monster?

"But I know it'll be worth it," Troy continues, giving my breast another vicious squeeze. "The daughter of a whore will fuck like a porn star. Those guys are all just jealous because I'm going to be getting my dick wet every night, while they'll be lying next to their cold, frigid wives."

He leans in closer, his breath hot on my face.

"You try to act like you're some good little girl," he says, a taunting edge to his voice. "But don't forget, I know what you did at our engagement party. I know you let one of those men fuck you upstairs. What did you let him do, huh? Did he bend you over? Hike your dress up and go to town on that dirty pussy of yours? Did he fuck you in the ass? You look like a bitch who likes it in the ass."

He shoves me back against the wall and presses up against me, sliding his hands beneath the fabric of the bodice of the dress. His fingers skate over my breasts, brushing my nipples, and nausea churns in my stomach

"Stop it," I hiss. "Not now."

"*Not now*," he mocks, putting on a high, feminine voice. "I bet that's not what you said to your gutter trash boyfriend. I bet you begged him for more."

His hands start roaming again, and he paws at my dress like he's looking for the zipper or a slit to get his hands in. "Doesn't seem fair that some random asshole gets to fuck you and I haven't yet," he slurs. "Maybe I should just sample you right now. So I can make sure I'm getting my money's worth."

Troy leans in, smashing his lips against mine in a forceful kiss. I fight against it, but he grabs my wrist with one hand, forcing it above my head and pinning it to the wall. His other hand starts groping me through the dress, finding its way down between my legs to cup my pussy.

Anger and panic surge through me, and when he tries to shove his tongue into my mouth, I bite down on it—hard.

He rears back, eyes flashing, and his fingers tighten on my wrist hard enough to bruise.

"We're not married yet," I warn him, panting for breath. "So unless you want to walk down the aisle with a bloody nose, you'd better stop."

His eyes narrow, his mouth hanging open a little as his hot breath gusts over my face. Then he grabs my chest one more time, groping me cruelly before he pushes away and steps back. His face twists into a sneer as he looks at me.

"You just bought yourself an extra hour, bitch," he says. "Once you've got my ring on your finger, I'm looking forward to breaking you. I'll make you bleed even though you're not a virgin."

There's a soft knock, and then the door opens. Troy doesn't look away from me as a woman I don't recognize pokes her head in.

"Excuse me, Mrs. Stanton said..." She trails off, glancing between us nervously. "Um, it's time to start."

"Huh. Maybe it'll be even less than an hour."

With that, Troy spits in my face and then walks out, slamming the door behind him.

I sag against the wall for a second, wiping my face clean with a shaking hand. It's harder to find my courage now, but I force myself to drag in a deep breath and then follow him.

26

RANSOM

THE CAR IS PACKED UP, loaded with anything and everything we thought we'd need for this. It's hard to know what to bring when you're running away from your old life, but Vic insisted on being prepared.

We're all piled in the car too, sitting at the drop point where we agreed to meet Willow to pick her up.

We're here, and our shit is here, and we're all ready to go... except for the fact that there's still no Willow.

Malice is full of nervous, angry energy, drumming his fingers on the steering wheel. Every time a car drives by, he cranes his neck to see if it's Willow, and every time it's not her, his mood seems to sour a little more.

"Has she called or texted at all?" he asks me for the fifteenth time in less than an hour.

I shake my head. "No. Nothing."

"Fuck." He hits the steering wheel with his fist. "What the fuck is going on?"

"Do you think..." I start and then trail off. I don't want to say it, but there's a lot that could have happened. She could have gotten caught on her way out. Her grandmother or one of the stooges who work for her could have intercepted her as she was trying to sneak away.

"Her last message said she was on the way to meet us," Vic points out.

I nod. "She said everything was fine."

"Well, clearly it's fucking not fine since she's not fucking here," Malice snaps.

"Calm down." Vic says it shortly, but I can tell he's anxious too.

We all are. As more time passes and we have no fucking answers about where Willow is or what happened, the tension in the car winds tighter and tighter.

Silence takes over again, but it only lasts for a few minutes. Malice's angry leg jiggling reaches a fever pitch and then he turns in his seat to look to at Vic.

"Check the security footage from around her apartment," he says. "If someone stopped her or came and took her or something, I wanna know who the fuck it was."

"On it." Vic pops open his laptop and starts searching, his fingers flying over the keyboard as he does what he does best. The tension in the car doesn't lessen, and Malice and I wait anxiously to hear whatever he's found.

I can tell it's on the tip of Malice's tongue to urge Vic to hurry up, but before he can, our brother makes a noise of disbelief.

"What is it?" I ask, craning my neck to look. "What did you find?"

"She went to the church."

"What the fuck?" Malice's head whips toward him. "That can't be right."

"It is," Vic mutters, his eyes scanning the screen. "She didn't get in the car we left for her. It's still sitting there. But I've got footage of her getting into the back seat of the car her grandmother had stationed outside her place. And that same car brought her to the church. There's a building across the street from the church, and I can see her pulling up and then walking in."

There's pin drop silence after Vic finishes speaking, as we all try to process what he said. Even *he* looks like he's working through it in his mind, when he's the one who saw it all on camera.

I know my brothers well enough to know that the same thought is going through all of our heads right now.

Why would Willow do this?

The silence stretches out for another few seconds, and then Malice explodes.

"What the fucking... fuck?!" he shouts. "What the hell was she thinking? We had a plan. We had a fucking deal, and then she goes and does this?"

He sounds furious, and I blink, still reeling from the shock. I can't even be angry or sad or anything other than stunned.

She hates Troy. Why the hell would she choose to marry him instead of running with us?

Distantly, I hear Malice's deep voice growling about how fucked up this is, but it's not until Vic speaks up again that I'm able to really focus.

"It's obvious why she did it," he says softly.

Malice rounds on him. "What the hell do you mean, it's obvious? I was pretty sure we had a fucking agreement. We agreed to give her a few more days, and if she couldn't find anything to use against her grandma, we'd run. She was out of time for her plan, so we had to do ours. And now she's turning on us?"

Vic shakes his head. "She's not turning on us, Malice. She's just... going through with the wedding. I don't know why she would choose to do that, but we can sit here and bitch about it, or we can go stop her."

That gets through to Malice enough for him to nod.

He cranks the car up and guns the engine, peeling out so quickly that Vic and I have to scramble to hold on and not get tossed around.

Now that some of the surprise has worn off, I'm catching up

with Malice in terms of how I feel. There's anger and agitation, and above all, the feeling of not understanding what's happened.

"She thought running was a bad plan to begin with," I bring up, half thinking out loud. "Maybe she came up with a better one?"

"There isn't a better fucking plan," Malice snaps. "The fucking wedding is today. What did she think she was going to find out this close to the deadline?"

"I don't know. I just don't understand. There has to be a reason."

"If there is a reason, then why wouldn't she tell us? If she had another plan, she would have told us," Malice insists. "That old bitch must have said something to her. Made some threat or something. There's no other explanation."

"There's one other explanation," Vic points out, interjecting in his quiet voice. "We protected her once with a massive lie. Maybe this is her way of doing the same."

As soon as he says that, the sinking feeling in my chest gets even worse. Because he's right. We left Willow in the dark once to protect her, because we thought it was the best way to handle a shitty situation. And it makes so much fucking sense that she would try to do the same thing if she thought she had to.

And I hate that. I hate being left in the dark because someone else made a decision to try to protect us.

I can tell Malice feels the same. His jaw is tight, his lips pressed together, and it looks like he's about to explode all over again.

I brace myself, but the feral yell he lets out still makes me wince. He slams his hands on the steering wheel and floors it, sending us speeding down the road even faster.

We pull up to the church with a squeal of tires after what feels like way too long. Malice parks across the street, and we can see that the doors are closed already.

"Fuck. The ceremony must be starting," I murmur.

"We need a plan," Vic says. "We need to get Willow out, but

there will be hundreds of witnesses. We can't just run in there, guns blazing."

"We don't have fucking time—"

Vic cuts Malice off, talking over him. "We have to be smart about this. There's only the three of us, and while I don't expect those rich pricks in the audience to be armed, there could be security. We're not taking any chances."

"He's right," I throw in. "At the very least, we're super outnumbered. And it's important that no one is able to identify us later. We'll need to keep a low profile if we can."

Malice grumbles but gives in. It would've been a hell of a lot easier if we could've researched and prepped for this operation days ago, but since we didn't, our best chance of getting Willow out now is to avoid doing something stupid.

"Fine. Then we sneak in," Malice says. "We go in the back and keep to the side halls as we make our way to the main part of the church. We don't let them know we're there until the last possible second."

Vic nods. "Then we grab Willow and get the fuck out the same way."

"We'll need masks," I add. "It'll make us harder to ID later. Vic, you'll need to be ready to wipe some footage too."

"I will," he confirms.

It only takes us another minute to sketch out a rough plan. It's how we usually do these things, coming to an agreement together, but this feels a lot more high stakes than most of the things we've done in recent memory. Even the last time Willow was kidnapped and we didn't know where she was, we had more planning behind our rescue mission. In this case, we just have to hope we can get in and out and away without it turning into a fucking bloodbath.

Malice pulls around to the back of the church, and we all share a look, arming ourselves and then tugging on ski masks.

I don't really want to start mowing down wedding guests, especially since everyone at the ceremony is likely to be wealthy and well-connected, but if I have to... fuck, I'll do what it takes to protect Willow.

The back door of the church is locked, but Vic drops to his knees quickly and busts out his lock pick. Fortunately, the lock isn't nearly as complex as some of the ones we've had to deal with, and it clicks open in less than a minute. Malice yanks the door open as Vic tucks his tools away, and we all slip inside, sticking together.

It's quiet in this part of the massive building, and I keep my head on a swivel, grateful for the old carpeting that muffles the sound of our footsteps.

I can hear the sound of music from up front, and I signal to my brothers and gesture with one hand. Vic nods, and as a unit, we start making our way toward the sound, keeping to the shadows.

Before we can get very far, a door swings open a few feet ahead of us and someone steps into the corridor. It's a young man who looks like he was hired to serve drinks or something, and his eyes go wide when he turns and sees us.

Quick as lightning, Vic darts forward. He grabs the guy and puts a hand over his mouth, then finds a pressure point on his neck, holding his fingers there until the guy slumps in his grip.

Malice yanks open another door cautiously, and when it turns out to be a closet full of cleaning supplies, he motions for Vic to stash the unconscious staff member in there. Then we keep moving.

Luckily, we don't run into anyone else, and we make it to what I'm pretty sure is the door separating us from the front of the church.

This close, I can make out the droning voice of the priest, speaking about marriage and the sanctity of that union.

Fury fills me, and I clench my free hand into a fist. It's all a fucking sham, and I wonder if this priest knows that. Or if he even cares. Maybe he's being paid off too.

We've kept this rescue mission covert for as long as we could, but this is the part where that has to end. Willow is out there, standing in front of a crowd of people, about to pledge herself to Troy Copeland—and the only way we're going to get to her is by stepping out in front of that same crowd.

We hesitate by the door for a second, each of us taking a second to steel ourselves for what's about to happen. My finger slides over the trigger of my gun, and I draw in a deep breath and let it out.

Then we nod to each other, the signal that it's time to go.

Malice kicks the door open, and we burst through it. I fire two shots into the air, and the loud pops cut off the priest's words. Screams break out among the guests almost immediately.

Willow is standing near Troy and the priest by the altar, dressed in an expensive looking wedding dress, and as more screams rise up, she turns toward us, her eyes going wide with shock.

27

WILLOW

No. They can't be here.

The three men standing in the doorway are wearing ski masks, but there's no doubt in my mind who they are. One of them holds his gun above his head and fires another two shots, sending people scrambling for cover.

The priest darts away, ducking low as he runs, and Troy curses and reaches out for me, but I step back on instinct. My heart is racing, torn between hope and despair that the men are here.

"Willow!"

My head snaps up when someone calls my name, and before I can react, one of the masked men—Vic, judging by his voice—grabs my hand, dragging me away from the altar as Malice and Ransom cover us.

The church is in total chaos now. Guests are screaming and running for the exits, some of them huddling on the floor by their pews, trying to get away from all of this.

As Vic pulls me away, I get a glimpse of Troy's angry face, and behind him, I see Olivia in the crowd, her delicate features contorted in fury.

But there's no time to dwell on that.

Vic is running and pulling me along, and I have to stumble to keep up with him, trying not to trip over the train of my dress. Malice and Ransom keep anyone from getting close, and I get yanked through a door and then hustled down the back halls of the church.

Once we're clear enough, Malice shoots me a look, fury burning in his eyes behind his ski mask.

"What the fuck were you thinking?" he demands.

I open my mouth, but before I can say anything, shouts and footsteps ring out from somewhere ahead of us. My head whips in that direction, my heart crashing against my ribs.

"Shit," Ransom curses. "We were right about Olivia having security here. They're probably about to surround the whole damn building. We need to move before we get boxed in."

Ahead of us, Jerome rounds the corner from an intersecting hallway, and there's another guard dressed in a black suit beside him, guns drawn as they try to block our exit.

Malice and Ransom move almost as one, firing at the two guards in our way.

Jerome gets clipped in the shoulder, grunting heavily, and both guards duck back behind the corner, using it for cover as they fire at us. Vic snags my arm, dragging me behind him as we evade Jerome's gunfire.

My feet get caught in the lacy white skirt of my dress, and I almost go down in a heap before I yank it out of the way, my heart thundering. Another volley of shots ring out, and Vic pushes me behind one of the pews that line the hallway, trying to find some kind of cover.

"More guards!" Ransom shouts, calling out to Malice, I think. "I count four of them now. Two on the left up ahead, and two on the right!"

"Fuck. Goddammit."

Malice is suddenly kneeling in front of me, pulling me from Vic's hold. He wraps an arm around my shoulder protectively, swinging his other arm around the end of the pew as he fires a shot toward the intersection in the corridors up ahead where more of Olivia's security team have joined Jerome, taking cover around the corner.

"We're not getting out that way," he tells his twin urgently. "We've got to double back. We need another way out of here. Something with a clear path to the car."

"On it."

Before I can ask what Vic means by that, Ransom and Malice both open fire on the guards up ahead of us, giving Vic cover as he stands up and dashes back down the hallway, retreating the same way we came from before splitting off in another direction.

Once Vic is out of sight, Malice drags me to my feet and hauls me backward too, ducking and cursing as a bullet slams into the wall less than a foot from us.

"There's a door back there," he shouts to Ransom. "We can cut them off!"

Ransom nods. "Yeah, I see it. Go, go, go!"

There's a set of double doors at the end of the corridor that must be fire doors or something, and Malice drags me down the hall and pushes me through them before he and Ransom shove them closed.

A heavy metallic clang rings through the hall as they latch, and almost immediately, shouts and footsteps rise up from the other side of the doors. Now that Malice and Ransom aren't holding Olivia's security forces off by returning fire, the men who were cutting off our path are trying to close in on us. And although there's a door between us now, I have no idea if it's locked, or whether the lock will hold.

Ransom must have the same worry, because he glances around quickly, then jerks his chin at Malice.

"Help me!" he calls.

There are pews set at intervals along the walls of this corridor too, and Malice and Ransom shove one in front of the doors, blocking them. Something heavy hits the door from the other side, and I yelp and duck down.

"Come on, Solnyshka." Malice grips my arm again, sharing a look with Ransom before glancing at the doors. "That won't hold them for long."

Ransom snorts, his eyes glinting behind his mask. "Doesn't matter. If it takes us that long to get out of here, we're fucked anyway."

I glance between them, my lungs burning. I feel like I can't get enough oxygen, even though I keep sucking in desperate breaths of air.

Things are happening too fast for my brain to process.

One second, I was standing in front of Troy, about to say the words that would bind me to him for the rest of my life, and now I'm running through the back halls of the church, getting shot at. Maybe I'm in some kind of shock or something, because none of this feels real. Part of me thinks I must still be standing at the altar, and that my mind is playing out this imaginary scenario to keep me from breaking down as I wed myself to Troy Copeland.

Malice gives a sharp tug on my arm, and then we're moving again, sprinting down the hall. Ransom is up ahead of us a little, reloading his gun as me move.

"What are we doing?" I pant. "Where's Vic?"

"He went ahead to find another way out," Malice says grimly. "He'll meet us."

I don't know why Vic has a better chance of finding a clear way out than the rest of us do, but maybe it's because he's the one who's the most analytical. Whatever the reason, Malice seems to think he's got it handled, and that's more than I can say for myself. I've probably spent more time in this church than any of the brothers, but right now, I can't even remember which room I got ready in, and that was less than an hour ago.

The sound of the guards trying to break through the barricaded door fades behind us as we run, and Malice takes a left and then another left, leading us away from the nave of the church where the ceremony took place and toward an area that seems like it's all offices and meeting rooms. My feet keep moving automatically, nearly tripping over each other as I try to keep up with the two brothers.

When a door suddenly bursts open from our right, the sound of it startles me almost as much as the sight of the two burly men hurtling through it.

They plow into Malice and Ransom like linebackers, and I skid to a stop as they roll across the floor, grunting and cursing as they grapple for control of their weapons. Malice elbows the one who tackled him in the face, but the man ducks his head to avoid the worst of the blow, gripping Malice's forearm and bashing it against the floor as he tries to break his grip on his gun.

"You fucking cunt."

The voice behind us is harsh and angry, and I hate that I recognize it.

Troy.

I whip around, but I'm too late. Troy grabs me by the front of my dress, tearing the delicate beadwork at the top as he hauls me toward him. His booze-tinged breath fills my nostrils as he bares his teeth.

"You're not going anywhere," he sneers. "You didn't think I'd bring a few of my own security team just in case your lowlife boyfriends tried to start some shit? Well, my men will deal with them, and then I'll deal with you, you little cunt."

"Willow! Fuck!"

Malice's cry breaks off in a grunt as he grapples with the guard he's still fighting. Ransom is trading blows with the other guard, his ski mask slightly askew as the two of them plow into a wall. Troy chuckles viciously, as if he's enjoying the show. He starts dragging me away, back toward the main part of the church, and I dig in my heels, clawing at his grip and hitting him as I work to pry his fingers off me.

I finally manage to wriggle free of his grasp, more beads tearing from my dress. But he reaches out in a flash and catches me again, grabbing my wrists this time, fury snapping in his eyes as he glares at me.

"You stupid bitch. I knew you were going to be—"

Whatever he was about to say is cut off by the sound of a gunshot. I swear I can feel the bullet whiz past me, and the noise is so loud that it makes my ears ring. As the loud *pop* echoes in the air, Troy stumbles backward and then drops to the floor. He goes down hard, sprawling on his back as a splotch of red blooms on his chest, widening quickly.

I slap my hands over my mouth to hold in a scream of shock as I stare down at his body with wide eyes.

My ears are still ringing, and my head spins as I glance over my shoulder.

Vic is standing at the end of the hallway, his gun drawn.

Malice and Ransom are between us, still dealing with Troy's security forces, but the fighting pauses for a split second as they all realize what just happened. Malice takes advantage of the opening, landing a crushing blow to the face of the guard he's been grappling with. The man slumps, losing consciousness, and Vic strides forward quickly, pointing his gun at the head of the guard who's wrestling with Ransom.

"Get up," he says coolly. "Right now."

The guard complies, holding his hands up in a sign of surrender. Vic nods to Ransom, who snatches his own gun up from where it skidded across the floor during the fight.

"Goodnight," Ransom mutters, stepping toward the remaining guard and cracking the butt of his gun sharply against his temple.

"I found a clear way out," Vic says, his voice even as he glances between his brothers and me. "All the exits are blocked, but there's a direct path to the car from a room up ahead. Follow me."

Without waiting for an answer, he turns and moves swiftly

down the hallway. Malice is on his feet a second later, grabbing me as Ransom joins us to follow their brother.

Vic leads us around another corner, keeping a wary eye out. I can hear shouts in some other part of the building, but I can't tell where they're coming from, and in the distance, I can hear the faint sound of sirens.

The guys must hear it too, because we pick up our pace as Vic jerks his head toward a room set off the hallway, and we all spill inside.

It looks like a nursery, probably a place where parents can leave their kids while they go to church, the room large and mainly open in the middle. But I don't see anything that looks like an exit, except the door we just came through... until Vic takes aim and shoots most of the glass out of the window at the far side of the room.

"Take Willow first," he says to Malice, who nods.

I barely have time to register what's happening before Malice is scooping me up and launching us both through the window, shattering what's left of the glass and sending us into a tumble.

We land on a grassy lawn outside, and Malice is up in a matter of seconds, grabbing me and dragging me out of the way as Ransom and then Vic come crashing through after us.

"The car's that way." Vic points to his right as he leaps to his feet. "Move!"

The world spins as Malice scoops me up again, sprinting to the car with his brothers on either side of us. He shoves me in the back seat, and Ransom slides in beside me, slamming his door.

Then Malice is behind the wheel, slamming his own door shut. He cranks the key in the ignition, and we peel out in a squeal of tires and a cloud of burning rubber and exhaust.

28

VICTOR

Malice's grip is tight on the steering wheel, his foot pressing the gas pedal to the floor of the car like his life depends on it. I've taken the front passenger seat, leaving Ransom and Willow in the back.

We hit a turn so fast that the wheels of the car bump over the curb nearby, and I shoot Malice a look before tugging off my mask and pulling out my laptop to get to work.

Olivia is a smart woman, and it'll only be a matter of minutes before she realizes her security team and Troy's men weren't able to contain us. Then she'll regroup and shift her focus to tracking us down. If I can slow that process down a bit, it'll give us a better chance of getting out of this mess.

"Take a left here," I tell Malice, guiding him along the best path to get us out of the city without being seen by dozens of security or traffic cameras. I'll have to wipe a few of them to make sure we're completely clear, but it should be doable.

Malice yanks off his own mask, shooting a glance at Ransom through the rearview mirror.

"The tracker," is all he says, but we all know what he means.

We knew this part was going to have to happen, although it should've happened under more controlled circumstances, not during a high-speed getaway.

Ransom nods, pulling out the first aid kit that we've stashed in the side of the car door. "I've gotta get that tracker out of you, angel. And I need to do it fast."

His tone is apologetic, and when Willow blinks at him, he grabs her wrist, rubbing his thumb over the place where her grandmother had the tracking device inserted under her skin.

"Do it now," Malice bites out. "The longer Olivia can track us, the harder it's gonna be to throw her off our trail."

Ransom grimaces but gets to work, pulling out the equipment he'll need to do the extraction. When he uses a scalpel to cut a thin line across the skin at Willow's wrist, she hisses out a breath, but I know from experience that a blade that sharp doesn't hurt very much when it pierces your skin. What truly hurts is everything that comes after, and I wince as memories of my father's "training sessions" rise up in my mind, momentarily distracting me from my task.

I shake my head and try to refocus, but Willow's groan of pain as Ransom digs for the tracker makes my stomach clench.

"Okay, it's out," he says, his voice soothing. He rolls down the window partway and hurls it out of the car, then returns his attention to Willow. "I'm just gonna do a couple stitches, and you'll be done. You're doing so well. You've got this."

More soft, pained noises come from her, and I resist glancing back to check on his handiwork. I know Ransom is capable of handling this, but I also know it'll irritate me that his stitches aren't as even as mine would've been. I wish I could've been the one to take care of the tracker extraction, but I'm needed up here.

"Another left into that alley," I tell Malice. "Then when it dead ends, take a right. We'll hook onto a side street."

"Got it."

"All done." Ransom sounds relieved, and I hear the rustling sound of him putting something back into the first aid kit. "How does that feel? You alright?"

"No." Willow's voice is soft, but it picks up strength and urgency as she speaks. "No, no, no, no, *no*..."

I glance over my shoulder to see her shaking her head, repeating the words over and over until her breath runs out. But even then, she keeps shaking her head, her mouth moving as tears well in her eyes.

"Hey. Breathe, pretty girl." My brother bats down the layers of Willow's dress and scoots in closer to her. "You're turning blue."

But I'm not even sure Willow hears him. Her face is flushed, and she rakes her hands through her hair, disturbing the elegant style it was forced into for the occasion.

"No. She's going to find us," she babbles brokenly. "She's going to find us, and then she's going to make our lives hell. Worse than hell because of how you just—just broke in there and started shooting and..."

She trails off, putting her face in her shaking hands.

"It's not that serious," Ransom tries to tell her, and when Willow's head snaps back up, her eyes are blazing.

"It *is* that fucking serious! Are you kidding? She has money and power and probably ties to who knows how many people who can hunt us down. You shouldn't have done it. You should have just—"

This time, she's cut off by Malice whirling around, almost jerking the damned car off the road as he faces her in the back seat.

"You don't get to decide what we do or don't do, Solnyshka," he snaps, anger in his voice and every line of his body. "We'll make that fucking decision, thanks very goddamned much."

The road splits up ahead, and there's a median between the two sides that Malice is currently barreling straight toward.

"Mal," I murmur, keeping my voice even. "Could you maybe keep us from dying in a fiery wreck?"

He looks back at the road in time to curse loudly and swerve, veering the car away from imminent danger.

"Thank you. Take the next right. Then straight down that road for six miles."

Ransom keeps talking to Willow in a low voice, stroking her arm, trying to calm her down. "Hey, it's alright. Vic's going to make sure she can't find us that easily. And we can handle whatever she throws at us. We're prepared for this. We've been through shit like this before, angel. It's not our first rodeo."

Willow just shakes her head, her mouth pressed in a thin line. I can see the strain in her, how wound up she is. She keeps twisting her head around to look behind us, like she expects her grandmother to be in a car, chasing us down the highway.

"Malice does have a point though," Ransom adds. "You went off and did something without talking to us about it first. You lied to us. What the fuck were you thinking? How could you just... go through with the wedding like that? Did you really want to marry that guy?"

We all know she didn't. Even if she had suddenly decided overnight that she hated all of us—a thought that makes my stomach twist unpleasantly—I know Willow well enough to know that she could never truly fall in love with a man like Troy Copeland. But I can hear the tinge of hurt in Ransom's voice as he asks, and I understand it.

Feelings aren't rational.

I've come to understand that more than ever as my own emotions become harder and harder to keep in check.

Willow sucks in a breath and stares down at her lap. "She... Olivia said that if I went through with the wedding with no more issues, if I did what she wanted and stopped trying to resist or find a way out... she'd let you guys go. She'd end your deal with X and let you live your lives, free and clear."

I blink in surprise as her words register. It's a good bargaining chip, all things considered, and it means Olivia was paying close attention to the relationship between all of us. Otherwise she wouldn't have known that tactic would work with Willow.

I turn in my seat to listen to her, my fingers going still on the keyboard of my laptop. It's unusual for me to have trouble focusing on the task at hand. Usually I can multi-task with ease, but right now, I'm more focused on Willow than anything else.

Part of me wishes I could climb into the back seat with her, to be closer to her and chase some of the pain out of her voice and her eyes.

It hits me hard, the scale of what Willow was willing to do for us. To tie herself—forever—to someone like Troy and a family like his. To be her grandmother's puppet and bear the weight of her legacy like that. It's a massive thing, and Willow was going to do it without question.

"Maybe it's not too late," Willow blurts, looking between all of us wildly. "Maybe you can take me back. I can, I don't know, grovel to Olivia and still marry Troy. Then you'll all be free."

My throat tightens, and Malice growls with rage beside me.

"No fucking way," he snarls. "And besides, your goddamned fiancé got shot by Vic. The wedding isn't fucking happening."

Willow shrinks back a little, looking even more upset. I know it's not because she's mourning Troy, but probably just the worry of what will happen now.

"She's not going to let this go. She won't. She's going to be even more angry that you shot Troy, especially if he's dead. She needed him for her plans to rebuild her estate, and his family will probably blame her if he died." Willow's eyes are wide with fear. "I don't know what she'll do."

Ransom wraps his arms around her and then pulls her into his lap, wedding gown and all. He holds her close, nuzzling against her neck, and I have to swallow past a lump of jealousy.

Not because I don't want Ransom touching her, but because I wish it was me.

The thought passes through my mind so naturally that it makes me blink in surprise, caught off guard by it. I've never been one to crave physical contact. Not since I was a child. I don't touch anyone that often, not even my brothers.

But ever since Willow came into our lives, she's thrown everything I thought I knew into disarray, making me question things about myself that I thought would never change. Making me want things that I've never wanted before.

I'm not even sure I could handle having Willow on my lap, but I want her there. I want to hold her. I want to be the one whispering soothing things to her and trying to calm her down.

"Vic," Malice grunts, snapping me out of my thoughts. "Wanna tell me where the fuck I need to go?"

I shake myself mentally, trying to refocus. We have to get out of Detroit without a tail if we want to have any hope of escaping Olivia. And that means I need to keep my head in the game.

I want to protect Willow, and right now, the best way to do that is to get out of this city in one piece.

"Over the bridge," I tell my twin. "Then cut down the first side street. Slight right."

Malice guns it once more, following my directions for the next several minutes until we get to where we need to go. It's a place on the outskirts of the city where we stashed the second car. At least we had already planned to leave today, even if we didn't plan on shooting up a wedding on our way out of town. We had time to prepare things, to have our escape route planned out and to set the pieces we would need in place.

We all pile out of the first car as soon as it rolls to a stop, and Malice and I work like machines, moving our stuff into the trunk of the second car. After one quick check to make sure we're not being followed and we haven't left anything, we hit the road again, leaving Detroit behind.

"Roomier in this car," Ransom comments after a few minutes, pressed right up against Willow in the back seat again. "I can stretch my legs out."

He makes a show of stretching out and making a blissed out

face, and Willow almost smiles. That makes Ransom grin even wider, as if he's happy to have gotten something close to a smile out of her.

"It's gonna be okay," he murmurs, his tone turning more serious. "You know that, right? Whatever happens, we're in this together. We're not going to just let her run over us. She might have power and money and connections, but she doesn't know what she's up against. Or what we'd do to protect you."

Willow runs her tongue over her lips and then nods, letting out a shaky breath. "Okay. I... okay."

He's so good at that. He always has been, ever since Willow came into our lives. Ransom calms her down, getting her to relax and even smile when it doesn't seem like she can, and it comes so naturally to him.

I glance down at the computer in my lap, focusing on what comes naturally to me. I go back through the security footage along our route and start scrubbing away any traces of us that I can find.

There isn't much there, since we took a good path with very few cameras, but the harder it is to track us, the better our odds will be.

But even as my fingers move across the keyboard and my eyes track across the screen, I'm still acutely aware of Willow. Part of my mind is focused on the task of wiping away all traces of our flight from Detroit, but the other part is focused on the soft sound of her breathing, on the small traces of her floral scent that tease my nostrils, and on the quiet words I hear her whisper to Ransom from time to time.

We have her back now, and we're not playing by her grandmother's rules anymore.

This time, no one will ever take her from us again.

29

WILLOW

It takes a long time, but eventually, my heart stops pounding so hard.

We put distance between us and Detroit, and after a while, I stop looking over my shoulder, expecting someone to be on our tail. Hours start to slip away as Malice drives, and as the road rolls by beneath us, my eyelids start to grow heavy.

It's been a long fucking day.

The adrenaline that poured through my veins during the escape from the church is fading, and I feel exhausted and shaky in the aftermath.

At some point, Ransom tugs me down to drape my upper body over his lap, and I go willingly, closing my eyes as he runs his fingers through my hair, pulling out the pins and combs that the stylist used to tease the locks into an elegant style for the wedding.

It feels good, his fingers gently massaging my scalp as Malice and Vic talk softly in the front, and I slip into a doze, lulled by the rumble of the car as the miles pass.

When the car finally stops, the sudden lack of movement wakes me up, and my heart gives a sickening jolt. My head snaps up, and a fresh wave of adrenaline surges through me all over again as I look around, trying to see where we are and why we stopped.

"Shh, it's okay," Ransom says immediately. He puts a hand between my shoulder blades and strokes his fingers there. "We're just stopping for the night. This is a safe place."

I swallow hard, forcing myself to breathe past the panic that's clawing at my throat and my chest. When I glance around through the darkness, I can barely see anything at all.

The car's headlights cut through the night, and I can just make out empty fields and a long, gravel path. Obviously we're somewhere pretty remote, and I guess that makes sense. It's better to keep off the grid if we want to stay off Olivia's radar. It's probably pretty unlikely that there are cameras or anything all the way out here.

"Where are we?" I ask, glancing at Malice and Vic in turn. "Is this a safe place to stay?"

There are a million questions in my head, but those are the most important two, I guess. The ones I need answered so that maybe I'll have a hope of not spiraling out of control.

"The middle of fucking nowhere," Malice answers, which is very him, but not exactly helpful.

I glance at Vic instead, hoping for more clarity.

"This property is up for sale," he says. "There's a farmhouse a little ways up that's furnished but currently vacant, and we'll stay there for the night. It's so remote that no one's shown much interest in it, which works for our purposes. We won't be bothered tonight."

"But it has like running water and stuff, right?" Ransom asks, frowning.

"And electricity, yeah. It'll do for now."

Malice drives up the long, winding driveway, and the farmhouse comes into view. It's a simple building, the wooden siding is dark in the headlights. We park behind the house, probably as an extra precaution to make sure no one sees the car, and then grab what we need before walking up to the door.

Vic crouches in front of it, and it only takes a few seconds for him to pick the lock and let us inside.

Ransom has his hand on the small of my back, and I let him lead me in. Malice holds a hand up and then nods at Vic, and the two of them split off with their weapons drawn.

"They'll do a quick sweep of the house," Ransom tells me. "Make sure it's empty and clear."

I nod, but my head is in chaos.

It feels so fucking strange to be here. I hadn't let myself think too far past the wedding, because with Troy's threats, I knew our wedding night was going to be the thing of nightmares. I'd tried to block it out of my mind for as long as possible, telling myself I'd deal with it when I got there, when there was no other way to avoid it.

But now I'm here, and the day went nothing like I thought it would. I'm standing in the entryway of a farmhouse, hours away from my old home.

A home I'll probably never go back to.

There's so much weighing on me. My head and my heart are a riot of emotions and thoughts that I can't even sort through. There's relief that I'm not currently married to Troy and worry for what comes next and anger that my plan was ruined and gratitude that the guys came to rescue me. It all blends together too intensely for me to be able to pick out any single feeling from the mad tangle, and my head throbs when I try.

After about five minutes, Malice and Vic come back.

"It's clear," Vic says with a short nod.

"Thank fuck," Ransom replies, groaning and stretching. "Malice drives like a fucking maniac, and I wanna soak up this time out of the car."

"Next time I'll just let Olivia's security forces catch up to us then. Or you can drive, since you wanna complain so fucking much," Malice grumbles.

Ransom just grins and walks into the kitchen to start opening and closing cabinets that are almost certainly empty.

Vic follows him, but instead of rifling through the cabinets, he starts setting up his laptop at the table, pulling out little devices and building himself what looks like a makeshift battle station.

I stand where I am, watching in silence for a bit, but eventually, the need to wash off the dried sweat and grime from the day wins out.

"I'm going to go clean up," I mutter and I walk off without waiting for a response.

It takes a few tries to find a bedroom, and when I do, I flip the light on and close the door. There's a large floor-length mirror behind the door, and I catch sight of myself with a start.

Fuck. I look like a wreck.

My makeup is smudged, mascara darkening the undersides of my eyes, my hair is a mess despite Ransom's ministrations, and my dress is torn and bloody.

There's a layer of dirt along the train from running through the halls, and grass stains from our fall out the window.

Just looking at myself in this fucking dress makes my heart pound and my stomach churn. I hate it. I hate everything about it. What it represents, how it looks. The way I had no say in any of it.

Suddenly, all I want is to rip this fucking thing off and maybe set it on fire. But getting it *off* is the most important part.

The woman who helped me into it what feels like forever ago made it look simple, but without someone else to help me, it's not easy at all. I end up scrabbling at my back, trying to find the ties and clasps that will undo it all.

I manage to undo a couple of them, but there are so many, and it's hard when I can't see them. Turning around in the mirror is useless, since I can't see that way either, and I just end up yanking at the heavy fabric, desperate enough to try to actually tear it off.

"Fuck," I pant, tears welling in my eyes. "Come *on*."

It's as if being trapped in this stupid fucking dress is just making everything harder, and my shoulder wrenches painfully as I reach back again and again, trying to find something that will get me out of this.

"*Please,*" I mumble to no one in particular. "I just want—"

The bedroom door opens, and I break off as Malice walks in without a word.

For a second, he just stands there, watching me as I struggle, and I glare at him, my heart racing.

"Aren't you going to help me?" I blurt, irritation prickling under my skin.

He just shrugs, his gray eyes dark. "I dunno. I figured you had it handled. Just like you had the wedding handled. Why would you want my help if you're just planning to do whatever the fuck you decide to do on your own?"

He doesn't even sound angry as he says it, but his words are deliberate, and they sting. I glare at him, clenching my jaw hard.

"Excuse me for trying to protect you," I snap.

Malice prowls closer, moving like a predator closing in on its prey. "Should I? We tried to protect you by keeping you out of X's crosshairs, and you didn't like that too much."

A noise that's halfway between a growl and a groan leaves me, and I blow out a breath. I hate him a little in this moment for throwing that in my face. It's even worse because he's right.

I did the same thing I got so pissed at the three of them for doing: making a choice and not letting them be a part of it. Not letting them have a say.

I know how they must feel about it, because it's how I felt when I found out. Angry, helpless, disrespected. I hated them for putting me in that position. Or at least, I tried to tell myself I did.

But I can't admit that I know he's right, or that I understand how he feels. Not right now.

Not when my emotions are reaching a fever pitch, anger and sadness and anxiety washing through me in waves. I'm so fucking worried about them and terrified of what Olivia will do.

I thought I could save them. I *tried* to save them.

And now they're on the run because of me.

"I knew what I was doing," I say, my voice tense and angry.

"And it would have been worth it. I could've kept you and the others from spending the rest of your lives in danger because of Olivia, or even worse, getting killed by her. You shouldn't have stopped me."

Malice's jaw goes hard, a muscle in his cheek jumping. "Stopped you from being sold off like a piece of cattle? Excuse the fuck out of us for thinking that would have been a shit deal."

I shove at his chest, trying to get some space from him. "You shouldn't have done it! You should have just let me make my choice."

Whatever space I gained, Malice takes back, getting right in my face. He doesn't stop when he reaches me either, backing me up until I'm pressed against the wall.

"*That's* the choice you were gonna make?" he snarls, his nostrils flaring. "Is that what you wanted? You wanted to be that fucker's wife?"

"No, but I—"

"But fucking nothing, Solnyshka! We had an agreement. We had a *plan*. We were gonna get you out of there, and instead, you decided to march down the aisle with one of the most disgusting pieces of shit I've ever met."

"It's *my* life!" I shout back. "If I wanted to do it—"

"What life?" Malice interrupts. "What fucking life, huh? You want me to tell you what your life would have been like with him? A living hell. I know his type, Solnyshka, and the things he would've done to you..." He breaks off, as if he can't force himself to continue that thought. When he continues, his voice is dark. "You were about to shackle yourself to a fucking monster, and you know that."

"Of course I fucking know that!" I blurt, shoving against him. "But how is this any better?"

"This way, we're all free!" Malice bellows, his voice echoing around the room.

"No, we're not. We're fucking fugitives!" I shoot back, frustrated tears burning my eyes. "I wanted to save you. Why wouldn't you let me save you?"

Malice goes silent, and the sudden absence of noise in the room makes our harsh breathing seem even louder. We stare at each other for a long moment, our chests rising and falling, our faces inches apart.

Then something in Malice's expression cracks. He makes a low, inarticulate noise and hauls me against him, closing the last shred of distance between us.

I gasp as his mouth meets mine, crushing and hot. Unrelenting.

He kisses me like we're definitely not done fighting yet, and the anger I heard in his voice is translated into the harsh press of his lips, the sharp edge of his teeth.

I'm stunned for a second, but then I come alive under his touch, my lips pressing back against his. I clutch at his shirt, my fingers curling into fists, as I pour all my feelings into the connection between us.

Our mouths crash and bruise, teeth catching on flesh. When Malice thrusts his tongue between my lips with a growl, it feels like he's staking his claim, and I meet it with my own tongue, letting them tangle together.

He grabs my shoulders and yanks me away from the wall, and I stumble, panting for breath. Before I can say or do anything, he's hauling me toward the bed with a look of single-minded determination on his face. As soon as we reach it, Malice lifts me like I weigh nothing and all but throws me onto it.

I bounce a little as my body hits the mattress, sucking in a sharp breath as I look up at him.

His gray eyes appear almost black as he stares down at me, his pupils blown out and overtaking the irises. His features, always so harsh and wild, look almost feral now. I can still see anger in his eyes, but there's something intense and possessive in their depths too, something that makes my thighs clench.

"I'm not gonna help you take that dress off," he says lowly, and

I swallow hard. "I'm gonna fuck you in it. To prove to the entire fucking universe that no wedding dress, no fake vows, no church or goddamned priest can change the fact that you belong to me and my brothers."

My heart slams against my ribs as he says it, the strength and conviction in his tone enough to leave me lightheaded. It's not the kind of vow someone would ever say at a wedding, but it means so much more than anything I could have said to Troy today in that church. Anything my grandmother could have forced me into.

This is *real*.

This is raw and primal.

This is something that nothing else in the world could ever touch, and I tremble in the face of it.

Maybe Malice can see the impact he's having on me, or maybe he's just feeling the weight of those words himself. But dark heat flashes in his eyes, and he stalks closer to the bed.

"Pull up your skirt," he commands, his voice like sandpaper. "I wanna see your pussy."

I swallow hard but do as he says, gathering the fabric of the dress in my hands until I can haul it up and over my hips. My cheeks flush, even though it's hardly anything he hasn't seen before.

The lacy white panties I have on already have a damp spot from my arousal, and Malice's nostrils flare as if he can smell it.

"Who the fuck are you wearing those for?" he demands.

"I... they came with the dress," I whisper, my cheeks burning impossibly hotter. "I didn't—"

"Take them off. Right fucking now."

I nod, scrambling to obey him. I slide the panties down my thighs, and Malice snatches them away, the fabric tearing in his grip. His eyes glint as he stares down at me, and I feel more on display than ever, like I couldn't hide from this man if I wanted to.

But in this moment, I don't want to. Not at all.

"Touch yourself," he orders, still standing at the foot of the bed like a vengeful god. "Rub that wet pussy for me, Solnyshka."

Hearing his nickname for me makes me moan, and I swallow again, my throat suddenly dry. I spread my legs, letting him feast his eyes on my pussy and the way my folds are slick with my arousal.

The first brush of my fingertips against my clit makes me gasp out loud. I close my eyes, tipping my head back as I circle my sensitive bud with two fingers, whimpering at the sensation.

"Don't close your eyes. Fucking look at me," Malice demands.

My eyes snap open, my gaze finding his immediately, and even though he hasn't moved, he seems closer than ever.

"Just like that," he grits out. "Don't you ever fucking look away from me, Solnyshka. Don't ever try to deny this. You're ours, do you fucking hear me? You belong to us."

I nod, my fingers moving faster at those words, as if something about being claimed like this makes me want to come for him even more.

"Every part of you is ours," he continues. "Your mind. Your heart. Your pleasure. Your pain. And we might share with each other, but make no goddamn mistake—any other fucker who touches you isn't long for this world."

My fingers slip and slide as I touch myself, more wetness coating them as my gaze stays locked on Malice. He drags his focus from my eyes down to my pussy and then back up, his inked forearms tensing as he clenches his hands.

"Look at you, soaking wet because you can't wait for me to fuck you," he murmurs. "Isn't that right?"

I nod again, and he scowls.

"Say it. Give me your words, Solnyshka. I know you can do it. Tell me how much you want my cock in that tight little hole."

"I... I want it," I manage to gasp out. "Please, Malice. I want your cock in my pussy. I want it so bad."

"Then show me. Use your fingers and show me how you want it. How you wanna get fucked."

I slide one finger into myself, my hips bucking forward at the intrusion. It's not enough. It's not even close to enough. Malice's cock is so thick that my finger pales in comparison, so I add another, working them in and out of me as deep as I can get them.

He just snorts, anger and lust warring in his expression. "That's it? You think that's how I'm gonna fuck you?" He leans closer, his voice dropping. "You know it's not gonna be anything like that slow, gentle shit."

And I do know. Malice doesn't do gentle. He doesn't ease me into it. Malice fucks hard and for keeps, and I whimper as I add a third finger, the stretch feeling so good to my lust addled body.

I pull all three fingers almost all the way out and then slam them back in, gasping and arching at the jolt of pleasure that it sends up my spine. I do it again, and then once more, but it's still not quite enough. Not to mimic the way Malice would claim me.

My other hand joins in, rubbing frantically at my clit while my fingers keep working, the wet, slick sounds of me fucking myself on my own hands echoing in the room.

And Malice doesn't look away, not for a second. He barely seems to blink, and I can feel his gaze like a physical sensation.

"Just like that," he urges. "Fuck yourself on your fingers. Get yourself all nice and warmed up for me. You're gonna need it, I fucking promise you."

"Malice, please," I gasp out. Pleasure spikes, and I arch harder, my legs splaying open even wider. "Fuck," I groan. "Fuck, I'm so… oh my god!"

"That's it. Come for me, Solnyshka," he croons. "Fucking come for me."

I don't need more urging than that. A sob rips out of me, and I slam my fingers in deeper, twisting and shaking as my orgasm hits me full-on. It steals my breath, and I'm left gasping for air as the sensations wash over me, leaving me a trembling mess.

Malice watches the whole thing, his cock a thick bulge against the front of his pants.

"Turn over for me," he says as the last tremors of my climax work through my body.

I try to obey him, but my limbs feel as uncoordinated as a baby deer's.

Malice makes a noise in his throat when I don't move fast enough, grabbing me around the waist and turning me over himself, then pulling me up onto my hands and knees. There's a second where I think I'm going to go right back down on the mattress, but my arms and legs manage to hold me up, and I drag in deep breaths, still trying to recover from the intense orgasm.

I can feel Malice staring at me, taking in my raised ass and my swollen, wet pussy. I know I'm a mess down there, and I tense in anticipation, desperate for him to touch me.

When he does, it's to slide the lacy garter from around my thigh and pull it off. He puts one large hand between my shoulder blades, pushing my upper body down onto the bed. With his free hand, he grabs my arms, wrenching them behind my back.

"Fuck," I groan, biting my lip.

Malice hums roughly under his breath, careful to avoid my stitches as he uses the garter to bind my wrists together at the small of my back.

"You're not going anywhere," he murmurs, leaning down, draping the hard lines of his body over me. "I know what you wanted to do today. But the only way you can protect us, Solnyshka, is by staying where you belong: right by our sides. Do you understand?"

I nod, my heart beating so fast that blood rushes in my ears.

The warm weight of his body disappears, but then I feel his fingers, thick and insistent, probing at my pussy. Two of them slide in with ease, slicked by my arousal. My toes curl, and I groan, pulling at the garter that's wrapped around my wrists, holding me tight.

"Malice," I whimper. "Fuck."

"Never again," he mutters, thrusting his fingers in even deeper. "*Never* pull that kind of shit again."

He doesn't let up, fucking me with his fingers hard and fast. I can barely breathe, my face pressed against the mattress, and I work my hips back, urging him on even more.

I feel him draw back a little, his fingers still buried inside me, and then his free hand comes down—hard—on my bare ass.

"Fuck!" I nearly scream, caught off guard by the sudden burst of pain.

"I'm not fucking kidding, Solnyshka." He spanks me again, hard enough that it sends a jolt of pain all the way through me. "Do you understand?"

I open my mouth, but all that comes out is a needy whine. It hurts, and I know I'm going to have marks on my ass, but I also want more. My head is spinning, the lines between pain and pleasure blurring more and more.

"You risked yourself," Malice says, bringing his hand down again. "You tried to use yourself as a fucking sacrifice for us." Another spank. "And you didn't even tell us." Another.

"I'm sorry!" I sob. "I'm sorry. I didn't—I just wanted—I couldn't let her—"

I shake my head, overwhelmed and choked up by the emotions coursing through me.

Malice brings his hand down once more, harder than all the rest, and I do scream then, my pussy clenching around his fingers.

It hurts, my ass one solid mass of burning pain, but it also feels so fucking good. I have to remind myself to breathe, my body throbbing from all the different sensations. This is half punishment and half something else, something deeper and more overwhelming. Something we both need.

When he pulls his fingers out of me, I whine pitifully, desperate for more.

Malice is breathing hard behind me, and I hear him fumbling

with his belt and pants. There's a split second warning, the feeling of his smooth crown pressing against me, and then he's plunging into my pussy, ramming his cock home.

If I wasn't already face down on the bed, I definitely would have collapsed from that. An intense wave of pleasure courses through me, punching the air from my lungs and making my muscles tighten.

His cock is so much bigger than my fingers or even his, and I can feel him stretching my inner walls, filling me up completely.

He grabs my hips and starts fucking me, setting a punishing rhythm that rocks me on the bed. His fingers bite into my skin, and I hope they leave marks behind.

I want to be able to see them in the morning.

To remember this.

Not that there's any chance of forgetting. Malice fucks me like he's trying to prove a point, pummeling into my pussy as if he's holding absolutely nothing back. The sound of skin slapping skin is loud in the room, and I don't think I've ever felt him get this deep before.

All I can do is take it, my wrists bound by the garter, not even trying to hold back the moans and pleas that spill out of my mouth.

It's like he's branding me with his cock, making sure that my body—and anyone who might think to touch me—knows that it belongs to him and his brothers.

He fists a hand in the skirt of the dress and uses it like a harness, lifting my hips even more. He tugs on it sharply, hauling me back into each powerful thrust as our bodies meet again and again.

"No one can ever give you what we can," Malice grunts. "No one. You'll never feel this good with anyone else. Will you?"

He punctuates those words with another snap of his hips, and my pussy grips his cock like it's trying to keep him from ever leaving.

"No! Fuck!" I sob, tears spilling down my cheeks and soaking into the mattress underneath my cheek. "No one, Malice, please! I can't—"

"Yes, you fucking can," he counters. "You can take it. You can take every fucking thing we give you. You were made for it, Solnyshka. You were made to take my cock."

"He's right about that," someone murmurs behind us, and I realize with a jolt that those last words didn't come from Malice.

They came from Ransom.

He comes around to the other side of the bed, and I can feel him watching as Malice keeps fucking me.

My entire body flushes, because I know what I must look like right now. My hands bound behind me, my face in the sheets, my ass burning bright red from being spanked.

I can only see Ransom out of the corner of my eye, but knowing he's in the room too adds another layer to all of this, making it even more intense.

Malice leans over me, his body pressing me down. His voice is low in my ear, and I shudder as the rough sound of it pushes me even closer to the edge.

"Look at him," he growls. "Look my brother right in the eye and come. Come for us. Let him see everything."

He fists one hand in my hair, yanking me upright. I cry out at the pain and pleasure of it, and Ransom's blue-green gaze is right there, cutting through me as Malice keeps fucking into me.

Ransom grins. His expression is less angry than Malice's was, but I can see the same fierce emotions lurking behind his eyes, and it almost takes my breath away.

Malice plunges into me again, and that's enough to spark my orgasm. It roars through me, hot and undeniable. I can barely breathe, can barely think, and my vision swims as I fall apart, coming in wave after wave of pleasure.

My mouth is open, and I realize that the high, keening noise in the room is coming from me, wailing my pleasure as I fall apart piece by piece.

Behind me, Malice keeps pumping, not letting up until he's swearing thickly and coming himself, filling me up.

I gasp for breath, but Malice isn't done with me yet. He wraps an arm around my waist, pulling my back flush against his chest, still buried deep inside me.

"Ransom is gonna come on your tits now," he pants. "Right on this fucking dress. He's gotta lay his claim too."

I moan thickly, my gaze darting to his brother. Without hesitation, Ransom moves closer, climbing onto the bed with us and shoving down his pants at the same time.

Even though I'm exhausted, the sight of his cock makes my mouth water, and I follow his movements with my gaze as he jerks himself off. He looks so fucking good like this, eyes narrowed, head tipped back and eyebrow ring flashing. His neck muscles strain as his hand flies over his cock, and it doesn't take long before his hips jerk, sticky jets of his cum spurting all over the front of my dress.

Marking me, just like Malice said.

Malice's hand tangles in my hair, and he tilts my head to the side a little. His lips find the curve of my jaw, and he presses a kiss there, his breath warm against my skin.

"Jeto ubilo by menja, esli by ja poterjal tebja. Ja chert voz'mi, zhit' ne mogu bez tebya, Solnyshka," he whispers hoarsely.

My head sags back against his shoulder, my body going boneless as all the emotions from our fight drain out of me. Malice finally drags his cock out of me, laying me down on the mattress, and I close my eyes, limp and exhausted. I can hear the two of them murmuring to each other, but I can barely focus on their words.

My wrists are unbound, and calloused hands rub at them, getting the blood flowing again and checking on my stitches.

"You alright?" Malice asks, a touch of gruff concern in his voice. I know he worries about being too rough with me, and I nod, blinking blearily up at him.

"Yeah. Are you?"

His eyes are still stormy, but they look different now, like the dark gray color of thunderclouds rolling away in the distance.

"I will be," he says.

Strong arms scoop me up, pulling me farther up on the bed, and I find myself held between the two of them. It's a surprisingly gentle moment after such a rough fuck, but I feel so much better than I did before.

Ransom strokes my hair, and Malice tucks himself in against my back, a line of protection and strength. His hand rests possessively on my hip, and even though I can't help but dread what our future will hold, I know that in this moment...

There's nowhere else I'd rather be.

30

WILLOW

We stay like that for a long time, and I doze a little between Malice and Ransom. I can hear their steady breathing and feel their heartbeats, and it soothes me. But there's still enough adrenaline leftover in my system that not even the exhaustion of being thoroughly fucked is enough to pull me under and put me fully to sleep.

My body is sore and worn out, both in good and bad ways. The warm, lingering throb from where Malice spanked me feels almost pleasant, but the sting at my wrist from where Ransom had to cut the tracker out is a reminder of everything that came before that.

I can also feel the sweat, grime, and cum drying on my skin, making me feel kind of gross after the long day I've had.

Neither of the brothers show any signs of moving, so I squirm between them after a while, making a face.

"I really do need to get cleaned up now," I murmur. "I'm even more dirty than I was before."

Ransom snorts, nuzzling against my neck. "Huh. I don't see the problem, angel."

"I agree," Malice adds, his voice rough and warm. "I like you filthy, Solnyshka. I like you painted in our cum."

His hand skims up my thigh and then over my pussy, not probing inside but settling possessively over the mound of it.

Ransom dips his head and finds my mouth with his, kissing me deeply. It makes me catch my breath, and I lean up into it, kissing him back. Warmth spreads through my body as I grind against Malice's hand a little. I'm definitely too worn out to go another round, but I like being touched by them like this, so possessive and familiar.

When they finally pull away, I can take stock of just how much of a mess I am. My makeup is probably ruined, my hair is a bird's nest, dirt and blood smear my skin, and when Malice pulled out of me, he left a trickle of his cum sliding down my leg.

My ass cheek still aches, and my pussy throbs from the hard fuck, but it's the good kind of soreness. The kind that does just what Malice probably intended, grounding me and reminding me that I'm his.

That I'm *theirs*.

"Alright, let's get you out of that damn dress," Ransom says.

"Thank god," I mutter.

He gets up and then holds his hands out to me, helping me to my feet. Malice gets up as well, and between the two of them, they rip away the laces holding the dress up. It slides down my body and pools at my feet, leaving me bare, and it's such a fucking relief to have it off me.

I glare at the messy pile of white fabric, liberally stained with grime and blood and cum now, then kick it into a corner, wishing I could burn it instead.

"I hope this place has hot water," I say, testing my legs to see if they'll hold me as I walk toward the ensuite bathroom.

They do, and I flip on the light, blinking in the brightness. It's not a fancy bathroom, but the shower looks clean, and that's all I care about. My body practically screams at me to get under the spray, my muscles aching for some hot water.

Ransom comes up behind me and skims his hands over my sides before dropping a kiss between my shoulder blades.

"You good?" he asks.

When I turn to face him, he searches my face, and I let him, not sure what he's looking for.

"Yeah. I'm good," I promise. "I'm just really tired. It's been a long-ass day."

He chuckles, reaching up to twist a lock of my hair around his finger. "You can say that again. Go ahead and get cleaned up, and if you need help with anything, give a call. We'll be downstairs."

I smile at him, then shift my attention to Malice, who's standing just a few feet behind him, still in the bedroom.

"Thanks," I murmur. It hits me suddenly that I haven't even told them how much it means that they came to get me. I was too busy being angry about it. "And thank you for coming to my rescue. I... really didn't want to marry Troy."

Malice huffs a breath, his eyes glittering in the soft light of the bedroom. "You sure put up a fight like you did. Here I was thinking you wanted to be that fucker's wife."

Clearly, he's still planning on giving me a hard time about it, but there's nowhere near as much heat in his voice as there was before. Things feel more settled between us now, and even if it takes a little while, I know we're going to be okay. I held on to my anger after they lied to me for a good long time, and even though the circumstances are a bit different, I guess this is one way in which Malice and I are more similar than I would've thought when we first met.

The two of them leave, probably to go scope out the house some more and consult with Vic, and I close the bathroom door, sighing into the silence.

The shower has one of those rainfall shower heads, and I turn the water on, letting it run a little hotter than I usually like it. Once the bathroom is filled with steam, I step into the tub and start washing up.

For the first time in a while, I feel like I can take my time. There's a target on our backs now, but I don't think Olivia will find us here. Not tonight.

So I stand under the hot spray as it pours down on my shoulders, soothing my aches and pains. Dirty, bloodstained water rushes down the drain, and I let it take the last of my anger with it.

It's too late to undo what happened, and as much as I wanted to protect the Voronin brothers, I was terrified to marry Troy. It's hard to stay angry at them for wanting to protect me when I just wanted to do the same thing for them. Hell, maybe it was stupid of me to ever imagine that they would stand by and accept that kind of sacrifice from me, when I definitely wouldn't accept it if our places were reversed.

We're too tangled up in each other, bound together in a way that's hard to even describe.

And now we're in this together, until the very end.

Whatever that end might be.

There are some basic toiletries on the shower shelf, and I'm not sure if they were left here by the previous owners, or if the guys put them in here when they did their sweep of the place. Either way, I'm happy to have them, and I lather my skin with soap before moving on to my hair and face. I scrub off all the makeup from the wedding, happy to have it gone.

When the water runs clear, I shut it off and step out. There's no towel, so I bend over and twist my hair above the tub, wringing it out as much as I can. When I glance in the mirror above the sink, I look a bit more like myself. Less like a miserable, terrified bride, and more just tired and worried.

After my skin has mostly air dried, I step back into the bedroom and find a small bundle of clothes on the bed that wasn't there before. Left by one of the guys, clearly.

It's a shirt that's too big for me, falling down past my knees and exposing my shoulder where the collar gapes at my neck. With it are a pair of sweats that I have to cinch tight to keep on my hips.

But it feels so good to be clean and dry and wearing clothes that weren't picked out by Olivia, so I'm not complaining one bit.

I comb my fingers through my hair then head down to the kitchen, my stomach grumbling. It hits me that I haven't really eaten anything at all today. I felt too sick this morning, carrying the weight of everything that was going to happen, and after that, we were too busy running for our lives for me to think about food.

"There are some snack bars in that box," Vic says as soon as I walk into the kitchen, nodding toward the counter. "And some bottles of water."

"How did you know I was starving?" I ask, glancing over.

A hint of a smile twitches on his lips, but he doesn't look up from his computer.

I smile back anyway and rummage through the box until I find an oatmeal raisin bar. It's not exactly what I wanted, but the guys packed for practicality, not taste. Either way, it goes down well enough as I devour it, chasing it with half the bottle of water in a couple of swallows.

The sound of Vic's typing is subtle background noise, and I lean against the counter, watching him.

"What are you doing?" I ask after a moment.

"Scrubbing the last traces of us from any footage near the church. Or on the way here. I'm trying to buy us as much time as I can before anyone finds us."

I touch the wound on my wrist where the tracker was, grateful they remembered to dig it out of me before we got too far away from the church.

"Thank you," I say. "For doing that. And I'm sorry I wasn't much help settling in here."

Suddenly, I feel guilty. While Vic was down here working, I was upstairs, fucking Malice and being marked by Ransom. That seems to be a trend, really. Victor doing the work while we're... occupied.

Vic's gaze flicks to me, and there's something different than usual behind his eyes. A spark that seems heated, but with an edge of something else I can't quite read.

"You were busy," he says simply. "I heard you with the others."

The eye contact turns charged in a way I can't define, the moment stretching out between the two of us. My heart flutters, and I remember how loud I screamed as Malice fucked me into the mattress and spanked me until I came.

Even though Vic didn't watch us, he was listening from down here. And it turned him on to hear it.

I swallow, taking another drink of water to steady myself as I hold Vic's gaze.

"You could have come up," I tell him. "I would have wanted you there."

His throat works as he swallows, and my stomach flips over as I think about what might've happened if he *had* come up. Would he have touched me again, like he did last time? Would he have kissed me? Would he have pushed past whatever is holding him back and done even more than that?

Vic's gaze bores into mine, almost like he's imagining every scenario I'm picturing, plucking them out of my head and seeing every filthy thing I wish he would do to me.

Every nerve ending in my body is practically screaming for him. Even though it's been days since he kissed me, I can still remember exactly what his lips felt like, and I want to feel them again, so badly.

The air is so thick I can hardly breathe, and when Malice and Ransom walk into the room, Vic and I don't look away from each other, neither of us reacting.

"Um... what's going on in here?" Ransom asks, stopping in place. In my periphery, I can see his head turn as he glances back and forth between the two of us.

"Nothing," Vic murmurs, still staring at me. "I'm just checking for any security footage that might've picked us up."

"How's it coming along?" Malice asks.

Vic blinks, finally wrenching his attention back to his computer. The little bubble that seemed to surround us breaks, and his voice is back to its usual tone as he says, "It's just about done. I'm covering our tracks from the last part of the trip up here. With the tracker out of Willow and the footage scrubbed, that should buy us enough time to make our next move."

"Yeah, about that. What *is* our next move?" Ransom grimaces. "We can't stay here, right? Charming as this mostly empty house in the middle of nowhere is, it's not really my dream home."

Malice answers before Vic can. "Fuck, no, we're not staying here. We can't stay anywhere for too long. It's too risky. We know Olivia has a shitload of resources, and we don't know how widespread they are. If someone spots us and reports back to her, then we're fucked."

"We keep moving," Vic agrees. "The more distance we put between her and us, and the more we vary where we stay, the harder we'll be to catch."

"Do you think she's going to have people out looking for us by now?" I ask, biting my lip.

"Hard to say," Malice muses. "She's clever, but I don't know how well she can anticipate what we'll do. She can probably guess that we wouldn't be stupid enough to hang around Detroit, but beyond that, I don't know how good she'll be at guessing our next move. We just have to be on our guard."

"We could head some place tropical," Ransom offers, grinning at his brothers. "Do some island hopping. Work on our tans."

"This isn't a fucking vacation, you know," Malice replies, rolling his eyes.

"And how would we get there?" Vic asks with an arched brow. "Just walk into an airport and show our IDs and let Olivia catch us? Use your damn head."

Ransom winks at me when I glance at him, and I know he's just kidding, trying to keep the mood light like always. I'm filled with a rush of gratitude for him and the way he never seems to let things keep him down for very long.

"The problem is going to be finding abandoned places to hunker down in," Malice says. "It might be better to sleep during the day and then drive at night. Put some miles between us and Detroit while everyone else is asleep."

"Yeah, or that might make us stand out more," Vic murmurs. "It could be best to blend in as much as we can."

Malice nods, acknowledging the point.

Ransom plays with his tongue piercing, sliding it between his teeth. "We also don't want to plan too far ahead, in case we need to pivot at the last minute. In fact, pivoting a good bit will probably do a lot to keep us one step ahead of her."

"Backup plans are always good," Malice agrees. "Maybe sometimes we stash the car in one place and then head to another."

"We should probably dump the car at some point anyway," Vic adds, "It will be harder for her to track us that way."

He opens his mouth to say something else, but before he can, something on his screen catches his attention. He sits up straighter, his eyes going wide as his shoulders tense.

"What?" I ask, leaning forward. "What is it?"

"We just got a message," he tells us. "From X."

31

WILLOW

My stomach drops, and I'm suddenly glad that all I've eaten today was that oatmeal bar, because otherwise I would probably be sick all over the shiny linoleum of this kitchen.

X and Olivia are one and the same, so whatever she's messaging them about cannot be good.

"Decrypt it," Malice says, his voice sharp.

"Working on it," Vic replies.

And of course it takes forever.

I have no idea how long these things usually take, but the minutes seem to crawl by. Malice starts pacing, and Ransom bounces his leg where he's still sitting on the counter. Vic stares at the screen of the laptop as if he can will the progress to go faster just with his eyes.

I just stand where I am, my stomach in knots and my heart racing.

Whatever she has to say, it's not going to be good. Although the men wore ski masks when they rescued me, there's no way Olivia wouldn't be able to guess who they were. She's going to be furious, and she's going to take it out on the guys.

Dozens of horrible scenarios play out in my mind, and I chew on my bottom lip, trying to breathe through the rush of panic and anxiety. Maybe she already knows where we are. Maybe she's already sent someone to get us. Maybe she's right outside, and she's just sending this message as a formality before she comes bursting in with her hired security team to drag us away.

I flick my eyes to the darkened windows, but I can't see anything through the inky blackness of night outside. Just the warm reflection of the kitchen we're all in.

I try to tell myself that it would be impossible for her to know our location. Vic covered our tracks, and it would have taken Olivia some time to regroup from the attack at the church.

We had a head start, and she would have been following the tracker, which we left behind early.

I force myself to take one deep breath and then another, trying to settle my heart down before it explodes out of my chest.

"Okay, here we go," Vic finally says. We all cluster around behind him to see the screen of his computer as the message loads.

The first thing I see is a picture of Troy.

He's flat on his back against the dull beige carpet of the church where he was shot, lying in a pool of his own blood. His face is streaked with more blood, and it soaks into the white of his dress shirt.

"*Fuck*," I gasp, and my stomach lurches even more. "You killed him."

"He got what he deserved," Malice bites out, no remorse in his voice at all. "Scroll down."

Vic obeys, scrolling down to the message itself.

And just as I expected, Olivia is pissed the fuck off.

Clearly my words of warning meant nothing to you, the message reads. *So I'll just have to show you how serious I am about this. There will be consequences for taking what wasn't yours.*

I clench my hands into fists, hating her even more. I hate how she talks about me like I'm a piece of property, like something she owned that the guys walked in and stole. It makes me feel even worse, and I swallow hard.

"Fucking *bitch!*" Malice explodes after a second, moving away from our little huddle. He goes back to his pacing, running a tatted up hand through his dark hair. "Who the fuck does she think she is? She doesn't own Willow. Willow's a goddamned person."

Warmth spreads through me to hear him say that, and I walk over to him, reaching out and resting a hand on his arm.

"She's terrible, I know," I whisper. "But she's wrong. I was never hers. Not really."

He looks at me, coal gray eyes burning, and when he yanks me against his body, I stumble but don't fight it. I let him hold me close, his nose buried in my hair as he breathes me in, hoping it will calm down some of his agitation.

"You know how rich people are," Ransom chimes in, his lip curling in disgust. "Everything is either property or an opportunity to them. They don't see the world like the rest of us."

"She can go to hell," Malice mutters. "And I'll be happy to send her there myself."

Vic starts to type something on the laptop, and my eyes fly open wide.

"What are you doing? Won't responding to her give away our location?"

He shakes his head. "No, that's not how it works. The connection is secure. And it's encrypted. Just like we couldn't find out where she was before, she won't be able to track this back to us."

I bite my lip, still unsure.

"Plus, this is a good chance to find out what she's up to," Ransom tells me. "If we get her talking, maybe she'll let some info slip. Give us a better idea of what she knows and how she's planning to track us down."

"You mean if we piss her off enough," Malice mutters.

Ransom grins, arching his pierced brow. "That too. People fuck up when they're angry."

Instead of comforting me, that just makes me worry more. Because he's right. People do fuck up when they're angry, and it's pretty safe to say that all the guys are angry at Olivia for what she's done.

"What if *we* let something slip instead?" I ask, making a face. "We could make a mistake just as easily as she could."

"Vic? Make a mistake like that?" Ransom shakes his head. "Maybe if it was Malice, but Vic would never be that sloppy."

Malice flips him off over my head, and there's a small hint of a smile on Vic's face as he keeps typing.

"What are you telling her?" I want to know.

"That she should be careful who she starts a war with," he replies.

There's an edge to his voice that makes him sound more like Malice than I've ever heard before, and I'm reminded all over again that the two of them are twins.

He sends the message, and now all we can do is wait. Malice goes back to his pacing, cracking his knuckles over and over again. Ransom raids the food box, grumbling under his breath about the things on offer, even though he was one of the people who packed it.

"Why the fuck didn't we bring any real food?" he complains.

"Because real food is perishable, and we don't know what our conditions are going to be like," Vic answers promptly.

Ransom makes a face. "And there's probably no fast food this far out either. Which sucks, because I could murder a fucking cheeseburger right now."

"Stop complaining," Malice snaps.

Ransom throws a granola bar at him, and Malice plucks it from the air easily before it hits him. He doesn't eat it though, just shoves it in his back pocket and goes back to his pacing.

I drop into a chair at the kitchen table, bouncing my leg and trying not to let the crawling feeling of anxiety get too bad. What's done is done, after all. It's not like we can go back and undo it.

Especially considering that picture of Troy's body. Malice was right. There's no one for me to marry to make amends now.

Vic's laptop pings after an hour or so, and then there's another wait as he decrypts that message as well. He turns the laptop so we can all see it, and there's another picture right at the top.

At first, it's hard to make out.

Something is burning, the flames bright, and the air thick with smoke. Whatever the building is—was—it's being reduced to ashes now, the walls black and charred.

I'm confused for a second, but then I recognize the area, and I gasp sharply as it hits me.

It's the guys' warehouse. Their home. It's burning to the ground.

Vic scrolls down to the message that goes with the photo, and Olivia has thrown his words right back at him, telling him he and his brothers should be careful who they start a war with.

Little slights can turn into grudges, and it doesn't take much to fan the flames, she adds at the end.

I frown, turning that over in my head. What the guys did here couldn't be considered a little slight. Not really. So clearly she's talking about something else.

"The Donovans," Vic murmurs before I can ask. "She got them to burn our place down."

"What the fuck?" Malice scowls. "Why the fuck would they do that?"

"'It doesn't take much to fan the flames,'" Vic reads out loud. "She probably offered them a good payday to take care of her dirty work for her. She knows enough about our business in Detroit to know that they've had a grudge against us, and she took advantage of that to recruit them for this job. They were already pissed at us, so it probably didn't take much."

"I can't believe she'd do this," I say, my throat going so tight that it's hard to breathe. "That was your home. That was... she's trying to take everything away."

I glance around as I speak, expecting to see anguish and fury on the three faces around me. But although all of the men look grim, their expressions haven't changed much from before we opened X's latest message. They're clearly pissed, but they've been pissed since the beginning. Olivia wanted this to be a personal attack, but they aren't rising to the bait like I would have thought.

"Don't you care?" I ask them. "She burned down your home. How can you be okay with this?"

Ransom shrugs, and when I blink at him in shock, he comes over and wraps an arm around me, trailing his fingers down the line of my jaw.

"We do care, angel," he says. "It's just that we expected this. Maybe not this exact scenario, but something like it. We may have left the warehouse in one piece when we headed out this morning, but we knew we were torching our old life. First, we thought we were all running away together, and then we had to literally go snatch you from your wedding. We knew we could never go back there."

He says it so calmly, like it's no big deal, but that's so far from the truth.

It's a huge deal, and the enormity of it hits me in a tender place.

The three of them were willing to give up everything. Their home, their livelihood, their foothold in the city, all of it. For me. And they did it willingly. I never asked them to, and I couldn't have ever even made myself think of asking, but they did it.

Maybe Malice is right. I can't protect them by trying to run off and make deals behind their backs. But I can do my damnedest to protect them now, by staying by their sides and seeing this through.

"Okay," I say, determination rising in me. "Then what's our plan from here?"

32

WILLOW

The kitchen shifts into hardcore planning mode from there. Even Ransom leaves the jokes behind, settling in at the kitchen table, his expression intent.

Malice seems to take point, listing out all the things we know about Olivia, unflinching and precise. He doesn't have any emotion other than anger as he ticks things off—her wealth, her status, the fact that she knows more about all of us than we know about her.

Vic writes it all down, keeping his eyes on the screen in front of him.

The picture it paints is pretty grim, all things considered. Olivia is powerful, and she seems pretty ruthless. She has connections and money and a grudge now, and we're going to be the only thing she has eyes for until she gets her hands on us.

"We just have to stay ahead of her," Malice says, leaning back in his chair. "Her shit isn't limitless. If we let her exhaust her money and her time trying to chase us around, that might give us an edge."

"She does seem pretty desperate to grow her fortune," Ransom agrees. "Which means it can't be in great shape now."

"It's not," I tell them. "All the things I wore to my engagement party were borrowed, which means she's trying to put on a show of having more money than she does to impress her peers. But that doesn't mean she's broke. Nowhere close to it. She still has a hell of a lot more resources than we do right now."

"It doesn't change the plan much. We keep one step ahead of her for as long as we can. If she sends people after us, we take care of them. We stay on our toes and watch each other's backs."

Malice sounds so sure of himself, so sure of *us* as a team, and the glowing feeling of realizing that I'm part of their unit now is only overshadowed by the gnawing worry about how this could spiral out of control.

The more people Olivia sends after us, the more bodies the brothers will rack up. That will make it even easier for Olivia to get them locked up forever if she catches us.

Assuming she doesn't just have them killed to begin with.

"She definitely wants Willow back," Ransom says, picking at a little hole in the woodgrain of the table. "So her coming after us isn't just about revenge. It's practical too. She still needs Willow."

"Yeah," I agree, even though it makes me grimace. "She needs me if she wants to expand her estate and tie her legacy to another wealthy family. It's not like she can auction herself off for marriage. So I still have value to her."

Vic nods. "That at least means she won't act rashly. She's not going to risk taking us out blindly if it means she might kill you along with us."

A prickle of fear creeps up my spine, and I lift one shoulder. "I don't know. I wouldn't put anything past her at this point."

"What do you mean?" he asks, looking at me intently.

"She... she killed Misty. Because she was an embarrassment to the family. And she killed my real mom too. My dad loved her, but she wasn't the right kind of person for Olivia's tastes. So she set our house on fire and killed her. She wanted me to die in that fire too."

I run my fingertips over my arm, feeling the ridges of scar tissue under the material of my shirt. The scars don't hurt, they haven't since I was a little kid, but I feel a phantom heat in them now, as if the flames are there, licking at my skin.

"Shit," Malice curses. "She really is a fucking monster."

"She cares about her family name more than anything," I say. "And the legacy she believes we're supposed to have. But Misty and my mom... they were inconveniences to her. They were in the way of the perfect future she had laid out. Stains on the family. She blamed my mom for 'seducing' my dad and trying to steal him away from the family."

The brothers all share a look, communicating silently in that way they have.

"That sounds familiar," Ransom mutters. "She really is obsessed with treating her family like property."

"So it's clear she's not going to back down," Vic murmurs. "She's not just going to cut her losses with the wedding and move on or give up. She'll be relentless."

My stomach churns just thinking about it. Malice makes it sound easy, staying one step ahead of her, keeping out of her grip, but I know it's not going to be that simple. There's no way it could be.

"We have to be really, really careful," I tell them. "If she catches us..."

"You'll be okay, at least," Ransom says.

"Define okay."

He winces and then nods. "Point. She won't kill you, but..."

"But I might wish I was dead by the time she's done shackling me into some horrible marriage. And if she hurts you guys, I..." I trail off, not even wanting to finish that thought. It hurts too much to even think about.

"Let's not dwell on that right now," Vic says, getting our attention back to the matter at hand. "We need a plan. Multiple plans, honestly."

"Detroit's a bust." Malice crosses his arms, making the tattoos on his biceps shift and stretch. "And anywhere close by is just asking for trouble. We're gonna have to put a lot of distance between us and this part of the country."

"Any kind of travel that requires us to have IDs right now is too risky. We don't know what strings she could pull to find out where we're going. And she might be expecting us to hop a flight somewhere and get out of here," Vic says. "So we're stuck to cars for a bit."

"But leaving the country might be a good idea," Ransom adds.

Everyone looks thoughtful at that.

"That's not a bad idea," Vic replies. He types a bit on his computer and then glances up at us, the cool light from the screen shining on his face. "Canada isn't far from here."

"Maybe too close, though," Malice argues. "Close enough that she might have friends or connections there."

Vic hums. "Possibly. Mexico?"

I chew on my lip, trying to remember my geography and just how many states are between us and Mexico right now. "That's pretty far, isn't it?" I ask.

"It is, but that's what we need right now. Plus, Olivia has dirt on all of us, just like she threatened. And none of it is vague or speculation. The jobs were for her, so she's got easy access to evidence connecting us to each of them. So we can't rule out her calling on law enforcement to help bring us in."

My stomach drops a little, because I didn't think of that. On the surface, Olivia seems like a respectable, wealthy member of society, and people like that always have better chances of getting what they want from the law.

The conversation keeps circling, the guys discussing who they know along the route to Mexico that might be able to help us, and whether it's safe to reach out to anyone at all.

Vic pulls up a map on his screen and turns it around so we can all see, charting different paths that can take us to where we want to go. It seems like such a massive distance, and the more they talk, hammering out the details, the more I worry that we're in over our heads.

Eventually, the day starts to catch up to me, and I can feel the late hour. My eyes slide closed, and I smother a yawn with one hand, blinking blearily as I fight to listen to everything they're saying.

"It's getting late," Ransom says after a few more minutes. "We should get some rest. Especially if we have a shit ton of driving ahead of us." He nudges me with his shoulder. "You're fading fast, pretty girl."

"No," I mumble, shaking my head. "I'm okay. We need to keep strategizing."

"We've just about done all we can for tonight."

He gets up and plucks me out of my chair, putting his hands on my shoulders to steer me in the direction of the bedroom. I don't fight him, my body sagging with exhaustion as my feet shuffle across the floor.

Another chair scrapes back from the table, and when I turn my head, I see Malice getting up too. Without saying anything, he follows the two of us, walking toward the bedroom in silence.

I don't bother to undress or anything, just crawl into bed, smothering another yawn. Ransom and Malice move to either side of me, the same way they did before, after they laid their claim on me, sandwiching me between them.

It should be claustrophobic, or at the very least uncomfortable, but it feels good to have them there, protecting me.

Soft footsteps echo down the hall, and Vic slips into the room then, flicking off the light. He settles in a chair in the corner, and I can feel his eyes on us as he makes himself comfortable. As my eyes adjust to the darkness, I look back, making out the shape of him in the darkness, aching for him to join us.

It's easier with Ransom and even Malice, the two of them taking what they want and giving me what I need in return. But

Vic holds himself apart, keeping his walls up, even though he lets me have glimpses behind them sometimes.

I've fallen for him too, the same way I have for his brothers, and I hope he knows that. I hope he understands that I want him just as he is, in any way I can have him, and that I always will.

I just wish he felt like he was a part of this. Because to me, he is. The four of us are a unit, and even though things have moved faster with Malice and Ransom, it's not complete without Vic.

My eyelids grow heavy, and even though my head is a mess, my thoughts a chaotic spiral, it only takes a few minutes for sleep to drag me under.

I WAKE with a start sometime later.

My heart is racing, but I can't remember any of my dreams. Just images and feelings, enough that I know my sleep wasn't restful by any means. With everything going on, that makes sense.

I still feel exhausted, tiredness and worry weighing on me, but when I try to close my eyes and go back to sleep, I realize it's not gonna happen. I'm too wired now.

The light coming in through the window is muted and pink-edged, so it has to be just after dawn. Malice and Ransom are still asleep on either side of me, and Vic is scrunched down in his chair, breathing softly.

Lying still starts to make me feel antsy, so I slip out of bed, holding my breath and creeping out of the room as silently as I can, careful not to wake any of them.

The house is silent as I move through it, and I step outside onto the small porch, taking a deep breath of the crisp morning air. I'm still wearing oversized men's clothes, and I wrap the big shirt a little tighter around myself.

There's still dew on everything and mist rolling over the fields, and it's such a different view than what I'm used to. In Detroit, even in the nicer area I moved to, there are always horns honking and the sound of people in the distance.

It's so quiet here, and that's somehow soothing and unnerving at the same time. I feel exposed without the chaos of the city to cloak us.

Movement in the field startles me, and I squint, going tense before I see that it's just a little rabbit hopping its way across the grass, heading for the distant tree line.

I watch its progress, letting out a slow breath—then I jump again when the door opens behind me.

I turn to see Vic stepping out onto the porch. He looks sleep rumpled, his hair and clothes a mess from spending a night in the chair, and he blinks in the early morning light before coming up to stand next to me.

"Are you okay?" he asks, voice pitched low, but somehow still loud in this early dawn stillness.

"I thought you were still asleep," I murmur back.

He shrugs. "I noticed you getting up, and when you didn't come back to bed, I thought I'd check on you. It's not really safe to be out here alone."

"Oh." I make a face. I'm still not used to being on the run. "Sorry, I'll be more careful. Thanks for coming to check on me."

He nods in acknowledgement of my words but doesn't take his gaze off me. "You didn't answer my question."

Right. Of course Vic would notice that.

"I'm okay," I say finally. "I just couldn't sleep anymore. I had weird dreams, and once I woke up, I was too wired to pass out again."

He makes a quiet noise. "I know that feeling. And yesterday was a long day."

"God, it really was. There's so much going on, and my brain feels like it's all over the place. I don't know what's going to come next, and it makes me feel like I'm staring over the edge of a cliff, about to jump off... with no idea where I'll land or if I'll survive the fall."

"You've been through hard times before and survived them," he points out.

"Yeah. But somehow this feels worse, because it's my own flesh and blood doing it. My grandmother—my last living relative—is the one posing the threat this time. I hate her so much, and when I think about all the awful things she's done, I wish I'd never met her."

Vic is silent for a second, and I wrap my arms around myself, half because of the chill in the air and half because I need the comfort of it. I can feel him watching me, but I wait to see if he's going to say anything else.

When he finally does speak up, his voice is even softer, and he sounds like he's almost unsure of what he's saying. "If she hadn't turned out to be a murdering sociopath, would you feel differently? Would you have been happy being part of her world?"

I wrinkle my nose a little as I think.

"I don't know. When she first showed up at that hospital, I was so glad to have found my family. Someone who could tell me about myself and my parents and all those gaps I've had since I was a little kid. But at the same time, I feel so stupid now for even considering wanting to be a part of Olivia's life. It's so superficial and fucked up. I never would have fit in there, and I was just kidding myself, thinking that I could."

"There's nothing wrong with wanting to be loved and accepted, butterfly. You've never known your family, and she was a chance to change that. It doesn't make you stupid for thinking it might work out. Or for wanting it to."

There's so much understanding in his voice that it makes a lump rise in my throat.

Of course he knows how I feel.

He knows all about wishing that a toxic relationship with a family member could be better.

Ransom might be the Voronin brother I felt the most safe with at first, but Vic and I have always had a strange bond that knits us together—from that very first time when we talked about peanut butter in his kitchen, to now.

He makes me feel safe, both because I know he'll do anything to protect me, and because he listens to me. I can be vulnerable around him without worrying that he's going to judge me or use it against me. He gets things about me that the others don't, and even though we've had plenty of long conversations on the phone, I sometimes feel as if I don't even have to say anything for him to understand what I'm thinking.

"I keep thinking I should have known it wasn't going to work out the way I wanted with Olivia," I admit softly. "The only time in my life I've ever felt truly accepted and like I truly belong—"

"—is with my brothers," Vic finishes for me. "I know."

I shake my head, frowning at him. "No, not with your brothers. I mean, not *just* with them. With all three of you. Your brothers and *you.*" I move a little closer to him as the morning breeze ruffles his hair. It's a bit longer than his usual short cut, as if he hasn't had time to trim it recently. "Do you know what I was thinking just now?"

He shakes his head, his face impassive.

"I was thinking that no one has ever made me feel as seen as you do. That we have a bond I didn't expect, but that I'm so happy it exists."

"I make you feel seen because I literally watch you all the time," Vic mumbles, his hands clenching and unclenching as if he's not sure what to do with them.

I huff a breath, taking another step toward him. "That's not what I mean. You watch me, yeah, but you also see me. It's different. I can tell you things, and you understand where I'm coming from. You seem to understand parts of me that I never even understood myself."

"Butterfly..."

His voice is very soft again as he whispers the nickname he gave me somewhere along the line, and he stares at me like he couldn't look away if the house exploded right next to us.

"Why didn't you come upstairs last night?" I ask. "Why didn't you come watch?"

The question has been sitting in my mind since our conversation and the loaded moment we had in the kitchen. He's watched me with his brothers before, so there was nothing stopping him from coming up and witnessing all of it.

But he chose not to. He stayed in the kitchen, even though I could tell he was turned on by what he'd heard us doing.

Vic's eyes flash, and the same thing I saw in them last night flickers through their depths.

It reminds me of a piece of flint being struck—a spark that flares and dies over and over until one day it catches, turning into a flame.

When that flame inside him lights, what will happen?

That thought makes my heart beat faster, and I stand still, not looking away as my question hangs in the air between us.

"I wanted to," he finally admits, his voice raw. "But if I had, I… I wasn't sure I could've just watched."

My eyes widen, a rush of heat pouring through me.

The admission that he would've wanted to join in with his brothers makes my heart beat faster, and it's on the tip of my tongue to ask him why that would've been a bad thing. But before I can get the words out, the door to the house bangs open, making us both jump.

"Ah. There you two are," Ransom pokes his head out, stifling a yawn. "We gotta get moving. Task master Malice says it's time to go."

33

MALICE

We load the car back up with the shit we took out of it for the night, and I stand on the porch, watching as Vic rearranges everything to best fit inside the trunk. He grabs his laptop bag and stashes it in the front seat, but everything else goes in the trunk.

I run down a list in my head, making sure we haven't missed anything, thinking of the next steps we need to take once we get out of here.

Something about needing a concrete plan snaps me into what Ransom calls my 'task master business mode', but whatever. Someone's gotta make sure we get where we need to go and don't get caught up in other shit.

The instinct to protect the few people in this shit world that I love is fucking strong. It was there for our mom before she died, and it's still there for my brothers. So strong that I went to prison to protect them, and that I'd do it again in a heartbeat.

Now that urge has expanded to protect Willow.

I watch her walk back into the house after passing the box of food provisions, and I track her movements, following the bright blonde glint of her hair before she ducks back inside.

Just thinking about yesterday, about her standing at that altar, about to marry some fucker who would have used and abused her, makes fury boil in my blood. I wish I'd been the one to kill Troy. It wasn't part of the plan, but if he was going to die, I wish I could have done it. At least he's gone. At least he can never put his grimy fucking hands on Willow again.

Her grandmother can get fucked too if she thinks she's going to get Willow back. She's ours, I'm gonna keep her safe no matter what it takes.

"Hurry up," I call, my voice carrying down to where Ransom and Vic are having a quiet argument about packing the car. "We don't have time for your fucking bickering."

They both look at me, then Vic plucks the bag out of Ransom's hand to slot it in place.

Ransom rolls his eyes but doesn't argue. He gives me a sardonic salute and then heads back into the house. When he and Willow don't appear after a few seconds, I go inside myself, glaring at them until they march their way back to the car.

"He's in a mood," Ransom whispers to Willow, loud enough for me to hear.

"Yeah, the mood to keep everyone from getting caught by a fucking crazy bitch with too much damned money and an ego trip," I grunt. "Just call me the asshole, I guess."

"We're going, we're going," Willow replies, smiling a little. It's strained, and she looks like she didn't get enough sleep last night, but she's moving.

I do one final sweep of the house to make sure we haven't left anything we need behind, and then walk the perimeter with a bottle of accelerant, splashing it liberally over the sides of the house. I toss the bottle in through the front door and then light a match, touching it to the trail of liquid on the porch.

It goes up immediately, and I jog to the car, sliding into the driver's seat.

Everyone else is already buckled in, and Willow sighs softly as she watches the house catch fire and start to burn. It goes up quickly, and this far away from civilization, it'll be down to ashes before anyone makes it out here to see what's going on.

"It was a nice house," Willow murmurs. "It's a shame you had to burn it down."

"Easier to cover our tracks this way," I tell her, starting the car and pulling back onto the gravel driveway. "Any DNA evidence we might've left behind is gonna burn with the house."

"Yeah," she says. "I get it."

I speed down the driveway and then pull out onto the road just as smoke starts to billow from the house. Not stopping to watch it go up, I get us going, glancing over at Vic in the passenger seat.

Usually the two of us would switch off driving, but right now, I need Vic on nav duty, letting me know the best route to get out of here without being detected. He already has his laptop open, a map pulled up on the screen.

"Just head back toward the highway," he says. "There's a back road we can take."

I nod and start driving that way.

Ransom is in the back with Willow, and that seems best for everyone. Even though she's trying to seem like she's not freaking out, I know she's probably stressed as hell about all of this. Ransom has a calming effect on her, and that's good right now. It used to make me jealous, how easily he could talk to her and get her to relax, but now I'm grateful for it. I can trust that Willow is in good hands with my brother.

We drive south, putting miles between us and the burning wreck of the farmhouse. Once we get about fifty miles away from it, my focus shifts to our next step.

"We need to get some money," I announce, and Vic nods.

Willow purses her lips, looking worried. "What does that mean, 'get money'? How are you going to get it? If you withdraw cash from an ATM, then there'll be a record of that, won't there?"

Ransom and I exchange glances in the mirror, and he grins before turning his attention to Willow.

268

"You're right about that, pretty girl. If we went to an ATM, it would be pretty easy to trace, so we won't do that. Malice was referring to getting money that doesn't strictly belong to us."

She breathes in sharply. "You mean stealing."

"That's one way to put it, yeah."

"But won't that be dangerous?"

"You mean more dangerous than being hunted by your bitch of a grandmother?" I ask dryly, one hand resting low on the wheel as I glance over my shoulder.

"We've done this before," Vic tells her. "We know how to pick an easy target."

"Yeah, but..." She shakes her head, still seeming skeptical.

I suppress a smile, moving to change lanes as Vic tells me to take the upcoming exit. Sometimes Willow still seems so shocked to have fallen in with a bunch of criminals. But Ransom is right. What we have in mind isn't something we've done recently, since the chop shop was doing a good business before Donovan and his gang decided to fuck with us, but we've done it before.

"What do you think?" I ask, glancing over at my twin.

"Convenience store is easiest," he says. "Anything bigger than that will be an issue. Small-ish town, probably. Let me see what we're near." He starts typing again, still talking as he does. "Small enough to not have too many cops. and probably slow ones at that, not used to being called out for robberies, but big enough that we won't stand out too much as strangers."

"Agreed. Anything too small, and everyone knows everyone, which will make it too hard to blend in."

"Exactly. Take a right up here."

I turn on my blinker. "Find us a place to stay tonight too. Somewhere out of the way."

"I'm on it."

After a quick stop to gas up the car and buy Willow some clothes that will actually fit her—along with some shoes that aren't the heels she walked down the aisle in—we drive for a good few hours before Vic guides me to a decent sized town.

"Okay, first things first," I say as I exit the highway. "We'll find someplace to drop Willow off, and then we should—"

"Wait, what?" she interrupts. "What do you mean, drop me off? You're leaving me?"

"Just long enough to do what we need to do," Ransom soothes. "It'll be better if you're not there."

"I can help!" she insists. "We're supposed to be sticking together. I can help you."

"*No*," I say firmly. "This isn't the first time we've done this, and we have our shit on point. We have a system, and we'll be fine."

"But—"

"But nothing, Solnyshka. We gotta keep you out of this shit as much as possible. If we get caught, you can keep running."

The look on her face is so mutinous that it makes me want to drag her into the front seat and kiss the fuck out of her, just to turn that spark into a full-blown flame. But she finally stops arguing, folding her arms and frowning out the window.

I keep driving, finding a little diner off the interstate where we can drop her off.

Ransom pulls a ball cap out of his bag and puts it on her head, covering the bright golden locks of her hair.

"You'll be okay," he says. "Just keep your head down and don't draw any attention to yourself. We'll be back as soon as we can." He pulls her into a kiss, and she goes willingly, even though it's clear she's still pissed.

After she slides out of the car, she turns back and peers through the open door at all of us.

"Be safe," she says sternly. "Be careful."

"Take your own advice," I shoot back, then watch as she turns and heads into the diner.

My hands tighten on the steering wheel, and something in me screams to snatch her back and not let her walk away from us. I can tell my brothers feel the same way, both of them looking unsettled and displeased about being separated from her.

"Let's get this done quick," Ransom mutters. "I don't want to leave her here longer than we have to."

"A-fucking-men," I grunt, and get us moving again.

Vic's already picked out a target for us, so we drive across town to the spot and scope it out. It's midsize, mostly a gas station, but with a little convenience store attached to it.

"Less likely to do regular deposits," he explains. "And probably staffed by bored kids who won't put up a fight."

"Perfect." I nod, then glance between my two brothers. "Usual plan. We work as a team. I'll handle the money. Vic, you handle the clerk. Ransom, you go to the back and see if you can find more cash waiting to be deposited, or anything else of value. We'll wait until there's no one else inside to minimize the risk."

The place isn't busy, so it only takes about twenty minutes before all of the pumps are clear. A minute or two after that, someone walks out the front door of the convenience store, and Vic nods. "I think that was the last customer inside."

We all pull our ski masks on, leaving the car parked down the road.

The shop is quiet, and the bell on the door jangles as we enter and fan out. The clerk, a bored looking guy in his twenties, looks up as we stride in. He barely even seems to notice us at first, but then he does a double take at the sight of our masked faces.

"What the hell?" he demands.

Ransom shoots out the security camera that's attached to the wall behind the counter, and Vic raises his gun, aiming it right at the clerk's face as the guy blanches.

"No sudden moves," Vic says, his voice passive and detached. "We're not here to hurt you. Open the register and give us all the cash you can put your hands on."

Ransom gives me a look, and I nod, watching as he peels away from the two of us and moves for the back. Luckily, this kind of place doesn't seem to be well-staffed or heavily trafficked, so there's probably no one waiting back there to fuck up the plan.

And if there is, Ransom knows how to handle himself.

The clerk raises both hands, eyes wide as saucers. "Don't hurt me, okay? I don't get paid enough for this shit."

"Just do what he fucking said," I snap.

"Okay, okay." He pops the register open and starts shoveling cash onto the counter, his hands shaking.

I pull a bag from my pocket and slide the bills into it, keeping an eye on the clerk as I do. Vic keeps the gun trained on him, never wavering.

"Is that it?" he asks, when the flow of cash has stopped.

The clerk nods. "Yeah, man. That's it. That's all that's in the register, I swear. You can check."

Vic glances at me and nods.

A few seconds later, Ransom comes back, holding up a deposit bag. Vic wasn't kidding about them not getting to the bank often, then.

Out of the corner of my eye, I see the clerk moving, and I snap my head around, pinning him with a glare as he moves to grab for his phone. Vic steps forward, pressing his gun to the clerk's temple.

"You just said you don't get paid enough for this shit," he says calmly. "Let's not make it so you have to pay with your life."

"Okay," the clerk says, raising his hand as sweat trickles down his brow. "Okay, fuck."

"We're done here," I tell my brothers. Then I step forward and then reach over the counter, grabbing the clerk by the shirt and hauling him over it. He yelps, babbling in his panic, and I drag him to the back through the Employees Only door.

"Please!" he begs, pure panic breaking across his face now. "Please don't kill me. I—I can give you all the money on me. I've got a few bucks in my wallet. Just—"

"Shut the fuck up," I grunt at him. "I don't want your money."

Keeping a hand on the guy, I yank open a utility closet and find a roll of duct tape.

That'll work.

I quickly tape up the clerk's ankles and wrists, winding it around and around so there's no way he'll work himself free easily. Then I add a strip over his mouth, cutting off his muffled noises.

It'll buy us some time to get out, and eventually someone will find him.

Once that's done, I leave him bound on the floor of the back office and head back to the front to find Ransom shoving bags of chips and cookies into his bag.

I roll my eyes and gesture for my brothers to follow me.

On the way out, Vic finds a sign on the door that says 'Back in 15' and flips it around so that it shows from the outside.

"There. That buys us at least fifteen minutes," he murmurs, and we pile back into the car and peel out.

"That was easy. It's about damn time something went smoothly," Ransom comments, prying open a bag of chips as we get back on the main road to go pick up Willow. "I feel like we were definitely owed a win."

I don't believe in that shit, in fate or being owed by the universe or whatever, but he has a point. If anyone is owed a break from things being a shit show, it's Willow, and what we did will help us keep her out of her grandma's clutches.

It's an uneventful drive back to the diner, and we all pile out to head in and get her. I scan the tables when we step in, my gaze skimming over everyone who's not my Solnyshka. It takes a second for me to find her, and when I do, I frown.

She's hunched down in a booth in the back, and there's some fucking guy leaning over her, obviously hitting on her.

That motherfucker.

Rage rises up in me, and I clench my hands into fists, about to step in... but before I can move, Vic storms past me, striding with purpose toward the corner Willow is sitting in.

34

WILLOW

"What's the matter, honey?" The man in the trucker hat leans closer, his voice a lazy drawl. His beer gut is pressed against the side of my booth, and I can feel him leering at me even as I keep my gaze firmly fixed on the table in front of me. "You looked so lonely over here, I thought you'd like a little company."

"No, thanks," I mutter, debating whether it would be worth it to push past him and get up.

But if I leave the diner, the guys won't be able to find me after they finish their job, so all I could really do is move to another booth. And I know this asshole will probably just follow me.

Undeterred by my obvious disinterest, the man reaches out, tugging a lock of my hair that's escaped from the hat between his fingers.

"You know, I always did wonder if blondes were more fun," he says with a sleazy grin. "Want to help me find out?"

"Don't fucking *touch* her, you son of a bitch."

The voice behind us is hoarse and furious, and it's the only warning the man gets before his hand is yanked away. His eyes widen as he stares at Vic, who's practically vibrating with rage.

"Vic!" I blurt, shocked, but it's like he can't even hear me.

He's entirely focused on the trucker, his blue eyes flashing.

The normally smooth lines of his face are contorted with fury, a vein pulsing in his temple as his nostrils flare.

"Someone should have taught you to keep your hands to yourself," he snarls. "It would have saved you a lot of pain."

"What the hell are you—"

The trucker never gets to finish that thought.

Vic slams his hand down on the table with a bang, then reaches for the metal container in the middle of the table that holds utensils and condiments. He hefts a steak knife and moves like lightning, stabbing it down through the guy's hand and into the table.

"Fuuuuuck!"

Instinctively, the man tries to pull away, and his curse turns into a howl of pain when it hits him that he's stuck. His face drains of all color, turning a chalky white, and he stares at the hand pinned to the table like a bug as if he can't quite comprehend what he's seeing.

His scream of agony was enough to catch the attention of everyone else in the diner, and they all look over to see what the commotion is all about. A waitress drops her tray with a shriek, and the trucker lets out another agonized groan.

"Shit," Malice bites out. He strides over and grabs Vic, dragging him away from the guy, who's sobbing in pain now. "Let's go. Solnyshka, come on."

I scramble to follow them, my heart racing.

Even though I saw what happened, it's hard to wrap my mind around the suddenness and violence of the attack. Vic just fucking went nuts on that guy.

Everyone stares as we leave the diner and get in the car, and Malice practically shoves Vic into the passenger side, slamming the door and getting in behind the wheel so that we can peel out. I barely have time to buckle my seatbelt as Malice drives, making a beeline for the highway.

"Keep watch for cops," he says over his shoulder, and Ransom nods, checking every so often to make sure that no one is on our tail.

"Clear so far," he calls out, but Malice doesn't slow down.

We drive until we're outside the limits of the town, several miles of highway stretching out behind us, and then Malice turns to Vic in the front seat. "Where am I going?" he asks.

Vic doesn't respond. His jaw is clenched, and his fingers tap a steady rhythm on his thighs, a sure sign that he's going through something.

"Vic!" Malice snaps.

"Not now," is all Vic says, and Malice snarls.

"I've got it," Ransom interrupts. He grabs the laptop from the front seat and takes over. "Exit twenty three, Mal."

With Ransom navigating, Malice seems okay to leave Vic alone for the moment, but the atmosphere in the car is tense. Ransom confirms that it's a couple more hours to where Vic picked out for us to stay the night, and he focuses on figuring out the best route to get there.

Luckily, it seems like Vic did a lot of the ground work already, so it's just a matter of following the path he laid out and telling Malice where to go.

The car is mostly silent, which just makes it even more uncomfortable.

Every so often, Malice will prompt Ransom for another direction, or Ransom will offer info about what's coming up next, but even that's done in short, to-the-point sentences.

Vic just keeps drumming his fingers on his leg, the rhythm steady and constant. He gazes out the window, and if I couldn't see him blinking in the reflection, I would think he was almost completely out of it after what happened.

About an hour in, I remember that we stopped in that town for a reason and chance breaking the silence.

"Did... did you guys get the money you needed?" My voice feels loud in the otherwise quiet car, and I make a face.

"Yeah," Malice answers, glancing at me in the rearview mirror. "No problems."

"In and out job," Ransom agrees.

"And you weren't seen or anything?"

"We cut the cameras," Ransom says. "And we were masked. There shouldn't be anything that can tie us to the robbery."

"Cops might connect it to the 'incident' in the diner though," Malice throws out. "And we weren't masked there. We'll have to keep our heads down."

That makes my stomach flip over with worry, and once again, I have to wonder what the hell Vic was thinking. The truth is, he probably *wasn't* thinking, just acting on pure instinct and rage, but that's always been more Malice's thing than his. Vic is usually the one cleaning up the messes that come from Malice's outbursts.

I chew on my lip for a while as we drive, until Ransom offers me some cookies from a bag, and I take a pack, more to have something to do with my hands than because I really want them.

"It'll be okay," he murmurs to me, and I give him a smile that I know looks forced.

The truth is, neither of us know what's going to happen or what's going on with Vic, and the more unknowns that stack up, the harder it gets to keep our heads above water.

Finally, we arrive at another empty, out of the way house, and Malice says this is where we'll stop for the night.

I glance around, checking out the location. It's not quite as remote as the other place we stayed, but it's clear there's no one around. All of the houses we drove past in the area seemed empty, and that helps me breathe a little easier as we pile out of the car.

"I think most of these places got foreclosed on," Ransom explains as we make our way to the back door. "Not great for the people who lived here, but pretty good for us."

Usually, Vic is the one who picks locks when needed, but he's still spaced out, following along behind us almost robotically. So Ransom kneels down in front of the door and handles it—maybe not as swiftly as Vic would have, but the door swings open after a few tries and a bit of cursing.

"Wait here," Malice grunts to me. He nods at Ransom, and the two of them do a sweep of the house to make sure things are secured.

Vic finally breaks out of his stasis enough to get his laptop out and set up his mini command center in the kitchen, but he still looks like he's going on autopilot, his expression completely shuttered.

It's a complete contrast to the look on his face in the diner. His expression then was *all* emotion, raw anger written across every line of his features.

He's never been that expressive before, or that... possessive. I don't think I've ever seen him react that way about anything, not even when he killed Carl for trying to blackmail me. It was like every ounce of his usual cool detachment was stripped away, leaving only pure feeling in its wake.

It was a bit terrifying, if I'm honest. But at the same time, there was definitely a part of me that liked it.

Because all of that emotion was for *me*.

Because some asshole who couldn't take no for an answer put his hand on me, and Vic didn't like it.

More than anything, I want to talk to him about it. To check in and make sure he's okay. But I can feel the waves of tension coming off him despite the blank look on his face, as if he's barely keeping himself from unraveling.

His brothers are giving him a wide berth too, watching him with wary expressions when they reconvene in the front room, declaring the house safe for the night.

"I'm gonna shower," Vic mutters, stepping away from the rest of us and heading down the hall.

Malice and Ransom stay where they are and watch him go, and for a second, I do too. But as I watch Victor slip into the bedroom, something breaks open inside me.

I just... can't.

I can't let him walk away from me right now.

I can't let this get swept under the rug.

I don't want him to go shower off all the agitation and then come back to us when he's shoved it all back inside, ready to pretend it didn't happen.

So I follow him, stepping into the attached bathroom on the far side of the bedroom and closing the door. It's not a large space, just enough for a shower, sink, and toilet, and there's nowhere for Vic to hide in here.

He's been ignoring me since the diner, but now he can't. Not when I'm this close.

He goes stiff as soon as the door closes, then slowly turns to face me. His eyes dart between my face, the floor, and the wall off to the side, like he can't decide which is the safest place to look.

"Vic," I say gently. "We have to talk about it."

"About what?" He shakes his head, and I can tell he's forcing himself to be blank. "There's nothing to talk about."

"Uh, I think there is. What the hell happened in that diner?"

He looks at me for a second and then away again. "You were there. It was nothing."

Those are two very different sentences, because I *was* there, and it was definitely *not* nothing.

"You stabbed a man," I tell him, as if he needs the reminder. "You pinned his hand to the table with a steak knife."

Vic's fingers curl into fists at his sides, and he shakes his head. I can see the tension in his muscles and the line of his jaw, as if he's working desperately to master himself. The edges of his control have been frayed, and are probably fraying even more right now, but I can't back down. Not this time.

"Why?" I urge. "What made you snap like that?"

Vic makes a noise in his throat, and before I can react, he's pushing past me, yanking open the bathroom door. He walks into the bedroom, but I follow him doggedly, my heart thudding in my chest.

He has his back to me, and I step around in front of him. I want to put my hand on his chest, but I stop myself, although I do move a little closer as I tilt my head up to meet his gaze.

"Listen to me," I tell him. "Please. I'm not mad, Vic. I just want to understand. What happened?"

"He touched you," Vic finally grates out. "And I... lost control. Like I *always* do when it comes to you. I can't control myself with you. That's why last night, I didn't—"

He breaks off, closing his eyes.

I stare up at him for a second, confused, but then it dawns on me.

"Why you didn't come up," I whisper. "Why you didn't come upstairs while Malice was fucking me."

"Yes." Vic's eyes open, the blue of his irises churning. "I used to be able push it all away, to keep things locked down. But now... it's like a door I can't close. And every time I open it a little wider, it gets even harder to push it shut."

Movement in the doorway catches my attention, and I glance over to see Malice and Ransom stepping into the room, probably summoned by our voices. I know they're both likely as worried about Vic as I am, but they don't tell me to stop or leave him alone, so I keep my attention focused on him.

"Is that what happened in the diner?" I ask.

"Yes." Vic taps his fingers against his thigh. "I saw his hand on your hair, and all of a sudden, I was moving. I didn't even think about it. All I knew was that I wanted to kill him for touching you." He draws in a ragged breath. "It's never been like that. Even when my father was hurting me, even when Malice got taken away, even when our mother died, I had control. I've always been able to hold myself apart from my emotions and be rational. But not when it comes to you."

"Is that such a bad thing?" I whisper.

"Yes," he rasps. "*Yes*. I have to be in control. I need to be."

There's something almost like desperation in his voice, and I know he's not exaggerating. Maintaining strict order in his life seems like it's all that keeps Vic together sometimes, and I understand enough about him to know that it was forged in the trauma he experienced growing up.

But I'm also afraid that he's going to tear himself apart if he keeps struggling so hard against his emotions. He'll bottle them up until they explode out of him like they did at the diner, making him feel even more out of control than ever.

I stare up at his handsome, anguished features, wishing so badly that I could make this easier for him. That I could help him somehow.

"What if…" I lick my lips, searching his face. "What if you *could* be in control? Even with me."

He huffs a breath. "That's not possible, butterfly. I've tried."

"But you've never been in complete control," I say. "Where every single thing that happened between us was up to you."

His brows draw together. "What do you mean?"

"You could tie me up," I offer, my pulse speeding up a bit. "Then you'd be in control of everything. Anything that happened would be completely up to you. You could touch me however you want, wherever you want. All of it would be your choice, under your control."

35

WILLOW

Vic blinks at me, his entire body jolting as if he's been zapped with electricity.

His fingers curl and uncurl, his jaw falling open a little... but then he snaps it closed, shaking his head.

"That's not a good idea, butterfly. What if I hurt you? What if I can't hold myself back?"

"I don't need you to hold yourself back. I *trust* you, Vic," I whisper fiercely. I glance over at Ransom and Malice, who have been watching this interaction silently. Malice gives me a tiny nod, so I press on. "And your brothers are here. They can keep watch and make sure I'm alright. Okay?"

I can tell it's a lot, what I'm proposing here. It's way out of his comfort zone.

Usually, he's the one watching while the others do things to me, and this would be flipping that dynamic completely on its head. But I feel like he needs it. He needs to understand that he can do whatever he wants, and nothing he does will disappoint me or scare me off.

He's kept himself in check, so tightly regimented for so long, that he panics when something throws his emotions out of order.

But I need him to see that he can let go of his tight grip on his feelings without losing control over *everything*.

And this is the only way I can think of to do that.

I glance over at Malice and Ransom again, half worried that they won't be on board with what I just volunteered them to do. Malice for one has never been a passive observer of anything, and both of them might be worried that this is too reckless or that I'll push Vic too far.

But they each nod again, agreeing to watch.

To let this happen.

My gaze shifts back to Vic, my heart knocking in my chest. He's already the one in control of this, because if he says no, I'll let it go. But I hope like hell that he'll trust me enough—that he'll trust his brothers enough—to try.

His eyes bounce back and forth between mine, hesitation and something like hope written across his face.

"Are you sure?" he asks.

"Yes," I promise him. "I just want you to be able to do what you want, Vic. Whatever it is. I want you to see that it will be okay."

Long seconds tick by, and I can tell he's debating internally, warring with himself and probably playing out a million different scenarios in his mind, trying to guess what will happen—another way he tries to keep control.

I don't move, and I don't say anything else, letting him decide.

Finally, slowly, Vic nods.

"Okay," he whispers.

My pulse immediately starts to race like a runaway train, but I do my best to keep my outward appearance calm as I step back and start to undress. I toe off my shoes and kick them away, peeling my socks off next. My toes sink into the plush carpet on the floor as I pull my shirt over my head, letting my hair fall around my shoulders.

Each new stretch of bared skin draws Vic's gaze, and I can see that he's hungry for it. His fingers twitch at his sides, like he wants to reach out and touch me, but he doesn't yet.

I keep going, taking off my pants and then removing my bra. On and on, until I'm naked in the center of the room, all three of the brothers looking at me.

I like having all of their attention, but right now, I'm entirely focused on Vic. On the way he sucks in a breath and lets his eyes trail over my body.

He doesn't move, so I climb onto the bed, lying down in the center of it before looking at Ransom and Malice.

"Can you help me?" I ask them.

"One sec." Ransom dips his chin, then strides out of the room.

He comes back less than two minutes later with a bundle of thin ropes, which I'm guessing he got from one of the bags the guys packed for our getaway. I don't ask where he got them from though, because in this moment, I don't really care. Instead, I focus on my breathing as he divides the ropes between him and Malice and the two of them approach the bed.

They each take a side, spreading my legs out and binding my ankles to the corner posts of the bed. When I try to close my legs, I get nowhere, and a little spark of electricity shoots up my spine at the knowledge that this is really happening. They do the same thing with my wrists, working carefully around the healing cut where Ransom sliced out the tracker.

Once they're done, I tug on the bindings, seeing how much slack I have.

The answer is not much at all. I'm not going anywhere until someone lets me go.

The air in the bedroom isn't cold, but it's still cool enough to make my nipples pebble a little, goosebumps dancing over my skin. I'm intensely aware of every single sensation I'm experiencing right now, from the slight chafing of the ropes to the softness of the blanket beneath my back.

Finished with their part in this, Malice and Ransom step back and stare down at me, heat burning in their eyes as they stand side by side at the edge of the bed.

I can imagine what I look like, spread open and spread out, helpless to do anything but lie here. There was definitely a time when I would have rather gnawed my own arm off than let the three of them see me in a vulnerable position like this, but now it feels natural.

It feels right.

Their eyes never leave me, but they move back to stand by the door again, letting Victor have the floor.

For a long moment, Vic doesn't move. He seems rooted to the spot, staring at me. Part of me wonders if he's even going to move at all.

My heart keeps pounding, and I can feel my body responding to the way Vic is looking at me. My clit throbs softly, and when I tug at the ropes, the reminder of how restrained and restricted I am sends a shot of arousal through me. A little whimper spills from my lips, and Vic groans in response.

"Willow..."

He sounds almost tortured, and I catch his gaze, trying to let him feel the connection between us.

"You're in control," I remind him. "Whatever you want, Vic. Anything you want."

Suddenly, he bursts into motion, crossing the space to the bed in a few long strides before kicking off his shoes and climbing up.

He kneels between my spread legs, and for a second, it doesn't seem like he knows what to do. Or what he wants to do first. His eyes dart all around, taking in the ropes around my wrists, the expanse of my skin on display, the way my breasts rise and fall with my heavy breaths.

It's like he's a starving man at a buffet, not knowing where to dive in first because it's been so long since he's had anything at all.

But then his eyes linger on my scars, and his hand reaches out, trembling a bit as he starts to touch me.

The first soft brush of his fingertips to my skin makes my breath hitch, every atom in my body focused on that tiny area. It feels so good. His hands are warm, and he trails his fingers along the edges of my scars, his gaze never wavering as he watches their progress.

He dips his fingers along the whirls and ridges of the worst of the scarring, and even though the nerves are a bit damaged there, the sensation is enough to have me panting and arching against the ropes.

I let him continue in silence for a while, but then I can't keep the words inside anymore.

"Do you... do you remember when you watched me in my room?" I whisper, and his eyes flick to my face. "When you told me to touch my scars for you, and I did?"

He nods, swallowing hard. "I remember."

"I remember wishing you were there. It was so hot over the cameras, listening to you telling me what to do. But I wished you were there to touch me yourself. To know how good it made me feel to be wanted by you like that."

"Like what?" His voice is ragged around the edges, and I can tell he's already starting to let some of his inner control slip.

Good.

"You're not turned off by my scars. You think they're beautiful. No one has ever looked at me quite like you, and I've had so many fantasies about what it would be like to have your hands on me. Just like this."

Vic groans, closing his eyes for a second. They pop open almost immediately, like he doesn't want to miss a second of this.

His touches slowly become less tentative and more possessive. He stops skimming his hands over me and lets them roam freely, touching me with intent. His palms slide over my sides and up to my chest, and when he gropes my breasts, I moan his name, arching under him.

It feels so good, and it's everything I've ever wanted from him.

It's nothing the others haven't already done, but this is new for Vic, who until now has only let himself look.

This is the first time he's ever touched my chest. The first time his fingers have pinched and tweaked at my nipples, and the pleasure from seeing him affected by it starts to build and grow inside me.

I'm panting before I know it, my pussy soaking wet. My body is buzzing from all of this, inviting more, drinking it up like I can't get enough.

Honestly, I can't.

Just as much as he's bingeing on me, I'm bingeing on him, addicted to his touch already.

"Please," I moan, my voice husky. "Fuck, that feels so good."

"I wanted to do this from the first minute I saw you," he breathes, and I know he's not lying. I don't think he *could* lie right now.

He drags his hands down my stomach and over my thighs, finding the scarring there and mapping it with his fingers. He dips between my legs, bypassing my aching pussy but stroking the soft skin of my inner thigh. I have to bite down hard on my lip to keep from begging him for more. I told him he could be in charge of this, and I want it to be his decision, but god, having him so close to my clit is only making it throb harder.

My toes are curling, my legs shaking with the effort of trying to stay still, and when Vic finally slides one finger up my slit, gathering my wetness before brushing over the little bundle of nerves at the top, it's more than I can take.

"Ahhh!" I cry out, my arms jerking against the restraints as an orgasm breaks through me like a bolt of lightning.

Vic's eyes flare wide, and then he's shoving his pants down, using the hand that was touching my pussy to jerk himself off. His strokes are quick and desperate, and I'm still coming when he shoots his load all over my stomach and breasts, spattering me with his release.

"Fuck. Oh god. Fuck. *Fuck.*"

His voice is wrecked, his body hunching over as he drags his fist over his cock one more time. He's breathing harder, and when he looks back down at me, the expression on his face is so hungry and possessive that it nearly makes me climax all over again.

"So beautiful," he murmurs. Then his gaze flicks up to my face. "Who's cum are you wearing, butterfly?"

"Yours," I whisper. "You marked me, Vic. You marked me up."

His chest heaves, and he reaches down to smear his cum, spreading it over my breasts and stomach like he's trying to rub it into my skin.

"My mark," he mutters. "*Mine.*"

His touch isn't tentative at all now. There's an edge to it, something almost primal as the heat grows in his eyes. He grabs my breasts again, squeezing them roughly. When he pinches my nipples, it's with force, and he twists one of them hard, making me cry out.

I writhe against the ropes, breathing hard.

"Yes," I gasp out. "Like that! Please!"

He plays with my nipples until I'm making little mewling noises, my head tossing restlessly back and forth. Then he drags his hands down again, this time letting his nails bite into my skin along the way. It burns slightly, but that edge of pain only stirs up the arousal growing in my belly.

This time, he doesn't bypass my pussy at all, and I whimper desperately as he cups it with his hand. He holds his hand there as if he's drinking in the heat pouring off me... then he lifts his palm, and brings it down with a hard smack against my sensitive flesh.

I cry out, surprised and so, so turned on. "Fuck!"

Vic exhales forcefully, and his hand shakes as he does it again, slapping my pussy harder. The pain reverberates through me, sharp and intense, but it feels so fucking good at the same time. He presses one hand to my stomach, pinning me in place, and then he starts raining blows down on my pussy, alternating between soft and hard, his hand coming away wet each time he lifts it.

I struggle against the binds, gasping and trying to remember how to breathe, his name spilling out of me like I can't remember any other words.

"Vic, Vic, Vic, Vic. Please. I'm so—"

I can already feel the pleasure growing, feel the sensations cresting and threatening to drag me under. Malice and Ransom are still watching, and the heat from their gazes adds to all of it, making it impossible to hold back.

Vic lifts his hand from my stomach and goes back to my breasts, playing with my nipples roughly, leaving them peaked and bright red from his attentions.

Every touch, every slap, every pinch puts me that much more on edge, but what affects me the most is just watching Vic. His expression is focused, ravenous, and intense, his eyes tracking over my body with every movement. It's like he's letting himself have everything he wants after spending so long in denial. Like he's drinking from a firehose after being in the desert for years.

He strokes his thumbs over my nipples, soothing the sting from the treatment just a minute ago, and somehow, that's enough to set me off again.

Another orgasm hits, making me shudder, and Vic is right there with me. He's hard again—I don't know if he ever softened at all—and he wraps a hand around his shaft and starts jerking, breath stuttering as he works himself.

"Never gonna stop," he groans. "Never gonna stop wanting you."

His climax hits quickly, his fist tightening around his cock, the thick, reddened head of it slipping through his fingers. The milky white ropes of his cum land on my thighs, pussy, and stomach this time, and he reaches down to rub them into my skin too.

"Fuck, this is everything," he mutters, his hands skating over my body. "Fucking *everything*. The way you look. The way you feel." He dips his head and drags his tongue along my collarbones, making my heart leap in my chest. "The way you taste. My beautiful, chaotic butterfly."

I've never had someone mark me like this. My skin is slick and sticky, coated in the mess of his cum, and it makes me feel filthy in the best way. I turn my head, silently inviting him to feast on the expanse of my neck, and he does it immediately, sucking and biting at the sensitive skin there.

"You're so perfect," he murmurs, sounding almost drunk. "So fucking beautiful. I watched you all that time, but I never thought—"

His voice breaks off, and he attacks my neck with renewed fervor, like he doesn't want to think about anything else.

My mind goes blank and hazy as he keeps working me over, his touch rough and possessive, punctuated by moments of softness when I need it most. It's as if during all that time he spent watching me, he was learning my body from a distance, his carefully observant nature logging everything away.

Twice more, he stops to jerk himself off desperately, pushed over the edge by the feel of my body beneath his hands. I'm a complete fucking mess by now, my skin covered in a light sheen of sweat from the way my heart is racing, and his cum smeared liberally over my torso.

When Vic reaches for his cock again, my breath catches, my eyes coming back into focus as I gaze up at him.

He's already come so many times that I'm amazed that he can get hard again. But this time, there's less franticness to his movements, as if he's worked off some of the desperate urgency that was coursing through his veins.

I watch his hand move over his cock, and the words pour out of me before I can stop them.

"Victor," I breathe. "Will you fuck me? I want to know what you feel like when you're buried all the way inside me. I want you to come in my pussy this time."

I'm careful to phrase it as a question, to give him a choice. He's already done so much more than I hoped, breaking out of his rigid restraint and allowing himself to let go. I won't demand more than he can give in this moment.

But Vic doesn't even hesitate.

His fingers uncurl from his shaft, and then he pulls his shirt over his head and shucks his pants all the way off, throwing them off to the side somewhere. My stomach flutters wildly, and I have to remind myself to breathe as he gets situated. He unties my legs from the bed, but keeps them spread open, lifting my hips so he can get a better angle.

Then the head of his cock is right there. I can feel it, pressed against my entrance, and my body thrills with it. I rub against him, whimpering softly.

As if he can't hold back any longer, Vic starts sinking into me. I can feel every single inch of his cock, stretching me open wider, even though I was already so ready for him. My arousal and the remnants of his cum on his cock ease his way in, and his jaw goes tight.

"Fuck," Vic gasps out. "You feel so fucking good, butterfly. You're so... so tight. So hot and wet and perfect inside."

I swallow hard, my legs wrapping around his waist as my body adjusts to him.

"You feel good too," I whisper breathlessly. "It's like I can feel you everywhere."

He stares down at me, and there's a look of wonder on his face, mixed in with the raw desire. I gaze right back, tears burning the backs of my eyes at the feel of being so connected with him after all this time. It's like something is slotting into place. Something finally there that was always meant to be.

At first, his strokes are measured and slow, a little clumsy. He's never done this before, and it shows a bit, but honestly, it doesn't matter. I meant it when I said there was nothing he could do that would disappoint me. His cock moves in and out of me, and every push and pull makes my body sing with pleasure.

He's so thick and hard, and every time he pulls out, the velvety skin of his shaft drags along my sensitive walls, sending sparks dancing through me. My wrists twist uselessly in the ropes that still bind them, and I lift my hips when I can, meeting his thrusts as we start to find our rhythm.

That look of wonder doesn't fade from his face. If anything, it just gets stronger as we keep going.

The pleasure and the pace start to build as Vic gets more used to things, and the natural instinct of his body starts to take over. His hands are tight on my hips, holding me in place, and he fucks me like there's nothing else in the world that matters.

Like our bodies were made for this.

He stares down at the place where we're joined, watching as his cock plunges into my pussy over and over again.

"Mine," he murmurs again, so low that I don't even know if he realizes he spoke it aloud.

My fingers curl into fists, like I need something to hold on to, and my palms tingle with the desire to touch him. Being tied up served a purpose, letting him choose how he wanted this to go, but we're over that hurdle now, and I want to be able to run my hands over his skin in return.

"Will you untie me?" I beg him, tugging at the ropes. "I wanna touch you. I wanna hold you while you fuck me, Vic, please."

He groans and stops for long enough to do as I ask, releasing me from the bed. My wrists are chafed a little from pulling at the ropes, but I don't even care.

Immediately, my arms wrap around his shoulders, feeling the heat of his skin and the flex of his muscles beneath my palms as he fucks me with everything he has, concentrating on nothing other than our bodies working together.

"I'm gonna come," he whispers finally, his voice strained. His face is only inches from mine, our harsh breaths meeting in the space between us. "You feel too fucking good, I can't—"

His angular features twist into a mask of pleasure, his neck muscles straining. I can't look away, and when I feel him start to swell inside me, I squeeze my inner walls around him. I swear I can feel the heat of his cum as it fills me up, and I pull him closer as I fall apart too.

He crushes his lips against mine, hungry and hard, and the two of us shudder together as pleasure flows between us in an endless loop.

His hips jerk, pressing his cock deeper inside me as the last of his release spills from him, and then he collapses on top of me, gasping for breath.

36

WILLOW

My heart is racing so fast that it's like a hum in my chest, and the room almost seems like it's spinning as I suck in lungfuls of air.

I cling to Vic, and it's such a wonderful novelty to be able to do that. I love the way he's melted against me, holding no part of himself back. He's a heavy weight, molded against my body, our sweat and his cum drying against our skin.

When I glance over toward the door, I realize with a start that the room is empty now except for us. At some point, Malice and Ransom must have left, letting us have this moment to ourselves.

They must've known we needed it.

I bite my lip, blinking back the rush of emotion that hits me with that thought.

I never saw this coming. The girl I once was would never have been able to imagine falling for any of the Voronin brothers, let alone all three of them. She never could've imagined being shared by them, and I think this thing between us took them by surprise too.

But I'm glad it worked out this way. I'm glad they didn't get jealous or angry toward each other, and I'm glad they never made me choose between them.

The bond between all three of them is so strong, and I love that Malice and Ransom look out for Vic. That they care about him enough to give him this.

Several long minutes tick by, and although I'd be perfectly content to stay like this forever, Vic gets too heavy after a while, cutting off my circulation, so I squirm under him.

He doesn't pull out, but he does roll us a little so we're both on our sides, facing each other on the bed. His softening cock is still mostly inside me, and I like the feeling of still being connected to him.

He must like it too, because he stays close, his face buried against my neck. I stroke his sweat-dampened hair and let my eyes drift shut, soaking up the feeling.

"I've been wanting to do that for so long," I tell him softly.

"I have too," he replies.

He sounds almost like he's in a daze, but not the same way he was after we left the diner. Not as blank and robotic as he was then, when he was trying to lock all of his raging emotions into a tiny box and bury it inside himself.

I rub one hand up and down his back, smiling.

"I've had fantasies about you, you know," I say. "About all the things I wanted you to do to me. I couldn't have imagined how good the real thing would be, though."

He hums against my skin, and it's silent for a second before he murmurs, "Back when we first met you, I... stole a pair of your panties. And then I jerked off with them."

My jaw drops in surprise. Part of me is shocked, because that seems incredibly out of character for Vic, but the more I think about it, the more it makes sense. And I can't even bring myself to be mad, because it's kind of hot. He wanted me, all that time ago, when I was so sure that he hated me. The attraction went both ways, and that's good to know.

"Huh," I say, my voice light and teasing. "Well, next time you get the urge to do something like that, you should let me watch. Maybe I'll even pick out the pair of panties I want you to use."

He groans and leans up to kiss me, taking his time with it. His mouth is hot and soft against mine, and he kisses me like he's never going to get enough of this. Like even after everything we just did, he's still starving for me.

I kiss him back, reveling in the feeling.

Eventually, his cock slips out of me, finally softened and resting on my inner thigh.

"I've never felt anything like that before," Vic admits after a while. "It was like I had no control, but it wasn't bad."

"Yeah?"

He nods. "Usually, being out of control is... terrifying. I don't know what I'll do or what will happen. I can't predict anything. But this... I knew you were with me."

"I'm always with you," I tell him. "Always. And I'm glad we did it. I'm glad you trusted me. That you trusted *yourself*."

He nods again, then huffs a quiet laugh. "I'm not a virgin anymore. I was so sure that was never going to change."

"Are you going to miss it?" I ask, pulling back a little to grin at him.

He snorts. "No. It wasn't a point of pride or anything. There was just no one I wanted before you. I didn't see the point in fucking someone just to do it. Just for some rite of passage. Until you came along, I was perfectly happy to jerk off on my designated days, just to take care of my body's needs. I would get pent up, and then I'd take care of it. I can't even say that I really enjoyed it."

Something about that makes me feel sad, but it's not pity. Vic built his life the way he did because he needed to. Because he didn't want certain things the same way Ransom and Malice did.

"But it's different now?" I ask.

"*Everything* is different now," he murmurs. "It still scares me sometimes, and overwhelms me a lot of the time, but... I think I'd rather feel things than not feel them. Especially when it comes to you."

"Thank you," I whisper.

"For what?"

"For letting me in like that. For opening yourself up to me this way. I know it wasn't easy."

Vic is quiet for a moment, and he turns his face more into my neck, almost like he's trying to hide a bit. It's adorable that a man who's so skilled and dangerous—a man who's literally killed for me—can also be so shy about some things.

My heart swells in my chest, aching pleasantly.

"It wasn't because I didn't trust you." His voice is a low rumble against my skin. "At least not after things changed between us. I wanted you. I wanted you even when I wished I didn't. It was like no matter how much I told myself that you were a bad idea and that I needed to keep my distance, I craved you anyway. But I didn't think I could have you, and... I worried that I would be a disappointment."

"In what way?" I ask, frowning.

He shifts a little against me. "Every way? I don't know. Mostly in bed. Compared to my brothers, I have no experience. And I saw first-hand how good they made you feel. How they opened you up and showed you how things could be. I didn't think I could measure up to that."

I grin, taking one of his hands and dragging it down my cum covered chest and stomach to my pussy. More of his cum is leaking out, mixing with the wetness of my arousal, and I let his fingers drag through the mess.

"Are you kidding me? Does this feel like me being disappointed? It was amazing, Vic. I've never experienced anything like that before. Feeling you mark me this way turned me on so much."

There's a sharp intake of breath, and Vic's nostrils flare as he lifts his head. When I let go of his hand, he doesn't pull away.

Instead, he presses his fingers inside me, slipping two right into my pussy.

I moan, squirming against him. My body responds immediately, although not as strongly as it did the first time he touched me like this. I'm worn out from the marathon before, even though I can feel my clit pulsing with a distant sort of need.

He starts fucking me gently with his fingers, and I can hear how wet the slide is, the mess of our combined arousal squishing in and out of me as he moves his fingers faster.

"Vic," I whine softly, pushing my hips closer even as exhaustion weighs me down. "I don't think I can come again. I'm spent."

He leans in and kisses me, heat searing through me as his mouth moves against mine. When he pulls back, his blue eyes are intent, and he doesn't look away for a second.

Watching me. Always watching.

"One more," he whispers. "For me. Give me one more, butterfly."

Something about the way he says it, the soft plea in his voice, makes me determined to do what he wants. My breath hitches and my heart stammers in my chest as I reach down to grip his forearm, rolling my hips as I ride his hand.

He adds another finger, thrusting all three of them as deep into me as they can go, and I let the waves of pleasure sweep me up.

His thumb finds my clit, toying with it lightly, rubbing in small circles that send jolts of sensation shooting through my belly. It's enough to make me catch my breath sharply, and when my orgasm hits, it almost takes me by surprise.

I clench around his fingers, gripping his arm and moaning his name, and when I come this time, it really is the last one I have in me. I flop against the bed, letting the aftershocks work their way through me, breathing hard, already half out of it.

He drags his fingers out of me, and I catch his forearm, forcing my eyes open so that I can meet his gaze.

"Will you stay?" I ask, a note of uncertainty creeping into my voice. It feels like something monumental has shifted between us, but I know that not everything can change in a single day.

In answer though, Vic gathers me in his arms, pulling me close.

He kisses the tangled strands of my hair, and when my eyelids drift shut, they stay that way. The last thing I hear as I fall asleep is him whispering in my ear, although I'm too tired to make out the words.

37

WILLOW

It's late at night when I wake up again, sticky with the remnants of sweat and Vic's cum on my skin. I lie on the soft sheets for a while, soaking up the quiet and savoring the feeling of Vic's breathing against my skin, basking in his closeness.

After several minutes, my stomach growls, and I realize that although I grabbed a bite at the diner, I haven't really eaten much at all today. I'm not going to be able to go back to sleep like this, so I pull myself up, careful not to wake Vic.

I'm surprised he's sleeping so deeply, but he's probably worn out from all the sex.

I slip into the bathroom and hop into the shower quickly to clean myself up. Part of me is sad to get rid of the evidence of what we did, but I can still feel the phantom pressure of Vic's hands on me, and I remind myself that there will hopefully be lots of chances for us to repeat what we did.

Vic's shirt is on the floor from where he threw it earlier, and I pull it on and then leave the bedroom, closing the door behind me.

At first, I think I'm the only one awake because the house is so quiet, but as I enter the kitchen, I notice Malice sitting at the table, carving off slices of an apple with a pocket knife.

"Hey," I whisper quietly. "I didn't know you were up."

He raises a brow and bites off a piece of apple. "I thought you'd be dead to the world until morning."

"I got hungry. Otherwise I probably would be."

"Sit," Malice says and then gets up, moving over to the box of food we brought in with us.

I take his seat since he's being all bossy, and he gives me a look as he brings over some cookies and a fruit cup, setting them out on the table for me.

I kick out one of the other chairs for him, and he takes it, watching me as I start to eat. I can tell there's something he wants to say, probably related to what happened in the bedroom earlier. It hangs in the air between us, but I don't poke at it, just eating pieces of pear and pineapple, licking the juice from my fingers.

"You're okay, right?" he asks finally. "After…"

I nod, not needing him to finish that sentence. "Yeah. More than okay. And thank you. For being there and then for giving us that moment alone."

Malice nods, gaze intense. "Seemed like you guys needed it."

"Which part?"

"All of it."

I can't argue with that. After what happened in that diner earlier today, things had reached a boiling point between us, and something had to give. It wasn't planned at all, but I'm glad it happened.

At first, I think that's going to be the end of it, but Malice surprises me by continuing on.

"You know, Vic's always been kinda… different, I guess. Even before our dad started fucking him up, he kind of held himself apart. He was quiet. Fierce, but quiet. So I worried about him. Then that piece of shit got his hands on him, and it just made everything worse."

"He told me a little about it," I say. "What your dad did, how it affected him."

Malice nods again. "When we killed him, our dad, it was

mostly for our mom and all the shit he put her through, but part of it was for Vic too. At least on my end. He never deserved any of that, and our dad was just doing it because he was a selfish waste of space who thought he could mold his sons into the perfect soldiers and build a name for himself in the criminal underworld. Now Vic has to deal with the fallout of that forever."

"None of you should have had to go through that," I say, meaning every word of it.

"Yeah, but especially not Vic. I just... I dunno. I was always worried he was never going to find anyone. Find love or whatever. I didn't even know if I believed in that shit for myself, but at least I had an outlet, you know? If I wanted to fuck, I could fuck. Ransom knows how to get along with people, so he was always going to find someone, but I thought Vic was always gonna be stuck behind a computer screen."

It's interesting, listening to Malice talk like this. I've always known the three of them are a unit, brothers who have each other's backs and would do anything for each other. But there's something about how Malice talks now that shows just how deep his love for Vic runs.

"I think... he would have said that was what he wanted," I murmur. "To just be alone with his screens."

"Yeah." Malice runs a hand over the stubble on his jaw. "But would it have been the truth? I guess I would have thought so before you came along. Vic always needed someone who was gonna be patient with him and understand where he was coming from."

"I didn't want to force him into anything. I mean, I know I pressed the issue today, but that seemed like... I don't know. I felt like he needed the release at that point."

"I think you're right." He nods. "And I think it's gonna be good for him in the long run. So thanks. For being so patient, and for knowing when to push."

I clear my throat as a lump of emotion settles there. "Of course. I've always cared about Vic, and that's not going to change."

Malice's expression turns intense. His eyes seem to bore into me, and I don't look away as he reaches out, gripping my chin and tipping my face up.

"The way we feel about you won't change either, Solnyshka," he says, his voice low. "You're our endgame. Nothing else matters."

My heart flutters, my stomach swooping down and then back up again like I'm on a rollercoaster. His lips quirk into a little smile, and just when I think he's about to kiss me, he lets me go and stands up instead.

"Wait here," he says.

I frown, watching as he leaves the kitchen, heading for the living room where he's left some of his stuff. When he comes back, he has his tattoo gun and supplies with him.

A quiet laugh bursts out of me, and I shake my head. "You left your whole lives behind, and you brought that with you?"

He shrugs. "Of course. What else do I need? As long as I've got this, my brothers, and you, I'm good. And it's a good thing I brought it, because I wanna give you another tattoo. Seems like it's about time."

My stomach flutters. He added to the first one already, but I like the idea of getting more. People always say that tattoos are addictive, and I understand that now. Or maybe it's just Malice who's addictive. Maybe it's about the feeling of his attention and concentration on me, watching him do something so skillfully, feeling him mark me permanently.

I nod, biting my lower lip. "Okay, yeah. Let's do it."

"Good. Come on."

Malice grins and jerks his head toward the living room. I follow him into the room, where he switches on a lamp and sets out his equipment.

"Strip," he commands, standing back and watching expectantly.

It's easy, considering all I'm wearing is Vic's shirt, and I take it off, leaving myself bare for Malice. He watches me, his eyes raking over my skin for a long moment before he points to the couch.

"Lie down on your stomach."

"Yes, sir," I mumble under my breath, and he snorts with amusement.

I make myself comfortable on the couch, resting my cheek on the cushion and watching as Malice strides over.

He kneels on the floor next to me, grabbing my arm and arranging it so that it drapes off the couch. I wait while he studies my skin like he's picturing a million different designs he could put on my body, and he mutters to himself a little before nodding. Then he picks up the tattoo gun and gets to work.

This time, he's working on my shoulder. It feels different than when he tattooed my chest, but there's still a burning bite that comes from the needle moving against my skin. I'm more used to it now though, and it doesn't shock me the way it did the first time.

I breathe through it, keeping my body relaxed.

The hum of the machine is loud in my ear, and I want to crane my neck to see what Malice is putting on me, but I stay put, letting him work.

"Shoulda woken Ransom up," he murmurs after a while, not taking his eyes off his work. He grabs a rag and wipes away some ink before getting back to it.

"Hm?" I ask.

"So he could distract you from the pain like that first time. When he touched you. Although..." Malice grins, his eyes darting up for a second. "The second time, you just touched yourself."

I smile back, replaying both memories in my mind. Warmth crawls through my limbs from the recollections of those two different nights.

"I needed it then," I whisper. "But not this time. I can handle it. In fact... I kind of like the pain now."

"Fuck," Malice mutters. "*Ty vygljadish' takoj nevinnoj, a potom govorish' takie veshhi. Ty svodish' menya s uma.*"

He glances up at me again, just long enough for me to see the heat curling through his eyes. I lick my lips, trying not to squirm from how much my body likes that look on him.

"You were so fucking gorgeous that first time," he continues. "Letting me mark you up, taking the pain even though it must have hurt like hell for a first-timer."

"I wanted... I wanted it," I manage to tell him, breathing a little harder now.

"I put my lucky number on you, and that was the night I knew I'd never find another woman who could match us as well as you could."

It's not the first time he's said something like that, and the conviction in his voice hits me hard. Malice is like a force of nature, dominant and gruff and protective, but when he makes declarations like that, something inside me goes all warm and gooey.

He keeps the needle moving over my skin, and as the buzz of the tattoo gun fills the quiet air, I realize I'm getting turned on. No one is touching me this time, except for Malice's hand on me, keeping me still and occasionally adjusting my position, and the needle on my skin—but that doesn't matter.

At this point, it's like a Pavlovian response. This kind of pain *is* pleasure to me now, and I whimper softly, squeezing my thighs together.

Of course, Malice doesn't miss it.

"What are you doing, Solnyshka?" he asks. "Are you rubbing your pretty little legs together, trying to get off?"

"I..." My mouth is suddenly dry, but we both know the answer to his question is a resounding yes.

"Fuck," he groans. "You're getting worked up just from this, aren't you? Just from the tattoo. No one touching you, nothing inside you. Just the needle on your skin. That's so fucking hot." He shakes his head. "I bet if you didn't have to stay still right now, you'd be humping the couch like a desperate little slut, wouldn't you? Or you'd have a hand between your legs, trying to get your fingers deep inside your wet pussy. Even after that fucking Vic gave you earlier, you're still not satisfied."

I whimper again, his words going straight to my head and to my core. I clench around nothing, and I really do wish I could work one hand down there and touch myself.

"Be still," Malice commands, as if he can sense where my thoughts are going. "I'm doing a more intricate design this time, and I don't wanna fuck up your tattoo."

He shades in something on my shoulder, the needle dragging over the same place for so long that it starts to ache. But instead of tamping down my arousal, the slow burn of pain just makes me wetter.

And Malice notices that too.

I whine softly, my inner walls clenching as my clit throbs. He doesn't stop tattooing, and I lose myself in the buzz of the gun, trying to be still as he keeps etching the design onto my skin.

He goes over a line, and the pain rises, almost more than I can stand. The need in my body rises with it, tightening and tensing, and just when I think I might be able to come like this, Malice pulls the gun back.

He wipes ink away, and I don't have to look at him to know that he's probably grinning, amused at teasing me this way.

Before I have time to catch my breath, he's back at it, going in with the gun again.

He repeats that process over and over again, bringing me higher and higher and then leaving me there on the edge. He's basically edging me, working me up more and more and not giving me any relief.

My body burns from the pain and from the arousal, and my heart is slamming against my ribs by now. I'm on the verge of begging, so close to release that I can almost taste it.

"Do you want to come, Solnyshka?" Malice asks mildly, his voice a low rumble.

"Yes!" I gasp.

"Then be a good girl and wait for it."

The needle digs into my skin again, and I bite down hard on my lower lip. He keeps working, and I can't even tell which part of my shoulder the needle is dragging across anymore. It's all one endless wash of sensation, punctuated by my shuddering breaths and Malice's occasional grunts.

"That's it," he murmurs. "Just a bit longer now."

The next several minutes pass in a haze of pain and arousal, and when he wipes the tattoo down one last time, he presses a bit harder than necessary, making me moan out loud.

"Such a good fucking girl," he praises. "Come for me. Now."

Before he even finishes speaking, my hand delves between my legs. I rub my clit furiously, grinding against my hand, and it only takes a second for the pleasure to spill over. My orgasm hits me hard, and I trap my lip between my teeth, trying not to wake up Ransom and Vic with my moan.

"Oh my god," I finally murmur, my head still spinning.

Malice pats my ass possessively, then spreads a little ointment on my shoulder. "Is that your new nickname for me?"

That makes me smile into the couch cushion, and I twist my head to look at him. "It would be if I didn't think it would go to your head."

He smirks, his harsh features looking even more angular in the lamplight. "Do you wanna see the tattoo?"

I nod eagerly, pushing myself up enough that I can swing my legs over the side of the couch. There's a mirror on the opposite wall, near what's probably a closet door, and I walk over on unsteady legs to see what Malice has put on me this time.

I have no idea what to expect, really, but what I see makes me stop in my tracks. The design is much different than the first two things he put on me, but it's so fucking beautiful. Clusters of wildflowers twine around a knife, the tip of which points down my arm. The flowers seem to pop, each petal rendered in beautiful shades of gray.

"Oh," I breathe, almost reaching up to touch the fresh ink before thinking better of it. "It's gorgeous, Malice."

I meet his eyes in the mirror and realize that he's come to stand behind me.

"It represents you," he tells me. "Soft and beautiful, but with a spine of fucking steel."

He leads me back to the couch and makes me sit down while he puts a gauze pad over the tattoo, his touch careful and almost tender. Then he scoops me up, making me yelp in surprise.

"Alright. Enough of this shit. It's bedtime," he grunts. "We've got a lot to do tomorrow."

I laugh, because it's very like him to have a sweet moment and then get all bossy. But I don't complain as he carries me to the bedroom where Vic is still sleeping. He settles me into bed next to his brother, and I slip under the covers, curling up with a yawn. Either the sex or the tattoo endorphins—or both—are wearing off now, and I can feel how tired I am all over again.

The bed shifts, and when I look up, Malice is getting in with us, sandwiching me between him and his brother.

"Sweet dreams, Solnyshka," he murmurs gruffly.

And despite everything, I think maybe they will be for once.

38

VICTOR

Usually, I have an alarm that wakes me up promptly at the designated time. Sometimes I even wake up before my alarm, my brain churning through a to do list or solving a problem that's been eating at me.

This morning, it's not an alarm that wakes me, but the sound of a familiar voice scoffing.

When I open my eyes, Ransom is standing on my side of the bed, his hands crossed over his chest. He stares down at me, and judging from the warm weight at my back, at Willow as well.

"Huh. I see how it is," he drawls, shaking his head. "Malice and I left you and Willow alone last night, and now I find all three of you in bed together? And no one thought to invite me to this little slumber party? I can't believe it. Betrayed by my own flesh and blood."

"For fuck's sake, Ransom," I mutter, stretching under the covers.

"Shut the fuck up," Malice grumbles, and a pillow goes sailing over the bed to hit Ransom right in the face.

He laughs, unbothered. "I don't blame Willow, of course. She just got swept along in all of this. I bet she would have woken me up and invited me."

"Mm-hm," Willow murmurs, still sounding half asleep. "I definitely would have. Malice carried me in here, and I didn't have a choice. Blame him."

"Oh, I always do," Ransom replies. "That's my motto for life, actually. When in doubt, blame Malice."

As my twin grunts something obscene about Ransom and rolls out of bed, I turn over so that I can see Willow's face. She's very close, and she looks so fucking beautiful with her hair messy from sleep and her eyes half closed. I search her face, trying to see if there's any regret there. If she has any doubts about what happened yesterday.

I remember her seeming happy before we fell asleep, but sometimes things change. Maybe she slept on it and realized it wasn't what she wants. That I'm not what she wants.

But when she meets my gaze, her brown eyes are soft and clear. A smile spreads across her face, slow and tender, and it's like the sun coming out from behind the clouds, warming me as I watch.

"Morning," she whispers, and she sounds unbelievably pleased to be waking up with me like this. It soothes the worst of my worries, and I swallow hard.

"Good morning, butterfly," I manage to rasp back.

Willow leans in like she's going to kiss me, but then she hesitates. She still seems unsure of the boundaries between us, so I take the lead for once, closing the distance and pressing my lips to hers.

My body reacts immediately, my cock stiffening. But even though it feels like an electric current is passing through me, it's not overloading my system the same way it used to. It still feels good, but pleasure isn't trying to strangle me anymore.

"I like this," she says softly as our lips part. "Being close to you. Touching you like this. I like it so much."

I nod, my throat dry. "Me too."

It feels inadequate, like there should be more to say somehow, but I don't even know where to start.

"Okay, enough lying around," Malice says, cutting into the moment. "We need to get moving."

Willow sighs softly but pulls away from me. As soon as she turns, Ransom slides into the place where Malice was and takes his own good morning kiss, threading his fingers through her hair as he pulls her close.

"Jesus fucking Christ. I said get *out* of bed, not get *into* it," Malice grunts as he heads for the bedroom door. "We're leaving in half an hour."

"Letting him think he's in charge was our biggest mistake," Ransom mutters with a sigh.

Willow chuckles softly, and we all climb off of the too-small bed. I grab some clothes, my toothbrush, and my personal tube of toothpaste from the bag I packed and then head into the bathroom to wash up and get dressed.

Part of me expects my obsession with Willow to be more of a distraction now, making it hard for me to focus on anything else now that I know what it feels like to kiss her and touch her and fuck her.

But it's almost the opposite.

It's as if now that I know those things, now that I'm not holding myself back anymore, it's easier to focus past the inner struggle that used to tear me up inside. My awareness of her has changed, the desire I always feel when I'm around her shifting to a constant steady drip instead of a torrent.

Once I've grabbed a quick breakfast, I check my computer for any messages from X, but the inbox is empty. That doesn't necessarily mean anything one way or the other. She definitely hasn't given up, not that easily. She'll still be searching for us, and that means we have to get away from this area quickly.

We're pretty far from the small town where we robbed the convenience store, but it will be good to get even farther.

Thinking about the robbery leads me to thinking about the diner. That shouldn't have happened, not if we were going to try to avoid being noticed. I'm usually much more rational and level-headed, able to think past my feelings and act strategically.

But then again, this isn't the first time I've acted before thinking when Willow was threatened. I killed Carl all those weeks ago in her old apartment, and I still remember the flash of rage I felt when I saw him trying to blackmail her.

He put his hands on her, so I killed him.

And I'm not sorry about it, just like I can't bring myself to be sorry for stabbing that trucker. I'm finally starting to accept that I'll *never* be rational and logical where Willow is concerned, and letting go of the need to try to be unclenches something in my chest.

She's my beautiful chaos. My butterfly.

And if she brings out a bit of chaos in me too, maybe that's okay.

Shaking my head to clear it, I close my laptop and gather the rest of the equipment I've got set up. Then I head out to where Malice and Ransom are loading up the car, pushing them both out of the way so that I can take over.

"Why do we even bother?" Ransom mutters.

"I have no idea," I deadpan.

Willow comes out with the food box, and Malice ducks back into the house to do one last check. The three of us get in the car while Malice handles spreading the accelerant and lighting it up, and we stay just long enough to make sure the place catches and starts to burn before we head out.

We keep driving, and I handle the navigation, back in my usual role. We're heading for a major city this time, rather than the out of the way spots we've been stopping at so far.

"Is that dangerous?" Willow asks when I mention our destination.

"We need to find someone who can make us fake IDs," Malice tells her.

"And good ones," I add. "We won't find that in a small town."

"Hopefully it'll be a big enough city for us to slip in unnoticed," Ransom says. "But we gotta take the risk if we're going to make this work."

Despite the tinge of worry in Willow's voice, the atmosphere in the car is much lighter than it has been before, and I focus on my computer, plotting our route and digging up information about who we can meet with when we reach our destination.

Even as I work, the awareness of Willow is always there, in the back of my mind. She jokes and laughs with Ransom in the back, the two of them playing some car game that seems to involve trying to think up the name of an animal that starts with the first letter of the first sign they see.

"Exits don't count," Willow complains at one point. "How many E animals are there, even?"

"Elephant, eagle, eel," Ransom says. "Uh... okay, that's all I got."

"Echidna," I throw in, not looking away from my screen.

"What?" My brother scoffs. "That's not a real thing."

"It is, actually," Willow responds before I can. I turn in my seat to smile at her, and she grins back.

"Just because you don't know what it is, doesn't mean it's not a real thing," I tell Ransom. "And if we were to get started on *that* list, we might be here for a while."

He flips me off as Willow and even Malice burst out laughing at my comment, and my lips twitch into a grin as I get back to work.

When we reach Oklahoma City, the first thing we do is stop for some real food, at Ransom's insistence. We've been mostly living out of our food box, supplementing it with whatever we could get easily while on the road, so it's been a while since any of us had an actual cooked meal.

We find a food truck parked on a street corner, and Ransom takes Willow with him, returning with two plastic bags loaded full of tacos and chips.

"Finally. A real fucking dinner," he groans as we eat.

Willow moans in agreement as she takes a bite of one of the

tacos, and the sound goes right to my cock. Memories of touching her and tasting her—of *fucking* her—fill my head for a moment, and I drag in a breath, tapping out a ten-count on my thigh as I ride out the sudden surge of emotions. It's easier to handle them than it used to be, but it's still a bit overwhelming sometimes.

Once we finish the food and throw away the empty bags, Malice starts the car again.

"You know where we're going?" he asks me.

"Not exactly," I tell him. "But I can get us to an area where we should be able to find what we need. We'll just have to ask around a bit."

I spent a good portion of the drive doing research on the city, and there's an area where criminal activity is definitely higher, so I guide Malice there.

There's a grungy looking dive bar on one block, and I point to it, recognizing the name. "Let's try that one."

The sky is a dusky blue as we park and get out of the car, the streetlamps that haven't burned out or been shot out flickering to life above us. Malice and I flank Willow, Ransom sticking close by as he brings up the rear. There are a few neon signs in the window, and the music is loud enough that I can hear it as we approach the bar.

It's as run down inside as it is outside, and I make a face when my shoes stick to the floor as soon as we walk in. The tables look like they haven't been thoroughly cleaned in months, if ever, and the people lounging at tables or clustered around the pool table in the back don't look much better.

I position myself so I'm not touching anything, mentally cataloging all the ways I would disinfect this place if I could, just to recenter myself a bit.

Willow, Ransom, and I hang back, letting Malice take point. In normal conversations, he's not the best with people, but he knows how to converse with shady types to get what he wants. He gives off an aura that makes it clear he's not fucking around, which is useful in these types of situations.

We watch as he walks up to the bar, leaning against it casually. He orders a drink and strikes up a conversation with the bartender, a short woman covered in tattoos herself.

She eyes him with a hungry look, and I feel Willow bristle a little at my side. Ransom laughs and runs a placating hand down her arm.

"It's just business," he murmurs. "He isn't interested in her. Trust me."

Willow nods, although she's still glaring daggers at the woman. "Right. I know. Fuck, I've been hanging out with Malice too much. His jealousy is rubbing off on me."

"Well, I don't think he'd complain about that one bit." Ransom wraps his arm around her, pulling her a little closer against his side. "You're sexy as fuck when you get all possessive."

After a few minutes, Malice slides the bartender a crisp bill and then comes back over to us.

"Got a lead," he says. "She wouldn't say anything specific, but there's a guy who deals in 'documents' down the block a little way. She said we could drop her name if we have any trouble."

"And what did you tell her?" I ask him. "About why you were asking?"

Malice shrugs. "The bare minimum. You know these types don't ask that many questions. She probably didn't give a shit one way or another, and it's clear we're not narcs."

That's true enough. I nod. "Alright. Let's go."

We turn toward the door, but before we can leave, it bursts open. Two cops come striding inside, walking with purpose.

They stop in the middle of the bar, glancing around quickly, and my entire body goes on high alert. Ransom sucks in a breath as Malice goes tense beside me. I clench my jaw, moving to stand in front of Willow, wanting to hide her from their view.

The police officers are both burly and tall, one of them nearly as big as Malice. He's got a short buzz cut and a thick neck, and the man beside him is slightly thinner, with a neatly trimmed beard. After only a slight hesitation, they start moving again, making a beeline toward a table near the back where three guys who look to be in their early twenties are sitting.

"Jacob Beeler? You're under arrest for possession of an illegal firearm, and for possession of a controlled substance with intent to distribute," the cop with the beard says. "Get up."

The man named Jacob stares up at the two police officers for a second, his face hard. He glances at his two companions, then rises slowly from his chair, anger flashing through his eyes.

"That's fucking bullshit, man," one of his friends spits out. "It wasn't him."

"Shut up," the taller cop snaps, grabbing Jacob by the arm and pulling a pair of cuffs from his belt. He snaps them on with a metallic *snick*. "You have the right to remain silent. Anything you say can and will be used against you..."

The conversation in the bar has died out, and even the music is lower now, everyone hunkering down at their tables as they watch the arrest take place.

The bearded cop is standing off to the side a little, and as his partner reads Jacob his rights, he scans the bar again—but this time, his gaze doesn't skip over us. He pauses as he looks toward our little group, his brows drawing together a little.

Malice nudges me subtly with his elbow, and I glance sideways at him. He tips his head toward the front of the bar and then looks at Ransom, who nods slightly, picking up the silent thought that echoes between all of us.

We need to get the fuck out of here. Now.

Ransom starts moving first, walking casually toward the door. I push Willow to follow, and then I start moving myself, with Malice close behind me. Although I don't look his way, I can feel the bearded cop's gaze tracking us.

"Wait a second," he calls suddenly. "Stop."

He steps forward into Malice's path, cutting him off. Malice stiffens, glancing at me over the cops shoulder.

"I know you." The bearded police officer steps closer to Malice, his hand moving toward his service belt. "There's a warrant out for your arrest."

I inhale sharply. *Fuck.*

If this was about the diner, or the convenience store we robbed, then it would be either me or all three of us being questioned right now. But Malice is the only one the cop recognized, which means this has to be Olivia's doing.

Apparently, she hasn't reported all of us to the authorities for the illegal things we did for X yet. She's probably saving that as her trump card, especially since she'll have to be careful not to implicate herself as well if she goes that route. But whatever strings her dead husband pulled to get Malice out of prison early, she's clearly gone back on that deal.

And now there's a warrant out for his arrest.

39

WILLOW

"Put your hands behind your back," the cop tells Malice, and my pulse jumps.

Malice hesitates, his jaw clenching. His gaze darts past the officer toward me and his brothers, locking eyes with Vic for a heartbeat. Then he shifts his attention to the man in front of him again and slowly starts to turn around, overlapping his wrists behind his back.

Some kind of silent communication seemed to happen between the twins in that look they shared, and I wait for Vic to do something—to execute whatever plan they were making in that wordless way they have.

But then Vic's hand closes around my upper arm, and he starts tugging me toward the door again. My eyes go wide, my feet sticking to the floor a little as I dig my heels in.

"Wait," I hiss, glancing between Ransom and Vic. "What are you doing? Where are we going?"

"We have to go, butterfly," Vic murmurs, his voice tight. "Malice gave us the signal: run."

What? I shake my head, panic rising up in me like a tsunami. *No. That doesn't make sense. We can't do that.*

"We'll figure something out," Ransom whispers, worry glinting in his eyes. "We won't abandon him, I promise."

But what are we supposed to 'figure out' if Malice is hauled off to jail? Are we supposed to run in there, guns blazing, and bust him out? The idea of him being locked up makes my stomach twist into a knot, and I don't see how the three of us could possibly pull off a jailbreak.

We can't let this happen. We can't let him be taken away.

Behind us, the cop who stopped Malice clicks a set of handcuffs onto his wrists, and his partner glances over at him.

"You good?" his partner calls, gripping Jacob Beeler's upper arm.

"Yeah." The bearded cop nods. "Got a parole violator here. He's wanted across state lines."

"Must be our lucky fuckin' night."

His partner grins, and Jacob's friends glare up at him from where they're still seated at the table. They look tense and furious, and one of them licks his lips and spits on the floor.

"Hey, cut that shit out," the cop holding Jacob warns.

Vic tugs on my arm again, pulling me toward the door. When I glance up at him, the look on his face fills me with dread. He's normally so calm, his features almost expressionless sometimes. I've learned how to read him better, and lately, he's allowed more of his emotions to show on his face, even smiling from time to time.

He's not smiling now though. He looks grim, his jaw set tight as his blue eye churn with fear and a flicker of self-doubt.

Normally, Vic has a plan, but it's clear he doesn't have one now.

He knows this is a bad idea.

That thought sparks something inside me, and I move without thinking. Yanking my arm out of his grip, I dart out from between him and Ransom. There's an empty metal tray on a nearby table, and I pick it up and hurl it as hard as I can toward the wall behind the bar. It hits the long shelf loaded full of liquor bottles, shattering two bottles with a loud crash.

The noise draw's both cops' attention for just a split second—but that's all it takes.

The guy who spit at the cop surges to his feet, knocking over the table as he pulls something from the back of his waistband.

"Gun!" the cop yells, releasing his hold on Jacob and lunging forward to try to disarm the man.

At the same moment, Malice slams his head back, connecting with the taller cop's face and making him reel back. A shot rings out, and more yells rise up in the bar, but I don't even know who fired.

Malice doesn't even look toward the altercation on the other side of the room. He wheels around and charges, barreling into the officer who was standing behind him. He plows his shoulder into the cop's solar plexus, sending him staggering backward before he can recover from the blow to the face.

A brawl is breaking out between the other cop and Jacob's friends, so there's no one left to stop Malice as he sprints toward us. Ransom grabs my arm in a vise-like grip as Victor shoves open the door, and Malice is right behind us as we spill out onto the sidewalk.

Another gunshot rings out inside the bar, and I can hear someone yelling, "Backup! We need backup!"

"Go!" Malice barks, and we dash toward the car, heads down.

I'm running so fast that my hands smack against the smooth metal siding of the car when we reach it, and Victor grabs the keys from Malice's pocket to unlock it. I open the back door and throw myself inside, sliding across the seat to make room for Malice, who dives into the car with his hands still bound behind his back.

Vic gets behind the wheel, and as I reach over Malice to close the back door, I can hear the telltale howl of sirens in the distance.

Backup is already on the way.

The engine roars to life as several more people burst out of the bar. I can't quite tell who they are in the dim light of the street, whether they're cops or patrons, and we don't stick around to find out. Vic peels away from the curb, driving like a machine.

The way he navigates us down the street is so different from how Malice does it. He's all precision and speed, taking each turn as fast as possible, but somehow not throwing us around in the car. Ransom is in the passenger seat giving him directions, playing the role of navigator like Vic usually does.

Malice straightens up on the seat beside me, grunting as he wrestles with the cuffs. He glances out the back window, his dark eyes glinting under the passing streetlights.

"We've got a fucking tail," he growls. "They're a ways back, though. We've got a few blocks on 'em. Floor it, Vic."

The sirens behind us get louder, their wails rising in the air, and Vic speeds up, weaving around cars as he checks the rearview. He takes each twist and turn that Ransom tells him to, and after a while, I can't see the blue and red lights behind us anymore, although I can still hear the sirens.

"Up there. Left, left, left!" Ransom says urgently. "Pull into that alley. Kill the lights."

Vic does, veering into an alley that's just barely wide enough for our car. Panic flashes through me at how boxed in we are, but he doesn't question his brother's judgement as he switches off the headlights and drives deeper into the dark alley, stopping when it dead ends in a brick wall and killing the engine.

Just about a minute later, several cop cars go screaming by, lights flashing.

We wait a few seconds, then a minute more, and when they don't come back, I slump against the seat, blowing out a shaky breath.

It feels too soon to say we're in the clear, but at least I can't hear sirens anymore.

"What the *fuck* were you thinking?"

The sudden boom of Malice's voice jerks me out of my

thoughts. He turns to face me, and it's so dark in the alley that his features are cast in deep shadows, making the anger on his face even more apparent.

"Do you have any idea how badly that could have gone down?" he demands, somehow managing to get right up in my face even though he's still constrained by the handcuffs. "I gave Vic the signal to run. You were supposed to get the fuck out of there. Not start a goddamned brawl!"

"And leave you behind?" I narrow my eyes. "No."

"For fuck's sake, Solnyshka! You can't keep risking yourself like this. That cop only wanted me, but they'll sure as hell be after all four of us now. Is that what you fucking wanted? Are you happy now?"

My hands are still shaking from the fear and adrenaline of everything that happened in the last fifteen or twenty minutes, so I let them ball into fists. I don't back down from Malice though, glaring right back at him.

"I was doing what you said," I tell him stubbornly.

"What are you talking about? I never told you to pull some reckless shit like that."

"You said the only way I could protect you and your brothers is by staying by your side. By staying where I belong." I hold his gaze, lifting my chin and letting him see the defiance in my eyes. "So that's what I'm gonna do. I'm not running, and I'm not letting you split us up. I don't care about your secret signals. Vic knew it was a bad idea too, I could see it in his eyes. We have to stay together."

"Not if the rest of you—"

"No!" I cut him off, my heart pounding. Yanking the neckline of my shirt aside, I gesture to the still healing tattoo he put on my shoulder. It's still bright and shiny from the fresh ink, the skin a little tender. "Is this really how you see me? Because if it is, then you don't get to pick and choose when you like this quality about me or not."

Malice goes still, blinking as he stares at the tattoo peeking out from my shirt. His nostrils flare as he breathes hard, and I can see several emotions playing out over his face in the semi-darkness. When he speaks again, his voice is as rough as gravel.

"Ransom. Get these fucking cuffs off me."

Ransom leans around from the front passenger seat, and Malice twists a little on the seat as his younger brother picks the lock on the cuffs, popping them open.

As soon as his hands are free, Malice reaches for me. He grabs the back of my head and hauls me in, dragging me onto his lap and crushing his mouth to mine. It's a rough kiss, even by Malice's standards, almost punishing, his lips and teeth clashing with mine.

When he finally pulls back, his eyes burn, and the hand at the back of my head fists my hair close to the roots, tipping my head up to meet his gaze.

"I love that about you all the time," he says, his voice low. "It's a fucking pain in the ass sometimes, but your fierce spirit is my favorite thing about you, Solnyshka."

My heart stutters in my chest. He didn't say 'I love *you*,' but it's the closest he's ever come to saying it.

I stare at him, my bottom lip trapped between my teeth, forgetting all about where we are and what's going on, until Vic speaks up from the front.

"We should move again," he says. "We need to get out of the city. And I need to get on my computer to make sure to scrub the tracks." He turns his head to look at Malice. "Do you want to drive?"

Malice doesn't look away from me for a second, just shaking his head. "Nah. I'm good right where I am."

Ransom chuckles. "Figures. The only one who can get Malice to give up a chance to drive is Willow."

"Well, one of you has to, because I have work to do," Vic points out. "Unless you'd like to get arrested for real tonight."

"I'll do it," Ransom offers.

He and Vic switch seats quickly, which is slightly awkward

since they can't open the doors, and then he starts the car up, pulling out of the alley. Ransom drives quickly but carefully, making sure to blend in with traffic and avoid any cops as we go.

Now that we're all back together again, I feel a little better, gradually letting the tension in my body bleed out. Malice still has me on his lap, and he pulls me closer with rough hands, shifting me around until I'm where he wants me to be.

He leans in, and his breath tickles my ear as he murmurs, "That little stunt you pulled kept me out of prison. Thank you, Solnyshka."

"You're welcome," I whisper.

His voice drops to a growl as he adds, "But that doesn't mean I'm not gonna punish you for it later."

I lean into his possessive touch and bite back a smile, my heart racing for an entirely different reason now.

40

WILLOW

We drive through the night this time, after a short discussion where we all agree it's probably for the best if we don't stop.

At some point during the night, Malice switches with Ransom, taking over as he navigates the back roads Vic has mapped out for us and giving Ransom a rest. I wake up in the morning with my head on Ransom's shoulder, feeling stiff and sore from being in the car for so long.

When we finally do stop a few hours after that, we pull into an RV park near San Antonio. The guys pay cash to rent one of the RVs, and it's clear this is one of those 'no questions asked' sort of places.

The guy taking their money doesn't give us a second look as he hands over a key and tells us a row number.

"Someone we used to do work for mentioned this place," Ransom explains as we hunt down the RV we'll be staying in. "He was coming back to Detroit with a bunch of stolen goods and didn't want to risk a hotel. Apparently, the guy who runs this place went above and beyond to not notice a damned thing about him."

"Convenient," I agree, nodding. That definitely suits our purposes.

We pile into the RV, which is definitely not a luxury. I think about those home improvement shows I used to watch all the time, and how people with too much money on their hands would buy buses and RVs and have them renovated into trendy little homes.

This is nothing like that.

The appliances are rusty and out of date, and the furniture creaks and sags as we all find different things to flop onto. Besides the bathroom, the rest of the RV is one long room, separated into a tiny kitchenette, a sitting room with mismatched furniture, and a bed that pulls down from the wall.

Ransom groans as he stretches out, cracking his back. "Jesus. I swear I can feel all the vertebrae in my back fusing. Road trips really are the fucking worst."

All of us are stiff and sore from that long drive all night, but being out of the car and having a chance to stretch our legs feels so much better. It was worth it, though, to get us away from the site of that altercation with the cops. Every mile we put between us and the bar in Oklahoma City eased some of the pressure in my chest.

It's too early to relax, especially when we're still on this side of the border, but we're close now, and we just have to keep going.

Malice pulls out a shopping bag and dumps the contents out onto the scratched up coffee table.

"Where did you get all that?" I ask him, eyeing the pile. There's hair dye, makeup, and a few boxes of colored contacts.

"We stopped at a shop on the way here," he says. "Sent Vic in while you were sleeping." He passes the box of hair dye to me. "We need to change our appearances a bit."

I nod, looking down at the woman on the front of the box, whose toffee brown hair tumbles in waves around her face. Now that we know there's a warrant out for Malice and the rest of us just helped him evade arrest, it'll help to look different.

"Dye your hair, and we'll go get our fake IDs. I bet the guy who runs this park knows a place."

"Okay," I murmur, taking the box and heading into the tiny bathroom. I take a minute to open everything and read the instructions, laying out the plastic gloves and the little brush that came with the kit as well.

When someone walks into the bathroom behind me, I turn and see Ransom coming in.

"Need a hand?" he asks, shooting me a lopsided grin.

I smile back. "Sure. That would be great."

He closes the lid of the toilet and then motions for me to sit down. I do, watching as he mixes everything up and puts on the gloves.

"Have you ever done this before?" I ask curiously.

Ransom nods. "A couple times when I was in high school. I dated this girl who changed her hair color like the fucking wind. One week it was blue, then the next it was back to blonde. I never knew how she managed it, so she invited me over to watch one time. Eventually, I learned enough to help her."

"That's nice of you," I say, keeping my tone neutral even as a wave of irrational jealousy rises up inside me.

He sees right through me, of course, and laughs.

"You don't have to be jealous of a girl I dated in high school, angel," he teases. "Last I heard, she was married to a woman anyway."

"I'm not jealous," I insist. "It's just interesting, hearing about you guys as kids. It's weird to think that you were ever young."

"Mm, I get that. Especially Mal and Vic, since they're both so serious in their own ways. Believe it or not, they were always kind of like that."

"I believe it. Especially considering..." I wave my hand, not wanting to bring up their terrible father right now.

But Ransom must get what I mean, because he nods. "Yeah. They kind of had to grow up pretty fast. We all did." Abruptly, he smiles. "Do you wanna hear a funny story about Malice?"

"Always."

Ransom's grin grows, turning mischievous. He takes the handle of the brush and uses it to part my hair, starting to apply the dark brown dye in sections. "So, even though Malice was always scowling and got into fights every other day, he was still pretty popular with the ladies."

"Understandable," I murmur.

"Sure. He was big, he was intense, he was brooding or whatever. They ate that shit up. Anyway, there was this big party close to where we were living at the time. Some kind of homecoming or graduation or something. Malice had gone out a couple hours earlier, and suddenly he comes home, bursting through the door looking more uncomfortable than I'd ever seen him before."

"What happened?"

"Turns out, some asshole was being a dick to some of the girls at the party, so they wanted to leave. It just so happened that Malice was walking past that house when they came out, and they immediately latched on to him. It was a smart bet, going for the big dude when some creep won't leave you alone. Only Malice wasn't the most... charming person ever."

I snicker softly, thinking of the standoffs I've had with Malice, how gruff and forceful he can be. Charming isn't a word most people would use to describe him. Honestly, *terrifying* would probably be a lot higher on the list. He used to scare me too, although it's hard to remember what that felt like now that I know him better.

"He apparently told them to get fucked and leave him alone, but they kept following him because just being around him was safer than being alone. Malice, not knowing what the fuck to do with this group of girls, came home to find me so I could get them to leave him alone."

I can just picture it in my head, a younger Malice with a gaggle of teenage girls following after him, trying to get him to walk them home. Just the thought of it makes me laugh, and Ransom joins in too.

"Never thought I'd see the day when Malice was afraid of something like that," he says.

"It makes sense, in a way. It's not like he could fight them or anything, so what else could he do?"

"Come beg his little brother for help, apparently," Ransom says, his blue-green eyes glinting with amusement.

He keeps working his way over my head, and the dye is cold and pungent smelling as he applies it, rubbing it in down to the ends of my hair. As he spreads the dye, he tells me more stories about when he and his brothers were younger, keeping me laughing.

"You should have seen it," he says, in the middle of a story about the first apartment the three of them shared together. "It was always a fucking mess, half because it was so small, half because Malice could never be fucked to do his dishes. It drove Vic out of his skull."

"Oh god, I bet."

"Finally he got so pissed off that he put on a pair of gloves and marched into the kitchen with this big plastic bin. He took every single dish that Malice had used and put it in the bin and then dumped the bin out on Malice's bed while Mal was out. Of course that led to Malice fucking losing it when he got home, but Vic didn't give a shit. He just calmly told Malice that he wasn't his fucking maid, and he needed to start carrying his weight or he could get out."

"Do you think he would have actually kicked him out?"

Ransom shakes his head. "Nah, but it was an effective threat. Plus, Malice does care a lot, and once he could tell how badly it was affecting Vic, he started to do better. By the time we moved into the warehouse, things were much easier."

I like that thought, the three of them working out their differences so they could keep living together. Even Vic, so particular about the way things need to be, was willing to work around Malice's idiosyncrasies, because he loves his twin.

"Okay," Ransom says. "That's enough about us. I want to hear more about you."

"I don't have many funny stories," I tell him. Most of my childhood stories are about Misty going on benders, or getting bullied in school or dealing with her shitty johns.

But Ransom dyeing my hair does remind me of something, and I smile.

"So, there was this time when I really wanted red hair," I begin.

"Oh, this should be good."

"There was this woman Misty knew, I don't know if she was also a hooker or just one of my mom's friends, but she would come by sometimes, and she had the most beautiful red hair. It was curly and bouncy, and I'd just stare at it in awe. I knew I was never going to get the curls like hers, but I figured I could manage the color if I worked at it."

Thinking about Misty hurts a bit, but I push that down to keep going. "I didn't have the money to buy any good dye, so I ended up stealing the first box I saw that looked like the right color at the store. I was wearing an oversized hoodie, and I tucked the box under it and no one stopped me. Turns out, trying to dye your hair with a shitty box dye that probably cost five bucks is a terrible idea."

Ransom laughs brightly. "What happened? All your hair fall out?"

"No, but it was close, I think. It came out so patchy, and the color was definitely wrong. It was more like a carrot-y orange than red, and that was in between the patches of blonde. And whatever was in it fried the hell out of my hair, so it was a dry, frizzy mess for weeks."

"Oof," Ransom says, trying to hold back his laughter. "At least you managed to fix it eventually. Your hair is beautiful now."

That makes my cheeks flush, even though it's far from the first compliment I've gotten from him. "It bounced back eventually. With a lot of conditioner."

"Did you steal that too?" he asks.

"Yeah, from Misty."

"You little rebel. I wish we'd known you back then. I bet it would have been fun."

I smile, a little wistful at the thought. "Yeah, me too."

Ransom steps back and takes the gloves off, tossing them in the trash. "Okay, you're done. Now we just have to let it process for half an hour or so."

Before I can reply, low, angry voices from the other room catch our attention. The two of us exchange glances and then step out quickly to see what's going on.

Vic is sitting in front of his computer at the little kitchenette counter, Malice standing at his shoulder, and there's a message pulled up on the screen. My stomach drops, because I can already guess who it's from.

"Olivia. What does she want now?" I ask, almost afraid to find out.

"She knows Malice was almost arrested in Oklahoma City, which means she knows we were there," Vic tells me, his voice tight. "She says we're not covering our tracks well enough, and that it's only a matter of time before we make a mistake. So she's offering us a deal."

"What deal?" My gaze flicks from Vic to Malice, who's gripping the back of his twin's chair hard enough that I'm worried he'll break it.

"She offered us ten million dollars to bring you back to her," Malice growls, sounding furious and disgusted.

"*What?*" My eyes widen, and I step closer to read over Vic's shoulder.

Sure enough, there it is. My stomach sours as I read the text, reminded of the way Olivia offered to sweeten the deal when she was trying to negotiate with me—offering me something I wanted instead of threatening me with something I didn't.

"She's so fucking manipulative," I whisper.

"We're not taking it," Ransom says immediately, and Malice grunts, as if that's obvious.

"Of course we're not."

I swallow hard, trying to be comforted by how quickly the men rejected her offer, instead of horrified by the fact that my grandmother is trying to buy me back.

And is that ten million dollars part of the money she would get from offering me up for marriage to some other family like Troy's after the brothers returned me to her? Or is she really so rich that she has that much wealth to spare?

I suppose it's possible that she doesn't have it at all and is just trying to bluff her way into getting the guys to bring me back. But either way, the light, comfortable mood from before is gone now, snuffed out like a candle flame. Tension fills the cramped RV, and Vic taps his fingers against the table, a relentless rhythm that shows how agitated he is.

"Should we tell her to fuck off?" Ransom asks.

Malice shakes his head, still glaring at the screen. If that laptop wasn't so precious to Vic, I have a feeling he'd be tempted to snap it in half. "No. That message doesn't deserve a goddamned response. I'm done talking to that bitch."

"He's right," Vic agrees. "There's no point in replying. For now, we just need to keep our heads down and get the rest of the way across the border. We stick to our plan."

Olivia's message kicks the guys into action, and they start to prep for the last leg of this trip while I wait for my hair to be ready to rinse. Once it is, I go back into the bathroom and get in the shower, stepping under the pitiful lukewarm trickle.

Dark brown water runs down my body to swirl down the drain as I wash the dye out of my hair, and I keep going until it runs clear. Then I wash myself up quickly and step out, clearing steam off the mirror with the towel in my hand.

As I catch a sight of my reflection, I have to stare for a second. It's me, but it sure as hell doesn't look like me. Something about my blonde hair made me look... softer, more innocent, I guess. The new dark color highlights my rough edges more—or maybe that's just from everything I've been through these last few weeks. I can see it in my eyes too. A new hardness, something sharper and less delicate than what was there before.

I shake my head, breaking myself out of my musing. After towel drying my hair, I rub a little lotion onto my new tattoo and then get dressed before stepping out into the other room.

"All done?" Malice asks, looking me over.

"Yup." I fluff out my still damp hair. "What do you think of the new me?"

He smirks, lifting a dark brow. "It's the same you, Solnyshka. Just with different hair."

That makes me smile, and I join them as we leave the RV. "So, it's fake ID time?" I ask, and Malice nods.

My body protests a bit as we pile back into the car, but at least it's just going to be for a short trip this time. We're in the car for maybe twenty minutes, driving into the city and then pulling up outside of what looks like a small, unremarkable storefront. It could be a convenience store or something like that, and there are signs for various brands of cigarettes and beer in the windows.

The bell over the door chimes when we walk in, and a bored looking girl is behind the counter, barely paying attention. When Malice walks up to the counter, she lifts her head and stares up at him.

"Can I help you?" she asks, raising an eyebrow.

"We're here to see Chuck," he says. "He missed our poker game last week."

His words make no sense to me at first, but then I realize it must be some kind of code. The guy who told the brothers about this place must've also given them that information.

The girl hesitates for only a second, her gaze flicking over the rest of us as if evaluating whether we're a threat. Then she jerks her chin. "All the way to the back. Hang a left past the Gatorade."

Malice grunts his thanks, motioning for us to follow. All three of the brothers are on alert, and I notice that they keep me between them, almost like they're forming a shield around me with their bodies.

When we make it to the back, the door is locked. Malice knocks hard, three times, and the door inches open a little.

"What?" someone barks.

"Aces wild," Malice murmurs, which I assume is also code. "We need some documents made."

"You can pay?" whoever's inside—presumably Chuck—asks.

Malice pulls out a rolled wad of cash, letting that speak for itself. There's a moment of silence, and then the door creaks open all the way.

"Come in," the man says.

He ushers us into a back room, stuffed absolutely full of various equipment. There are cameras and a massive printer and some other devices I can't even identify. Chuck is a tall guy, almost taller than Malice, with tired eyes and twitchy hands. He's on the skinny side, except for a slight potbelly that hangs over his belt.

"What are you after?" he asks, adjusting his belt and glancing at Malice, seeming to suss out that he's the one in charge.

"We need passports made."

"Four of 'em?"

Malice nods. "And they need to hold up."

Chuck sniffs. "They always fucking hold up. Don't worry about it. Payment first."

He names an amount of money that makes my stomach drop, but Malice doesn't even blink. He nods and hands over the cash, and Chuck counts it meticulously before nodding. He moves around the small space easily, setting things up.

Then he takes a closer look at each one of us, sizing us up as he rubs his hand over his chin. His attention lands on me last, and one of his eyebrows slides upward a little, his gaze tracking up and down my body. I've been ogled much worse and much more obviously by guys at the strip club I used to work at, so I barely even register the fact that he's checking me out—but all three of the Voronin brothers react immediately.

Vic and Ransom move in protectively on either side of me as Malice steps toward Chuck, narrowing his eyes.

"We're on a tight schedule here," he snaps. "So move it along."

"Alright, alright. Jesus. I'm moving."

Chuck holds up his hands in a gesture of peace, slumping his shoulders a little as if to make it clear he's not trying to start some shit. He clears his throat and motions to the empty wall where a backdrop has been set up to look exactly like the one at the DMV.

"Whoever's first, then," he says, glancing toward us but avoiding looking at me.

It's a pretty straightforward process, getting the fake passports made. He takes our pictures and asks us some questions, assigning fake names and ages but using our actual heights and weights. He does a few things on his computer, muttering to himself under his breath as he works, then we wait while he prints the photos and assembles the little booklets.

He hands me mine, still barely looking at me, and I take it, opening it up and reading the name written next to my picture: Christina Peters.

Once he's given each of the guys their passports as well, he jerks a nod at Malice and shuffles back over to sit at his computer. Without another word, we leave the little back room and head out through the front of the store, passing by the girl who greeted us.

On the drive back to the RV, I shove my fake ID into my pocket as the guys fall into their usual habit of batting around ideas, strategizing about our next step.

"There's no point in drawing this out," Vic is saying. "We need to get out of here, especially now that we know for sure there's a warrant out on Malice."

"It'll take a couple days to get everything we need together," Ransom chimes in. "Is it safe to stay at the RV park?"

Vic considers that and then nods. "Safe as anything else. I'll keep an eye on police chatter if I can, and see if I can pick anything up. But at this point, we're close enough to the border that we just need to make a move."

"We'll need a new ride," Malice grunts. "I'll see what's around."

Ransom's blue-green eyes light up. He straightens up beside me, the sleeves of his dark t-shirt stretching a little as he rests his arms on the back of the seat. "Oh, about that. I have a great idea."

Victor and Malice share a loaded look in the front, and I glance between the three of them, confused. "What? What's your idea?"

Ransom shoots me a look, grinning broadly. "Don't worry, pretty girl. It'll be fun. Trust me."

41

WILLOW

"This is *not* going to be fun," I tell Ransom definitively the next day. We're standing outside the RV, four large motorcycles lined up and ready in front of us.

I stare at them, my gut churning with nerves. *This* is what he wants to take over the border? I guess I should have expected it. All the guys are into cars, but Ransom in particular has always been crazy about motorcycles.

Even my sour expression isn't enough to dim the brightness of his enthusiasm. He grins widely, excitement sparking in his eyes.

"I know you probably think I suggested this just because I like bikes," he says.

"Oh, is there another reason?" I deadpan, my hands on my hips.

"Actually, yeah, there is. It'll be good for us to separate at the border, for one thing. Anyone looking for us will be looking for four people together, not four separate people. Even with us changing our appearances, a group of four is going to stand out."

I make a face, reluctantly admitting that he has a point about that.

"For another thing," he goes on, "With helmets on, it'll be harder to ID us on the road. We'll have to take them off to get across the border, but it gives anyone looking for us fewer chances to pick us out on traffic cameras or security footage."

"Ugh, fine. I guess that's true."

"Lastly, I know you enjoyed the times when I took you out on my bike before. But it'll be even better this time. You'll be the one in control."

"Umm." I grimace. "That's what I'm afraid of. I have no idea how to control one of these things."

Ransom smiles, leaning on one of the bikes. "That's what I'm here for, pretty girl. I'm not gonna let you go crashing into a ditch or anything."

"Thanks for putting that image in my head," I mutter under my breath.

My heart beats wildly as I stare at the bikes. I'm terrified of the idea of handling one of these things on my own. Even though it was thrilling as hell to speed down the road on a motorcycle with Ransom steering, doing it by myself is a whole different ballgame.

But he has good points as to why this makes sense, and we're so close now. Too close to let something like this stop us. So I drag in a deep breath, trying to steel myself.

"Okay," I say, puffing out my cheeks. "Teach me."

Ransom's handsome face lights up even more, pride and adoration shining in his eyes. He comes over to me and takes my face in his hands, kissing me soundly on the mouth. When he pulls back, he looks exhilarated, like he can't wait to do this.

"I knew from the first time I got you on my bike that I wanted to do this with you," he murmurs. "And you're so much bolder now than you were then."

"Am I?" I mutter, even though I know he's right.

"Hell yeah, you are. You've gotten all assertive about what you want in bed and what you want from us. You're embracing your kinks and even bossing Malice around. You've gotten used to being a bad bitch in charge, and you know it. This is just an extension of that."

I can't help but chuckle, feeling pleased and a little better about this whole thing. My cheeks flush from the praise, and my body hums, warmth stirring in my belly at the reminder of how things have shifted between all of us.

But I need to focus.

"Let's do this," I tell him, giving a sharp nod before I can change my mind.

Ransom motions for me to pick a bike, and I do, going with one that's been painted a bright, sunny yellow. It gleams in the light, and Ransom chooses the black one for himself. We grab some helmets and push the motorcycles over to a dirt road that winds away from the RV park, my pulse racing with every step we take.

But Ransom is a good teacher, especially when it comes to stuff like this. Stuff he really cares about.

"Do you remember when I taught you about this before?" he asks. "When we were hanging out in the garage?"

I nod. "Most of it, I think."

"Show me."

So I do. I point out parts of the bike that I can remember, telling him what they do and how they impact your ride. The parts I can't quite remember, he fills in, going over it in a way that doesn't make me feel like I'm stupid.

He talks about it all thoroughly, explaining how to make the bike go faster, how to brake safely, how to lean into turns and use your body with the bike instead of against it.

Next, he has me sit on my motorcycle and mime what I would do when I start it up, nodding and adjusting my grip in places.

Once I'm able to repeat it back to him, he smiles and then leads me over to his motorcycle.

"Okay, I'm going to control the bike first, going over everything we just learned," he says. "I want you to mimic it behind me, and then we'll see if you're ready to try it on your own."

"A-alright."

My voice shakes a little, but there's still a feeling of excitement in my chest when I get on behind Ransom. He puts my helmet on for me, making sure it's secure before giving the top of it a little tap. Then he starts the bike up, and I match his hand movements, going through the motions of what he just showed me. When he kicks off, I wrap my arms around his waist, and I lean when he leans into turns, getting a better feel for how to move with the bike, reading and guiding its momentum.

"In theory, it's like an extension of yourself," he says once we've stopped. "In a car, you're just piloting it, and you can't really feel how it's connected to you. But on a bike, your control is everything."

"What if my bike won't listen to me?" I mumble, and Ransom belts out a laugh.

"It's not a horse, angel. It's not like you have to break it first. Don't worry, you're gonna be great."

He takes me out on his bike once more, this time having me talk him through the process as he starts it up and we zip around the RV park in a quick loop.

When we get back to where we started, he nods to the motorcycle I chose.

"Now it's your turn."

I swallow down the panic in my throat and go to the bike, throwing my leg over it. It feels odd, being the only one on this massive machine, and I take a second to adjust myself, breathing in and trying to soothe my own nerves.

"First thing?" Ransom prompts me, and I nod, focusing.

I know how to do this.

I go through the steps we just walked through over and over again, but somehow, I still jump when I get the bike started up.

"Just go to the end of this little road," Ransom calls over the noise.

Just to the end of the road. Right. I can do that.

It's... a very wobbly start.

I get a couple of things mixed up and almost lay the bike down once or twice, scrambling to lean the right way and remember what I'm supposed to be doing.

But I keep practicing, riding up and down the short stretch of road over and over.

Ransom is a good teacher, which helps. He doesn't rush me, instead re-explaining anything that I'm struggling with.

"Think about it like this," he says at one point when I'm having a hard time with the throttle. "You want a firm grip, but not too firm. Like if you were jacking me off, right?"

My face floods with heat. "*What?*"

"Go with me on this," he says, grinning sinfully as he flicks his tongue out, making the ball of his piercing catch the sunlight. "Too loose, and it does nothing for me. You may as well not even be holding on to my dick. Too tight, and it's too much, which also isn't super useful. You want the right amount of pressure, keeping a firm grip without locking your wrist. So just imagine that the right handlebar is my dick."

His explanation does make a certain amount of sense, and I adjust my hold on the handlebars, making Ransom nod.

"There you go. Much better."

From there, he corrects my posture on the bike. "You're too stiff. You're riding it, but you have to put your hips into it. Just like if you were riding a guy."

Oh my god. Clearly, I'm going to be blushing a lot during this lesson.

But it does help, in a way. It's not hard to imagine that it's a hard body between my legs instead of a hunk of metal, and I adjust how I'm sitting, letting my hips lead more.

"Perfect," Ransom praises. "Told you, pretty girl. You're a natural."

We keep at it for hours, until I can make it down the road and back without any issues. Turning around trips me up at first, but eventually, I manage it smoothly. I lean into the little bend in the road and pull up to a stop near Ransom without even wobbling once.

We go from there into moving faster, closer to the speed we'll need to get down to the border. It's exhilarating and exhausting, but each time I manage to do it right, it feels so good.

Once Ransom seems satisfied that I know enough, he nods.

"You're killing it. You feel up to going for a longer ride?"

"Okay." I nod, wanting to keep up the momentum.

He straddles his own bike and kicks it into gear, revving it and taking off down the dirt road. I follow, slowly at first, but then picking up speed as we ride.

This far out, there's not much around, just this dirt road with trees on either side of it. No cars, no other people on the road. Ransom picks up speed, and my heart leaps with excitement as I catch up to him, controlling the bike better than I expected.

The wind whips past me, and the adrenaline in my body builds. Finally, I can understand what Ransom loves about this so much. There's a freedom to it, and something oddly sensual, without that separation that comes from being in a car.

When I lean the bike into a turn, I can feel the connection, the way it responds to my movements, and it feels incredible to have that kind of control.

After a little while, we stop, pulling over onto the shoulder in a wooded area.

I get off the bike and tug my helmet off. The breeze ruffles my hair, and I can't keep in the little whoop of excitement that spills from my lips. I'm exhilarated, my heart pounding for a reason other than fear for once, and it makes me happy.

Ransom is grinning as he gets off his own bike. He strides over to me and scoops me up as my helmet drops from my hand and tumbles to the grass beside us. He twirls me around, laughing, and then kisses my forehead when he sets me back on my feet.

"I knew you'd love it," he says, his lips brushing my hair. "I fucking knew it."

"Yeah, you were right. Don't let it go to your head."

"Too late."

We smile at each other as he draws back, but then suddenly I think about Ransom's bike back home, and how he worked on it so lovingly. I think about their shop and how it was reduced to ashes. All their hard work—gone.

My smile fades, melting off my face like a piece of ice dissolving on a hot day.

"I'm sorry about your bike back home," I murmur. "It's probably burned now with everything else. I know it meant a lot to you."

He shrugs. "It did, but I can always get another bike."

I run my fingers lightly down his neck and along the curve where it meets his shoulders, feeling the strength of his muscles beneath his dark tee. "I hope... I hope all of this will be worth it."

"It *is* worth it," he says, conviction clear in his voice. "Because *you're* worth it, and you'd better fucking believe that."

As if to prove his words, or maybe to consecrate them like a vow, he palms the back of my neck and presses his lips to mine.

42

RANSOM

Willow makes a noise against my mouth as I kiss her, a sound that's both surrender and yearning at the same time, and her arms wind tighter around my shoulders. She molds her soft, delicate body to mine, going onto her tiptoes to erase some of the height difference between us as her tits press against my chest.

I swear I can smell the wind in her hair from our bike ride, and I bury my fingers in the strands as my lips slant over hers. Seeing her with that bike helmet on and the Harley between her legs definitely belongs in the top five sexiest things I've ever witnessed in my life.

Like a fucking goddess of the open road.

I thought the Willow who was a good girl on the outside and a bad girl on the inside was the sexiest thing I'd ever seen, but I was wrong about that. This is. Willow embracing who she is, being the bad girl I always knew she was.

It's fucking addictive, and such a goddamned turn-on.

Even when our kiss breaks, I keep my lips hovering over hers, only a hairsbreadth separating us as I push her newly dark hair behind her ear.

"You have no idea how fucking sexy you are, do you?" I whisper. "How much you get me going with every little thing you do. My alluring little vixen."

She grins, and I can feel it more than see it. "I thought I was your angel."

"You can be both. You *are* both."

My hands roam down her sides and over her ass, and she inhales sharply as I grab her thighs to scoop her up. She wraps her legs around me immediately, clinging to my shoulders as her thighs clench my waist. I can feel the heat of her body through two layers of clothes, and the feel of her in my arms, so eager and willing, goes straight to my cock.

"You know, we've been out here for a while, pretty girl," I murmur, dropping my head to nip at the soft skin of her throat. "We didn't bring any snacks, and I'm fucking starving."

She chuckles, and I can feel the vibrations of it beneath my lips. "Yeah? Too bad there's nothing out here for you to eat."

"Oh, but there is." My grip on her ass tightens, hitching her against me so that her pussy grinds against my stomach. "*You*."

She moans quietly, rolling her hips like she can't help but chase the friction, and my cock goes rock hard in my pants, pressing painfully against my fly.

"Shit," I groan, and then I'm moving.

I set Willow down so that she's perched sideways on my bike and go for her pants, grinning when she lifts her hips to help me. I get them down enough that they're pooled around her ankles, and Willow toes her shoes off so that I can drag her jeans and panties off and toss them to the side. Her top is still on, but I don't have the patience to get her more naked than this.

Not when my body is thrumming with arousal, and she's right there, wet and ready for me.

I drop to my knees on the gravel in front of her, spreading her legs wider as she braces her hands on the bike seat. Her pussy lips are already wet and flushed, and I throw her legs over my shoulders and then bury my face between her thighs, letting my tongue seek out the taste of my favorite fucking meal.

Willow gasps as I start eating her out, squirming in place and clenching her thighs around my head.

"Someone could see us," she pants, fisting a hand in my hair even as she speaks and dragging my face closer to her pussy. "They could—*fuck*—they could drive by."

I glance up at her long enough to smirk. "They won't. And even if they did, they'd never get the chance to tell anyone. I'd hunt them down and kill them, because no one gets to see you like this but me and my brothers."

She moans, her head tipping back, and I go back to work, determined to make my girl come. I swirl my tongue around her folds, lapping at her as she gets wetter and wetter. When I move up to suck at her clit, she jerks against me, trying to muffle the noise of pleasure by biting down on her lip.

"Don't be quiet, angel," I mutter against her soaked flesh. "Let me hear you. Let the fucking birds and the trees hear you."

She does exactly what I'm asking for, letting her mouth fall open on a cry as I find a spot she really likes. She's so fucking responsive, and I keep going, taking my cues from her noises, working her up and tasting everything she has to give me until I can feel her thighs trembling in my grasp.

I press the flat of my tongue against her clit and lick hard, and she almost wails in pleasure, sending a flock of birds scattering from a nearby tree.

"That's more like it," I murmur as I work her through it. "Fuck, I love making you scream for me."

Willow gasps for breath as I slowly detach her delicate fingers from my hair and get to my feet, wincing as the movement makes my pants press harder against my stiff cock. The only thing that turns me on more than eating Willow out is fucking her, and even then, it's a close second. I could live off her pretty cunt for the rest of my life and die a happy man.

I didn't mean for our lesson to get sidetracked like this, but watching her learn how to ride a bike was so damn hot I couldn't help myself. My cock is still pulsing angrily, demanding to get inside her tight, wet heat, so instead of helping her put her pants back on, I pick her up again. Her legs go back around my waist, her arms over my shoulders.

"You've been doing such a good job today, pretty girl," I tell her. "Your balance and control are getting so much better, I think we can level up a little. Do you trust me?"

She nods, her cheeks flushed.

"Good." I grin and get on my bike, starting it up a second later.

The way the bike rumbles under us, and I can tell from the way Willow jumps that she can feel the vibrations. I can too.

"Remember when we did this before?" I murmur. "I let you hump my bike until you came all over it, riding the seat like you couldn't get enough." Her blush deepens, but she nods. "I was never jealous of my fucking bike before that day."

Her laugh is breathy, and her fingertips slide through the hair at the nape of my neck, her nails scratching lightly at my scalp. "You don't need to be jealous."

"Maybe not. But I want my turn."

Her brows draw together, a little line appearing between them as she looks at me quizzically. I reach up and take one of her hands, guiding it to my crotch. My cock throbs through my jeans, and Willow lets out a quiet whimper as her fingers tighten around me a little.

"Feel that? Feel how fucking hard I am for you?"

"Yeah," she breathes back. "I can feel it."

"Do you want my cock, angel?"

Willow nods, her eyes hooded. "Always."

"Then take it out," I tell her, revving the engine a little. "And then sit on it. I don't want my bike to be the one getting you off this time. I want you to come on my dick while we ride."

Her eyes flare wide, shock and desire flashing in them. I grin at her, lifting one eyebrow to show that I'm serious.

There's a split second of hesitation, but it doesn't last longer than that. She really is a wild thing at heart, and I love helping her realize it. Her hands fumble for my belt, and she undoes my pants quickly, shoving them down enough to free my shaft from my boxer briefs. It's a bit of an awkward maneuver, and I shift my weight a little on the seat to help her.

"There you go," I murmur as she wraps her small hand around me, making my balls tighten. "You think you can ride me like this?"

Her chin dips in another little nod, her gaze laser focused on my dick as her fingers slide over the rounded silver of my piercings.

"Then climb on. I've got you."

Willow adjusts her position, resting her heels on the seat behind me as she braces her arms on my shoulders to help her rise up and then sink down. The head of my cock breaches her tight core, and I hiss through my teeth, cursing under my breath as she gets situated. She feels so fucking good. So tight, so hot, so perfectly wet. And judging by the way she moans, the thrill of this is doing the same thing for her that it's doing for me.

"You know what to do," I tell her, dragging my teeth over her earlobe before releasing the clutch. "Make yourself feel good."

"Fuck. Ransom," she whimpers, clinging to me tighter.

Pulling onto the road, I let the bike roll forward—not at my usual speed, but fast enough that Willow will notice.

When she starts to move, it's hesitant at first, the same way she was when she was controlling her own motorcycle for the first time. She's shaky, like she's afraid to move too much and make us crash. The black tarmac passes by under us, and I shiver as she gives an experimental undulation of her hips, resisting the urge to buck up into her. Someone's gotta keep this bike upright.

"That's right, you've got it. Fuck, you're so tight like this," I say through gritted teeth. "You like the thrill, don't you, pretty girl?"

I tighten my hands around the handlebars of the bike, then huff a laugh as I remember what I told her before about how to hold on. *Not too loose, but not too tight either*. Her pussy has my cock in a vise grip though, and damn, I'm not complaining.

"Don't hold back," I tell her. "I've got this. I'll keep us on the road. You focus on getting yourself off. Because I wanna see that. I wanna see you fucking yourself on my cock like you can't get enough."

Willow moans, and I can hear the quiet sound even over the roar of the bike. She starts getting more confident, and even though she can't get the leverage in this position to ride me hard, every small movement is enough to make us both groan.

A turn comes up, and I tilt us into it, groaning when moving my hips forward buries me even deeper in Willow's pussy.

"Oh fuck," she gasps. "Oh my god."

"Does that feel good? Are you gonna come all over me?"

She nods frantically, her inner walls clenching around me, rippling all along the length of my shaft. She's grinding hard against me, and I know she's probably getting friction right on her clit.

"Tell me," I urge. "Let me hear you."

"God, you feel so good," she breathes. "You're so deep, and the vibrations are... fuck. You don't need to be jealous of your bike. *Ever*. This is better. So much better. I can feel—"

She cuts off with a sharp gasp and grinds down even harder, like she's just found a spot that she doesn't want to let up from.

"What can you feel?" I pant, starving for more of her words. I fucking love when she lets go like this.

"You. You, you, *you*. Your cock. The piercings. I can feel all of it."

Her arms are wrapped tight around my shoulders, her legs hugging my waist as her heels press against my ass. She tips her head back a little, and her luminous brown eyes are glassy with pleasure as the dark strands of her hair dance around her face.

"You're so fucking good, angel," I praise. "Come apart for me. I wanna feel it when you lose it and go all tight around my dick. I wanna fill you up with my cum while we're on my bike."

"Yes!" she nearly wails, and I can feel how close she's getting.

I'm right there too. The pleasure is molten hot, building in my balls. It started off slow and gradual, but now it's like a rising tide that won't stop, stealing half my focus as my body responds to what she's doing.

It's a fight not to close my eyes and just fuck Willow hard and fast, and I suck in a breath, swerving a bit at the last second to avoid plowing into an embankment that causes a sudden turn in the road.

Willow doesn't even seem to notice, and I get us back under control just in time for her to arch her back and cry out my name, the sound cutting through the quiet, still air. Her pussy clamps around me like it wants to milk my cock of everything it's got, and that's enough to set off my own orgasm.

"Shit," I groan.

I skid to a stop, pulling the bike over to the side of the road and cutting the engine. As soon as my hands aren't needed on the handlebars anymore, they land on her hips, guiding her up and down on my cock. I drag her down hard a few times, filling her up as deep as I can, and then blow my load inside her, choking out a rough grunt as I wrap my arms around her.

Willow clings to me, panting hard, and I rest my face in the crook of her neck. I can feel her heart racing and her body trembling, and it's a point of pride to be the one who did that to her.

When she can finally breathe again, she pulls back, and I lift my head to look at her. Her eyes are bright with adrenaline, her cheeks flushed. She looks different with the dark hair, but it's still her. She's still beautiful and bold and brave, and I can't get enough.

"You know," she comments, "I think I'm really getting the hang of this riding thing."

I burst out laughing, smacking her bare ass lightly with one hand.

"You definitely are." Then I grimace, looking over my shoulder toward the road behind us. "We should probably head back. This road is pretty much deserted, but I don't want to leave the other bike for too long."

"More lessons before it gets dark?"

"You're insatiable, aren't you?" I tease.

Her expression turns more serious, the spark of happiness in her eyes turning to one of determination. "I just want to be ready. We're so close, and I don't want to fuck this up."

I nod, reaching up to drag my knuckles along her jaw. We *are* close. But that doesn't mean we're safe yet.

I help her climb off my cock and clean up a little, then she clambers back onto the bike and I wheel it around, heading back to where we left hers.

43

MALICE

Three days later, I'm up early, too agitated to sleep.

It feels strange to have stayed in this one place for several days, after being on the move so much. This is the most I've ever traveled, the farthest from Detroit I've ever been. Up until now, my brothers and I were content to stay put where we were. We made a home and a name for ourselves in the city where we were born... and now we're about to cross the border into a whole new country.

Never really saw that coming.

But then again, I didn't see Willow coming either.

She blew into our lives like a tornado with silky blonde hair and brown eyes like a doe, fierce and vulnerable and brave all at the same time. And she changed fucking *everything*, altering the dynamic of our little unit and writing herself into our very DNA.

We've prepared as much as possible for our entry into Mexico, and we all agreed last night that today is the day we'll head to the border and try to cross.

Everyone else is still asleep, and despite the urge I had to rouse them from bed so we could get moving already, I decided to give them a few more minutes of rest. So the RV is quiet as I stand by the window and stare out of it, lost in thought.

Willow has spent the last few days practicing on her bike with

Ransom, and she's getting good. When I talked to him last night, he said that she's solid enough on the basics to be safe riding on her own, and to pass as a biker, not drawing attention to herself.

That's the most important part of this.

All of us have to blend in. There can't be a single thing about us that stands out or draws attention.

Vic has spent every single moment of the past few days getting ready for the crossing—doing research, learning which lines we should get in at the border, what time of day to go to have agents who will be less sharp, less likely to put in the effort of scrutinizing us too closely.

He's even done a couple things that might help throw Olivia off our trail too, manipulating surveillance footage in a completely different city to make it look like we headed west after leaving Oklahoma City instead of south. If that works, it'll send Olivia on a wild goose chase and give us more time.

We're so damn close. Everything is done except for the physical crossing, and that's the biggest part.

Realistically, I know we're as prepared as we can be, but that doesn't stop me from feeling antsy as fuck.

I look around the RV as dim sunlight creeps through the window. Willow is breathing softly with her head on Vic's chest on the couch. Ransom is on the pull down bed, sprawled out under the scratchy as fuck blanket that came with it.

The sight of Vic cuddling with Willow is one I never thought I would see, and it makes something squeeze in my chest. It's a soft emotion, one I've only ever felt when it comes to the three people in this little shithole of an RV.

I turn away, looking out the window as the sun starts to rise.

In quiet times like this, I can't help but think of our mom. She liked to get up before dawn too when she had the time, even if she'd had a long shift the night before.

I remember coming downstairs to see her standing in the kitchen with a cup of tea in her hand, reading one of those romance novels she loved so much. It was probably one of the only moments of peace she got, being a mom and a nurse and dealing with our shitbag dad all the time. I never wanted to disturb her, so I'd just stand on the stairs and watch the way the morning sun slowly started to fill the little kitchen, spilling light around her until she finally put her book aside and stood up.

As usual, there's a pang in my chest that comes from thinking about her, and I unconsciously rub the tattoo on my arm that bears her name. It still fucking kills me that I wasn't there to protect her.

I'll protect them though, I silently promise her spirit. *Ransom and Vic. I'll keep them safe. We just need to get through today.*

I close my eyes and take a deep breath, trying to calm the jangle of nerves in my chest.

My thoughts are churning so loudly in my head that I don't even notice that Willow is awake until she steps up behind me, wrapping her arms around me from behind.

I tense for just a second, then relax, and Willow rests her forehead against my back, her hands splaying over my chest and stomach. I close my eyes, leaning into her touch. As always, I crave it, soaking it up like some sort of drug I can no longer live without.

"I thought you were asleep," I tell her, keeping my voice low.

"Yeah, I was," she murmurs back. "How long have you been up?"

I shrug. "A while."

There's a moment of silence, and it's surprisingly comfortable. After everything we've been through in the last few weeks, it's strange to have this moment of peace between us. Everyone else asleep, just the two of us standing together as the sun comes up.

After a while, I turn in her arms, wanting to see her face.

Even though it's early, she looks rested enough. Her pale features are smooth, and the morning light catches on the strands of dark hair that I'm still getting used to seeing. She gazes back at me, searching my face, and I don't try to hide what I'm feeling from her. After coming this far, there's really no point, and I don't want to hide anything from this woman.

Willow reaches up, tracing the lines of my face with one gentle finger. "You're worried."

I just shrug again, because I don't think she needs to hear me confirm it with words.

"It's always you, isn't it?" she murmurs.

"What do you mean? Always me what?"

She bites her lip, like she's trying to figure out how to answer before she speaks. "Always you who has to protect people. Who takes all of it on your shoulders. You're the glue that holds your brothers together."

I blink at her, caught off guard. It's not what I was expecting to hear, and I don't even really know how to respond. She keeps watching me, and I know she's taking in every shift of my expression, trying to suss out what I'm feeling.

It should be uncomfortable, or at the very least fucking invasive, being scrutinized like this.

But it's Willow, so it's not.

"We all need each other," I tell her finally. "We're a team. A family."

She nods, agreeing with that. "I know. And I love how you take care of each other. But you're the head of that family. The natural leader. Even Vic looks up to you, and you're basically the same age. You're the one they turn to when they're unsure, the one they'd follow anywhere."

"I'm not sure I'm up to it," I admit, my throat tightening. "I'm not sure I can keep them safe. And if I can't, then I don't deserve this role."

"Yes, you do," Willow argues gently. "You've *been* keeping them safe, Malice. You went to prison so they wouldn't have to. You were about to get arrested again the other day, and you told us all to run."

"Yeah, I remember that." I narrow my eyes. "I also remember you starting a bar fight."

Her eyes flash, the hint of a smile tugging at her plush lips. "And I remember you getting mad at me for that. Because you wanted to protect us. You're good at protecting us," she insists. "And we believe in you."

I swallow hard, hit hard by the fierce devotion she's offering. Of anyone I know, she has plenty of reasons to not want to follow me. I'm not infallible, and I've made plenty of mistakes in my life. Hell, I was ready to kill Willow for being a witness to our takedown of Nikolai Petrov before Ransom stopped me.

But here she is, offering me her trust, giving me the strength to get through this shit because she believes in me.

My arms tighten around her suddenly, crushing her lithe body against mine as I bury my face in her hair. I know I'm probably holding her too hard, and it can't be comfortable for her—but still, somehow, it's not enough. I hate every single barrier that keeps us apart. My clothes, her clothes, the tiny atoms of space that exist between us.

Emotions well up in me, and I feel like I'm choking on them for a second before they take over, almost as natural as breathing. I open my mouth, and the words spill out before I even realize I'm about to say them.

"I fucking love you, Solnyshka."

Willow stiffens.

She pushes against my chest, squirming out of my grip, and when I release her, she leans back and stares up at me. Her eyes are wide, her jaw hanging slack, and she blinks several times, not saying anything.

When she's silent for almost a full minute, I clench my jaw, trying to rein the emotions in.

Maybe I shouldn't have said it.

At least not now, when everything is so fucking uncertain.

"You don't have to say it back," I mutter, looking away from her.

"No, I—" She reaches up to rest her fingers on my jaw, turning me back to face her. Her voice is barely more than a whisper as she breathes, "I... love you too."

It knocks the wind out of me. Her voice is soft, but those four words hit me like a blow to the chest, and I kind of understand now why it took her a minute to respond when I said them to her. I feel like the world just shifted around me, like the man I was a second ago isn't the man I am now.

Because Willow Hayes loves me.

"Yeah?" I rasp, searching her face.

She nods, her head bobbing quickly as she sucks in a breath. "Oh, fuck yes."

I pull her against me again, kissing the fuck out of her. It's probably too hard, just like the way I held her before, but Willow meets my tongue stroke for stroke, the fire inside her rising up to match the inferno in me. When we finally break apart, her lips are swollen and pink, and it's a good fucking look on her.

"I didn't believe in love for a long time," I admit in a low voice, brushing my thumb over her bottom lip just because I can. "Or attachments. I had my family, and after we lost Mom... I knew how much there was to lose when you gave a shit about someone. I thought loving anyone other than my brothers would be a weakness."

Willow grimaces, her face scrunching up a bit. "Well, I mean, look at how much you've lost since I came into your lives. How much you've had to give up. Maybe you weren't wrong, and it is a weakness."

She looks sad to be saying it, and I shake my head, smiling at her, fierce and possessive.

"No fucking way. There's no way you could ever be a weakness, Solnyshka. You're my greatest strength."

She blinks, and for a second, it looks like she's about to cry. But then she goes up onto her toes, and I cup her face in both hands so I can kiss her again. She makes a soft sound against my lips, and it heats my blood. Without even really thinking about it, I back her up to the wall, pinning her there with my body, still devouring her mouth with everything I've got.

All I want in this moment is to fuck her against this wall. To make her fall apart for me. To make her scream that she loves me as her pussy takes my cock and my cum.

But we don't have time for that.

Reluctantly, I pull back, smiling in satisfaction at the wide eyed, flushed look on her face.

"Alright," I grunt. "Let's get this fucking day over with."

Willow nods, determination clear in the set of her mouth and the way she holds her shoulders.

"Okay," she agrees, and together, we go to wake my brothers.

44

WILLOW

Once Ransom and Vic are up and we've all gotten ready, we leave the RV park and hit the road.

All four of us are on our bikes, and for a little while, I let myself enjoy the sight of Malice and Victor on their motorcycles up ahead of me, riding with ease. They're not quite as skilled as Ransom, who's bringing up the rear of our little group, but they both look right at home as they lean into the wind.

I'm surprised how comfortable I've gotten on my own bike, honestly. I probably have to keep my mind on the task more than any of them do, reminding myself of everything Ransom taught me as we go along, but I feel more confident than I would've imagined at the beginning of this.

I've come to really enjoy motorcycles, in the last few days especially, mostly thanks to his enthusiasm for them.

But even with part of my brain focused on making sure I don't hit a bump wrong and lay down my bike, I can't stop my mind from drifting back to what happened with Malice this morning as we stood together in front of the window. The view wasn't much to write home about, just dusty asphalt and the other RVs around ours, but that was still one of the most unforgettable moments of my life.

My heart swells when I think of the words I never expected him to say. Maybe I should've seen it coming, though. So many of his actions made it clear how he feels about me, and the fact that we're here now, leaving everything they've ever known behind, is proof of that.

Maybe that's why I wasn't waiting for the words.

Other people have said they loved me, and then treated me like shit. Misty said it often enough, usually when she was drunk or high, or when she was trying to get me to do something for her. She'd say it, and I'd fold, but in the back of my mind, I knew that people don't treat someone they truly love the way Misty treated me.

Olivia acted like she loved me, welcoming me into her life, buying me expensive things, telling me she wanted to make sure I had what I needed. Acting the way a beloved family member should act. But it was all a game to her. All a trick to get me to do what she wanted, to use me for her own ends.

Malice never said he loved me until today, but he and his brothers have protected me. He's looked out for me and gone after anyone who tried to hurt me. He fucks me like I'm the only woman in the world, the only woman he'll ever want to be with again.

So I think a part of me knew how he felt, even before he said it.

After another couple hours of riding, signs for the border start to pop up around us, and my heart rate speeds up.

We're so close now, so fucking close to reaching our destination and having Olivia's threat ease up a bit. Hunkering down in Mexico won't make her go away—not by a long shot—but it will give us some much needed breathing room.

But we have to get there first.

Victor makes a gesture with one hand, and we all stop our bikes, pulling off to the side of the road and dismounting so that we can do one final check-in.

The plan is set, and we've gone over it several times to make sure that we all know what to do. We've all rehearsed our cover stories until we know them backward and forward, and we know what order we'll go in as we approach the border. We need to leave a bit of space between ourselves, so that it won't seem like we're together, but not enough that we'll be too far away from each other if something goes wrong.

"Everyone got their IDs?" Vic asks, tugging off his helmet and holding it at his side with one hand.

I nod, removing my helmet too and triple checking my bag to make sure I've got the fake passport we bought from Chuck. Ransom plucks the little blue booklet from my hand, opening it up and then looking at me.

"And what's your name, miss?" he asks, putting on an official sounding tone as if he's a border agent.

"Christina Peters," I reply.

"Date of birth?"

I tell him the birthday that's listed on the passport, and he nods.

"How much do you weigh?"

I squint at him, pursing my lips. "Wow, that's a rude thing to ask a lady."

He laughs, but there's a tightness around his eyes. I can tell he's just as worried and tense as the others are, despite the fact that he's trying to keep things light by joking around.

"What brings you to Mexico?" he asks.

"I'm on a break from school, just trying to see new things before I get locked into a job I'm probably going to hate," I answer immediately, making a face that I imagine an overworked college student would make.

Ransom gives me a look of approval. "I think you've got it."

The others have their own fake identities, and they've changed little things about themselves. Malice has cut his hair a little, as well as stopped shaving, and he's wearing blue tinged contacts, the natural color of his eyes turning them almost a stormy cobalt. He has makeup covering most of his more noticeable tattoos, helping him to stand out less.

Vic has let his hair grow out longer since we've been on the run, and I can tell it bothers him. He's constantly flicking it out of his eyes, but now he steels himself, mastering that impressive control to ignore it. His eyes are green thanks to another set of contacts, and when he looks at me, it's startling.

Ransom's hair is more buzzed on the sides now, and his eyes are a muddy brown from the contacts he's wearing. But even that can't hide how attractive he is.

We stand there together, none of us in a hurry to leave just yet, even though we need to. We have a window of time that we need to get through the border, in order to take advantage of the research Vic did, but tension hovers in the air between us. Like none of us want to admit that this could be the last moment we're all together or even all alive.

But we all know it.

Ransom pulls me close and kisses my forehead. "I'm proud of you," he says.

"For what?"

"For handling your bike like a boss bitch. For coming this far. For never giving up." He shrugs. "Take your pick."

I hug him tightly. "Thank you. For everything."

I don't even know how to start numbering all the things he's done for me. Being there when I needed someone, when I was alone and scared at their house for the first time. Keeping me alive, when his brothers would have killed me in a heartbeat. Being open and strong and kind and funny. It's too much to say.

But there's a look on Ransom's face like he knows what I mean anyway, and we share a quick kiss.

He pushes me over to Vic next, and I stand there for a second, not sure how to approach this. I know Vic needs his control to get through today, and I don't want to shatter that, but if this is the last time...

He makes the decision for me, striding closer and reaching up to touch my face.

"You can do this," he murmurs softly. "You can do anything."

I laugh, feeling emotional all of a sudden. "I don't know about that."

"I do," he says, eyes blazing. "You've done the impossible before."

He's talking about him and his brothers, maybe. How I managed to win them over.

"Can I hug you?" I whisper, and he nods, just once.

I put my arms around him, and he stiffens for a second before melting against me. He breathes out a ragged sigh, and I hold him tighter, memorizing the way he feels against me, the way he smells.

When he pulls back, his eyes are a swirl of emotion, all of it so close to the surface. It takes my breath away, the split second or so that I get to see it, before those walls come back up because they have to.

He kisses the corner of my mouth and then moves away, fingers tapping at his thigh, pulling himself back together.

That leaves me with Malice. He steps toward me, his dark hair gleaming in the sunlight as he drops his head.

"You remember what I told you this morning?" he asks.

My heart flutters, and I arch a brow at him, because there's no way I'll ever forget that. "Of course I do. Do you remember what I told *you*?"

We believe in you. I love you.

Malice nods, his eyes on fire with determination. "I remember."

I step into his arms, and he holds me tight, almost too tight for just a moment. I breathe out a long sigh, clinging to him, not wanting to let go.

But of course we have to. Long before I'm ready for it, he steps back. He goes back over to where his brothers are, and I watch the three of them have a silent conversation. Malice looks to Vic first, and Vic nods. The two of them don't touch, but they don't have to. Their connection, their bond is plain to see. Then Ransom and Malice grip each other's forearms, and Malice claps Ransom on the shoulder before they break apart.

As one, they turn back to me, and I take a deep breath.

Here we go.

We all head back to our bikes, mounting up again.

It's only another half hour or so to the border, and by the time we get there, my nerves are a mess. It's a good thing I have to focus on the bike, and I'm actually grateful that Ransom suggested this way of getting there. If I had to sit in a car with these nerves, I'd be close to barfing out the window right now.

We're far from the only people trying to get into the country, and there's a line to go through the checkpoint, which then splits up into separate lines, each going to a different border agent.

The guys and I are all separated, staggered with space between us, the way we planned it.

So far, nothing has gone wrong, but as the line inches forward, my brain conjures up all kinds of ideas of what could be waiting for us when we get there—the worst of which is a sudden flash of certainty that Olivia beat us here and will be right there, waiting to identify us and have us hauled off.

But I shake myself out of that negative line of thinking. We know she's been tracking our movements, trying to figure out where we've been and guess where we might be going, but despite all of her resources, she's only one woman. And if Victor's decoy worked at all, she should think we're heading toward Los Angeles right now instead of toward the Mexican border.

Finally, I get to the border agent. I take a deep breath as I roll to a stop, trying to act calm, as if I do this sort of thing all the time.

The agent is a woman who looks like she'd rather be anywhere but at work right now, and she takes my ID and glances at it. I pull my helmet off so she can see my face, and she nods.

"Reason for visiting?" she drones.

"Just a little vacation," I reply with a shrug, trying to keep my tone casual. "I graduate soon, and I wanna see stuff before I get chained to a desk." I make a face at that last bit, she snorts, nodding.

"Tell me about it. How long are you staying?"

"Just a week," I reply. "That's as long as I could get away."

Out of the corner of my eye, I see Malice approaching the agent in his line. He looks so different with his tattoos covered and the dark scruff on his face, but I'd recognize him anywhere.

The agent looks at his ID and then back to him, and a slight frown crosses the man's face.

My stomach drops.

Fuck. Does the guy recognize him?

A loud noise in the line behind Malice draws everyone's attention. A horn honks and a dog barks, high pitched and grating. The agent with Malice frowns, leaning up to see what the commotion is, and then waves Malice through, handing the ID back before he goes.

I have to fight not to breathe an audible sigh of relief, and my heart unclenches a little as I shift my focus back to the agent in front of me.

"Enjoy your trip," she says, passing me back my fake passport and waving me through.

I put my helmet back on and roll my bike forward, my hands shaking a little.

After driving past the border, I put some distance between us, forcing myself to keep going for a bit longer. I want desperately to turn back to check on Ransom and Vic, to make sure they get through okay, but I can't draw attention to them. Or to myself.

So I keep going until I get to the spot we designated, parking the bike and tugging off my helmet to wait for the rest of them.

Malice shows up a couple minutes later, nodding at me, and then Ransom and Vic arrive, right on each other's heels. As we reconvene, the knot of worry I've been nursing since Malice almost got arrested finally loosens enough that I can breathe.

We did it.

We *did* it.

Ransom pulls his motorcycle up alongside mine and takes off his helmet, grinning as he shakes out his hair. The bronze highlights in the brown strands glint with the movement, and he leans over and kisses me, his bike still humming beneath him.

"Welcome to Mexico, pretty girl," he says when he pulls back. "We made it. I think this calls for a celebration."

I couldn't stop the grin that spreads across my face if I tried. "What did you have in mind?"

45

WILLOW

It turns out that what Ransom has in mind is margaritas.

The city we crossed over into is called Nuevo Laredo, and Victor guides us to a neighborhood in the far west part of the city, a place he's scoped out during all of his research over the past several days. Malice pays a guy in cash to rent a small house for a few days, and although it's nothing fancy, there are flowers blooming on a trellis outside, and the inside is considerably roomier than the RV was.

We get groceries from a little shop up the street, stocking up on food and tequila, and it feels almost... normal.

Back at the house, Vic digs into the fresh ingredients he bought at the store to make us all dinner, presiding over the kitchen with a spatula in his hand and threatening to smack Ransom with it every time his brother gets close enough to try to steal something from the pan. Eventually, Ransom learns his lesson and retreats to make margaritas, juicing limes and muddling fruit, then mixing it with tequila and triple sec.

The food is incredible, better than anything I've eaten since before the aborted wedding that they stole me away from, and the margarita is sweet and refreshing. Even though Malice cuts us all off after one drink, insisting we need to stay sharp, just in case, the slight buzz of the booze in my system is enough to make me pleasantly relaxed.

After dinner, Ransom and I step out onto the tiny back patio behind the house, listening to the distant sounds of the city. Someone on the next block is playing music, and the melodic notes make it all the way to our little backyard oasis, filling the air with their quiet sound.

When Ransom notices me bobbing my head along to the music, he pulls me into his arms, swaying his hips against mine.

"I have no idea what I'm doing," I tell him, shaking my head.

"That's not true. I saw you at Sin and Salvation," he whispers in my ear, his breath tickling the lobe. "I fucking *know* you can move."

I grin, letting him slip his muscled leg between my thighs as he presses me closer against him, his hand splayed over my lower back. The warmth of being pleasantly tipsy trickles through me… or maybe it's not even that. Maybe it's just the happiness and relief that we made it out of the country and into Mexico in one piece.

I know there's more to figure out, and we can't stay here forever. For one thing, the money will run out before too long, and if the guys have to rob some place again, there's more risk of them getting caught.

We need to come up with a better long-term plan to keep Olivia off our asses, but that can wait for another day.

For right now, tonight, I'm happy.

Malice ducks out of the house as we dance, tall and imposing, dressed in dark jeans and a t-shirt that shows off the tattoos on his arms. He's removed the jacket and the makeup that covered them up earlier, and all the men have taken out their colored contact lenses as well. He looks different with the scruff that covers his jaw, but still as brutally gorgeous as ever.

He strides toward us, and when Ransom takes my hand and spins me around, Malice steps closer, resting one hand on my hip as he sandwiches me between him and his brother. I can feel the strength and heat of them as a new song starts up in the distance, and I let my head fall back against Ransom's chest, my eyelids drooping a little as I move my hips sensually, lost in the feel of it.

A few female voices catch my attention, and I glance at the street, I can see a group of women passing the house. They eye Malice and Ransom with interest over the low wall that borders the backyard and then look at me between them, envy flashing across their faces.

I just smile and keep dancing.

They should be jealous.

I have three gorgeous men who care about me, and that's an incredible feeling.

Somehow, the Voronin brothers all want me. They want me enough to leave everything else behind, and although I once tried to protect them by leaving them, I'm starting to believe that our future together could be bright. That it could be something incredible.

The women continue on by, disappearing down the alley, but I still feel eyes on me, so I turn my head the other way. Vic has come outside too, and he's leaning against the side of the house near the door, watching us intently.

It feels different than it used to, when he would watch because he thought that was as close as he could get. Now, it feels like he's watching just because he wants to. Because he likes what he sees.

I meet his eyes, and a spark of electricity arcs between us. I have a feeling that if I keep dancing with Malice and Ransom, it won't take long for Vic to move closer and maybe even join us.

But I can still feel the heat of that spark in my blood, mixing with the incredible feeling of being surrounded by his two brothers, and the truth is, I want to do more than just dance with the three of them.

So I move before Vic can, stepping out from between Malice and Ransom. I shoot a single glance at them over my shoulder, then walk into the house without a word.

Even without looking back again, I can tell they're all following me, and something about that realization makes my heart beat faster. I'm finally starting to accept how deeply and truly these men are mine. That they would follow me anywhere.

The house has a separate living room and kitchen, which feels like a luxury after all that time in the RV. I step into the brightly furnished living room and then stop and turn around. Malice, Ransom, and Victor stop too, their expressions heated and intense as they gaze at me.

I took the initiative by coming inside, and I take it again now, moving closer to kiss each one of them. I start with Vic and end with Ransom, lingering just a little between each kiss. That clicks the tension building between all of us up a notch, and their focus on me is laser precise.

"No more dancing, angel?" Ransom asks as our kiss breaks, his voice husky. "What do you want to do instead?"

Instead of answering him, I just *show* him, dropping to my knees in front of him. He sucks in a breath and looks down at me with hooded blue-green eyes.

I tug open his button and fly, then work his pants and boxer briefs down enough to free his cock. He's already hardening, and his shaft is a warm weight in my hand. I trail my fingers over the piercings and slide my thumb over the head, enjoying the soft groan that spills from Ransom's mouth.

Then I take up exploring him with my own mouth. I lick up the underside of his cock, taking my time allowing my saliva to coat his shaft. I play with each little ball of his piercings, feeling the differences between where he's pierced and where he isn't.

"Fuck," Ransom groans. "You drive me crazy."

"That's the idea."

I smirk a little and keep it up, easing my mouth over the head of his cock and sucking shallowly, flicking the tip of my tongue right over his slit.

When he's breathing harder, I pull back, licking my lips. The other two have moved in closer, which makes this easier. I turn to Malice next and get his pants open as well.

His tattooed shaft is a familiar thickness, already hard when I pull it out. He's not as content as Ransom to just let me do my thing though, and he threads his fingers into my hair immediately, fisting the strands as I start sucking his cock too.

"Shit," he hisses. "Take it, Solnyshka. Swallow me down. Show me what a good girl you can be."

His hips buck forward, making my eyes water a bit, but I relax my jaw and let him have what he wants. He uses his grip on my hair to keep me in place and starts moving, fucking my mouth with deep thrusts that hit the back of my throat.

I moan around him, looking up at him through my lashes, and the possessive desire darkening his expression makes my clit throb. I slide my tongue over the smooth underside of his cock, swallowing around him when he stills for a moment with his cock buried deep.

His muscles are hard as steel beneath my hands when I press against his thighs, and he releases his hold on my hair, letting me pull back. A thin line of saliva connects my lips to his cock as he slides out of my mouth, and I draw in a deep lungful of air before licking my lips and turning to Victor.

Of the three of them, he's the most tense. His fingers are already tapping at his thighs, and I count the rhythm in my head. *One, two, three, four, five, six...*

Instead of just taking what I want, I pause, waiting to see if he'll let me.

Something flickers in his eyes, but then he nods, letting out a breath as his shoulders relax a little.

My heart leaps, and I shuffle closer to him on my knees, carefully drawing him out of his pants. As apprehensive as he seemed, he's also obviously turned on, the large vein along his shaft throbbing. As soon as I touch him, his cock starts leaking precum, and I groan and lick it up, savoring the salty tang.

"You taste good," I tell him softly. "I wanted a taste so bad when you were marking me with your cum. I wanted it on my tongue, not just my skin."

Vic lets out a shuddering breath, his hips stuttering forward.

"Pretty," he breathes. "You're so fucking pretty like this."

His cock pulses warningly as I wrap my lips around him, and I only bob my head a couple of times, not wanting to overwhelm him too much yet.

I move back to Ransom then, setting a rhythm of my own. Heaving breaths and low grunts fill the room as I alternate between the three of them, going back and forth, my mouth and jaw adjusting to their different sizes.

Vic comes first, unable to hold back, his hands gripping my head as his hips jerk toward me. He gives me exactly what I told him I wanted, filling my mouth with his cum, and I swallow it greedily, some part of me still not quite believing that this is real. That I can really have him like this.

"That was..." He shakes his head as his shaft finally slides out from between my lips, looking down at me with awe in his vibrant blue eyes. "I thought it felt good to fuck you, butterfly, but that was... the way you..."

"She's got a good mouth, doesn't she?" Malice asks, pride in his tone as he fists his cock, his gaze locked on me. "There's nothing quite as hot as watching you try to take all of me between your perfect little lips, Solnyshka. I think Vic feels the same way."

Vic makes a noise of agreement, and Ransom does too. The sounds go straight to my clit, and I squeeze my thighs together before I move back over to kneel in front of Malice. Tilting my chin just a little to keep eye contact with him, I make a show of clasping my hands behind my back, a silent signal that I want him to take total control.

A deep noise rumbles in his chest, and he wraps his hand around the dyed strands of my hair, bringing my face closer to his cock. When the smooth head bumps against my lips, he growls, "Open."

I do, letting him inside, and he doesn't give me any more time than that to adjust. He fucks my face, working his cock deeper each time, his thick shaft sliding between my lips as I keep them wrapped around him, making sure my teeth don't scrape his length as it slides in and out. I open the back of my throat, keeping my jaw loose and gagging a little as my heart hammers in my chest. My clit is throbbing, my entire body burning with arousal, and when the coarse dark hairs at the base of his cock brush against my nose, I moan around him.

He once warned me that he breaks everything he touches, but I don't feel broken now. I feel strong and filthy and powerful.

Malice strokes in and out of my mouth a few more times, grunting with each rough thrust, then tightens his hand on my hair, making my scalp sting as he yanks me off his dick.

"Open," he says again, his voice strained. "Hold out your tongue."

I obey immediately, and he fists himself with his free hand, using the saliva that still coats his cock to slick the glide as he strokes quickly, keeping his crown right near the tip of my tongue. When he explodes, his cum shoots into my mouth and over my tongue, and I shiver at the feel of it. His chest heaves as he looks down at me, and I don't move, letting him see his release sitting in my mouth, a tiny bit of it spilling from one corner.

"Swallow," he rasps.

I close my mouth, savoring the distinctive taste of his cum before letting it slide down my throat. I lift a hand and wipe up the little trail that dribbled down to my chin, licking my fingers to clean them.

Malice's nostrils flare, and he lets go of my hair, his hand gentle as he smooths down the strands. I feel like I'm practically vibrating with arousal as I glance over at Ransom, who's watching me as if this is the best fucking thing he's ever seen in his life. Instead of making me come to him, he steps closer as I turn to face him, reaching down to trail his fingertips along the side of my face.

"Saved the best for last, huh?" he jokes with a wink, and I bite back a smile. I'm breathing harder, and he must be able to see the way my eyes are glazed over with arousal, because he adds, "You've gotten yourself all worked up, haven't you, pretty girl? Why don't you get yourself off while you suck me? Make yourself come with my cock in your mouth."

Almost as if I've been waiting for permission to do it, I slide one hand into my pants, finding my clit with my fingertips as I wrap my other hand around him and slide my lips over his pierced cock. He wasn't wrong. I'm so close to the edge, so wound up from the heat in the air and the incredible feeling of making his brothers come. My hand moves fast, my fingers circling my clit with firm strokes, as I hollow my cheeks and work Ransom's cock in tandem.

"Fuck," he groans, and I can feel his legs shaking a little as he presses deeper into my mouth. "Fuck, fuck. *Fuck!*"

His upper body bows over me a little as he comes in my mouth, and I almost don't swallow in time because my own orgasm hits me at the same moment. My movements lose coordination, but I keep sucking on his cock, mewling around him as pleasure wracks my body.

I'm completely breathless by the time I finally pull back, my heart galloping in the aftermath of my climax.

Ransom helps me to my feet, giving me a deep, filthy kiss, like he wants to taste the remnants of himself on my tongue. Then he presses another little kiss to my nose.

"It was a long-ass day," he tells me. "I think we'd better get you to bed."

"Fuck, yes." Malice scoops me up and tosses me over his shoulder, startling a laugh out of me as he carries me down the short hallway to the bedroom. He drops me onto the large bed, and I bounce a little as I hit the mattress.

"This is *so* much better than that pull-out bed," I groan,

spreading my arms out and savoring the feeling of cool sheets under my heated skin. "It's nice to be in a bed that's not built for someone the size of a toddler."

Malice chuckles as his brothers come to stand beside him. "Only the best for you, Solnyshka. You deserve a big-ass bed to get fucked in."

"Like the queen you are," Ransom adds, grinning.

"Are you wet for us?" Malice's gaze slides over me. "Are you nice and wet and ready?"

"Yes." I nod, but he shakes his head.

"I think you could be wetter." He flicks his gaze over toward his twin. "Vic. You want to get her all warmed up for us? You want to taste her?"

Vic stiffens, his breath catching. The banked arousal in my body instantly flares up to eleven as I realize what Malice is doing. He's letting Vic take the lead, giving his brother a chance to touch me first. To eat me out.

I can't stop myself from squirming on the bed, my hips shifting restlessly as my clit responds to Malice's words. I tug my shirt off and reach behind me to unclasp my bra, arching my back a little. Then I shove my pants down, kicking my shoes off and working them down before shimmying my panties off too. Vic stands like a statue, watching as I do all of that, and when I'm fully naked, he finally moves. He shucks his own clothes, folding them and setting them aside on the bed in a perfectly Vic way before climbing onto the mattress with me.

He spreads my thighs, and the feel of his hands on my bare skin is just as thrilling as it was the first time he did it.

But this time, he doesn't just touch me with his hands.

Settling more comfortably between my legs, he lowers his head. He's moving so slowly that I can feel the warmth of his breath before I feel his tongue, and when he finally licks his way up my slit, I make a hungry, shocked noise.

"You like that?" Malice asks. "You like my brother's tongue on you?"

"Yes!" I pant out. "So much!"

Vic seems encouraged by the undeniable honesty in my voice, and he keeps going. He laps at me the same way he explored my body the other night, with a kind of single-minded thoroughness and focus that takes my breath away.

My second orgasm hits me before I even see it coming, and as I quake through the aftershocks, he barely even slows down.

"She likes when you fuck her with your tongue," Ransom comments, his voice heated. "As deep as you can go. Then when you start to feel her clench around you, lick her clit. Fast. Hard. She can take it."

"*Fuck*," I moan as Vic follows Ransom's directions.

My hands flail around desperately for something to hold on to, and I fist the sheets as Malice and Ransom keep telling Vic everything I like.

I'm not sure he would even need the advice, since he's watched so many times, and it's clear that he's observant as hell. But the sound of their deep voices describing everything they like to do to me only heightens my arousal as Vic experiments, his fingers digging into my thighs to keep me open for him as his relentless tongue moves over every part of my pussy.

He makes me come again, his name a loud cry on my lips this time. And then again. And again. He doesn't seem like he ever wants to stop, and by the time he finally pulls back, he looks almost as wrecked as I feel.

His normally neat hair is messy from where I think I had my fingers in it at one point, his lips and chin are wet, his cheeks flushed, and his eyes dark. His cock is rock hard again, and he hisses as he fists himself at the base and squeezes, like he's trying to hold back an orgasm.

"I think..." He drags in a breath. "I think she's ready for you."

My gaze tracks him as he moves off the bed, and he doesn't look away from me either. Distantly, I'm aware that Ransom and Malice are both tugging off their shirts and discarding the rest of their clothes, but it isn't until Malice climbs onto the bed with me that I wrench my focus away from Vic.

"You want more?" Malice asks, crawling up so that his large body looms over mine. He's hard again too, the heat of his cock brushing against my lower belly. "Do you want this?"

I lick my lips, and my voice is scratchy when I finally find the words to reply.

"Yes. Please."

I reach up to touch him, but he grabs my wrists before I can, pinning them over my head against the sheets with one hand. The stitches from where Ransom removed the tracker came out yesterday, but he's still careful of the pink, healing skin.

I spread my legs for him, letting him see what a slick wet mess I am for all of them, and he curses under his breath as he uses his free hand to guide himself to my entrance. His hips drive forward as he pushes all the way in, and I gasp at the intrusion. After coming so many times, I'm swollen and sensitive down there, which makes him feel even bigger than usual. It's just this side of pain, but it feels so good too.

He fucks into me hard and fast, like waiting this long to claim me has pushed him right up to the edge. His cock fills me completely, and each hard, almost punishing thrust rocks me to my core.

I'm pinned down and filled up... and I love it.

"Watching you scream for Vic got me so fucking hard for you," he growls. "Our greedy girl. So. Fucking. Greedy."

Each word is punctuated by a thrust so deep I can feel it all the way through me, and the bed rocks beneath us, its joints squeaking.

I don't say anything back. I can't. Every time he bottoms out inside me, it punches all the breath from my lungs, so I just wrap my legs around him, my nails digging into my palms and sweat slicking our skin as he pounds into me.

When he comes, he drops his head to the crook of my neck with a feral grunt, and I squeeze around him, my legs shaking. I can't even tell if I'm coming again, or if it's just the leftover pleasure from all the orgasms Victor gave me, but it doesn't matter. It's exactly what I need.

Cum drips from me as Malice pulls out, and when he moves out of the way, Ransom takes his place.

"Such a good girl for us," Ransom murmurs, giving me a little smile as he lifts my hands and kisses my wrists where Malice held me down. Then he drapes my arms over his shoulders, gripping my hips as he notches himself at my entrance and slides inside.

The piercings along his shaft feel huge as they rub against my walls, and I'm already so close, just from him pressing inside me.

He starts off with a few measured strokes to let me recover a little, then picks up the pace, fucking me almost as hard as Malice did, hunger burning in his blue-green eyes. He leans down and kisses me as his hips keep working, mouths and teeth and tongues colliding as heat builds between us.

By the time I feel another orgasm cresting, I'm a mess, sweaty and writhing under him. It hits me hard, and I let out a ragged cry, clenching around him.

"God, fucking... Willow!"

He groans my name as he follows right after, grinding his pelvis against me as his cock jerks and swells. He keeps doing that as we ride out our orgasms, the pressure on my clit dragging mine out until I feel like I might never stop coming. My heart is a heavy drumbeat in my chest, and I have to take a second to catch my breath before I can unwind my legs from his waist and let him pull out.

Instead of shuffling off the bed like Malice did, Ransom just flops to the side, and my gaze returns to Vic. Tonight has been a lot, and I wouldn't blame him if he can't handle any more. Hell, I'm not sure *I* can handle any more.

Of course, as soon as I have that thought, Vic moves toward the bed, and my exhausted body immediately sparks back to life a little. If Vic is going to fuck me, I want that so badly, no matter how worn out I am.

I watch Vic as he crawls onto the mattress, settling between my legs.

"Beautiful," he murmurs, reaching up to smooth my sweaty hair back from my face. "You have no idea what you look like when you're letting them have you."

"Is that why you like to watch so much?" I whisper.

He smiles, lifting one shoulder. "It might be. But I think it's just you. I can never take my eyes off you."

I pull him down into a heated kiss, and he groans against my lips, his movements a little clumsy and desperate as he guides himself into me at the same time. My pussy is slick with my own arousal and the combined cum of both of his brothers, but Vic doesn't seem to care.

He presses his huge cock into me, and I'm grateful for the extra wetness to help him slide in smoothly. Once he's fully seated, he grabs my hips for a second, his jaw going tight as he steadies himself. Then he pulls me up, changing our positions so that I'm half in his lap.

My arms shake a little as I cling to him, worn out from the marathon of fucking and coming. But he cradles me close, not letting me fall, and when he thrusts his hips up, I can feel how deep this angle lets him get.

There's more confidence in the way he fucks me this time, and it doesn't take him as long to find his rhythm. He's getting more experienced, but more than that, I think it's because he's learning how to let go with me, learning that it's okay to chase what feels good, to give in to that craving.

It's something I had to learn too. It took me a while to stop second guessing myself or feeling like there was something wrong with me for the things that turn me on.

For needing it rough.

For liking when Malice degrades me.

For wanting to be claimed by three different men.

But I'm finally starting to accept those things about myself, and it makes me want to show Victor how much it means to me that he's fucking me like this. I feel like a rag doll, limp and spent, but I clench my walls around him, pressing wet kisses to his neck and sucking on his earlobe as I push myself toward another orgasm.

"You feel so good, Vic," I whisper. "This feels so good."

"This is where you belong," he pants. "With us. Like this."

I nod my agreement, because there's nowhere else I'd want to be. Vic bounces me on his lap, working me up and down his cock, and when he pulls me down hard and pulses inside me, I swear I can feel some of his brothers' cum leaking from me to make room for his.

That thought—knowing that all of them have come inside me, that I'm full of all of them—triggers the orgasm I've been working toward, and I shudder weakly against Vic as my eyes roll back.

He splays his hands over my back and leans forward, laying me down on the bed again as he finally slips out of me. I really am spent now. There's nothing left in my mind but a blissful haze, and I'm just moments away from falling asleep.

When something warm and wet settles between my legs, I whimper and try to shove it away.

"Can't... come again," I mumble.

Ransom chuckles. "No one's asking you to this time, pretty girl. But as hot as it is seeing you drip with our cum, we need to get you cleaned up a little. You just rest. We've got you."

The washcloth goes back between my legs, and the warmth of it does feel soothing as he carefully wipes away the sticky mess. When he's done, the mattress shifts a bit, and then someone lifts me while the covers are pulled down. They set me down and tuck me beneath the sheets, and I blink my eyes open long enough to gaze up at the three of them.

"There's only one bed," I remind them.

Malice looks at the bed with a doubtful expression on his face. "Yeah, but it's too small for all of us. Someone can sleep on the couch, and there's a—"

"Stay," I mumble. "Please."

I don't have the brain power to be more articulate than that, but fortunately, I don't need to be. After a few low, murmured words, the three of them shuffle onto the bed with me, Victor on one side and Malice and Ransom on the other.

"Don't fucking try to cuddle with me in the middle of the night," I hear Malice grunt.

"Aww, you used to love our cuddle time, Mal," Ransom shoots back.

"That was when you were three, and it was because you wouldn't fucking nap if I didn't go in there and sit with you. Mom made me."

"Sure she did."

"She didn't," Victor whispers in my ear. "Malice just liked to look out for him."

A tired smile tugs at my lips, and I nestle deeper into the little pocket between all of them, warm and cozy and content.

46

WILLOW

A LIGHT BREEZE ruffles my hair as I step out of the front door. It's chilly this morning, dew still clinging to the grass outside. I wrap my arms around myself, smiling as the sound of laughter rises up in the distance—one voice young and bright, the other deep and resonant.

"Malice took her for a walk again," Ransom says from behind me, wrapping his arms around my waist. "She was begging him to go exploring. She's just as brave and adventurous as her mother."

I grin, leaning back against his chest. "Well, the three of you brought out that side in me. So it makes sense that you brought it out in your daughter too."

His head drops, his lips brushing my temple as he murmurs, "Nah. That's definitely not all because of us. You get credit for it too."

My heart swells, warmth expanding in my chest from the fond, proud tone of his voice. Deciding I'll have plenty of advance notice when Malice and Dayana get back from the sounds of their voices, I turn around to face the man behind me. His lips tilt upward as our gazes meet, the eyebrow ring he's had for as long as I've known him glinting as he cocks a brow. I go up onto my toes, and he meets me halfway, erasing the distance between our faces as we kiss, slow and unhurried.

His hair is a bit shaggy these days, the bronze and brown locks wild and unkempt in a way that I know makes Vic secretly dream of attacking him with a pair of clippers one night just to get it back in order. But I think it's sexy.

I slide my fingers between the strands, loving the way they feel against my skin, and when I drag my nails over his scalp, he makes a sound into our kiss.

Even when our lips finally separate, we don't let go of each other. I slide my hands down his back, keeping my arms wrapped around him as I rest my cheek against his chest, listening to the steady beat of his heart.

"Did Vic go with them?" *I murmur.*

"Nah. He's working on a shopping list. You know how he is, he hates when we forget something."

I laugh quietly, because I do know. This far out from civilization, a shopping trip is a day-long undertaking, which is why Vic always insists on being the one to write the list. When we first settled out here, I thought the guys would miss living in the city, but it turns out that Malice wasn't lying when he told me once that all he needed was me, his brothers, and his tattoo gun, and he'd be happy. Ransom added 'motorcycles' to that list, and Vic added 'computers,' and since they've each got what they need in that regard, none of them seem to miss Detroit all that much.

I certainly don't.

It's been years since we fled from Olivia, and she's never managed to find us. We've built a life for ourselves down here in a remote part of Mexico, and when I think of the city I used to live in, it's never with longing or nostalgia.

Why would it be?

Just like Malice said, everything I need is right here.

Sweet, childish laughter rises up again, still at a bit of a distance but coming closer. I can't make out Malice's words as he responds to Dayana, but whatever he says makes her laugh harder.

Ransom and I finally break apart, and I turn again to watch Malice and our daughter emerge from the trees up ahead, following the path back to our house. There's no one else around for miles, nothing but lush forest and a back road that eventually connects to a larger highway, so I don't worry about the noise as Dayana catches sight of us and lets out a happy cry.

She starts to run toward us, and Malice jogs to catch up with her, taking her hand to keep her from tripping on any loose rocks or roots.

Her blonde hair streams behind her, her cheeks round and soft and her blue eyes shining with excitement.

"Momma, momma!" she calls, and I kneel down to greet her as they reach us. "We saw a pretty bird!"

"Yeah?" I smile at her, brushing her wild hair back from her face. She'll be four soon, and I can't believe how big she's getting. "Did you stay so, so quiet so it wouldn't fly away?"

"Yes!" She nods proudly.

"At first," Malice adds, crossing his inked arms over his chest as he grins. "That lasted for about five seconds."

I laugh. "Better than I would've done."

"Oh, I know you can't keep quiet, Solnyshka." His gaze turns heated as those dark gray eyes find me. "But I like it when you're loud."

I flush, heat rushing through me. As I straighten, Dayana holds up her hand to me, slipping it easily into mine, and the three of us turn to head back into the house. Vic is in the kitchen, and he looks up from his computer as we enter. His gaze shifts from me to Dayana, and if possible, the adoration in his eyes only grows.

He pushes his chair back from the table and pats his thighs, and Dayana lets go of my hand and trots over to him, crawling happily up to sit on his lap. He wraps his arms around her, gentle and protective, and she nestles into his embrace like there's no place better in the world.

She's not wrong about that.

"How's the shopping list coming?" I ask, walking over to press a kiss to his lips.

He lets go of Dayana with one hand and catches the front of my shirt, pulling me closer and extending the kiss, his lips moving hungrily against mine before he finally lets me straighten up again.

"It's almost done," he answers as I clear my throat, my heart beating a little harder. "We should be—"

"Willow."

Malice's voice behind me interrupts Victor, and my brows pull together. There's something off about his tone. Something urgent and hard. But that doesn't make any sense.

"Sorry," I say, shaking my head and returning my focus to Vic. "What were you saying?"

"I said we should—"

"He's going after Willow! Fuck!"

This time, it's Ransom's voice that cuts in, so loud and full of fear that it makes me gasp.

My heart lurches as a large hand closes around my wrist, and—

My eyes pop open, my body jolting with the force of being dragged awake so suddenly.

The hand on my wrist tightens, and I realize with a shock of panic that it wasn't just in my dream. Someone really did grab me, and in the darkness of the bedroom, a figure looms over me.

"No, you don't, you son of a bitch!"

Ransom's voice is like a growl, and a second later, he plows into the shadowy figure above me. The two of them go stumbling across the room and crash into a wall, and I realize that near the doorway of the room, Malice and Victor are wrestling with another man dressed in black.

Fuck. Oh god, fuck!

I scramble out of bed as Ransom ducks a punch from the man

he's up against, my heart crawling up into my throat. I feel dizzy and disoriented, my mind reeling from the sudden shift of my dream to this. But I know I can't afford to hesitate. I don't know who these men are, but they must've broken into our bedroom as we slept, and they're clearly skilled fighters because it's taking both Malice and Vic to hold one of them off.

That leaves Ransom on his own to face the other one.

Shit.

Adrenaline rushes through me, clarifying my thoughts as I glance around the room. The bedroom is sparsely decorated, but there's a wicker chair in one corner, and I pick it up and bring it down as hard as I can against the back of the man fighting Ransom.

The wicker snaps and cracks, hardly enough to do any real damage—but it gives Ransom an opening. He lunges in, landing a hard punch against the man's face. He follows it up with two more, and when the man staggers a little, Ransom grabs the back of his head and yanks it downward, lifting his knee to crack it against the man's skull.

The guy in black grunts and goes down, and behind me, I hear the sound of frantic scuffling. I whirl around, worried that the man Malice and Vic were fighting has managed to hurt one of them, but instead I see that Vic has their attacker in a headlock. He holds the man tight, bracing one hand against his bicep as his forearm slowly cuts off the man's air supply. The man struggles for another several beats and then finally goes limp.

"Fuck!"

Malice bites out the curse as Vic deposits the man on the floor and stands warily over his body, as if prepared to fight him again if he has to. Ransom does the same with the other man as Malice strides out of the room and then returns a moment later with a gun in his hand. He's still naked, just like his brothers are, and in the dark, their tattoos look like shadows crawling over their bodies.

"Should we try to wake them up and interrogate them?" Ransom asks.

"No." Malice shakes his head grimly. "We don't know if others are coming. There's no fucking time for that."

Without breaking stride, he stalks to the bed and grabs a pillow off it. Then he kneels down by the unconscious man Ransom is standing over, holds the pillow to his head, and pulls the trigger.

Even muffled like that, the gunshot is loud, and I jump, my heart crashing against my ribs.

"This isn't a time for mercy either," Malice says in a hard voice, his gaze flicking up to me before he grabs another pillow. "These two fuckers broke into the house. They were armed, dressed in tactical gear, and one of them had a syringe of what's probably some kind of knock-out drug. They came to take you, Solnyshka."

He drapes the pillow over the second man's head, the muffled bang of the gunshot punctuating his words.

My skin goes cold, goosebumps breaking out over my naked body.

"Get dressed," Vic says, leaving his post near the downed man now that it's clear he won't be getting up again. "We need to leave. Now."

He grabs his clothes and starts tugging them on, and I rush to do the same as his brothers get dressed too.

"Who were they?" I whisper as I pull my shirt over my head, my pulse racing as I glance at the two still forms on the floor.

"We don't know." Malice shakes his head and crosses to the little window on one side of the bedroom, tucking his gun into the back of his pants as he peers out. "They're not cops, but Olivia must've sent someone else after us. Private security or her own personal guards. Bounty hunters, maybe."

Goddammit.

My stomach twists with worry, and I bite my lip as Malice nods to his brothers and the four of us slip out of the bedroom.

How did this happen? Did someone see us at the border? Or maybe the women who passed by while we were dancing recognized us somehow. Maybe it wasn't jealousy I saw on their faces, but something else.

How the hell could Olivia have found us so quickly? Vic did everything he could to throw her off our trail. She was supposed to think we were in Los Angeles.

The small house is still and quiet, but it's not a comforting sort of silence. My heart is beating so loud that I feel like the thud of it must be audible for miles, and I blow out a slow breath, trying to get it under control. Vic grabs his laptop and stuffs it into a backpack, and I start to move toward the other bags containing our meager belongings, but Malice holds out a hand to stop me.

"No time," he repeats. "Grab your passport and that's it. We need to get the fuck out of here in case those assholes had backup. Vic's got his computer, and that's enough. Everything else, we'll replace."

I nod, swallowing hard. I stuff my fake passport into my back pocket, and the brothers arm themselves and pocket theirs too before Ransom grabs the keys to the bikes.

We head outside, all of us on high alert. The street is quiet and dark, and I have no idea if it's very late at night or very early in the morning, but I guess that doesn't really matter. The guys scan the area around the house, keeping me between them as we move. Ransom's hand is at my lower back, urging me on, and he glances at Malice over my head.

"Do we head deeper into Mexico or back to the states?"

"I don't know. Let's get the fuck out of here first, and then we'll —*shit.*"

The curse comes out hot and angry. He stops in his tracks, and as I follow his gaze, my heart drops.

Our bikes are parked where we left them, but it only takes one glance to see that the tires have been slashed.

Those men must've done it before they attacked us. So we couldn't escape.

Panic crawls up my spine, a creeping feeling of dread and

claustrophobia, even though the street ahead of us is wide open and empty.

"Those goddamn cocksuckers," Malice growls.

The tires are obviously unsalvageable, and none of the men even stop to try. Malice grips my arm, tugging me along with him as his brothers fall in around us, jogging away from the house quickly. I pant as I try to keep up, my breaths coming out short and choppy.

When the rumbling of a car engine sounds behind us, Malice's grip on my arm goes even tighter. He pulls me down another street, picking up the pace—but instead of passing by, the headlights of a Jeep flash as it turns onto the same street we did.

Following us.

"Shit!" Ransom blurts. "We gotta go!"

We break into a dead sprint, and the car's engine revs as it speeds up after us. We veer again, Malice nearly yanking me off my feet as he cuts through the yard of a house to our right.

"We need to lose them," he says grimly, hopping a fence at the back of the property and then reaching back to help me as Ransom lifts me over. We start running again, cutting down the alley, but up ahead, the Jeep swings into view where the alley intersects with the street.

My feet skid against loose gravel on the road as we stop and double back, cutting through another yard as male voices call to each other from the Jeep. There's more than one person in the car, clearly, and I can hear their deep voices in the distance as we keep running, someone calling out our location to the driver and the driver responding.

"Keep going," Malice grunts beside me. "Don't stop."

My lungs burn as we keep running, taking little side streets, ducking through alleys, trying to leave the Jeep behind as best we can. But although we have the advantage of being able to fit through smaller places on foot, the Jeep is boxing us in, staying on our tail when it can and reappearing to cut us off when we try to lose it.

"*Fuck* this," Ransom swears as we stumble onto a new street. "Olivia can go fuck herself."

But even as he says that, the Jeep is there somehow. It cuts sideways, hurtling straight toward us, and as Malice pulls me into a sprint again, I glance backward over my shoulder. The blaze of the headlights is nearly blinding, but as the Jeep veers to avoid a pothole, I get a glimpse past them into the car.

With a sickening jolt, I realize that I recognize the person in the front passenger seat.

It's not a stranger, and it's sure as hell not Olivia.

Somehow, it's Troy.

My foot catches on an uneven piece of concrete, and I nearly go down. Vic grabs me, pulling me sideways and into another alley away from the Jeep.

I'm breathless, struggling to compose myself, lightheaded and exhausted. There's a stabbing pain in my side, and I feel like my legs could give out at any moment, but I force myself to keep moving, pushing myself farther. We have to get away.

"I saw... who was in the... Jeep," I pant, gasping for air and trying to force the words out. "It was... Troy."

"What the fuck?" Malice snarls. He whips his head around to look at me, not stopping. "Are you sure?"

I nod shakily, my skin somehow sweaty and cold at the same time. "I saw him. He's not dead. He must have... must have survived."

Vic makes an angry noise behind me. "That means Olivia had help. Fuck, I didn't know. I wasn't counting on that."

"Come on!" Ransom hisses, urging us on. "We can figure it out once we get out of here."

We put on more speed, pushing ourselves to the limit as we keep running.

The headlights have faded, and after a few more minutes of

racing down side streets, it seems like maybe we've managed to lose the Jeep. I don't hear it or see it anymore. We vault over a fence or two, running blindly through the dimly lit outskirts of Nueva Laredo. I have no idea where the hell we're going, and I'm not even sure Vic knows at this point.

Our footsteps finally slow a little, and I suck in ragged sips of air as Victor glances around quickly, as if trying to get his bearings.

We step out onto a new street—but as we do, the roar of an engine rises up from nearby like the sound of an angry animal.

The Jeep races toward us, its headlights off now, blending in with the darkness. It's so fucking close already, too close to evade, and as it bears down on us, Victor lunges in front of me protectively, reaching for his weapon.

A loud *bang* rings out.

For half a heartbeat, I think he's the one who fired, but then he stumbles back, his knees buckling as he goes down.

I scream, shock lancing through me.

The Jeep keeps coming, veering slightly just before it reaches us. The whole side of the car is open, and as it passes by, a hand reaches out, grabbing for me. My scream is cut off abruptly as I'm hauled up into the Jeep, my arm almost wrenched from its socket by the speed.

Malice and Ransom are both shouting something, their deep voices cutting through the air as the Jeep speeds away. I can make out the three shapes of them in the darkness, one of them on the ground. It's too dark to tell if the shadowy form on the ground is moving, and the thought that it might not be makes my stomach drop like a rock.

I struggle against the burly man holding me in the backseat, trying to elbow him in the face, the throat, *anything*. But he wrenches my arms behind my back, making me cry out in pain as my shoulder screams in protest.

Troy turns around and leans toward me from the front passenger seat, gripping my chin as the Jeep bounces over the rough road. His face is cast in harsh shadows, making him look like a monster, a thing of nightmares, as he jerks my chin to pull me closer.

"Did you miss me, baby?" he asks, his voice low and ominous.

He crushes his lips to mine, his fingers digging into my cheeks as he kisses me hard. Then he releases me suddenly, and a hand claps over my face, holding a cloth soaked in something pungent and sharp. I rear back, struggling harder, kicking and writhing... but my limbs are already losing strength.

The hand over my mouth and nose doesn't budge, and as the drug seeps into my system, the world falls away into nothingness.

BOOKS BY EVA ASHWOOD

Clearwater University
(college-age enemies to lovers series)
Who Breaks First
Who Laughs Last
Who Falls Hardest

The Dark Elite
(dark mafia romance)
Vicious Kings
Ruthless Knights
Savage Queen

Slateview High
(dark high school bully romance)
Lost Boys
Wild Girl
Mad Love

Sinners of Hawthorne University
(dark new adult romance)

When Sinners Play
How Sinners Fight
What Sinners Love

Black Rose Kisses
(dark new adult romance)
Fight Dirty
Play Rough
Wreak Havoc
Love Hard

Dirty Broken Savages
(dark new adult/mafia romance)
Kings of Chaos
Queen of Anarchy
Reign of Wrath
Empire of Ruin

Filthy Wicked Psychos
(dark new adult romance)
Twisted Game
Beautiful Devils
Corrupt Vow
Savage Hearts

Magic Blessed Academy
(paranormal academy series)
Gift of the Gods
Secret of the Gods
Wrath of the Gods

Printed in Great Britain
by Amazon